WESTERN

Rugged men looking for love...

The Maverick's Christmas Kiss
JoAnna Sims

A Proposal For Her Cowboy
Cari Lynn Webb

MILLS & BOON

JoAnna Sims is acknowledged as the author of this work
THE MAVERICK'S CHRISTMAS KISS
© 2024 by Harlequin Enterprises ULC
Philippine Copyright 2024
Australian Copyright 2024
New Zealand Copyright 2024

First Published 2024
First Australian Paperback Edition 2024
ISBN 978 1 038 93532 8

A PROPOSAL FOR HER COWBOY
© 2024 by Cari Lynn Webb
Philippine Copyright 2024
Australian Copyright 2024
New Zealand Copyright 2024

First Published 2024
First Australian Paperback Edition 2024
ISBN 978 1 038 93532 8

MIX
Paper | Supporting responsible forestry
FSC® C001695

Published by
Harlequin Mills & Boon
An imprint of Harlequin Enterprises (Australia) Pty Limited (ABN 47 001 180 918), a subsidiary of HarperCollins Publishers Australia Pty Limited
(ABN 36 009 913 517)
Level 19, 201 Elizabeth Street
SYDNEY NSW 2000 AUSTRALIA

Cover art used by arrangement with Harlequin Books S.A.. All rights reserved.

Printed and bound in Australia by McPherson's Printing Group

The Maverick's Christmas Kiss

JoAnna Sims

MILLS & BOON

JoAnna Sims is proud to pen contemporary romance for Harlequin Special Edition. JoAnna's series The Brands of Montana features hardworking characters with hometown values. You are cordially invited to join the Brands of Montana as they wrangle their own happily-ever-afters.

Books by JoAnna Sims

Montana Mavericks: The Trail to Tenacity

The Maverick's Christmas Kiss

Harlequin Special Edition

The Brands of Montana

A Match Made in Montana
High Country Christmas
High Country Baby
Meet Me at the Chapel
Thankful for You
A Wedding to Remember
A Bride for Liam Brand
High Country Cowgirl
The Sergeant's Christmas Mission
Her Second Forever
His Christmas Eve Homecoming
She Dreamed of a Cowboy
The Marine's Christmas Wish
Her Outback Rancher
Big Sky Cowboy
Big Sky Christmas

Montana Mavericks: Six Brides for Six Brothers

The Maverick's Wedding Wager

Visit the Author Profile page
at millsandboon.com.au for more titles.

Dear Reader,

Thank you for choosing Dawson John and Marisa Sanchez's opposites-attract romance just in time for the holidays!

Dawson John is a handsome, wealthy rancher born into a powerful family in Bronco, Montana. When it comes to women, he's looking for fun, not forever. Until sassy Marisa Sanchez waltzes into his life and Cupid's arrow with her name on it pierces his heart. How can he convince her that he is husband material? For the first time, Dawson can't get what he wants with a wink and a smile.

Marisa Sanchez is a music teacher from a barely blue-collar family in Tenacity, Montana. When a video of her multicultural approach to the previous year's Tenacity holiday show goes viral on TikTok, Marisa is offered a job producing the Mistletoe Pageant in the neighboring town of Bronco. And this is where her life unexpectedly collides with swoon-worthy Dawson John. Marisa has always dreamed of a humble, hardworking Tenacity man dedicated to community service for her husband. A devil-may-care cowboy like Dawson did *not* fit that bill!

Will Dawson and Marisa's holiday fling be little more than a shooting star streaking across the Montana night sky: white-hot and gone too soon? Or will Dawson and Marisa find a way to bridge their differences and forge a love that will last them a lifetime?

My best always,

JoAnna Sims

PS: My website, joannasimsromance.love, is under construction. Watch this space!

Dedicated to Jacqueline Sumner-Davis

Thank you for being the sister I always wanted.

You are brilliant, beautiful and as tough as tungsten steel.

I love you and I am so grateful to have you in my life.

Your Big Sis

PROLOGUE

Tenacity Elementary School
Tenacity, Montana
December 2006

IT WAS TWO weeks until Christmas Eve, and eight-year-old Marisa Sanchez had just performed in the Tenacity Elementary holiday show. Like many of her peers, she had auditioned for the holiday show, but only she had won the coveted spot of the star on top of the singing Christmas tree. Her mother was a seamstress by trade and, with materials that she had been provided by the school, she had designed and sewn the costumes.

Dressed as a puffy, bright yellow five-point star with a small hole in the top point for her face, Marisa was now standing in line to greet the music teacher, Mrs. Jankowski, who had produced the holiday show. Her parents and her brothers, Julian, Diego and Luca, along with her sister, Nina, stood beside her. Marisa's face was flushed and her dark brown eyes were shining from her triumphant performance. Yes, it was difficult for her to wait, but the wait was totally worth it to spend a moment with her favorite teacher.

Before taking her turn with her teacher, Marisa tugged on her mother's hand to get her attention.

Her mother leaned down and asked, "Yes, *mija*?"

"Remember how scared I was?"

"I do," her mother said.

"Guess what?"

"What?"

Marisa smiled up at her mother. "Once I got onstage, I wasn't scared anymore. I was the very best Christmas star I could be."

This made her mother laugh. "Yes, you were, *mija*. A perfect Christmas star!"

When it was *finally* their turn, Marisa threw herself into Mrs. Jankowski's arms and hugged her tightly.

"My beautiful little star!" The music teacher returned her hug. "You were the perfect topper for our Christmas tree!"

"Thank you, Mrs. Jankowski," Marisa said with a happy grin.

"You are welcome, precious one." Mrs. Jankowski gave her one last big squeeze before she turned her attention to Marisa's parents, shaking hands first with her father and then her mother.

"Mr. and Mrs. Sanchez, thank you so much for coming," the music teacher exclaimed. "I hope you all enjoyed the show."

"We loved the show," Nicole said. "We didn't know that Marisa could sing just like a pretty little songbird."

That made Mrs. Jankowski's smile broaden. "Your daughter is very talented. She has a beautiful voice and she is picking up the piano so quickly."

"Thank you so much for everything you have done for our daughter," Will said while Marisa basked happily in the praise of her teacher.

"Of course!" the teacher said with a nod before she added, "And thank you, Mrs. Sanchez, for making our costumes. The Kindergarten Christmas show never looked so good!"

"I was so pleased to be able to help," Nicole said, putting her arm around Marisa the Five-pointed Star.

"Well," Will said, glancing at the parents and students waiting to greet the teacher. "We'd better let you go."

As her family moved on, Mrs. Jankowski had one final had one final word for her parents. "Please consider getting music lessons for Marisa. I would start with voice and piano, as she is really quite gifted."

Marisa waved goodbye to her teacher as she walked with

her family to the parking lot. As expected, the older siblings held the hands of their younger siblings, and because it was her special night, Marisa walked between her parents holding their hands and swinging every couple of feet. Marisa was feeling so happy, but there was something bothering her. When Mrs. Jankowski had mentioned lessons, a dark cloud of worry had passed over her parents' faces. Their house was full of love and family and laughter, but money was always tight. Even at her tender age, Marisa was aware that, even though they were rich in the love department, they were considered poor when it came to money. Many times when she asked for something that she saw other kids in school had, her mother, with a deep sadness in her eyes, would tell her that they would have to wait. Her father worked on a ranch and rented land to farm, growing hay for the animals. Will also regularly took on odd jobs to make ends meet while her mother sewed nearly seven days a week.

Once their family of seven was seated in her father's van, her mother met her husband's eyes. "Lessons. Can we manage that?"

Will was silent for several seconds, then he broke the gaze with his wife and stared out of the windshield that had a small crack in the center, his hands gripping the steering wheel so tightly that his knuckles had blanched white.

"We will figure it out, my love," her father said. "Somehow, someway, we will get our sweet angel those lessons. You heard her teacher—she is talented."

"I can take on more sewing," her mother said with a nod and a look of determination on her face.

"And I can take on more handyman jobs," her father agreed, his jaw set.

"She can have our mowing money," Julian said, and her brothers Diego and Luca nodded their agreement.

Will Sanchez looked back at his boys. "Thank you. You make us so proud."

Little Nina piped up and said, "Marisa can have my birthday money."

"My lovely Nina," her mother said, "you are such a sweet thing."

"Wait a minute! Am I going to take music lessons?" Marisa

asked, her eyes, wide with hope, dancing between her parents' faces.

Her mother smiled at her. "We will have to see what Santa left under the Christmas tree for you."

CHAPTER ONE

TWENTY-SIX-YEAR-OLD MUSIC TEACHER Marisa Sanchez peeked out from behind the stage curtain at Bronco Theater to see how many folks answered her advertisement for open auditions to perform in the annual Mistletoe Pageant, a show full of singing, dancing and holiday cheer. A very nice crowd of potential performers were seated in the curved rows of the theater. Relieved, Marisa let go of the curtain with an excited smile on her face. She loved a challenge and the town of Bronco had certainly given her one: she had been hired to organize and direct the annual Mistletoe Pageant.

Marisa took one more quick scan of the crowd and that was when her eyes zeroed in on a dusty-haired cowboy finding a seat in the back row of the theater. He wore casual western clothing that had an exacting fit across his broad shoulders and tall, muscular frame. The quality of his clothing, along with his confident swagger, screamed "money" and "privilege," which was always a turnoff for her. His companion was a willowy, leggy blonde with a face meant for modeling. That cliché made Marisa dismiss the cowboy as shallow and self-important.

"Marisa?"

At the sound of a voice behind her, Marisa startled and spun away from the curtain as if she had been caught in the act of doing something wrong.

"Yes, Agnes?"

Agnes Little, her "go-to" person at the Bronco Theater, was a dear woman in her late sixties who had worked at the theater for decades.

"Would you like to get started?" Agnes asked. "It's six minutes past one."

"Yes. Thank you so much for keeping me on schedule."

"My pleasure." Agnes beamed at her. "If you stand right there on that mark, I will open the curtain for you."

Marisa took her spot on the mark, closed her eyes, took in a deep breath and knew that once the curtain opened, those pesky nerves would evaporate. Agnes walked over to the thick cord that would allow her to manually pull open the heavy maroon curtain.

"Ready?" Agnes asked.

She was ninety percent ready and ten percent slightly nauseous. Her norm.

After one quick silent prayer, Marisa opened her eyes, chin up, shoulders back, and said to Agnes, "Let's get this party started."

"DAWSON!" CHARITY PUT her hand on his arm and shook it. "That's her!"

Dawson John wanted to focus on his phone while mentally willing time to pass at warp speed so he could get out of this musty, old relic of a theater and once again breathe in the fresh Montana air.

All he had done was offer Charity a lift to her audition because her truck was in the shop; he had planned on dropping her off and picking her up after it was over. But then Charity, as usual, had to go and complicate it. Now she wanted him to stay for moral support.

"No good deed goes unpunished," he muttered as he sent a text then slipped his phone into the front pocket of his designer button-down shirt.

Charity had turned around so she could take a selfie with the woman on the stage in it. And for some unfathomable reason,

Charity had the exact expression on her face as when she had gotten her first Range Rover.

"Are you okay?" he asked her.

"I am." Charity pointed to the stage. "That's Marisa Sanchez! I'm a total fan girl. I can't believe she's actually here!"

"Who the heck is Marisa Sanchez?" he asked, feeling an odd combination of irritation and curiosity.

"For us theater geeks, she's kind of a big deal right now. One of her videos went viral on TikTok," Charity explained.

Dawson turned his attention from his phone to take a good look at the amazing Marisa Sanchez. There, standing alone and poised at center stage, was a woman who looked to be around Charity's age—maybe a bit older. She was rather short—he liked his women tall. She had straight long hair as glossy as a raven's wing. He had always preferred blondes. She had a curvy hourglass figure, and while some guys were into that, he favored women with an athletic build. Women who could keep up with him when he rock climbed, white water rafted or BASE-jumped. The wondrous Marisa Sanchez looked more like the type to curl up on the couch with a good book. After a quick appraisal of her, Dawson could not fathom why these artsy folks in the theater were acting as if they had just found Elvis alive in Bronco Theater.

His phone rang, and he was happy for the excuse to exit stage left.

Charity managed to take her eyes off her idol for a second to ask him, "Where are you going?"

He held out the phone for her to see. "I have to take this."

"Okay." Charity frowned at him. "Promise you'll be back in time for my audition."

He made a cross over his heart and winked at her, then he answered the phone while he headed out to the lobby.

"Natasha," Dawson said with a pleased smile, "how did you know I needed to be rescued?"

"Now why would a strapping cowboy like you need to be rescued by little ole me?"

"You'd be surprised."

"Maybe I would," the woman on the other end of the line said. "Maybe I wouldn't."

Dawson had eaten the night before at The Association, a private dining club for wealthy ranchers where the John family had a long-standing membership. Besides appreciating the excellent food, spirits and backroom deals at the club, Dawson loved catching the eye of the beautiful women employed there. It was a perfect scenario—most of the women were just passing through on their way to find a bigger and better life outside of Montana. Romancing women with an expiration date was zero risk and all reward for him. Simple. Clean. No fuss, no muss. Last night, he had met a sexy redheaded bartender named Natasha, and he was eager to make her time in Bronco memorable.

"Are you willing to take my word for it?" he asked flirtatiously.

"Not a chance. I gave up trusting cowboys like you a long while back."

"Been burnt?"

"Plenty."

"I guess I bet on the wrong horse." Dawson frowned. It felt odd to be rejected.

"Now, Dawson." Natasha's voice turned silky and sensual. "Don't go hurting my feelings by giving up so easily."

"You're beautiful and you know it."

"The same could be said of you."

Dawson went quiet while he conducted a cost-benefit analysis. Perhaps Natasha was turning out to be way more of headache than he was looking for.

After a short silence between them, the bartender said, "I'd be happy to take you out for a nice, long ride if that's all you're after."

"No attachments?"

"None whatsoever."

"Is there a secret password to this nirvana of which you speak? *Open sesame*?"

That made Natasha laugh and he liked the sound of it. "Offer me a nightcap, Dawson. The rest will come easy between us or it won't."

"Lovely. Natasha, would you like to have a nightcap with me?"

"Pick me up after my shift. Eleven o'clock sharp. I don't wait."

"Neither do I."

MARISA HAD STOOD on the stage looking out at the people who were there to audition. There were moms and dads with their children, and that brought up so many emotions tied to her childhood in school plays and at the community theater. These experiences had quite literally brought her to this moment in her life. She also saw some folks standing for her and clapping *very* enthusiastically while simultaneously filming her on their phones. She imagined that these might just be some of her TikTok fans, which was still an odd concept for her to get her head around.

"Thank you so much, Bronco!" Marisa smiled broadly and clapped her hands for them. "It is my pleasure to be here with you. Thank you for coming. Let's make this the best darn Mistletoe Pageant that Bronco, Montana, has ever seen!"

She made sure that she looked at all sides of the theater to acknowledge everyone. For barely a moment, Marisa's eyes caught and held the gaze of the perfectly made cowboy in the back row. He didn't look away and neither did she. And then something truly unusual and notable happened: those familiar, sweet, darling butterflies turned into a giant boulder roiling around like a washing machine overloaded with towels.

The cowboy was first to break eye contact and then he got up and left the theater. And that action made her smile falter for a second. It felt like a rejection and that irritated her and she brushed that feeling aside and refocused her attention to what was really important: musical theater auditions!

Marisa had forgotten that audition day, while at times exciting and invigorating, could also be long and exhausting. Marisa worked her way through the alphabetized list of children first and then the adults, and after she had finished the *I* names, she decided to take a fifteen-minute break.

After accepting a burnt cup of coffee from Agnes, Marisa returned to her place at the piano. She flipped the *I* page over to *J* on the adult list and called the first name on that page.

AFTER SECURING A date with Natasha for the evening, Dawson took his time returning to the theater. Charity had always been involved with the arts and he wanted to support her, he really did. But sitting in a theater for an entire afternoon while listening to people butchering holiday classics? No thanks. After he strolled around town a bit, he returned to the theater and he took his seat next to Charity. She was sitting forward on her seat, her arms crossed in front of her body, and she barely glanced his way.

"What'd I miss?" he asked her in his best cajoling voice.

She didn't respond, and that's the moment he realized that he'd screwed up royally.

"Hey." He leaned over and whispered, "I'm sorry."

"Where have you been?" she whispered back, still refusing to look at him.

"Ah, heck, Charity. I hate this sort of thing. You know that."

"Yeah, I do," she replied. "But I thought you loved me enough to suffer through it."

Dawson felt like he'd been punched in the nose; the way she put it made him feel like the biggest jerk in the world.

"I do, Charity. You know I do. Have you gone yet?"

"No. Not yet."

Dawson saw Marisa glance their way and Charity saw it too.

"Shhh. We aren't supposed to be talking during someone else's performance."

Dawson's hackles went straight up and he wanted to say, in a louder voice, that it was a free country and he could do whatever he wanted to do wherever he wanted to do it. But because Charity was already pretty sore at him, he decided to follow the rules. He even clapped for the young man who had just finished his audition to show Charity that he *was* there to support her.

"Charity?" Marisa called the name. "Charity John?"

Charity stood up and he could tell by the expression on her face that she was feeling uncertain. He stood up too, gave her a bear hug and said, "You've got this, Charity. Go show Miss TikTok what *you* can do."

IN HER PERIPHERAL VISION, Marisa had noticed the cowboy return and take a seat next to his companion. Their talking had been a distraction, and if they hadn't stopped when they did, she would have marched up the stairs and told them to knock it off. Now that Charity walked by on her way to the stage, Marisa realized the young woman was a knockout with large eyes surrounded by long, dark lashes, a petite nose, and a toothy white smile that lit up her face. She had sweetness about her that Marisa hadn't expected.

"Hello, Charity," she said. "Nice to meet you."

"It's really great to meet you, Marisa," Charity said in a breathy voice. "I love your videos."

"Thank you. The pleasure is all mine," Marisa said. "What will you be sharing with us today?"

"'Last Christmas' by Wham," Charity said shyly. "I know it's a strange choice."

Marisa took the sheet music that Charity had handed to her and flipped through the pages quickly. "I don't think it's a strange choice. I think it's an insightful choice."

This compliment earned a smile from Charity that started with her lips and ended in her eyes. "Thank you. I was so worried about it."

"Let that worry go," Marisa said. "You had a brilliant idea. Now, get up on that stage and own it."

AS DAWSON WATCHED Charity onstage, he actually began to worry for her. She seemed so nervous and so young standing there that he found himself silently praying for her success. Instead of sitting down, he kept standing and gave her two thumbs-up signs, which made her smile. The moment Charity began to sing, he felt the hair on his arms stand up. It had been a while since he had heard her perform; he had no idea how beautiful her voice had become. Dawson started to clap for her, calling out encouraging words. He thought he was helping until he saw a look of horror mar Charity's face as she shook her head at him and faltered. Marisa stopped playing, stood up and marched up the aisle to him.

"Hey! Cowboy. Please don't clap or stomp your feet or whistle or yell during the audition. It is very distracting. If you can't follow my rules, I will need you to wait outside until your girlfriend has finished."

Dawson watched Marisa walk away from him before he slumped back into his seat. He could feel the disapproving gazes of the audience and the humiliation emitting from Charity. Screw up number two! But he knew he could make amends with his sister later. Right now he was too focused on the mind-altering thing that had just happened to him.

He'd been run over by a freight train named Marisa Sanchez.

CHAPTER TWO

DAWSON WOULD NEED time to process this moment. All he had done was look into Marisa Sanchez's stormy, soulful brown eyes and he had experienced what he could only describe as an entire system meltdown. His heart was pounding in his chest as if he had just climbed up the peak of a high altitude mountain. He couldn't seem to take his eyes off of the woman at the piano and, in all honesty, he didn't want to.

Charity finished her song and everyone, including him, clapped enthusiastically for her. Charity sent him a sweet smile; that meant she had forgiven him. After a brief conversation with Marisa, Charity returned to their row of seats.

"You were amazing." He hugged her, then they sat down. "You're a star."

"Thank you. I really liked having you here with me."

"Except for when I interrupted your audition."

"I forgive you, of course," Charity said and then whispered, "I want to watch the rest of the auditions. I can catch a ride home. I know several people here."

"No," he said quickly. "I'll hang out and watch."

Charity looked at him with a truly surprised expression on her face. "Why would you do that?"

He tried to act nonchalant. "I know I haven't always liked things like this…"

"You loathe them."

"That's a strong word."

"An accurate word," she said quickly as the next performer's name was called. "You barely made it back in time to hear me sing!"

Dawson was about to debate her more, but Marisa looked at them both and he clammed up. He stayed even when one of the singers sounded like a bullhorn on a foggy day; he stayed even when a singer was so off-key that it hurt his ears. He stayed through every mind-numbing, ear-splitting performance. And watched Marisa.

Finally, a young man took the stage and he began to sing "Oh Come All Ye Faithful." Even Dawson could hear that his pitch was perfect and his voice filled the room taking everyone, including him, on an emotional journey. When they reached one of the quieter moments of the song, when the young man was about to take them back up to a peak, Dawson's phone rang loudly. He had turned up the volume so he could hear it over the singing before he knew he was breaking a rule. Several people around them groaned and swiveled their heads to give him a well-deserved death stare.

"Turn it off!" Charity whispered harshly to him.

"I will!" He fished inside of his shirt pocket for the phone only to recall that he had put it in the back pocket of his jeans. He stood up, grabbed the phone and fumbled to shut it down, while Marisa glared at him.

"Turn it off!" Charity said again, burying her head in her hands.

"I'm trying! Can't you see that I'm trying?"

He grabbed the phone, hit the red button to hang up, turned off the volume, and then apologized to everyone around him; he was about to sit back down when he saw Marisa pointing at the door. Sheepishly, Dawson ducked out of the theater and stood alone in the lobby.

He looked at the door he had just walked through, puzzled. He had never believed in love at first sight. And now he was pretty sure that he was wrong about that.

He was also pretty sure, but not entirely sure, that the woman of his sudden onset affection disliked him intensely.

"Well, lookie here! Dawson John in my theater? All grown up!" Agnes gave him a tight hug before she stepped back to beam up at him from her short stature. "Are you auditioning?" Agnes Little had taught music at his elementary school. She had taught the Abernathy and Taylor kids as well as his brothers and sister. She was beloved by the parents and the children who had her for a teacher. Now, in her second act after retirement, Agnes wore as many different hats as needed to keep the doors of the community theater open for performances throughout the year, especially the annual Mistletoe Pageant.

"Me?" He winced. "Not a snowball's chance."

Hands on narrow hips, Agnes asked, "Now, you aren't still bent out of shape about the cactus incident, are you? It's not kind to hold a grudge against someone of my age."

"You told me that I was talented at standing stiffly onstage."

"Yes." She nodded. "Yes, I did. And it was true. You were very good at that and it wasn't a skill that just anyone had, so it made perfect sense to cast you as the important role of the cactus." Agnes continued, "And it would break my heart if I had ruined musical theater for you in any way."

"I'm okay," he said.

Agnes shot him a smile, pat him on the arm and said, "I'll sleep better tonight. Now that's the God's honest truth. Good to see you. Say 'hi' to the folks. Work to be done, so I'd best shuffle off…"

"What do you know about Marisa Sanchez?"

Agnes turned around and looked at him. "Not much. She's a music teacher, so I feel a kinship with her. She cares about kids and the planet."

"She's a force." For some reason, he *needed* to tell someone, anyone, about what had just happened to him. Struck by lightning and left lovesick.

"From my limited knowledge—" she shrugged "—I think that sums her up, yes."

Dawson looked at Agnes and couldn't seem to form the thoughts in his mind into actual words.

"Dawson. I love you, my boy. Did you know that the older you are, the quicker you get old? When we started this conversation, I was sixty-seven. Now I'm knocking on the door of sixty-eight. Blink twice if you can hear me."

His next words were blurted out. "I interrupted Marisa's auditions. How do I apologize?"

Agnes shook her head, looked down at the toes of her sensible black shoes and said, "Love. It's always love, isn't it?"

"I don't know what this is," Dawson said with a confused shake of his head. "All I did was look into her eyes and then…"

"Lightheaded, heart racing out of control?"

"I feel like my heart is suddenly too big for my body like that Grinch guy." He wiped off his forehead and then looked at his hand. "I'm sweating. It's hot in here. Is it hot in here? Or is it just me?"

"It's just you."

"I don't feel well at all, Agnes." He said, "I think I need to go to a doctor."

"Well, I'm not a doctor per se, but I do have a pretty good idea what's ailing you."

He looked at her intently, awaiting her next pearls of wisdom.

"My diagnosis?" Agnes stated, "You have a classic case of love at first sight."

Dawson shook his head. "No."

"Yes."

"That can't be right. Can it?"

"I know what I know."

Dawson still felt completely perplexed, like a cartoon character that had been run over and stood up flattened.

"Then what should I do?" he asked. "I don't think she's at all fond of me and we haven't even met."

"That's a brainteaser, no doubt about it," Agnes agreed. "Can I give you a bit of advice?"

"No."

"I recommend that you say you're sorry with hot chocolate."

He furrowed his brow. "That doesn't seem like much of an apology."

Most women he'd met along the way would throw that hot

chocolate in his face right before they dragged him through the mud on social media and then put the final nail in his coffin by blocking him on their phone.

"That's your absolute best advice?"

"Yes, it is," Agnes said. Then she added, "Heavy on the marshmallows." She heaved a sigh. "Well, I've got a tight schedule. Good luck to you!"

Agnes was a woman who had a keen sense about people. She was known for it. And did he really have a better idea for how to smooth over things with Marisa? No. He didn't. The apology tools in his toolbox would work with most women he knew, but not Marisa Sanchez. He'd bet money on that. It was Agnes's advice or nothing.

AFTER THE LAST audition ended, everyone began filing out of the theater. Marisa felt drained from the long day but also excited by the level of talent she had seen in Bronco. And even though she was ready to wind down after a hectic day, she spent time with the performers who wanted to speak with her when the auditions were done. She noticed Charity John walk toward her as the line finally began to dissipate.

"I am so sorry about the clapping and the cheering and the phone ringing," the blonde said, apologizing.

Marisa smiled a tired smile and wanted to set her mind at ease. "It's fine, Charity. No real harm done. Just maybe remind your boyfriend to turn the volume off on his phone next time."

Charity laughed. "Dawson isn't my boyfriend. He's my brother."

"So that's who he is." Marisa didn't understand it and she couldn't even find words to describe it, but knowing that the cowboy wasn't Charity's boyfriend made her feel...inexplicably happy.

Charity continued, "Honestly, you probably won't see Dawson again. He was only here today to give me a ride. My mechanic texted me earlier and said that my truck is ready."

"Oh. I see." Was that disappointment she heard in her own voice? *Odd.*

Charity continued, bringing Marisa's focus back to their

conversation. "Thank you for your coaching today. It was a big help."

"You have a gift, Charity. Your voice is a gift."

A pretty blush appeared on Charity's high cheekbones. "Thank you. I'm worried that I picked up some bad habits from my time in beauty pageants. Mom started me when I was a baby." She laughed and it was a pleasant tinkling sound. "I actually have a crown from when I was one year old!"

Marisa smiled along with her. Charity was exactly the type of person Marisa enjoyed; she was kind, gentle and didn't take herself too seriously.

"Do you still participate in pageants?" Marisa asked.

Charity furrowed her brow and shook her head. "No. I broke my mom's southern belle heart, but Miss Bronco 2022 was my last."

"Well," Marisa said, "now I understand why you have so much poise onstage. You look right at home."

Charity hugged her tightly and said, "Even if I don't get a singing role, I promise I will be here to help you any way I can."

"I really appreciate that. I'm in a new town, and I could use all the support I can get."

Charity looked at her directly. "You can count on me, Marisa."

"Thank you."

The door to the theater opened and she saw the cowboy—Dawson—now she knew his name, walked through. Charity waved at him, thanked her again, and then easily took the stairs two steps at a time to reach her brother. When she reached him at the top step, Charity waved goodbye. And, as quick as a flash, Marisa met Dawson's steady gaze again. As brother and sister disappeared into the theater lobby, Marisa was left standing by the piano, temporarily frozen in her spot. Then, she felt a wave of dizziness and that made her put her hand on her stomach and sit down heavily on the piano chair.

She closed her eyes, fighting an uncomfortable woozy sensation that was followed by her heart racing so quickly that she wondered if she had developed some sort of cardiac problem.

"Miss Marisa?" Agnes found her slumped forward, her arms

resting on the closed keys, her head down and resting on her folded hands. "Are you okay?"

Marisa sat up slowly. "Yes. I'm just tired. Or coming down with a bug. Or both."

"Can I get you something to eat?"

"No." Marisa shook her head, "My aunt and uncle expect me later. Is it okay if I stick around for a bit? Music always helps me clear my head."

"Well, of course you can," Agnes said. "And we can talk about the auditions tomorrow when you're not so tuckered."

"Thank you."

"You do seem a bit flushed in the cheeks. What *are* your symptoms?" Agnes asked in a no-nonsense tone. Like a detective searching for clues.

"Dizzy, I guess, and lightheaded. My heart was racing."

Agnes looked at her and after a moment said, "There seems to be a lot of that going around today."

"Really?" she asked, putting her hand on her forehead. "*Is* there a bug going around? I can't get sick now. I don't have time to be sick."

"Don't you worry about that, dear one," Agnes said. "The kind of sickness going around this theater can't be healed with medication."

AFTER DROPPING CHARITY off at the mechanic's and making sure that the truck was back in working order, Dawson headed straight to a nearby coffee shop and ordered two large hot chocolates *with* marshmallows on the side, then drove back to the theater to hopefully catch Marisa before she left for the day. When they were on the way to the mechanic, the only subject Charity wanted to talk about was Marisa. And he didn't mind one bit. He wanted to know more about the director of the Mistletoe Pageant, so he listened carefully. Just before they arrived, Charity told him that Marisa was such a hard worker and so dedicated that she was going to be creating a new arrangement for a Christmas carol, and wasn't that amazing?

What was amazing to him was the information Charity had given him. Marisa would be at the theater, and he needed to apologize quick before her possible bad opinion of him was set in stone. Maybe it was a long shot, and maybe this was a fool's errand, but he *had* to try. And even though he felt a twinge of guilt for keeping his plan from Charity, if something came of it, she would be happy, and if it didn't, he could walk away without telling anyone about his failed attempt at winning Marisa over.

MARISA CLOSED HER EYES, felt the keys with her hands and listened to the notes with her heart. One measure at a time, she listened carefully, stringing more notes together in a way that remained true to the song "Jingle Bells."

"I've never heard 'Jingle Bells' played like that before."

Marisa's fingers froze, and she opened her eyes to find Dawson John standing a couple of feet away from her; they were the only two people left in the theater.

"I love the original arrangement, of course, but I also think that it's fun to jazz it up a bit," she said, not at all sure why he hadn't left with his sister.

"I liked it. I'm Dawson, by the way. Dawson John."

"Yes. I know." Her tone was more abrupt than she had intended. "Charity told me."

After he didn't fill in the silence, she added, her guard up, "I'm Marisa. But I think you may already know that."

Marisa *had* never "swooned." Prone. Yet, up close, Dawson John was so incredibly handsome with his tanned skin, dusty-blond hair tussled in a very sexy way, his icy-blue eyes, strong nose, perfect jawline, perfect teeth and lips that were meant for kissing, Marisa was certain she *was* on the verge of a swoon. He could easily be mistaken for a Hemsworth brother from an American mother; he looked as if he had stepped right out of magazine or onto a movie set where he, obviously, would be playing the role of leading man. Those broad shoulders, those heavily muscled arms and legs, and gosh darn it, he smelled delicious—vanilla and spices found in a pumpkin pie all rolled into one—and she was *very* hungry.

"Is there something I can do for you, Dawson?" Marisa managed to ask the question in a breathy voice that did not even remotely sound like her own.

"No. Maybe. Yes."

In that moment, he seemed more human to her, and when she laughed, and then he laughed with her, the fog of an uncomfortable awkwardness between them lifted.

Dawson held up one finger. "Wait right here."

"Okay."

Marisa watched Dawson jog up the steps, retrieve a bag and walk back to her quickly.

"Why did you hide that bag?" Marisa asked. "You don't have a knife in there, do you?"

Dawson smiled at her while he opened the bag from Bronco Java and Juice.

"No." He laughed. "What I have in here is an apology. And I hid it just in case you kicked me out again."

"Only if you ignore the rules," she countered, her curiosity officially piqued. "What's the apology for?"

"Breaking your rules." He took two cups out of the bag labeled Bronco Java and Juice.

"I don't think you need to apologize. It occurred to me that you'd missed my audition rules, and I felt bad about how I spoke to you. So, I apologize. My only excuse is that I'm super stressed out about this job."

"I couldn't tell. You looked perfectly at ease, quietly confident. Impressive, really," Dawson said. "How about I forgive you and you forgive me?"

Marisa smiled at him, and she had a gut feeling that she would remember this moment for the rest of her life. She held out her hand to shake his, and the minute their hands touched, a spark of electricity jumped between them.

"Did you feel that?" he asked her in a direct manner she liked.

Of course she had—she couldn't have missed it! "I did," she admitted, and then she did her best to redirect the conversation. "What's in the cups?"

There was that swoonworthy smile of his. "Hot chocolate. For two."

Her eyes widened in surprise. "Agnes?"

"Agnes."

"Why don't we sit down on the stage? I don't want to have

anything liquid around this piano or on the floor. I want to stay on Agnes's good list."

"Ditto."

They both walked up the stairs to the stage and sat down together.

Marisa sat cross-legged, picked up her cup, held it in her hands to enjoy its warmth and then she took a small sip of the piping hot liquid.

"Is it good?" he asked.

"It's so good," she said with a thankful smile. "I really appreciate this, Dawson. You didn't have to, but thank you."

"My pleasure. But how about I make it even better?" He pulled out a baggie of small marshmallows he had asked for on the side. He showed her the bag and she laughed.

"You have excellent intel, don't you?"

He sprinkled some marshmallows into her cup and then dropped some into his.

"I suppose I do. I've never really needed it before, but it did come in handy this time."

Marisa wasn't sure what he meant when he had said *I've never really needed it before* but didn't ask. Things were easy between them, oddly comfortable; she didn't want to rock that boat. But it did not escape her that she wasn't at all certain why Dawson John was with her right now. This was too elaborate for only an apology from her point of view. What exactly was his ulterior motive? She wanted to know, so she asked.

"Are you trying to influence my decision about Charity?"

Dawson looked at her with a frown on his perfectly symmetrical face. Could she be reading that correctly? Had there been a flash of hurt in those ocean-blue eyes?

"No," he said, "I'm not."

"Then why?"

"Why am I here?"

She nodded wordlessly.

After several silent moments and after Dawson had stared out into the empty rows of seats.

When he turned his eyes back to her face, her unexpected companion said, "I'm here because of you."

WHEN DAWSON CONFESSED that he wanted to get to know her better, it felt as unbelievable as if he had announced that he was Santa Claus. And this wasn't a put-down of herself. Not at all! She believed that she was an attractive person, starting on the inside. But she also knew that she wasn't a Heidi Klum or Sofia Vergara. She had always been a cute "brainy bookworm," a shy girl, but performing from a tender age had made her feel more at home onstage than offstage. Eventually her love for performing and music had even earned her a full-ride scholarship to the prestigious Berklee College of Music in Boston.

During her first year in Boston, she had formed a band with her then roommates named Row House Four, which had played gigs all over the city. The band's success had gone a long way to building her confidence offstage. Many men approached her when their set ended but none of them had been a Dawson John type.

"Thank you again for the hot chocolate," she said.

He smiled at her in a way that made her feel nervous and jittery on the inside. "I'm glad you enjoyed it."

She checked her phone. "My aunt and uncle are expecting me."

Dawson looked reluctant to end their time together, and she felt the same way. But she also knew that she had a big job to do in Bronco and this *spark* they seemed to have between them should be left on the stage, where it could fizzle out on its own.

Before he easily jumped down from where he sat, he put the empty cups in the bag.

"I can help you down," Dawson said to her.

Marisa had the distinct feeling that if she let Dawson John touch her once, even in the most innocent of ways, she was going to keep on letting him touch her in perhaps some *naughty* ways.

"Thanks," she said. "I've got it."

She walked over to the piano, hoisted a heavy backpack on, then grabbed an overstuffed bag filled with sheet music and other tools of her trade.

"Allow me." Dawson reached for the bag.

She handed it to him and found herself smiling at him. She couldn't seem to stop herself from smiling at him!

Together they walked up the stairs, and when they reached the top, Dawson opened the door for her.

"So what's next for you?" he asked.

"After dinner, I'll start sifting through the performers today so I can post them on the theater website tomorrow so I can begin rehearsals."

"So all work, no play?"

"Yes," she said. "But I did enjoy getting to know you."

"Thank you. Me too."

Out in the parking lot, he matched her pace while they walked over to her car.

"Is this a 1982 Ford Falcon?"

"1984." Marisa put her bookbag in the back seat and he followed suit.

"It's completely refurbished," Dawson said, admiring the two-toned silver-and-purple car with its distinctive three windows that together resembled a trapezoid.

"I had a friend in high school who was obsessed with rescuing eighties cars from the junkyard and restoring them. I had some money saved up and he gave me the family discount," she said with a shrug of one shoulder. "Now I am the proud owner of a Ford Falcon.

"Well," she said, opening her door, "I guess I'll see you around?"

"I was actually thinking about stopping by rehearsals."

That surprised her. "I don't typically let the public come to rehearsals. Parents of my young performers, of course, but Charity...*if* she makes the cut, is an adult."

"Can you make one little exception?"

She smiled with a small shake of the head. "I have a feeling that happens quite frequently for you, doesn't it?"

"I'll have to plead the fifth on that one."

"So, I guess I'll see you around?"

"I hope so," he said. "Just do me one favor."

"What's that?"

"If you do allow me to come to rehearsals, please don't kick me out a second time. I do have a reputation to uphold."

She got into the car, tossing him a small smile before closing her door. "I make zero promises."

AFTER HIS IMPROMPTU "date" with Marisa, Dawson headed to the family ranch, the Double J, a sprawling cattle spread located in Bronco Heights, the town's upscale counterpart to Bronco Valley. Whenever he needed to clear his mind and work his way through a problem, he got himself on horseback and went for a long ride. He brushed down a beefy Quarter horse gelding named Scottie.

"How's your day been?" he asked the horse as he picked out his hooves. "Mine's been odd—real odd."

Dawson put the saddle pad on the horse's back, and then swung the saddle over and put it down gently.

Once the bridle was on, Dawson led the horse out of the barn, hooked his left foot into the stirrup, reins in hand, hand resting on the thickly muscled neck of the horse, and then mounted, his right foot finding the stirrup. After a few more tail swishes, Scottie settled down and walked out from Dawson's leg. Dawson didn't have a plan other than *ride until life makes more sense*. Still feeling like that flattened cartoon character, he rode right up until the sun was setting and dusk was upon him. And, after hours of riding, his mind was still bent all out of shape. He wasn't the falling-in-love kind. He certainly didn't go around falling for women who were literally his exact opposite! Marisa Sanchez was an artistic kind of person, and he was definitely *not*! But in spite of it all, Marisa had something special that he must have been unknowingly craving his entire adult life.

It was dusk by the time he returned to the stable. After brushing the sweat from Scottie's back, he handed him over to the stable hand taking care of evening feeding at the barn, and then got in his truck and drove to the main house. What was really eating at him was the undeniable fact that he didn't feel one iota better after his ride. If he was hoping to figure out his strong attraction to Marisa Sanchez, that strategy had failed miserably.

Instead of going through the house where he might have had

to talk with his parents, he walked around the long way to the outdoor kitchen that overlooked bucolic, snowy fields that had been harvested for hay stocks as winter was on its way. Dawson found a nice whiskey in the outdoor kitchen, poured himself a glass neat, and then sat down in one of the high quality rocking chairs put there for this exact purpose by his mother, Mimi. It was cold even with his thick, warm coat but he didn't much care. He needed this time alone to think and to figure out how in the hell he had managed to get himself in this mess. He was on his second round of whiskey when the door opened behind him. He looked back over his shoulder, hoping it wasn't his father, Randall, or his mother. They were the last people he wanted to encounter.

"I didn't know you were home." His brother Maddox stepped out onto the lanai.

"Hiding out, big brother," Dawson said. "Buy you a drink?"

"What are you drinking?"

"Whiskey. Neat."

"Can I fill 'er up?"

"Why not?"

Maddox brought the bottle of whiskey over, topped off Dawson's glass before pouring one for himself. His brother took a seat next to him, they clinked glasses, and after taking a deep draw, Maddox made a noise in his throat from the oddly pleasurable burn of whiskey.

"So what's going on?" his brother asked.

Randall and Mimi had four children: Jameson was the eldest, Maddox second in line; Dawson was the third and last brother, while Charity was the only girl and the baby of the family. His parents were wealthy and liked to show it. They also were always trying to climb their way up the social rung to reach the status of the two wealthiest and influential families in Bronco, the Taylors and the Abernathys. And for his parents, part of that competition included their children making acceptable matches when it came time to marry.

"Nothing much," Dawson said pensively.

"Well, that was a load of hogwash right there."

Dawson remained quiet for a bit, and his brother didn't push him. Jameson and Maddox were happily married; Maddox and his wife, Adeline, had given their parents a grandchild, a boy, named Matthew. Did it really matter who Dawson ended up marrying? The fact that he had begun to contemplate the topic of marriage was yet another layer of *what the hell is going on*?

"I'm here if you want to talk about it, Dawson."

"Honestly?" he said after draining his glass and putting it down on a side table. "I don't even know where to begin."

"That doesn't sound good."

"No," Dawson agreed. "It doesn't."

Maddox looked at him with an intense gaze. "Now you've got me worried."

Dawson didn't respond.

"What's this about, D? Seriously. Now I've got to know so I can help you if I can. Please tell me you haven't gotten someone pregnant…?"

That question made him chuckle—that would be worse than falling in love with a woman who didn't meet the Randall and Mimi standards for their children, all in the pursuit of reaching that top rung on the food chain.

"No." He smiled at the thought. "It's not that."

"Well, thank heaven above for that." Maddox poured himself another whiskey. "But it does have something to do with a woman?"

Dawson gave a small nod and put his empty glass off to the side.

"Not a woman who would pass our parents' *Marry debutantes from other cattle families*?"

"That's about the size of it."

They shared a comfortable silence. His brothers weren't just siblings, they were his best friends. And Dawson knew he could trust Maddox explicitly.

"Let me run something by you."

"Shoot," Maddox said.

"From my way of seeing it, Charity is the princess," he said. "Jameson is the heir. You're the spare."

"Mom and Dad would love you using all of these royal family terms." Maddox laughed. "What does that make you?"

"It makes me *I don't care.*"

Maddox laughed out loud before he said, "Well, you may not care, little brother. But I guarantee this—Randall and Mimi sure as hell *will* care."

"Yeah. I know," Dawson conceded. "But we love who we love and if they don't fit neatly into that 'daughters of cattle barons only' box, that's when changes need to be made."

His brother looked at him with both concern and shock, "Love?"

"Maybe," Dawson said with an image of Marisa's sweet face and sparkling eyes in the forefront of his mind. "Just maybe."

Maddox leaned toward him, looking at him straight on, "If there's someone you want, Dawson. Someone that you know, in the deepest part of your soul, that you love, just put on your armor and prepare yourself for battle. That's the best advice I can give you."

CHAPTER THREE

DAWSON HAD AWAKENED the next morning with a slight hangover and to an irate text from Natasha, telling him to lose her number after he stood her up on the same day he had asked her out. He felt bad about it—he really did—and he apologized, but he was pretty sure that she had blocked him. But in his defense, Marisa Sanchez had kicked his legs right out from underneath him. How could he be expected to go out on a date after those impactful encounters with Marisa? After trying to make things right with Natasha, Dawson jumped in the shower. He had hoped that he would wake up right back to his old familiar, carefree, pre-Marisa life. That didn't happen. Now, all he could think to do was get that pass to attend rehearsals once they got started.

"You look tired, Dawson," his mother commented when he joined his parents at the table for breakfast. "And I think you need a haircut."

"I'll look into it," he said while he filled his plate with stick-to-your-ribs breakfast fare that his mother had prepared for them.

Halfway through his second helping, Charity burst into the room and raised her hands above her head and said in a very happy voice, "I did it! I'm in the Mistletoe Pageant!"

Dawson was happy to have his mother's attention switch from him to his golden-haired baby sister.

"That's real nice." Randall turned down the corner of the newspaper to look at his daughter. "Congratulations."

Mimi smiled at her daughter while carefully buttering a piece of toast for her husband. "That's wonderful, sweetheart, but I'd go easy on breakfast if I were you. You know what they say. A moment on the lips…"

Some of Charity's initial excitement waned and Dawson felt for her. Their parents were well-meaning, but they sometimes managed to dampen any good news with cautionary tales. Dawson got up, hugged Charity and congratulated her.

"What role will you have?" Mimi asked as she handed her husband the toast.

Charity sat down and gave herself big helpings of eggs, sausage patties, cheese grits and a biscuit. Dawson smiled as he poured his sister a full-to-the-rim glass of orange juice and then passed her the honey.

"I have one solo, one group song, and I'll be in the whole choir performances. *And* I am in two dance numbers. One number will include Bollywood moves!"

Randall lowered the paper again, stared at her over the rim of his reading glasses and asked, "Now what are you going to be doing?"

"I watched some Bollywood movies and they are so bright and energetic. But how would that work with our traditional Christmas songs?" Mimi's lips were pursed disapprovingly. "I don't think I like the sound of that at all."

"Well, some of the Christmas songs won't have traditional music arrangements. Instead their arrangements will be influenced by jazz, rock, Motown, and even hip-hop."

"No. That's a terrible idea!" their mom exclaimed.

"Times change, Mom. And we have to change with them," Charity said.

"That's a matter of opinion, little one," Randall said, returning to his paper.

"I for one am thrilled to see the pageant evolve," his sister said. "I'm proud to be a part of it. How do you feel about it, Dawson?"

"Me?" he asked, drinking down a third glass of orange juice. "I feel great about it. Can't wait to attend."

"Thank you, Dawson." She smiled at him.

"You are most welcome, Charity." He winked at her. They were overacting for sure, but this game was one that all of the John kids played to good-naturedly tweak their parents a bit.

The more she talked about her roles in the pageant, the more concerned her mother's face became. Mimi seemed un-impressed with direction of the once "set in stone" traditional Mistletoe Pageant.

Mimi folded her napkin and put it on her plate. "I'm very happy that you will play a large role in the pageant because you sing like an angel and you look like an angel."

"Thank you, Mom."

She held up a finger to stop her daughter. "But I am very concerned about what I'm hearing. Why in the world would the committee hire someone to run the pageant who isn't even from Bronco? And I don't think her idea is the right direction for our Mistletoe Pageant. We need the classics that are part of our tra-dition. That's what Bronco wants. That's what Bronco expects."

"I'm not positive, but I think there will be classic Christmas carols," Charity explained.

Her mom continued with a heavy sigh. "I want you to be happy, Charity, you know I do. I will be there in the front row cheering you on. But I'm afraid this new idea is doomed to fail. There is no way the Abernathys or the Taylors will stand for this."

Dawson left the breakfast table feeling unsettled about his parents' reaction to the direction Marisa was taking the Mis-tletoe Pageant. He supposed it made sense that he felt protec-tive of the Tenacity native because she had stolen his heart with just one look. What he saw was a train wreck unfolding in slow motion before his very eyes, and he was at a loss as to how to stop the crash from happening. Marisa was in real danger of having a revolt on her hands. Yes, there was a solid faction of young Broncoites who were more flexible and willing to buck tradition, but others, especially the old guard, could be as inflexible and unyielding as stainless steel. When news got out that Marisa was turning the whole Mistletoe production on its head, Dawson could absolutely see a boycott of the entire show by the old guard. He didn't want to see this happen for a multitude of reasons: he loved his town and the holiday season and he didn't want to see anything ruin that tradition for Bronco. He also didn't want his sister to get caught in the cross fire. But perhaps more importantly, and certainly more selfishly, Dawson did not want Marisa to become persona non grata in Bronco before he had even managed to ask her out for their first date!

"I've got to find a way to get through to her," Dawson told himself as he got behind the wheel of his GMC Denali Ultimate. "Somehow, someway, I've got to open Marisa's eyes to the reality of Bronco. For her sake and for mine."

MARISA HAD AWAKENED the morning after the auditions feeling exhausted but determined. She was grateful that her uncle Aaron and aunt Denise had allowed her to crash at their house in Bronco Valley. From the minute she walked in their door, the smell of good food cooking in the kitchen made her feel right at home. She knew that she had a safe harbor to dock her boat during her short stay in Bronco. She posted the list of performers who would have roles in the production. She also included a list for those who did not earn roles to help with building the sets. Then, she spent the day with her extended Bronco family to recharge for the first day of rehearsals.

The next day, she was greeted warmly by Agnes.

"Welcome back!" Agnes beamed at her. "How are you feeling?"

Marisa shrugged out of her jacket nd then took off her gloves and winter hat. "Thank you, Agnes. I feel pretty good. I wish I'd managed to get more sleep, but my mind was whirling with song arrangements and dance sequences! On the down side, I have some real concerns about the timeline."

"Let's go have a nice cup of coffee and let's see if we can muddle our way through some of your concerns."

Marisa followed Agnes to the kitchenette backstage, once

again feeling grateful that Agnes had taken such an interest in the pageant.

"I'm sorry I don't have hot chocolate." Agnes put a cup of freshly made coffee down in front of Marisa before joining her at the table. "I forgot to stop by the store today."

Marisa blew on her coffee. "Please don't go out of your way just for that. A hot cup of coffee is wonderful. Thank you."

"So," Agnes said, "let me have it. We can troubleshoot together."

Marisa breathed in deeply and then let out a long sigh. "I'm just out of my depth here, Agnes. If I had more time, I wouldn't have any trouble pulling this off. My mom will be coming in from Tenacity tomorrow to measure the performers for their costumes. She always makes the costumes for my shows."

"Good news."

"Yes," Marisa agreed. "The local band has already been practicing the updated versions of some Christmas classics. They've sent me videos, and that's actually going better than expected. They are so talented."

Agnes listened, giving her a nod every now and again to let her know that she was listening.

"But," she continued, "in three weeks, the singers need to be hitting all of their marks with unfamiliar arrangements, and I have to manage to teach people who don't dance how to dance in ways completely new to them. As for the sets, I have some of the sets that I use in my Tenacity holiday show stored in my aunt and uncle's garage, and so many people signed up to help with that. It's just a lot. When I organize and direct the holiday show in Tenacity, I've known almost everyone for years and we work together like clockwork.

"But I don't have that here. I know from experience that it can be super challenging to work with people I haven't worked with before. Rapport usually takes time that is not an abundant resource right now." Marisa sat back in her chair and asked, more to herself than to Agnes, "Did I bite off more than I can chew with this job? Does Bronco always have such a tight timeline?"

"Okay, last question answered first. Yes, we always have a tight timeline, but because we're always putting on the same ol' pageant with the same ol' singers and dancers, we don't need a whole lot of time."

"And now I'm shaking things up."

"In more ways than one." Agnes gave a nod. "And to your first question, no you haven't bit off more than you can chew. Rapport can be built quickly if you're kind. And from what I saw during rehearsals, you are kind and supportive and caring, and I know each and every one of those performers, young to old, and they will work hard for you—just as hard as I know you will work for them."

"Well, thank you, Agnes. You give good pep talks."

"I call it as I see it."

Marisa stood up, pushed in her chair, rinsed out her cup and set it aside. And then something other than rehearsals came to mind.

"By the way…"

Agnes was busily sweeping the floor. "Yes?"

"Guess who stopped by the other day bearing the gift of hot chocolate and marshmallows?"

A very sheepish expression appeared on Agnes's face. She stopped sweeping, leaned on the broom handle and said, "I have no idea."

That made Marisa laugh, and it felt good to laugh. Calmed her nerves a bit.

"But," Agnes said, "did it work?"

"Did I accept the apology?"

"Did you?"

Marisa laughed. "Of course it did! When Adonis in a Stetson shows up with hot chocolate and marshmallows, you forgive!"

"He is such a handsome man," Agnes said with parental-like pride. "I had him for kindergarten to fifth grade for music."

Marisa couldn't stop herself from asking, "What was he like as a boy?"

"Darling, cute as a button, mischievous…" the older woman said, then turned back to her work. "Now go have yourself a great rehearsal, Marisa! And don't forget to have a good time. Otherwise, what's this all for?"

Marisa did feel better after her talk with Agnes, and she

walked out onto the stage to greet the performers already gathered in the theater seats. Her gaze naturally went up to where she had first laid eyes on Dawson, but he wasn't there. And she felt disappointed. Maybe he hadn't enjoyed their meet-cute as much as she had. Dawson John and all he had to offer had played tug-of-war in her mind, fighting for her attention while she was in the casting process and during her restless sleep. Her brain had found a balance, sharing the time pretty equally split between Dawson and plans for the Mistletoe Pageant.

HER DISAPPOINTMENT WAS fleeting as her excited jitters for the first day of rehearsals propelled her to the edge of the stage. With a genuine smile on her face, she opened her arms wide as a welcoming gesture and called out to audience, "Good afternoon, Mistletoe Pageant performers!"

She began to hand out packets of songs and began to review them with the singers. The groups broke off and began to read over their songs and parts. They got Now that rehearsals were underway, Marisa made the rounds and worked with individuals or groups to rehearse the show. Marisa could see right away that she had passionate, hard workers in the boat with her and they were all prepared to row the boat with her.

"Hi!" Charity John took a straight line to her and gave her a huge hug. "Thank you for believing in me. I won't let you down."

"I do believe in you, Charity. Now it's time for you to believe in yourself."

When Charity arrived alone without her brother Marisa had to push aside her renewed disappointment.

"The show must go on," she said quietly to herself. And, truthfully, he wasn't her type and she was pretty certain that she wasn't his, and this attraction he felt for her could be an anomaly not a total change of heart. Her disappointment came from a place in her heart that wasn't the least bit rational. That's why she needed to acknowledge it—and *ignore* it.

Charity took the stage, her hands gripping the pages of her solo parts as she stood on her mark.

Marisa sat down at the piano and began to play Charity's solo in a modernized rendition of "Let it Snow." Charity's first, second and third attempt were shaky and pitchy. And, Marisa could see that Charity was becoming frustrated to the point of wanting to walk off the stage. So, Marisa left the piano and walked over to the stage and gave her some tips on posture and breath control. Charity was about to try to put the tips into practice when her shoulders slumped even lower as she said, "Great. Just what I needed."

Marisa turned and saw Dawson standing just inside the door; he raised his eyebrows at her and she nodded "yes" to his question. She had to turn away from him so she didn't start staring and even thought Charity was noticeably frustrated by her brother's appearance, *her* heart was beating as fast as a humming bird's wings. That man had an effect on her that was beyond her control to stop.

"Will you please excuse me?" Charity asked.

Marisa nodded and returned to her piano bench. Somehow, sitting at the piano gave her something to focus on other than Dawson while she insisted that her brain *stop* paying so much mind to that cowboy!

"WHAT ARE YOU doing here?" his sister asked him in an annoyed tone.

Dawson pulled up straight and gave her a grin. "I thought you'd like me to be here on your first rehearsal day."

His baby sister frowned at him. "Well, I don't. But since you're already here, make sure you turn off your phone!"

"Already did it."

"And don't clap or cheer for me." She pointed at him. "Not one word! Not one peep out of you or I will have Agnes remove you from this theater and ban you for life!"

"What about the Mistletoe Pageant?"

"Banned for life!" Charity raised her voice, something that was out of character for her.

"I'll be on my best behavior," he said sincerely. "I promise."

Charity gave him a sour look before she turned on her heel and quickly returned to the stage. She wasn't the only one who ignored him. After their first eye contact, Marisa did not look at him even when he tried to will Marisa to look over at him, to throw him a bone, but she didn't and it irked him! He hadn't experienced that before and he certainly didn't like how it felt In just a short amount of time, Dawson realized that Marisa was fiercely independent, talented, kindhearted, and a take-charge type of woman. How did one approach a woman like her?

"Carefully," he whispered under his breath. "Very carefully."

After watching the rehearsal, Dawson was amazed not only at what Marisa was doing with the show, but with his sister. She really shined onstage, and he was so proud of her. "You were amazing, peanut." Dawson used his childhood nickname for his sister. "I've never heard you sound like that before."

"Thank you," Charity said, slipping on her jacket, which she had laid across a nearby chair. "Marisa is a musical genius. The way she explains things! The way she models what she wants me to do, it's beyond. She's on a whole different level."

"You get some of that credit too, you know."

"I know." She nodded. "But Mom has had me in lessons as soon as I began to talk it seems like. In over ten years of lessons, not one of my coaches got me to where Marisa just did in fifteen minutes."

Charity zipped up her jacket, threw a backpack over one shoulder and then looked at him. "Are you coming with?"

Dawson had been wondering exactly how to get by with his "romance Marisa" plan without Charity noticing, and then he realized he couldn't. She was too smart and too observant.

"No," he said. "I think I'm going to stick around."

She narrowed her eyes. "Why?"

His eyes moved past his sister to watch Marisa working on a song at the piano. Charity must have followed his gaze because she let out a harsh whisper. "No. *No!* You have women all over the state of Montana ready to worship at the feet of the incredibly handsome, athletic and wealthy Dawson John! Leave Marisa alone!"

"I just want to get to know her, Charity. Nothing more to it than that."

Charity balled up her hands into fists, squeezed them tightly and then said, "If you screw this up for me, Dawson, I promise you I will never forgive you. You have no idea how much this means to me."

"I think I might," he said gently. "I'm not going to do anything to hurt you."

"But you might do something to hurt Marisa."

Dawson wanted to reassure his baby sister that he had no intention to hurt Marisa in the pursuit of love. How could he? In all of his thirty years, he now knew that he hadn't ever been in love. Not really and not like this. Hell, for all he knew, *he* could be the one who'd be left with a broken heart.

Charity studied him with worried eyes. "I can't change your mind."

"No," he said. "Not on this one."

Charity hooked arm through the other strap on her backpack so it was held evenly between both arms. "At least promise me that you will tread lightly, Dawson. She's...special."

"I promise," he said sincerely. "I promise you that I will."

CHAPTER FOUR

"HI, DAWSON." MARISA stopped at the last row and greeted him with a sincere, kind smile that reached her lovely dark brown eyes. They were the last ones left and he preferred it that way. An audience could complicate this budding friendship in ways that he imagined could have Marisa running as far away from him as humanly possible.

He had a reputation as a playboy and people gossiped about him—a lot. He hated to think what they might say if they saw him chatting up the new girl in town. He didn't pay attention to the chatter, but Marisa *might*, and he was willing to bet she wouldn't like it.

"Hi, Marisa." He stood up and took her bag off her shoulder and put it onto his. "Do you have time for coffee? Tea?"

"Or me?" she asked teasingly.

"Whoa! Slow down, Ms. Sanchez. I'm a slow burn, not a flash in the pan," he said, grabbing his Stetson from a coatrack and putting it back on his head.

That made her laugh and he loved the sound of it.

"I'm always in the mood for hot chocolate," she told him.

"I know a place with excellent hot chocolate and abundant marshmallows."

"Lead the way, kind sir."

Together they walked to the parking lot and then to her Falcon.

"Are we walking or driving?" she asked.

"Driving. I wouldn't mind a ride in your car. It's cool."

Marisa tossed her thick curls over her shoulder sassily and titled her head flirtatiously. "Of course it is. Didn't you get the memo, Dawson? *I'm* super cool."

MARISA CRANKED THE engine and asked, "Where to?"

"Take a left and then drive for a piece."

"As the crow flies?" she bantered, enjoying his company as if she had known him for a long time.

"Spoken like a Montana girl."

"Well—" she turned onto the road "—I'm from here. Just down the road, you know."

Dawson turned toward her, admiring the smooth ride of the vehicle. "I've heard that, yeah."

"Born and raised in Tenacity, an hour or so away from Bronco. Maybe it isn't everyone's cup of tea, but it's my own little slice of heaven on Earth."

"It's good to love where you come from."

"Yes, it is."

After a short silence, Marisa said, "Your shoulders take up too much room in my Falcon! It never felt small before."

He winked at her. "I've never had any complaints. I've been told my shoulders are one of my best features."

"What are your worst features?"

Dawson rubbed his chin, pretending to be in serious thought. "Now that you ask, I'd be hard-pressed to find one."

"May I suggest that enormous ego as a possible flaw?" she asked. "I bet that's what's taking up all the space in here! Roll down the window and let me have some air!"

Their conversation turned to small talk and then Dawson pointed to a little roadside greasy spoon and a gas station on the outskirts of town that didn't appear to get a lot of customers.

Marisa pulled in to a spot and turned off the engine. She looked at the restaurant with curiosity. "Eat, Gas-n-Go? This is the place?"

"This *is* the place."

She took the key out of the ignition. "Okay."

Dawson took his hat off the dashboard, stepped out of the car, put his hat back on and said, "Hold up! Let me be a gentleman and open up your door."

"Okay," she said, "if you want to."

"Lately, I do," he said. He walked quickly to her side of the Falcon, held out his hand for her to take and helped her out.

"Thank you."

"You're welcome."

They walked in together and the decor was sixties chic with real splatters of grease and some handprints of children on the newsprint wallpaper peeling off the wall.

They were greeted by an older gentleman with an unlit, half-smoked cigarette stuck to his lip.

"Take your pick." The man nodded toward the three tables with faded blue tops and orange scoop benches. "Menu's on the table."

She sat down and looked around with a pleased smile. "I love this kind of place."

"Me too." Dawson pulled on a menu that was stuck to another one. He peeled them apart and handed Marisa hers.

"Hungry?" he asked.

"I am, but my aunt and uncle expect me to eat a healthy meal with them," she explained but scanned the menu for another time.

"Ready?" the man asked.

Dawson put the menus back in their holder and held up two fingers. "Two hot chocolates, heavy on the marshmallows."

In no time at all, the man delivered their drinks, and her large mug was overflowing with marshmallows that were already melting into the hot chocolate.

Dawson held up his mug. "What should we toast to?"

"A successful pageant!"

They touched mugs. "Here's to the most amazing Mistletoe Pageant Bronco has ever seen."

Marisa took that first wonderful sip of the chocolatey beverage and closed her eyes to fully enjoy the feeling of the warmth spreading from her mouth to her belly. When she opened her eyes, Dawson was studying her.

"I've never seen anyone enjoy hot chocolate like you do."

"Well," she said, "maybe you've never met anyone like me before."

"Now that's the darn truth." He smiled at her in a way that made her blush and feel a tad insecure.

She put her hands on her mug to warm them. "Let me ask you something."

"Shoot."

"I may not know Bronco very well, but I'm sure there are a few places to get hot chocolate without the long drive. Why'd you pick this place?"

Without any hesitation, he said, "It's away from prying eyes. I have a way of finding myself the topic of the gossip column in the local newspaper a time or ten. It's not a lot of fun."

She took another wonderful sip of the drink. "Oh. That makes sense. And thank you, actually. I'm not sure I want to draw attention to myself other than for my role as the director of the pageant."

"You're welcome, then. I'm glad I got it right."

"You did." She smiled at him. "One of my videos from Tenacity's last Christmas choir went viral on TikTok…"

"Charity mentioned that…"

"I didn't expect it, and it still feels weird when someone outside of my circle recognizes me. I have so many new followers and that I don't mind, but I did become a bit of a celebrity in Tenacity."

She showed Dawson the video that had started the whole "local celebrity" deal. "Actually, this video actually got me this job."

"How so?"

"The committee for the pageant heard about my arrangements of holiday classics, and next thing you know, here I am!"

"Well," he said, "thank you, TikTok."

Marisa didn't quite know how to respond to Dawson's out in the open interest in her. She liked it and she liked him. She could even concede that they made sense in a greasy spoon on the outskirts of town, but in town *out there* with all of their friends and family involved? That couldn't make sense.

"You have a marshmallow mustache," he told her.

"So do you."

He opened his phone, turned the camera around to look at himself and he said, "Gosh darn. You're right. Come on over here and let's get a picture."

Laughing, she came over to his side and sat down next to him. He put his arm around her and then held out the phone and took a picture of them to immortalize their twin marshmallow mustaches.

"It's a good picture," she said.

"Agreed. We look good together," Dawson said, pulling up his Instagram and pushing buttons, leading her to believe that he was really going to post that picture while she watched in absolute horror.

"Wait!" she said in a loud voice. "You aren't going to post that, are you?"

"Well, I was."

She shook her head. "No."

He looked confused. "Why not?"

Marisa returned to her side of the table, leaned her body forward and said, "You can't post that!"

He waited for her to explain.

"Dawson! I've already told you that TikTok changed my life in ways both good and bad. Once that content is out there, it's out there for *life*."

When he still didn't look convinced, she told him to close Instagram, and after he did, she sat back relieved and then asked, "Tell me the truth. Am I someone you would typically go for?"

He didn't respond.

"Okay. Bad question. How's this. I don't want to hurt your feelings, but *you* would be a seismic shift in my social media," she said, "and even though I haven't poked around in your social media..."

"Hurt."

"But I very much doubt that I would see too many Marisas."

"There's only one Marisa."

"Dawson! I'm serious."

"So was I..." he said. "And who cares anyway?"

"For one, I do!" she said. "I have friends who have dated for six months before they post. It's almost as serious as an engagement announcement." Dawson seemed deflated and that made her feel sad. "That doesn't mean we can't still be friends."

After a silence, Dawson said, "If we are seen together in Bronco, we could end up in the paper."

"Well, I don't want to have all of the mothers of eligible daughters hating me and boycotting the show. But if we are just having innocent fun and we end up in the paper, at least it will stay *local*, not like social media."

After another silence, he said, "Okay. We'll do it your way. You have a point, anyway. The folks who write about me in the paper would probably take note if I posted marshmallow mustache pics with a beautiful stranger in town."

"We can't build a bubble around us. But we can pick and choose some ways that we put ourselves out there."

"Agreed."

Marisa checked her own phone and saw that she had forgotten to turn her phone from silent to vibrate and had missed both a call and a text from her aunt.

"I've got to get back," she said.

Dawson took out his wallet and put money on the table. "Okay, let's get you back."

ON THE WAY to town, Dawson felt odd inside, like his skin didn't fit him any longer. He was an adrenaline junkie, always had been and most likely always would be. But sitting in that diner with Marisa felt like a new untapped adrenaline. The shiny silkiness of her hair made him want to comb his fingers through it and feel it on his skin. Her lips were full and those dark eyes, so insightful and kind, cut straight through to his soul. She was a curvaceous woman he thought her curves were beautiful and sexy and enticing; and that made him realize that what he was feeling for Marisa went way beyond the physical. This was uncharted territory for him and that tipped him off balance.

With so many obvious differences between them, and no doubt a dump truck load of differences yet to be uncovered,

Dawson just didn't know how to capture the heart of a woman like Marisa Sanchez. But he wanted to learn.

"You're awfully quiet," Marisa said as she drove them back into town. "Everything okay?"

"Sure," he said, not wanting to overwhelm her with the very serious thoughts he was having about her. He did not want to scare Marisa away by coming on to strong. He needed to slow down, give her time to get to know him.

"So," she said, "what do you think about the show so far? I mean obviously it's the first day and that's always hectic and jumbled."

That question hung in the air between them and when she glanced over at him, awaiting his response, he did his best to be diplomatic. "I think the first rehearsal went well."

She nodded and waited, no doubt catching the subtle hesitation before landing on "well."

"And what you did with Charity—honestly, it was like you gave her a fifteen minute master class. I've never heard her sound like that before."

She continued to nod and wait, giving him all the space he needed to give her an appraisal.

"But…"

She raised her eyebrows. "But…?"

"I think," he said slowly, wishing he could go back in time and cut this encounter short before she could pin him down on his opinion. Unfortunately, he was trapped in her car and he had no where to go. All roads led to bad news. "And, this is only because you are new to Bronco and Bronco hasn't had time to adjust—"

"Adjust?"

Damn it! Wrong word. Wrong word!

He took in a big breath and blew it out slowly; it was the sigh of a defeated man. "There might be some people in town—you know, people who prefer their holidays 'classic'—" Dawson made finger quotes around the word "—and are resistant to change. I just wonder how they gonna feel about some of the changes you're making to the pageant."

He could see the furrow in her brow and new the wheels were

spinning out of control in her head. "What does this Bronco old guard have to do with my rehearsal?"

At the look on Marisa's face, Dawson felt like those weird trapezoid Falcon windows were closing in on him.

Marisa's eyebrows furrowed. "But that's why I was hired! Someone here saw my videos from last year's Tenacity holiday show and the committee hired me to *start* new traditions. Why would the town council hire me if they *didn't* want a refresh?!"

Marisa's voice had raised and she was gripping the steering wheel tightly. He *knew* talking about the pageant was going to ruin what had been a nice time together.

Not another word was spoken between them until they arrived at the theater parking lot and she parked and turned off the engine. Staring out of the windshield, Marisa was frowning deeply, her eyes confused and concerned, and he felt as if the progress he had just made with the pretty director had just been swept away.

"No." She shook her head. "That can't be."

He didn't know the right words to say so he remained quiet.

She looked into his face and studied him carefully. "Is your family a part of this group of people that don't like change?"

"Yeah. They are." What else could he say? He had to tell her the truth even if it meant she backed away from him. If Marisa ever caught him lying, he felt instinctively that Marisa would shut him down and never let him back in.

"Is that how you feel?" she asked.

"No. But, I do think that too much change over a very short time will not go over well in Bronco. The Mistletoe Pageant is hallowed ground."

"Then why hire me? I just don't get it."

"Look," he said, "I could be wrong."

"That's true." She nodded with a hopeful expression. "You could be."

"Maybe we could figure out exactly how Bronco feels."

"How?"

"We make a wager."

"What are the terms?"

"How about you have a pop-up concert in the park across

from the city hall. This time of year, there are a lot of people passing through the park, watching the city begin the routine of putting up Christmas decorations downtown."

"I could set up my portable keyboard."

"You could alternate between modern takes on Christmas songs and then classic takes."

"Maybe the same song back-to-back?"

"Sure," he said, "why not?"

"I wonder if Charity would be willing to be my accompaniment?"

"She'd do it. I'm sure she would. She thinks that you can walk on water."

"I just love her so much already," Marisa said sincerely while she held out her hand to him.

After some moments of thought, Marisa said, "It's not the worst idea I've ever heard."

"Gee, thanks?" He said half in jest. Marisa did not give him any leeway he had grown accustomed to from the opposite sex.

"You're welcome," Marisa said and then asked, "What would I win? I do feel confident that I *will* win."

"Besides the invaluable knowledge gained from the focus group? The loser takes the other one out to dinner."

"Full disclosure. I have a bologna budget."

"I know a great burger place."

"Or a greasy spoon on the outskirts of town where you can eat *and* get your tires rotated?"

That made him smile; he found himself smiling quite a bit with the lovely Miss Sanchez.

"If you win, you choose."

Marisa gave a shrug. "I'm pretty sure I'll win."

He loved the fact that he had turned the conversation around and now Marisa, a woman who liked to win, was fully invested in this wager and not stuck on whether she could win over some stuffy ranchers.

"All right, Dawson John. I'm in. Tomorrow in the park. Afternoon after rehearsals, so it won't be impossibly cold. Get ready to lose."

"I'll look forward to it." He winked at her and smiled to

let her know that he was being ironic. He believed, without a shadow of doubt, that he would win. Either way, win or lose, he was the winner—he had managed to find a way to share a meal with the object of his sudden-onset affection.

THE NEXT AFTERNOON, after a rigorous day of rehearsals, Marisa rode with Charity to Bronco Park. She had been disappointed when Dawson hadn't come to watch the rehearsals and was looking forward to seeing him in the park. He was beyond handsome, a real, living Greek god in human form, and she had judged him unfairly. She had assumed that he would be completely off-putting and shallow. If he had those sides of his personality from a lifetime of getting what he wanted based on his looks alone, he didn't show them to her.

"I love this park!" Marisa exclaimed. "It seems so odd to me that I visited my aunt and uncle several times when I was growing up, but I don't remember them ever bringing me here."

Charity parked her truck and shut off the engine. "This park and all of downtown is transformed into a Christmas wonderland. This time of year we have so many musicians and carolers performing in this park. When I was growing up, and during my beauty pageant days, I sang here sometimes."

"Well, that's good news. You can show me the ropes."

"Of course I will," Charity said sweetly. "Oh, here comes Dawson now."

And there it was, that same nervous stomach, that same shallow breathing and tingling sensations in her lips, fingers and toes. The mental fluctuation were annoying—one minute she was ready to enjoy a fun, casual, short and sweet holiday romance with Dawson and the next she wanted to push him away so she wouldn't get too attached. The part that wanted to push him away was the part of her that knew Dawson John, as much as she enjoyed his easy company, was not the type of man she would seriously pursue as a possible love match.

They came from backgrounds so different that they may as well have been raised on different planets. Perhaps they could have some fun, make a few memories, and perhaps, let this undeniable chemistry between them play out as a holiday tryst.

But could she imagine a long-term romance with him? *No.* She was convinced that she would not fit fully into his world and she was pretty certain her way of life, one of hard work and community service, would grow tiresome for a man like Dawson in less than a month's time.

"Hey there, ladies." Dawson smiled at them.

Charity hugged her brother quickly.

"Seems like a perfect day to win a wager!" Dawson rubbed his hands together.

"Well, thank you, Dawson," Marisa gave him a cheeky smile. "Are you already accepting your defeat?"

"Not a chance!" he countered. "What can I help you with?"

Dawson carried her portable keyboard while she carried her stool and sheet music, and Charity carried a case full of tambourines and bells.

Dawson and Charity helped her get set up and then she put an old coffee can on the top of her keyboard. She donned a Santa hat that matched her Santa scarf and her Christmas tree sweater that had actual blinking lights.

Dawson had been watching her again, and one side of his lovely lips were turned up in a crooked smile that only added to his already ridiculous handsomeness.

"Are we ready?" Marisa sat down on her stool.

"Ready," Charity said, holding two silver bells in her gloved hands.

"What's my role?" Dawson asked.

"You need to find us some people," Marisa said, as she handed him a small container of red chips and blue chips.

"Poker chips." He smiled. "Where'd you pick up these?"

"Turns out Agnes loves a poker night." She laughed. "So, reindeer red will be for classic arrangements and sleigh bell blue will be for a modern take on holiday classics."

"You don't play around." Dawson whistled, clearly impressed by her plan to tally the town's preference.

"Not when it comes to work," she said. "The results of this focus group will inform my decisions for the show. I really don't think that the good people of Bronco will side with you. But we shall see!"

"I do want to apologize right up front for the loss you are about to experience." Dawson flashed a teasing smile.

"Cocky. I hope you're not a sore loser." She teased back and then said, "People choose the colored chip that corresponds to their preference and then drop it into this coffee can right here. Is that clear?"

"I think I've got it," Dawson said, still in a teasing tone. "May the best man win."

Charity rolled her eyes at her brother, "You're the only man here, Dawson."

"I know. I'm the best man here right now, so I guess I'll be taking home a win. Get it?"

Marisa said to Charity, "Let's see how this man will take defeat when the two best women win."

"He'll probably cry," his sister said.

"You know what? I thought that about him when I first saw him." Marisa nodded. "A very big crier."

DAWSON COULDN'T SEEM to take his eyes off Marisa; she looked adorable in her Santa hat, scarf and ugly Christmas sweater. When she played the keyboard, she emitted a joyousness that seem to come from her very soul. She loved making music and he loved watching her perform. Yes, he had known she was an incredible musician, but he hadn't yet heard her sing more than a few notes as an example for the singers auditioning for her. The way her voice sounded with its crystal clear pitch and roundness of the notes, he found himself mesmerized by her.

"Dawson!" Charity sent him a disapproving look. "You're supposed to be bringing us voters! Quit ogling Marisa!"

Dawson rarely felt embarrassed, but the fact that he was caught gazing at Marisa and listening to her sing a jazzed-up version of "White Christmas," by his baby sister no less, he got a very large taste of embarrassment and he didn't like the way it made him feel at all.

"Well," he said sheepishly, "you shouldn't be singing so pretty if you wanted me to be able to work."

Marisa smiled at him in a way that put him at ease like no one in his life had ever done before. He had grown up with type

A personality parents who pushed all of their four kids to constantly strive for an impossible level of perfection. Randall and Mimi love their children but the high expectations they had for their children felt too heavy to carry. Perhaps that was what he had always rebelled against.

The kindness and acceptance that Dawson felt with just one simple look from Marisa had not been something he was accustomed to. His parents had mainly showed their love for their children with the best material objects that money could buy. And in that moment, he wondered if Marisa's more humble upbringing, just based on what he knew of her aunt and uncle, was the better option for raising children.

"Dawson!" Charity yelled at him with her eyes wide and questioning with a hint of disapproval mixed in.

"Get ready to buy my dinner!" Marisa called after him. "And Charity's dinner too!"

CHAPTER FIVE

IT WAS OVERCAST and cold in the park; it looked like a snow sky to her. And, even though she was wearing gloves with the tips of the fingers exposed, her hands were beginning to ache.

"How are you doing?" Charity asked.

"My fingers are cramping up," she admitted.

"Should we take a break? Or call it a day?"

Charity John was such a sweet, dear young woman and, in her mind, that light reflected on Dawson. They were raised in the same family, so Dawson couldn't be completely different. Could he?

"And why do you even care?" she asked out loud.

"Would you repeat that?" Charity asked.

"I was just wondering if your brother would tip the scales in his favor."

"No," Charity said. "He's competitive and doesn't like to lose..."

"Me either."

"But he's not a liar and he's not a cheater."

"Well, that's good know."

Charity stopped playing the bells and walked over to her. She took one look at her exposed fingers, which had begun to turn white.

"No. This has to stop." Charity took off her own gloves to feel

Marisa's hands. "Your fingers feel like ice cubes. We need to get them warmed up. Let's call it quits before you get frostbite!"

"No." Marisa dug in her heels. "This is important to me, Charity. I need to know what Bronco wants—classic, modern, a mixture of both?"

"Well, then, at least take a break," Charity suggested.

"Okay," Marisa agreed. "I can do that. But I don't want to leave my instruments."

"I'll stay here," Charity said before she yelled for her brother to come over.

Dawson turned, looked over at them before he quickly left the small group of people with whom he was talking and walked with long strides over to his sister and Marisa.

"What's wrong?"

"Nothing really." Marisa downplayed the situation.

Charity disagreed. "It's something. Her fingers are ice cold but she won't call it quits."

"Stubborn," Dawson said, concern present on his face. "How about we scrounge up some hot chocolate for you?"

Marisa gave in; she hated it, but she knew it was the best thing for her to do in that moment. She wasn't giving up, she was just taking a break from the focus group.

Dawson put down the chips and offered her his arm; he was always a gentleman with her and while she appreciated it and found it charming, she didn't accept it. She looked up into his gorgeous face just in time to see a flash of rejection in his striking eyes.

"Thank you, Dawson," she said to soften the blow. "I think we should stick to our agreement from yesterday. Keep it casual while the good people of Bronco get to know me better."

Dawson's lips turned down. "Maybe I overplayed my hand. I don't want you to get the wrong idea. Bronco is a friendly town. Always has been. Just some are more tied to our traditions than others."

She reached over and touched his arm. "No. I'm grateful that you told me. In all seriousness, I don't like to be wrong, but I may very well be wrong. I was hired because of my popular TikTok videos, but that doesn't mean that my take on the classics and will work here. What if ticket sales are down because of my modern approach? I would be truly horrified and incredibly sad if I did anything to ruin the show that is the kickoff for the whole holiday season! Especially this year because Agnes told me that part of the proceeds of ticket sales this year is going to fund a summer theatre camp!"

Dawson gave a slight nod that signaled to her that he had heard her. He was pensive for the short walk to a small, locally owned coffee shop. When they arrived, Dawson held the door open for her and she smiled at him.

"Thank you, Dawson," she said, glad to have her hands warming up in the pockets of the coat she wore. At the beginning of the pop-up performance, she had left her coat unbuttoned so her cheerful Christmas tree sweater was on display. Now, warmth was the priority.

Dawson walked in behind her. "My pleasure. Some women take offense."

"I was raised by an old-fashioned man," Marisa explained. "But I don't expect it. And I understand women who want to stand on their own. And if that includes opening their own door?" She shrugged. "Who am I to say they're wrong?"

That finally got a smile out of Dawson and that felt gratifying. How could she have missed something like his smile after only one or two days of knowing him? That was downright bizarre and inspired internal curiosity for one minute before her logical brain refocused on the task at hand—producing and directing the best darn Mistletoe Pageant show that Bronco had ever seen. A show that even the stuffy old guard would approve!

"Good morning, Mr. John." Even though the man behind the counter was much older, he spoke to Dawson in a respectful, deferential manner.

"Good morning, sir." Dawson was very polite in return, and that put a check in the column for the *things that I actually like about Dawson John* on her mental checklist.

"What can I do you for?"

"I've heard around town that you've got the best cup of hot chocolate in Bronco."

The man seemed pleased by the compliment. "I do make a mean hot chocolate. How many can I get for you?"

"Three." Dawson held up three fingers before he took his wallet out of his back pocket.

"I'm buying." Marisa pulled out her wallet too.

"Absolutely not," he argued. "It would be my pleasure."

"It would be *my* pleasure," Marisa said. "When I win today fair and square, I'll happily let you buy my dinner."

The man behind the counter delivered hot chocolates with lids on them. He'd overheard the small debate and he said, "Best just let her have her way, Mr. John. I'm a much happier man once I figured that out after twenty years of marriage."

"Thank you," Marisa said with her debit card in her hand.

"Is there anything else I can get you?" the gentleman asked. "Sticky buns, muffins, all made fresh today."

"I'd love to." Marisa put her card in the reader. "But if I did, I would have to curl up on one of your lovely benches while I recovered from a sugar coma."

The man laughed and then handed her a receipt and asked, "Now where have I seen you before?"

She tucked her receipt into her wallet. "I'm not sure."

"This is Marisa Sanchez," Dawson said. "She's producing the Mistletoe Pageant this year."

The man thought for a moment and then snapped his fingers. "Are you any relation to Stanley Sanchez?"

"He's my great-uncle."

"Well, then, that must be it. He was in here not too long ago and showed me some videos of you singing and playing the piano." He nodded. "I knew you looked real familiar."

"I hope you will come see the show this year."

"Me and my wife, we never miss it."

Marisa and Dawson carried the cups out to where Charity was waiting for them.

"Mmm." Charity made a happy noise after her first sip. "So good."

"I agree." Marisa smiled as the hot liquid warmed her from the inside out. "It's my absolute favorite holiday indulgence."

Marisa finished her hot chocolate and then sat back down

behind the keyboard. She was about to get started again when Charity spotted a friend on the other side of the park.

"I'll be right back! I haven't seen her since she left for college in August!"

"Good help," Dawson said, "is hard to find."

"A constant struggle, yes."

"I think your cold finger routine was a stall tactic. That's how I knew you're running scared," Dawson said. "Are you ready to get back to work?"

"Why are you still standing here talking smack?" Marisa stretched her fingers.

"You actually went there."

"Yes, I did," she retorted playfully. "And don't go using your good looks to sway voters to your side of the argument."

"Hey," he said, "I don't need to cheat to defeat."

Marisa began to play scales to warm up her fingers. Dawson picked up the tokens and that was when a young woman appeared on the main steps of city hall. She folded her arms tightly in front of her body in an attempt to keep warm without a coat. The woman, attractive with her blond hair styled into soft curls, waved her hands to get Dawson's attention.

"Dawson!"

He turned around, looked for the person addressing him, and then he smiled appreciatively at the well-dressed woman.

"I thought I saw you over here!" the woman said, shivering in her pencil skirt and silky blouse. "The mayor would like a quick word."

Dawson kind of shrugged before he put down the clipboard. "I'll just be a minute."

Marisa sent him a small smile and then began to play "Rudolph the Red nosed Reindeer." It was one of her absolute favorite songs all the way back to when she was a child. She had never tried to put her modern spin on this classic; it was perfect just the way it was written. As she played a small group of people began to congregate around her and, loving the energy any size audience could bring, Marisa forgot all about her cold fingers or Dawson walking off with a beautiful blonde. As she sang, the crowd grew and then she began to take requests, all the while encouraging the spectators to vote.

She was so happy, totally in her element, and having a great time catching vibes from the crowd that at first she didn't notice a police officer winding his way through the crowd until he was standing in front of her keyboard and watching her intently.

When she finished the song and after some flattering applause that also made her pretty sure she was about to win this wager, she asked the officer if everything was okay.

"Well, between you and me and this oak tree, you need to have a permit to play in the park."

"Oh!" Marisa exclaimed. "I didn't know." She was an avid rule follower! Always had been. "I'll pack up right now."

"No need. Just get a permit next time."

She didn't think there would be a next time, but she told him that she would.

"Don't stop on my account," said the officer. "I love music in the park. I think I saw you on the theater website. My wife *loves* musical theater, and she was first in line when tickets went on sale for the Mistletoe Pageant."

"I hope she will enjoy the show."

"I bet she will."

"Thanks, Officer," she said with a grateful smile.

DAWSON WAS SPEAKING with the mayor, Rafferty Smith, about the Mistletoe Pageant—he had heard that Charity was in the show and he wanted to know what Dawson had to say about how Marisa Sanchez was doing. Dawson only gave Marisa rave reviews and he could do it without stretching the truth. Dawson was impressed with Marisa's talent both as a musician-vocalist and a teacher. It wasn't the right moment to share his concerns about how the old guard of Bronco would respond to Marisa's take on a holiday show, especially when the focus group results hadn't been tallied.

"Thank you for your time," Mayor Smith said.

"My pleasure," Dawson replied. While he was shaking the mayor's hand, out of the corner of his eye he saw a police officer standing with Marisa.

"I'm sorry," Dawson said, "I've got something pressing to attend to."

"I understand." Rafferty nodded. "I've taken up too much of your time as it is."

Dawson left the mayor's office and rushed out of city hall, taking the steps two at a time, and running pretty darn fast in his cowboy boots over to where Marisa was talking to a police officer.

"Everything okay here?" Dawson asked.

The officer turned around, and that's when Dawson realized that the police officer was a high school buddy.

"Big D!" The officer stuck out his hand for him to shake. "How have you been?"

Dawson shook the officer's hand with a broad smile. "Good to see you, Mateo! How's the wife and kids?"

"We're good, man. Everyone's good."

"I'm glad to hear it. We're all good too." Dawson looked at Marisa. She'd stopped playing, which had caused the crowd to move away naturally. She looked upset and Dawson discovered that he didn't like how it felt to see Marisa upset. Strange times. "So, is everything okay?"

"We needed a permit," Marisa said.

"Wait a minute," the officer said to Marisa. "Is Dawson involved in this? No wonder you didn't have a permit! D has never been one for following the rules."

Marisa seemed hesitant to say one way or the other, so Dawson quickly turned it back on himself. "Guilty as charged. If we need a citation, please make it out in my name, not in Marisa's."

Officer Lopez smiled at Dawson. "No citation. Just a friendly reminder that if you want to play in the park, get a permit first."

"Done." Dawson shook the officer's hand again.

Even though he had smoothed things over, he could see that Marisa was unhappy and she was beginning to pack up.

"I hope you aren't leaving on my account." Officer Lopez seemed genuinely concerned.

"I think it's for the best," she said. "The temperature is dropping and I can't play with my gloves on."

"Well," his high school buddy said, "would you be willing

to sing one more song for my wife? She read your bio on the theater website and she even found some of your videos on Tik-Tok." He looked over at Dawson.

Dawson was relieved to see Marisa stop packing as the lure of a fan with a favorite-song request seemed to overcome her frustration about the permit deal.

"What's your wife's favorite song?"

"Do you know 'Last Christmas' by Wham?"

And that singular question made Marisa smile and then laugh, and the happy light returned to her eyes, which made him smile too.

"I know it well!"

"Can I get this on video?" the officer asked.

Marisa said, "Of course," as she sat down on her small stool.

Just then, Charity rounded the corner, spotted the officer and then broke into a run. Winded, she asked, "What's going on? Dawson, what did you do *this* time?"

"It's okay, Charity." Marisa met Dawson's gaze after she took him out of the hot seat with his sister. "You're just in time for Wham!"

Charity's large blue eyes lit up, her face registered sheer joy and she clasped her hands together and hopped up one time, both of her feet coming off the ground.

"Duet?" his sister asked.

"Absolutely duet!" Marisa waited for Charity to get situated and for the officer to start recording before she put her fingers to the keys.

Dawson could hear that Charity's voice blended with Marisa's in an interesting way. It was like an extra layer that captured the ear. And he wasn't the only one who liked this matchup; a new crowd was drawn to them, more votes were cast and, in the end, the officer was the last to cast a vote before leaving with his video of his wife's favorite song.

As usual, Dawson couldn't seem to take his eyes off the pretty musician. The way Marisa took Charity under her wing and worked to show her voice off while taking a supporting role really touched him. His relationship with his sister was a special one for both of them. They loved each other, they were honest with each other, they could be each other's worst critic or biggest fan. He loved everyone in his family, but everything he knew about unconditional love he'd learned from his baby sister. Even listening to Marisa perform a song that was on his *most hated* list, Dawson saw how her incredible voice cut through the human condition filled with rules and roles to reach the heart of a person. Marisa was someone very special—not just a great singer or a great musician—she was a star with a heart of gold.

"I'm tired now. Hungry and cold too," Marisa admitted. "Let's just get going."

Charity stopped her movement. "Before we know who won?"

Marisa nodded to the coffee can. "Would you like to do the honors?"

Charity dumped the chips into her hand and then counted quickly.

"Well?" he asked impatiently. "Who won?"

Charity looked at him with her best deadpan expression, building the suspense like a true performer, and then finally sang the name, "Marisa!"

Dawson frowned. "By what margin?"

"One vote." His sister grinned. "Where are you taking us for dinner?"

ONE OF DAWSON'S favorite places to eat was DJ's Deluxe.

"Dawson must be trying to impress you," Charity said.

Marisa had heard of DJ's Deluxe because her cousin Camilla had worked there before opening up her own restaurant called The Library over in Bronco Valley.

"Are you sure they have seats available? It's packed," Marisa said, her stomach beginning to growl the minute she walked through the door of the upscale barbecue place. Whatever they were cooking, it smelled amazing.

"We'll get a table," Dawson said without concern.

"I don't feel like I'm dressed for this place."

"You look great," Charity was quick to say.

The hostess walked up to the podium and, just like everyone they had encountered today, Dawson was given special treatment.

"Hello, Dawson." The tall, reed-thin hostess smiled at him.

"How are you, Kirsty?"

"I'm doin' better now that you're here," the hostess said. "Will you be sittin' at the bar or do you want a table?"

Marisa's sharp, discerning eye went straight to Dawson's face but couldn't read it.

"Table. For three please."

Kirsty picked up three menus and led the way to a centrally located table. It seemed like the best table in the restaurant. Kirsty handed them all menus and said, "Enjoy your meal."

"Thank you, Kirsty."

Dawson held out a chair for his sister and turned to do the same for Marisa, but she sat down before he could. She was still feeling stunned at how Dawson had managed to get the best table after walking past a line of people that spanned the lobby and the sidewalk on the outside of the establishment.

This was supposed to be fun for all of them, so Marisa decided to let the line of questioning die out while she looked over the menu. The more she looked, the more shocked she became. She hadn't seen a menu priced like this since she'd lived in Boston for college—and on her work-study budget, she'd definitely avoided places like that back then. For Pete's sake, a simple salad was thirty dollars!

Who would pay thirty bucks for a bowl of leaves? Even if it did have some of Montana's finest goat cheese on top!

"What's wrong?" Dawson asked her.

"Nothing's wrong, really," Marisa said, and then asked, "Just as a point of clarification, are these prices for a single entrée or a whole family deal?"

CHAPTER SIX

"I'M TREATING, REMEMBER?" Dawson said to her, and she appreciated his attempt to put her mind at ease. But it felt wrong to spend so much money on one meal.

Finally she decided to go with barbecue chicken and a small salad on the side.

"How is it?" Charity asked her when their meals were promptly delivered and they began to eat.

"It's so good," she said and meant it. She couldn't remember having better barbecue anywhere.

The taste of the meal didn't change how she felt: this one dinner would probably cost the same amount that her family would have spent on groceries in a week. It would've been rude to mention it, so she didn't. She did her best to enjoy the meal and put the inflated cost as much out of her mind as possible.

"So, what did you think about the focus group results?" Dawson asked her after he had wolfed down a huge premium cut steak with a side of broccoli.

Marisa put her fork down, wiped her mouth, then said, "I'm shocked, really. I thought that I would win easily. Not just by one vote."

"But you did win, Marisa," Charity reminded her. "So, I do think that Bronco is ready for some progress."

"Maybe," Marisa said, "but I need to do some rethinking though. I need to thread the new into a tapestry of tradition."

"Now, you're talking." Dawson smiled at her. "Anyone up for dessert?"

"No. No. No." Marisa shook her head. "I'm full."

"Me too," Charity agreed. "There is a part of me that would like to order a huge piece of their famous three layer Death by Chocolate cake just because I know Mom would clutch her pearls at the thought of me eating all those calories. But I'll have to give Mom apoplexy the next time."

The waitress returned and asked if anyone would like to finish the dinner with a cup of coffee.

"Yes, please," Marisa said, and then covered a yawn with her fancy napkin. "I still need to figure out how to marry tradition while still bringing my own style to the pageant. I've been thrown a curveball."

Dawson waited for the coffee to be poured before he said, "I feel like this curveball was my fault."

After adding two sugars and some cream, Marisa gratefully took a sip of the strong coffee. "I wish you wouldn't feel that way. Truly, Dawson. Yes, I have to rethink my approach, but I'm so grateful to have the time to design a show that Bronco—all parts of Bronco—will love. That's always my primary goal when producing a show like the Mistletoe Pageant. I want to create memories that will last a lifetime."

"You did win," he reminded her.

"I did," Marisa agreed. "But by a nose. I need a much wider margin if I'm going to design a show that is a success. And the only time I will truly know if I succeeded in that main goal is on opening night!"

"It's going to be great." Sweet Charity always tried to make people feel better.

"Well," Dawson leaned back, looking well-fed and happy, "I'm glad I didn't end up on your naughty list."

"Just give him time," Charity said.

That made Marisa laugh. It was so easy to be with Dawson and his sister. And she loved how they both worked overtime to make her feel comfortable in a town that, at times, felt very far away from her hometown of Tenacity.

The day in the park had tired her out and she couldn't stop yawning. "If I don't get home and get into bed, I might just embarrass the both of you by falling asleep in this chair."

They all prepared to stand up when a gentleman stopped by their table.

"Dawson John! How the heck are you?"

Dawson stood up and shook the man's hand. "DJ Traub! The man who single-handedly put Bronco on the map for our barbecue."

"How was the food tonight?" DJ asked. Marisa hadn't met the owner of DJ's Deluxe, but Camilla had talked about him often and had only positive things to say.

"Damn delicious!" Dawson sat back down. "Can you join us?"

"No," DJ said. "Not tonight. But I thank you for the offer."

"Next time, then."

"You bet." DJ nodded before he turned his attention to Charity. "Is this little Charity all grown up?"

"Hi, Mr. Traub."

"Oh, Lord, no. Mr. Traub is my father. Just DJ."

DJ walked to Marisa's side of the table and introduced himself.

"Now, didn't I see you in my Facebook feed a couple of nights back?" the owner asked her.

"Possibly. I'm Marisa Sanchez. I was interviewed about the Mistletoe Pageant by a blogger who covers all things Bronco."

"That's it. That's it. Now are you any relation to Camilla?"

"She's my cousin."

"Boy, did I hate to see her go," DJ said in a booming voice. "She was one of my best employees. But I can't stop progress. I'm glad she's got her own place now. Tell her I said hi, will you?"

Marisa nodded. "Of course I will."

"How's Thunder Canyon treating you?" Dawson asked. "And how's your family?"

DJ and his wife, Allaire, spent most of their time in their

hometown of Thunder Canyon, several hundred miles away. They had another barbecue restaurant, the much more casual DJ's Rib Shack, known for its secret sauce—the recipe of which DJ still refused to reveal, even after over a decade in business.

"Right as rain," DJ said. "Right as rain."

Soon after the owner left their table, the three of them decided to head out. They all had busy days, and Marisa had so much thinking to do and she could only do that alone in a quiet space.

The minute they walked outside, a frigid gust of wind felt like pinpricks on her face. She ducked her head and walked quickly to Charity's truck.

"Drive safe," Dawson said to his sister as he held her door open.

"Yes, Dad."

Then he ushered Marisa around to the passenger side and opened the door.

"Thank you for dinner, Dawson." She held out her hand for him to shake. "And for the eye-openers." When he gripped her hand, she felt the oddly familiar warmth and excitement that only his touch seemed to induce.

"I hope to see your real soon, Marisa."

She smile at him shyly. "Me too." He shut her door, and she watched through the window as he walked to his vehicle.

Charity pulled out of the parking lot slowly. "Dawson likes you."

Marisa felt both excited and terrified. For her, she had always kept romance at bay. When she was in Boston, she kept her schedule crowded with her education and gigs with her band. Even when her fans asked her out after a gig, and some were nearly as handsome as Dawson, but no one was as handsome as Dawson, she had turned them down. When she had graduated from Berklee and returned to Tenacity, she had focused on building a career, finding ways to serve her community and making sure she contributed to her family.

She was not a naive woman, but while she had dated before, she was a novice when it came to love. Had she ever before felt this electricity light up her entire body like whenever Dawson was around? No. Not even close. While she couldn't deny it, she also didn't have time to turn this molehill into a giant mountain. Her focus was the Mistletoe Pageant; that's what needed her full attention, not some crush she had developed for one of the wealthiest, most influential, ridiculously handsome eligible bachelors of Bronco, Montana!

"I like him too." Marisa did her best to sound nonchalant.

"No," Charity said. "I mean he *really* likes you."

"You don't approve?" She could hear some defensiveness in her tone. It was an old insecurity raising its ugly head. She was confident in herself now and embraced her curves, but it hadn't always been that way.

Charity glanced over at her briefly. "Not because of you, Marisa! I would never think that! You are one of the most amazing women I've ever met. I look up to you."

"Thank you."

"God. I hate that you thought I wouldn't approve of you for my brother."

"It's been a long day for all of us. I'm tired, Charity. Don't pay any attention to me."

There was an awkward silence before Charity added, "Dawson dates around, plays the field, but hasn't really had a serious relationship yet. And he's *thirty*, right? I just don't want him to hurt you."

"He won't." Marisa said, and she felt confident in that statement. She shared undeniable chemistry with the ultra-handsome cowboy and she genuinely enjoyed his company, but she had no intention of even cracking open the door to her heart.

"I hope not," Charity said uncertainly. "I've never seen him like this before. The way he looks at you. The way he is so concerned about you…"

"I'll be okay." She did her best to reassure her young protégé. "I have three weeks to launch this show. I have to focus on that."

Charity dropped her off at her car, which she had left in the theater parking lot.

"Text me when you get home?" Charity asked her.

"I will." Marisa shut the passenger door. "Get some rest. We have a long day tomorrow."

"WHO THE HECK told you all of that?" Dawson asked his brothers Jameson and Maddox.

"Dad told us, but I don't know which part of the grapevine got ahold of his ear," Maddox said, holding the board in place while Dawson hammered a nail long enough to hold the wood in place.

Fixing fences was something the John brothers did together that allowed them to catch up without interruption.

"That means Mom knows," Dawson said.

"I don't think so," Jameson said. "Dad doesn't want to be bothered, and if he thinks Mom will chew on his ear for several hours, that's strong motivation to keep his mouth shut."

"I agree," Maddox said. "So what part of the gossip is true?"

Dawson grabbed a thermos of water, took a long draw out of it and then handed it to Maddox. "A fraction as usual. I didn't have to stop Charity from getting arrested, I didn't get into a fight with a police officer, I didn't make out with the mayor's secretary and I didn't take two women out on a date. Yes, I took two women out to dinner but Charity was one of them!"

"Is that Marisa sitting with you at the table?" Maddox asked.

"Her name is Marisa Sanchez," Dawson said, annoyed. "And yes, she was there."

The brothers moved to the next part of the fence that needed mending, and Dawson wished that he could steer the conversation away from Marisa entirely. He felt out of his depth with her—she always managed to find something that put him in a negative light, and he was beginning to think her reciprocating his sincere feelings for her was a total impossibility. Even the reserved table had been a point of contention. He'd taken many women to DJ's Deluxe, and not one of them had ever complained about the reserved table or the prices on the menu. He had hoped to impress Marisa, and that had backfired on him pretty epically. He had hoped that a day out on the range with his brothers would be a way for him to lick his wounds in peace. But all his brothers seemed to want to talk about was Marisa.

"So who is this girl to you?" Jameson asked.

"She's closer to thirty, so 'girl' doesn't really apply."

Jameson looked up at him, hammer in hand, and after a second said, "You've got it bad, little brother."

"Why? Because I don't think you should refer to her as a girl when she is clearly a grown-ass woman?"

"Yeah." Jameson went back to his work. "That's the sum of it."

Dawson lifted up a board from the trailer hooked to their ranch truck and carried it over to Maddox.

"A *woman* from Tenacity isn't going to get by Mimi," Jameson added.

"Well, I wish you good luck, little brother." Jameson stood upright to take the pressure off his back. "I want you to be happy, and if this Marisa does it for you, I'll stand right there beside you."

"Second that," Maddox said.

"Well, I don't think it's going to come to that," Dawson told them. "She doesn't feel that way about me."

Maddox looked at him disbelievingly. "That can't be right. What put that into your head?"

Dawson went back to the trailer for another board. "She's different from anyone I've ever met. She's more interested in giving back to people in her community than going out on expensive dates. She almost lost her mind over the prices at DJ's Deluxe."

"She sounds like a departure for you," said Maddox, "Not the obvious choice."

"She is different," he agreed. "A once in a lifetime kind of woman."

Maddox and Jameson exchanged a look before his oldest brother asked, "Does she think you're a once in a lifetime man?"

"Damned if I know! She thinks the special treatment I get because of our last name is a mark against me! Like last night, there was a line and we go to jump the line and got seated quickly at one of the best tables. Now there isn't anything I can do about that, now, can I?"

"Not a thing," Maddox agreed. "You didn't choose the family you were born into."

Dawson said, "I only have three weeks to show her that we can make it work with us."

"How do you know it will?" Jameson asked.

"Gut feeling," Dawson said.

Jameson hammered in a nail and then took a break long enough to ask, "Do you want a piece of advice?"

"Not really." Dawson had now grown tired of the conversation. Nothing his brothers could say would stop his heart from aching. He wanted to impress Marisa, prove that he was worthy, but all of his old tools in his "romance the ladies" toolbox didn't really work all that well on Marisa. Maybe his brothers were right; maybe his feelings for Marisa were doomed to cause him pain. But that didn't change how he felt about her.

"Well, you're gonna get it anyhow because it's my job to look out for you," Jameson told him. "Whatever you think you feel for this woman—"

"Marisa…"

"Rethink it real quick." Jameson continued, "She's not going to pass muster with Randall and Mimi. That's the real bottom line. And *if* what you're telling us is true—that you truly do care for Marisa—then you'd be selfish to put her through it. Unless you're absolutely sure she can stand up to the pressure. If you're not one hundred percent on that…" He shrugged. "Then maybe Maddox is right. Go fish in a more acceptable pond."

Dawson had respected Jameson as the eldest of the siblings, but today more than any other day in recent memory, he wanted to punch Jameson right between the eyes.

DAWSON SPENT TIME mulling over what his brothers had said to him. Was he being selfish in this compulsion that was driving him to seek Marisa out? It certainly hadn't been planned. When he had driven Charity to her audition, he couldn't have known that he would meet a woman who had changed him so profoundly on the inside. Yes, of course, there were differences between them, but why did that have to be a deal-breaker? There were plenty of marriages between couples who were polar opposites. So after a full day of thinking about his predicament, Dawson decided to call Marisa just to check on her.

She answered the phone on the second ring. "Hi, Dawson."

"Hi, Marisa." His heart had begun to race with excitement

at the mere sound of her melodic voice. "How are you How'd it go today?"

Dawson had checked with Charity that rehearsals had concluded for the day, and he had planned his phone call accordingly.

Marisa let out a long sigh, and that told him everything he needed to know without her saying it.

"Would you like to talk about it?" he asked as gently as he could.

"Well," Marisa said, "the focus group..."

Dawson cursed silently—he knew he had really screwed things up with that suggestion. At that point, he had been interested in finding a plausible reason to spend time with Marisa, but he also knew that he wanted her to consider how the old guard might feel about the major changes she had made to a dearly held, time-honored tradition of the Mistletoe holiday pageant. Ever since he was a little boy, his family attended the holiday show and then followed that up with a family trip to the Mistletoe Rodeo. In fact, all of the John siblings had participated in the rodeo over the years.

"I feel real bad that I talked you into that stupid focus group," Dawson told her. "I can tell you have had some time to think it over and you don't sound happy."

"I have. And I wish you'd stop blaming yourself. Was it the result I expected? No. But it's reality and I have to make some tough decisions to pivot back to a more traditional show. It'll take time and I don't have a whole lot of that."

He said, "I feel like I've got to do something to make amends here, Marisa. What can I do?"

There was a long silence on the other end of the line, followed by another heavy sigh, before she said, "Thank you, truly. But some things I just have to figure out on my own."

"Just talk to me," he prompted her. "I'm a great sounding board."

He hadn't meant to make her laugh, but he was still glad he did.

"I don't really see you as the sounding board type."

"Well," he said, "just goes to show you that you can't judge a book by its cover, now, can you?"

"I suppose not," she said. "I'm still trying to figure out how to take the feedback from the focus group and change the show accordingly. I guess I really thought I'd win everyone over a hundred percent and have no holdouts."

He waited for her to continue, grateful that she was talking through her thoughts with him. It kept her on the line and it kept her connected to him and that's what he wanted: to help and to stay connected.

"My problem is that once I have a vision set in my mind, I can be quite rigid about it. And that makes it difficult for me to change it last minute."

"I shouldn't have talked you into that focus group idea," he repeated.

This time she addressed that concern. "Dawson, no, of course I don't like to hear that some people aren't wild about my plan for the show. But I'm grateful that you helped me figure out a way to understand what people are thinking and feeling and how I can make adjustments. My dilemma now is that I need to manage to stay true to myself, honor the reason I was hired in the first place, while meeting Bronco where it is now."

"What can I do, Marisa?" he asked again. "I want to help."

"I feel like I'm on the verge of a breakthrough that would allow me to take the pulse of Bronco as a whole, to experience it in a way that would shine a spotlight on the path forward."

After a minute of racing through possible scenarios to help Marisa, Dawson asked, "How about this idea? How about we return to the scene of the crime?"

"Do you mean, Permit-Gate?"

Dawson laughed. The fact that Marisa could make him laugh whenever he spoke to her was a powerful drug.

"Yes," he said with good humor in his voice.

"Not that I doubt your sincerity, Dawson. But how would going back there help me? I feel like I understand that the old guard wants to hold on to tradition. I've run up against this at times in Tenacity, and I'm one of their own!"

"No," he disagreed. "I don't think you have, honestly. I'd

like to describe Bronco as it will be during the first week of December."

"I don't think so... I feel like I've playing hooky too much with you because you're fun to hang out with."

"Thank you. You're fun too. Can you trust me on this, Marisa? I believe in my gut that this is what you need. I can paint the scene for you and show you pictures that I've taken over the years."

When she didn't respond, he asked, "What do you think? Meet me at Bronco Java and Juice tomorrow after rehearsals?"

"Okay," she finally said. "Maybe it won't help but it doesn't hurt to try."

CHAPTER SEVEN

THE NEXT DAY, Marisa had found it very difficult to focus on re-hearsals when she knew that she would be seeing Dawson at the end of her day. She couldn't change her growing feelings for the handsome Bronco cowboy—that was the stuff of the heart—but she did recognize that, even if they did have a sweet and spicy holiday romance, it could only be *that*. Using her mother's own recipe, Marisa *was* happier when Dawson was around, she did miss him when he was away, but she could not see him in her future in the one-horse town of Tenacity.

The man she imagined who would eventually be her husband didn't have a face, but he did have traits and qualities that had always been nonnegotiable—humble, hardworking and willing to share her passion for community service. She had to give back to Tenacity! What would she have turned out to be without the support of her community? Even the plane ticket that flew her to start her college career at Berklee was paid for from a collection plate that had been passed around in their church. It wasn't his fault really, but Dawson could never understand what it felt like to do without. He could never understand what it felt like to have an entire community rally to lift up one of their own so she could succeed. And, while he could never understand it, she knew that she could never forget it.

"Hi there." Dawson had arrived before her and had seemed

to be standing by the front door of Bronco Java and Juice so he could open it for her.

"Hi, Dawson," she said, with that same, wonderful, warm and tingly feeling that swept over her body whenever he was near her.

She walked in, pulled off her gloves and hat, and then Dawson was there to help her take off her overcoat. Underneath her dark blue conservative long coat, she had donned one of her favorite ugly holiday sweaters that portrayed the first Christmas flight of Rudolph the Red-Nosed Reindeer. Her favorite part of this sweater was the fact that Rudolph's red nose actually blinked.

"That's a nice sweater."

"Why thank you, Dawson. Would you like to borrow it sometime?"

"Super tempting." Dawson smiled at her. "You love Christmas, don't you?"

"What tipped you off?" She returned his smile.

"Wild guess."

Together they walked up to the counter and he ordered coffee for himself and then looked at her before he said, "One large hot chocolate, with extra marshmallows, right?" At her nod, he added, "Go grab a seat and I'll meet you there."

While she waited for him, she tried very hard not to stare at him. How could a human be that perfectly made? Dawson walked with the confidence of a man who had been given every physical advantage. His features were strong, symmetrical, from his jawline to the dimple in the chin to the firm shape of his lips. A sonnet could be written about the kissability of Dawson John's lips. The man should be in Hollywood making blockbuster movies to give the women of the world something to fantasize about this holiday season, not ordering a hot chocolate for her.

"Sorry," he said, "no marshmallows today."

"It's okay. Thank you," she said, when he joined her at the table and handed her the cup. She blew on the hot chocolate to cool it off but she just couldn't wait, so she took a sip and promptly burned her lips and the roof of her mouth.

"I'll never learn," she said.

"Burn your mouth?"

"Absolutely I did."

"Was it worth it?"

"Absolutely it was."

"Well, just in case they were out," Dawson said, tugging a small bag out of his shirt pocket. "Perhaps this will help cool it off."

"Dawson John! Are you ridiculously handsome *and* sweet?"

Dawson flashed her that winning smile with a wink and a look in his eye that set every bell and whistle in her body.

As Marisa watched Dawson fill her cup, she felt like her love-meter siren was blasting in her ears. Had any man been so attentive to what made her happy? Yes, she had been pursued back in her college days, but it had been easy for her to resist their often half-hearted attempts. There was nothing half-hearted about Dawson's gestures toward her. The man carried a baggie of mini marshmallows in his shirt pocket just so he could, in her mind, see the smile that it brought to her face.

"How is it?" he asked.

"Perfect now," she said, then asked, "So, I'm assuming you do have a job other than providing me with marshmallows and helping me understand Bronco better."

Dawson laughed. Just yesterday his brothers had been complaining about his recent absences from their ranch work. "I admit I've been playing hooky with you, but my brothers owe me some from their days when they were romancing soon-to-be wives."

Marisa's heart felt like it skipped a bit when Dawson mentioned "wives" as it related to him playing the same kind of "love" hooky. Did Dawson think of her in that way? As a wife? They hadn't even had a first real date unless coffee at the Eat, Gas, Go counted.

After they finished their drinks, they both put on their winter gear. He held the door open for her, and she walked out into the chilly November day. They walked together across the street to the park where she had won their bet by one vote. She wasn't a whiz at statistics but that margin could not be viewed as significant. For all intents and purposes, it was a tie.

On the way across the street, Marisa's foot hit a slick patch of ice and as her foot slid forward, tipping her off balance, she reached for the only thing sturdy enough to stop her from falling.

Holding on to Dawson's arm, Marisa fought to steady herself. He stopped walking, put his hand under her elbow and helped her to stand upright.

"Better?" he asked.

"Yes," Marisa said, annoyed that she had just played a damsel in distress with Dawson coming to her rescue.

She had to stop focusing on Dawson's handsomeness, the woodsy scent of his skin and the way he looked at her with those ocean-blue eyes, making her want to spend all day just swimming in them. She was here on a mission to save the Mistletoe Pageant, *not* to ogle a cowboy.

Dawson looked over at her, seemed to be about to say something to her when he slipped on an icy patch in his fancy cowboy boots. She reached out to break his fall, which was a fool's errand in the light of the fact that he was much taller and his body was heavy from tightly packed muscles.

Somehow, Dawson managed to stop his fall while not pulling her down. After a quick minute, he said, "We appear to be having some difficulty walking today."

Marisa, as she often did with Dawson, laughed happily. "What's wrong with us today?"

Dawson met her gaze and for the briefest of moments, he let her see what was hidden behind his incredible eyes and, on a soul level, she knew exactly what he was feeling because she was feeling it too.

Chemistry.

Undeniable attraction.

Even possibly, love.

She was conscious of the fact that Bronco, while not as tiny as Tenacity, was still small enough for the gossip mill to be fully operational. No matter what romantic notions she was having for Dawson John, Marisa was keenly aware of the fact that he was the son of a highly influential family. From her experience, she wouldn't be his family's first choice in the love department, and it was impossible for her to imagine Dawson getting the green light from her father or her brothers.

"I'm ready to be inspired," she told Dawson, clinging to a tiny ray of hope that he could help her break through her creative block. "Are you the ghost of Christmas past, present or future top help me see the errors of my modern musical theater ways?"

"I think you've got a handle on the present…"

"Maybe."

"And I'm not psychic, so I've got no business trying to make any predictions."

"Except to tell me that my show, as it stands right now, might draw the wrath of the old guard and cause a boycott of the Mistletoe Pageant!"

Dawson frowned at her. "I did make that prediction, didn't I?"

"That would be a yes, Dawson. But… I think that you can predict the future. There have already been some complaints on the theater website."

"That was lightning quick even by Bronco standards."

"Maybe Bronco doesn't want a stranger to run a historical event."

"Well, I'm not happy to be right about that," he said, and then tried to lighten the mood. "So, I'll be your ghost of Bronco Christmas past…"

"Eeeeew," she teased him, and he was glad she was willing to follow him back to their playful mood. "Spooky!"

DAWSON FELT AS if he'd never truly known what it meant to be happy. He had never expected any woman, or any one person, to make him happy—he knew that this was his job to do. But when he was with Marisa, he recognized that pre-Marisa, he hadn't drilled down to his soul, hadn't uncovered what could make him feel satisfied, content, filled to the brim with joy. Post-Marisa…he knew it exactly. He was certain what he felt for her was love. Plain, simple love. Now that didn't mean that a relationship with Marisa would be plain or simple. As much as he professed his "I don't care" attitude when he was talking with his brothers, there was a very real part of him that wanted his parents to approve of his choice and embrace the woman he intended to marry.

Could that ever happen if his chosen was Marisa Sanchez who would be a wonderful daughter-in-law but didn't come from a cattle baron family? Dawson answered his question with a small shake of his head before he shut down that part of his brain and focused his attention on helping Marisa. At the most basic level, he had discovered Marisa wanted Bronco to love her version of the Mistletoe Pageant.

Dawson pulled up some pictures he had taken at the tree lighting ceremony the year before.

Marisa studied the pictures and then looked at the undecorated park before her. "So, the tree goes right there?"

"Yes," he said. "Tree lighting always happens on the first Saturday in December. The streets are lined with vendors and performers—"

"All with permits," she interjected with good humor.

"Yes." He laughed. "Most certainly."

"Tell me more," she urged him, and he enjoyed watching her as she worked through her creative process, certain he had never met, and would never meet, a woman who was as gifted as Marisa. She was a genius; he was convinced of it. And admitting that to himself exposed a fault-line crack in his rock-solid self-esteem. Was he good enough for a woman like Marisa? There wasn't a frivolous bone in her body; quite the opposite in fact. She was incredibly focused and determined, and she was driven by a deep desire to serve.

They sat down on a nearby bench while he painted a picture of the idyllic Bronco holiday cheer. Every streetlamp, every traffic light, every window in the historic Bronco City Hall building would be dressed with lights and garland and wreaths. Kids would be entertained by face painting and ornament decorating, and bursting with energy from too many cups of hot chocolate. A modern touch had been added, Dawson told her—the many selfie stations replete with holiday cutouts.

"It all sounds so…" She paused, seeming to look for the right words. "Perfect."

"For us here in Bronco, that month leading into the new year is something that we look forward."

"Even cowboys like you?" she said quietly.

"Even cowboys like me," he agreed. "Maybe especially cowboys like me."

"How so?" She looked at him suspiciously and teased, "Are you a spy for the old guard?"

"You never know," he said. He winked at her, enjoying the feel of her body innocently resting next to his on the bench. "John men aren't raised to be emotional."

"But you love the traditions just as I love mine in Tenacity. I also love the excitement of creating something new—something that could become one of those traditions over the years."

"I think that describes me too." Dawson met her gaze. "And when I was a boy, I could just be a boy when my family came to this park. I didn't have to worry about being tough or the best this or that. I could just be…"

"You," she said. "No strings attached."

"Right."

After some thought, Marisa said, "I think that I've been so determined to fulfill the order, I guess I can put it like that, of the why I was hired in the first place. If my video hadn't gone viral, I wouldn't be sitting here on this bench with you right now. I would be back in my safe playground in Tenacity, where most of my ideas, no matter how outside of the box, are embraced by my community even if they don't like them."

"I think that's right."

"That's what you've been trying to show me."

"I feel like I didn't show it to you in the right way," he said. "And I'm sorry for that."

She turned toward him, touched his arm and said, "You showed me in the best way, Dawson. I don't know how you *knew* what I needed but you did know."

He put his hand over her mittened hand. "Then, I'm glad I could help."

Marisa turned her body forward but left her hand on his arm for a couple of moments longer. He fought the urge to reach for it, to hold on to that hand for the rest of his natural born days.

But his brother's warnings worked on his mind, twisted things up for him, so he didn't act on impulse. Instead, he told himself to enjoy Marisa in this moment and let destiny work out some of the parts that seemed impossible between them.

"The memories you have of Christmas here in Bronco are close to my own memories of the holiday season in Tenacity."

Dawson listened to her, wanting her to talk more so he could always have the memory of her silky, smooth voice burned in his brain.

"My parents didn't have a lot of money. There were five of us kids, so that's a lot of mouths to feed."

"Christmas must have been incredibly difficult for my parents. They always wanted us to have everything that we wanted, but they couldn't provide it. I believe, even though they've never said it and I've never asked, that this caused my parents deep pain that they carry even to this day."

"What traditions did you have growing up?" he asked.

Marisa smiled. "We had wonderful traditions. Even though there wasn't money for all of those store-bought things that we wanted, and I can only speak for myself, I always remember our Christmas Eve and day being the best days of the year. My mom would make us all matching pajamas. She even made a pair for our dad."

"And he wore them?"

"He did." Marisa recalled the holidays with a bright smile. "He was and still is such a strong man—a man among men—but for us and for his wife, Will Sanchez put on those pajamas and wore them with pride."

"Sounds like a man I'd like to know."

Marisa looked up into his face and he could see his comment about her father had struck a chord in her. "He is a wonderful man. His whole purpose in life is to take care of his family. That's what drives him."

"We always watched *It's a Wonderful Life* while we trimmed the tree. My parents had some ornaments from their childhood—a wooden sleigh carved by my father's grandfather and my mom had a small handmade doll that her mother had made for her. The doll looked just like my mom and had a matching Christmas dress. And, of course, mom and dad hung up every handmade ornaments us kids made. Each year, they get more and more tattered and we beg her to throw them away, but she just puts a little tape over the rips and hangs them for another year."

"I like the sound of your family Christmas."

"It's always seemed so magical to me. I want to carry on these traditions with my own family one day." In the short time they had spent together, marriage and family had come up several times. Other women had brought up the subject, hinting about marriage and or a long term commitment but he let that topic die as soon as it was raised. It was different with Marisa. The topic of family, kids, marriage were not shut down on his end and he could see Marisa as a wonderful mother as she continued her description of her family traditions. "When we were little kids, we always tried to wait up for Santa but we never could. I remember falling asleep on the couch with my siblings and then waking up in my own bed, bright and early on Christmas morning. While Dad was filling up on homemade Christmas cookies and milk, he must have carried us, one by one, to our beds."

"It sounds like you have a close family."

She nodded. "I do. We were always rich in love."

"I admire that."

Marisa had an odd look in her eyes when she looked up at him, but the thoughts behind that expression weren't vocalized.

"I'm close with my brothers," Dawson said.

"And your sister."

He nodded his agreement. "My folks are a different breed really. Too much keeping up with the Joneses and not enough enjoying what we have right now."

"They can't be all that bad. You seemed to have turned out all right, and Charity is one of the sweetest people I've ever met in my life."

"Charity is the crown jewel of the family, I'll give you that. But us John siblings made a concerted effort to go down the exact opposite path than the one our parents set up for us. In my mind, life's too darn short to spend so much time worrying about what other people think. But they're my parents and I love them."

"We don't always agree with our parents. I think it would be odd if we did." Marisa said to him kindly, "I see you with your sister and I know what kind of man you are on the inside. A family man."

As if the universe had given them a perfect chance to get their focus back on Christmas Bronco style, big, fat, snow flakes began top fall from the sky.

Marisa held out her gloved hands to catch snowflakes that had begun to fall. "It's snowing!"

The falling snowflakes grabbed his companion's attention, and Dawson was glad for it.

Marisa spun around in a circle, head back, arms outstretched as she tried to catch the fluffy snowflakes on her tongue.

"Isn't this just the most magical time of the year, Dawson? In just a few weeks, it'll be Thanksgiving."

"Of course," He smiled at her as he enjoyed her ability to be perfectly in the moment.

Dawson acted on sheer instinct, not giving it much thought at all when he took her into his arms, in broad daylight, in one of the most traversed parts of town, and spun her around in a circle before letting her twirl under his arm. After several fast twirls, Marisa laughed and told him that she was dizzy. He stopped twirling her and then held her close to his body until the dizziness subsided.

"I love to twirl!" Marisa stepped back once she was seeing clearly.

He almost let it slip—it was right there on the tip of his tongue. *I love you.* Three simple words he had never said to anyone other than his relatives. I. Love. You.

"Thank you for this, Dawson," she said after he walked her to her car. "It's exactly what I needed."

"Then I'm glad," he said, his hands on her driver's-side door. "I like spending time with you."

"I like spending time with you," Marisa said unexpectedly.

"Maybe we could spend some more time together while you're still here in Bronco."

"This weekend I'm letting everyone off from rehearsal," she told him.

"What would you like to do?"

"Well, I like to dance," she told him.

"As you wish."

Dawson shut her door and watched her pull out and drive away. He had just secured an official date with the pretty pageant director. How would he manage to keep her at a safe distance when all he wanted to do was take her into his arms, kiss her like she'd never been kissed before in her life, and hold her close for the rest of their days. He didn't know how he would do it, but if he loved her, and he truly felt that he did, then the best thing he could do was let her go. He couldn't stand the idea of his lovely Marisa ever being on the receiving end of Randall and Mimi's disapproval. Now that he was certain that he had fallen in love with Marisa, her happiness outweighed his own. At the end of this, he had to let her go, and he would let her go. In the meantime, he wanted to make as many memories with Marisa as he could, and he would hold those memories close in his heart for the rest of his days on this Earth. Of that, he was certain.

"So, WHAT DO you think?" Marisa asked Charity.

It was the end of their last rehearsal before the weekend they would be off for rest and reenergizing before the major push to opening night.

Charity, as always, was the last one to leave the theater, helping her pack up for the night. "I think it's a perfect blend between Bronco's traditional soul while moving the dial just a smidge in the direction of newfangled tunes that will lead to our ruination." Her voice carried a teasing tone.

Marisa shook her head. "That was eerily descriptive."

Charity laughed good-naturedly. "Oh, Marisa, relax! I was totally kidding. My prediction? You are going to be the toast of the town!"

As they walked out of the theater together, Charity said, "I'm kind of shocked that Dawson helped you figure things out. I wouldn't have cast him for that role."

Marisa couldn't help but smile; without saying it directly, Dawson's sister had just told her that her brother was behaving out of character. It made her feel special, and she had given up trying to lie to herself about her deepening feelings for the cowboy.

"He's taking me out dancing." Marisa felt close enough with Charity to give up that secret.

Charity titled her head to the side when she heard that news. "A real date?"

"I suppose." Marisa shrugged. "I...like him."

"He likes you too," Charity said easily. "I wasn't okay with it in the beginning."

Those words felt like a deep cut. "You didn't approve of me for him?"

Charity's lovely features crumpled as she reached out to touch her arm. "Marisa, no! That's not what I meant at all! Please believe me! I love Dawson. Always have, always will. But I didn't think he was the right one for you, not the other way around."

"Oh." That was the only thing she could think to say.

Charity shrugged one shoulder. "So I've given it long deliberation and I've come to a decision." The frown she wore turned into a brilliant grin. "I'm going to give him one chance with you."

CHAPTER EIGHT

MARISA TOOK EXTRA care with her outfit, her makeup and her hair. It was Friday night, and Dawson would be meeting her at the theater where he would take them both to a place called Wild Willa's Saloon. She had decided to leave her ugly Christmas sweaters in the drawer and put on one of her sassy Rank 45 rodeo button-down shirts in a maroon-red that showed off her black hair and dark brown eyes in their best light. She didn't typically wear makeup but did use a sparing amount for her date with Dawson. The mascara made her eyelashes look thick and long and hopefully it would draw Dawson's attention to her instead of any other women who would be at the bar.

"Where are you off to looking so pretty?" Her great-uncle Stanley stopped by the bathroom on his way to his own bedroom.

"I'm going to go kick my heels up a bit," she told him. It was the truth if not the whole truth.

She wasn't sure that she wanted her family to know about her budding friendship/relationship with Dawson. Besides, her great-uncle was already sad enough. After losing his wife of sixty years, the family had convinced him to leave his life in Mexico to start anew in Bronco, Montana. It wasn't long before lightning had struck Stanley twice and he fell in love with the elderly, free-spirited town psychic Winona Cobbs and proposed. Everyone believed that Stanley and Winona would enjoy a short courtship before they tied the knot. But when Winona disappeared on their wedding day without saying a word, Stanley experienced his second heartbreak. The entire Bronco Sanchez family tried their best to support him while he figured out what had happened to his beloved bride-to-be.

"Good girl," Stanley said, his shoulders drooped forward. "You deserve it. You've got the strong Sanchez work ethic."

Marisa hugged Stanley. "Thank you. That means a lot to me coming from you."

Stanley held on to her a while longer before he shuffled down the hall. Then, he stopped and turned back to her. "If you ever find love, *mi sobrina*, hold on to it real tight and don't ever let it go."

"I will, *tio*." She promised him, wishing that he could find Winona.

Not wanting to explain herself to anyone else in the small, cozy house, Marisa grabbed her car keys and coat and slipped out quietly into the frigid winter air, feeling like a teenager sneaking out of the house for the first time.

She drove the short distance to the theater and felt relieved when she saw that Dawson had beaten her to it. She parked next to his massive GMC truck, and he was there to open the door and hold out his hand for her to take as she got out from behind the wheel.

"Cold enough for you?" Dawson asked.

"I've got Montana blood running through my veins, same as you, don't forget," she bantered. "This is beach weather."

"You look mighty pretty, Ms. Sanchez."

He offered her his arm and for the first time, she took it. Why pretend that she wasn't interested? Why pretend that she didn't want to be next to him? As far as she could tell, the feeling was mutual.

"I was just thinking the same thing about you!" She felt giddy like she had just had two glasses of pink champagne.

Marisa climbed up into the passenger seat of Dawson's truck, then he shut the door before he walked quickly around the truck to join her in the cab.

"Are you ready for a good time?" Dawson asked her.

"You have no idea."

Dawson drove them to the Wild Willa's Saloon while she told him about the changes in the show she'd decided on following the focus group and the walk down Bronco Park Christmas memory lane.

"So far, things are going rather smoothly. I met with the band earlier today, and they're really nailing the jazzed-up versions that I'm keeping in the show, and the dances are starting to come together…"

"And Charity?"

"She is my best performer. Such a quick study. I really can't imagine the show without her."

Dawson pulled into the crowded parking lot; they weren't the only ones who were looking for a good time. It had been such a long time since she had gone on a date that she began to have a severe case of anxiety. She was stepping out with Dawson John, and it struck her as a potentially horrible idea.

"Wild Willa's Saloon." Dawson shut off the engine. "Home of the Get Lucky Bar, the one and only bar that is shaped like a four-leaf clover."

"It looks crowded."

"Friday night."

Marisa wanted to find a way to back out of the date; she was fairly well-known around town because she had been in the newspaper and on the local news, and Dawson was Bronco elite and it seemed like everyone knew him. What if Bronco didn't like the idea of her dating one of their favorite sons? Could this one night unravel all of the work she'd done on the show to fit the town's expectations?

While Dawson walked around to her side of the truck, Marisa truly contemplated backing out. But the brief exchange with her great-uncle Stanley, so sad and downtrodden while he mourned the loss of his beloved Winona, smacked her right in the forehead. She knew what he was saying to her—don't forgo love for work.

Dawson opened her door, held out his hand and asked, "Ready?"

"Yes, I am." She took his offered hand. "More than ready, I think."

DAWSON FELT PROUD to have Marisa on his arm as they entered one of his favorite watering holes. He was certain that he'd run into plenty of people he knew; he was taking Marisa to a place that would put a spotlight on them. But he didn't care. He only wanted to make Marisa happy, to show her a good time, to enjoy each other.

No doubt they were going to run into women he'd dated casually over the years and friends that he'd grown up with. And all of them were going to be curious when they saw him with a woman who was nearly the exact opposite of his so-called "type." But over the last couple of weeks he figured out that the women he'd been dating weren't actually his type. Marisa was. But how could he have known it without first meeting her?

"You want a drink?" he asked her.

"Sure," she said. "I'll take a beer."

"Tap or bottle?"

"Bottle."

Dawson ordered two bottles of beer for them before he led the way through the crowd to find an empty booth near the dance floor that was situated in the center of the four-leaf clover.

"Here's to an excellent Mistletoe Pageant." He held out his bottle for her to clink.

"Here's hoping." She took a swig of her beer and then said, "This place is cool."

"I've always thought so," he said, avoiding the eye of a couple of women he had dated a couple of times.

"Hey!" Marisa exclaimed. "That's my band!"

The local band that had been working with Marisa on the pageant walked from the bar and began setting up their instruments.

"Live music Friday nights," he said.

"I'm going to go say hi to them."

Dawson watched Marisa walk over to the small stage, and he had to admit that he liked what he saw of her coming and going. She was petite with an hourglass figure that he had learned to appreciate. She wore slender fit jeans that hugged her in all of the right places. He would be a liar if he hadn't tried to imagine what it would be like to hold her in his arms, skin to skin.

And he wasn't the only one in the bar appreciating the view as she walked in a confident, head-held-high gait, a lovely swing in her hips. He caught several men admiring her, and he didn't feel threatened at all—he knew that if Marisa came with him, she would leave with him. And he felt completely secure in that knowledge.

"Hey, man." One of his friends from high school stopped at the booth.

"Hey, Sam." Dawson stood up, shook hands and then sat back down. "Good to see you."

"Did I see you come in with Marisa?" Sam took a seat.

"You did."

"I've been working on building some sets for her," his old friend said. "You've got a tiger by the tail with that one."

That made Dawson laugh and relax some. Sam Scott was a good guy—nonjudgmental. They had been fierce rivals during their high school football years and had managed to become friends after they had graduated. They shared a passion for the outdoors, fast cars and any sport that got the blood and adrenaline pumping.

Marisa came bouncing up to the booth, her eyes shining and a broad smile on her face that only served to endear her to him more.

"Sam!" she said. "Aren't you supposed to be working on my set?"

"Just takin' a little break." Sam stood up, gave her a friendly hug, and then let Dawson have his time with Marisa.

"I didn't know you knew Sam." She took another swig of her beer.

"Since high school."

"He's pretty amazing. I've worked with a lot of carpenters, but he's a genius when it comes to woodwork. I'm thinking of asking him to come to Tenacity to refresh some of stage props for our Christmas show."

"Should I be worried?" he asked, teasing.

She gave one shoulder a shrug. "Only when it comes to woodwork."

The band finished setting up and then the relatively empty

dance floor became crowded. Marisa finished off her beer and then jumped up to join the line dancing that had just started. Sometimes he forgot that, at her core, she was a down-home Montana country girl. Marisa knew all of the line dances from the Cowboy Cha Cha to the Tush Push. At first Marisa started in the back row but worked her way right up to the front row. Next thing he knew, Marisa was giving some of the novices a tutorial.

Dawson did the right thing and ordered them another round of beer. After all of that dancing, Marisa would be parched. After another tutorial to Double D, Marisa headed his way, her face glistening with sweat, her face beaming with joy.

"Wow!" She sat down across from him. "I can't remember having more fun! This is exactly what I needed."

"Happy to oblige."

"How do you always know what I need?" She asked him a pointed question, but he didn't know the answer. Lately, he'd managed to do the right thing with her; he didn't want to press his luck too much, even though they were currently sitting in the Get Lucky Bar.

"Don't you want to dance?" she asked before he could reply.

"I'll wait until we get to the couples dances. Then I'll show you all of my moves, little lady." He gave her a wink. "So far, I've had a good time just watching you."

Her face was rosy from dancing, but he thought he saw an extra blush on her cheeks.

"You are beautiful, Marisa."

She ducked her head, the first sign of shyness she had exhibited that evening. Then, she glanced up at him and said, "And you're very handsome, Dawson. But I have to imagine you know that already."

He leaned forward, reached for her hand and told her, "Everything matters more when I hear it from you."

Dawson saw the surprise alight in her eyes, and he saw her process his words and then meet his gaze straight on. He had just opened the door for her to see what was in his heart and what was in his soul. She couldn't mistake his feelings for her after that. Surely she couldn't.

"You aren't what I expected," she said.

In that moment, Dawson felt like the world had faded to black, and only the two of them existed in the small space of the booth.

"You weren't what I expected either."

There was a long silence between them, and he wondered if they had both said too much for an evening that was supposed to be lighthearted and fun. That's when the band came to their rescue, moving on from line dancing to swing dancing. This was the perfect chance to get Marisa into his arms and keep her there for a good long while.

"Are you ready to be impressed?" he asked.

"Show me what you've got, cowboy."

EVER SINCE SHE had arrived in Bronco, Marisa had felt hemmed in, under a microscope, and worried about every move she made. No, she had never been a party girl—she had always provided the entertainment. But she had literally and figuratively let her hair down at Wild Willa's Saloon! If she had to analyze it, she felt comfortable with Dawson. She felt accepted by this man in a way she had only felt with family and close friends in Tenacity.

"I've got to give you credit," she said as Dawson whirled her around the dance floor. "You know your way around a dance floor."

Dawson pulled her closer and held on to her tightly as if he were afraid she would vanish into thin air. When her big, strong, strapping cowboy had to take a break from dancing, she found her way to the microphone onstage. When she had said hello to the band, they had asked her to sing with them. Dancing with Dawson had truly been the highlight of the evening, but singing onstage was a very close second.

"A very good friend of mine requested this song," Marisa said. "So, Dawson, this one's for you."

Marisa counted off the beat and then she began to sing "Ask Me How I Know" by Garth Brooks. If there was a message for her in these lyrics, she didn't want to ask. This budding romance would be a shooting star, fast and brilliant but gone too quickly leaving only a trace of light in its wake.

She sang several more songs before the four beers she had consumed began to wear her down. At the edge of the stage, Dawson was waiting for her. He put her hands on her waist and lifted her up and then put her down gently next to him.

"You ready?" he asked with an odd expression on his face.

She nodded. "I think I might've overdone it."

"You can sleep it off tomorrow." Dawson helped her into her coat and walked behind her to the front door.

It had turned bitterly cold, and Marisa was shivering as she climbed into the passenger seat, grateful that Dawson had remotely turned on the truck and gotten the heat started. Then he got behind the wheel and leaned toward her to push the ignition button.

"You smell good," she said, and then let out a dainty burp. "Sorry."

He grinned. "I don't need to ask if you had a good time." Dawson put the truck in Reverse. He had stopped drinking hours ago after his second beer.

"No," she said, her eyes half-closed, as she used the seat controls to lean back her seat. "You probably don't."

"I'm taking you to your aunt and uncle's house."

"Shoot! That's right. I can't drive like this."

"No, you can't." And then asked, "What will your family think, me dropping you off?"

"I don't know. They are early to bed, early to rise kind of folks. I'll just tiptoe in and in the morning get up super early and tiptoe out to catch an Uber."

"Not so sure your plan is flawless but I wish you good luck. If you need me to pick you up and take you to the theater, the only payment I'll need is a smile."

"Dawson John! You are what *mi abuelita* would call a smooth talker."

"I'm also a truth talker and I want to see you as much as I can for as long as you'll let me."

She didn't seem to hear him. Instead she exclaimed, "Hey!"

She reached over and tapped his arm with less than perfect precision. "My backside is getting toasty warm."

He nodded sagely, but there was a twinkle in his eye. "Heated seats."

"Oh," she said, closing her eyes. "I need to put these on my Christmas list."

THE NEXT MORNING, Dawson joined his family for their regular Saturday brunch. It was the one time during the week that their family came together. All of the siblings, plus wives and now a grandbaby.

"Now, Charity," Randall John said in his booming voice. "I've been getting all of this garbage on my phone, and I wish it would stop. It keeps on chiming, and beeping and buzzing and I don't want any of it, you hear?"

"Phone." Charity held out her hand.

She quickly searched his phone and then said, "Those are people reacting to my social media advertisements. It's a good thing, Dad."

Randall looked over to his wife. "Now what did she just say?"

"I'm sure I don't know," Mimi said. "What did you say, baby?"

"It's my advertising campaign for the Double J," Charity said but talked really slowly and a bit loudly.

"They can hear your words, Charity. They aren't deaf," Maddox said, bouncing his son in his arms. "Fast or slow, they aren't going to get it."

Charity rolled her eyes and made an annoyed noise in her throat. She had been handling the ranch's digital footprint, hiring a firm to revamp and maintain their website, using advertising dollars for social media, all the while tracking advertising reach and activity so she could adjust according to client interactions and interest.

"She's making deals, Dad," Jameson said. "But she doesn't use a handshake—she uses a computer."

"That's why our online sales have increased two hundred percent over the last year," Dawson added.

"Well," Randall said, "that's real nice, baby girl. Good work. Now, get it off of my phone."

Charity held out her hand again, took her father's phone, scrolled quickly and then handed it back to him. "I turned off notifications."

"Fine. Good." Randall slipped his phone back into his shirt pocket.

Dawson was just musing about how calm and peaceful this meal had been. There was usually some sort of drama or trauma being aired out at the family table. A few notifications from Facebook was pretty benign.

"What is this?" Mimi's eyes were glued to the screen of her phone. "Dawson. What have you done?" she said in a shocked whisper.

"So much for a quiet brunch," Charity muttered.

His mother looked up from her phone and repeated the question, her tone was very clipped.

"What now, Mimi?" Randall asked, followed by a frustrated sigh.

"What did you do?" Maddox asked him.

"You know exactly what he did," Jameson said as he continued to enjoy his breakfast. "Can you pass me those biscuits, Charity?"

Mimi reached for the newspaper still in the protective sleeve next to her husband's plate and opened it to the gossip column. She stared at it while a vein in her forehead began to bulge. "How could you do this, Dawson? Out in plain sight for everyone in Bronco to see!"

"Do what?" Dawson asked.

"You know exactly what you did, Dawson. And you know exactly why I wouldn't approve!" Mimi snapped.

"Now calm down, Mimi," Randall warned his wife. "You've got to watch that blood pressure."

"I wouldn't have high blood pressure if your son would do what he was born to do!"

"I'll take the baby," Maddox's wife, Adeline, said quietly, taking the child in her arms and leaving the dining room.

Mimi picked up the paper, slapped at it, and wrestling with it until she was able to flip it around. There on the gossip column page were several pictures of Marisa and him on the dance floor. The caption on the article was "Dawson John Gets Lucky."

"Oh, now, Mimi, that's nothing. He's just dancing like boys do," Randall said, but Dawson knew that his mother would not be thrown off the scent.

"He's a man, not a boy," Mimi said with a biting tone, "and he should know better. You're toying with that young lady, and even though you don't often show it, I raised you better. She comes from a good family who values tradition..."

"But not good enough to carry the John name. I'm not toying with her, Mom. You're dead wrong on that point," Dawson said with an edge to his voice that he had never used with his mother before. "Marisa *is* from a good family. A top-notch family from my vantage point. And she sure is heck worthy of the John name or the Taylor name or the Abernathy name or any damn name she chooses. You're just too focused on appearances to see it!"

The table went quiet. Then Mimi stood up, dropped her napkin on her plate and, with her head held high, said, "I will not sit here and field insults from my own son." Mimi paused with her hands gripping the back of her chair, and Dawson's stomach twisted when he saw that his mother had unshed tears in her eyes. "There's a lot about the world you don't yet know about, Dawson. And clearly, my mistake was spoiling you." His mother walked out of the dining room stiffly.

Everyone looked at each other in confusion. Charity got up and said, "I'll go," following her mother to try and calm her down.

"Dawson," Randall said with a tone that brooked no argument, "you need to apologize to your mother. She brought you into this world. You might not agree with her, and that's your right, but you will damn well show her the respect that she is due."

"I will, Dad." Dawson said, "That...didn't go as I had planned."

Randall looked at him with disbelief. "Oh, it didn't? Looks

to me like you wanted to push your mama's buttons, and I believe you succeeded."

Dawson had to admit to himself that his father was right. Yes, he did know that he would end up in the gossip column again eventually and then after the shock of it, a conversation would be had.

Wasn't that why, initially, he'd tried to go to out-of-the-way places with Marisa? To avoid all this? He sighed.

"Well, I am sorry," Dawson said to his father. The rest of his family quietly finished their food and quickly left the table to start their days. "I didn't mean to hurt Mom's feelings."

"Maybe not, but you did."

"I just want her to give Marisa a chance. That's all. One chance."

Randall rested his forearms on the table, fork and knife still in hand, and he pinned him with an intense gaze that made Dawson sit up straighter.

"Now you listen here, son. What your mama wants and what I want—there is no daylight between them. We want you to marry a girl who can handle ranch life because it's a tough life. We may not be the richest ranching family in town—yeah, I know it. Just don't let your mother ever hear me admit it. But we have a lot of land and a lot of responsibility."

Randall went back to pushing his brisket hash around his plate, then put his fork down and looked at his son. "The problem with you is that you've never struggled, you've never been without wealth and the influence that comes with it. But I promise you this, son, if you ever lost it, you'd do whatever you could to get it back. Your mother just wants the best for all you kids and to see that our grandchildren and great grandchildren are provided for. And that none of you ever have to struggle to build a legacy the way we did, even if you still have to work hard. After all, there's nothing wrong with hard work."

"Understood, Dad," Dawson said.

"Listen, I can see that this isn't going to be the last we see of Marisa. I've got two good eyes and so does your mama. But for now, all you are going to do is apologize and thank your mother for doing her very best to take care of her family."

After his father left the room, Dawson sat at the dining table alone with his uneaten breakfast on his plate and no appetite for cold eggs and now-soggy toast. And he still sat, trying to process the scene that had just unfolded. In his younger years, he'd be off to the next adventure, his mother's feelings be damned. But now? He'd grown and he had changed. And it hurt him that he had hurt his mother so deeply.

Charity walked into the dining room, came around the table and hugged him.

"How's Mom?"

"Better. Resting." Charity said, "Don't be too hard on her, Dawson. She does want what's best for us, even if we disagree on how to get there."

"I know she thinks she knows what's best." After a moment, Dawson said to his sister, "I have real strong feelings for Marisa, Charity. Real strong."

"I know you do," Charity said. "So do I."

He didn't say it aloud, but he knew in his heart that Marisa was his future, and no matter what he needed to do to get his parents to accept her, he was going to do it.

CHAPTER NINE

MONDAY MORNING, MARISA was back at work with rehearsals. She had nursed a hangover most of Saturday and then had to explain herself when more pictures of Dawson and her looking very cuddly and enamored with each other appeared for a second day in a row in the *Bronco Bulletin*. She had known that going out with Dawson John would cause some ripples, but pictures in the newspaper with the caption "Outsider Waltzes Her Way into Dawson's Heart?" was much more exposure than she had wanted or anticipated.

"Good morning, Agnes," Marisa said, folding the Sunday paper and tucking it into the compartment on the piano seat.

Agnes handed her a cup of cocoa with three jumbo marshmallows. "So I gather you had a good time Friday night."

Like Agnes, everyone in Bronco had probably seen the paper. "Not enough to ruin the show." She sat down heavily and drank the hot chocolate down, ignoring the burn on her tongue, the roof of her mouth and down her throat.

"You didn't ruin the show," Agnes said. "In fact, if I know my Bronco the way I think I do, you're going to be filling even the cheap seats up there in the balcony. Everyone is going to want to know who this mysterious outsider is. It's not every day that a filly manages to lasso Dawson John's heart."

"Can we please stop speaking in metaphors? I'm not a filly and I haven't done anything to Dawson's heart."

"Okay. So you're in denial. Not a bad thing considering everything that is left to do before the show."

"Are you being helpful now, Agnes?"

"No," Agnes said, unfazed. "Probably not. I think you'd better sit down."

"I am sitting…"

"Then stay seated."

"Please don't say something like—"

"Your drummer is in the hospital."

"Are you serious?"

"As a heart attack."

"But I just saw him on Friday! Is he okay?"

"Heart attack," Agnes said. "Needs surgery."

Marisa had dropped her head into her hands, but then she looked up and said, "Agnes, that was a terrible turn of phrase in light of the fact that he actually *did* have a heart attack!"

"I know," the older woman agreed. "I caught that right after I said it. At my age, sometimes it comes out right and sometimes it doesn't."

DAWSON HAD STAYED in contact with Marisa via text, but he had backed away after three days of gossip column photos. Monday the caption said, "More than Just Friends?" He had apologized to his mother. Meant it sincerely, but the daily pictures in the newspaper overshadowed everything else, including the apology. His mom was not moving from her position that he needed to find a wife from a landholding cattle family and if she was a debutante how could that hurt? But he was rock solid on his position too; these feelings he had for Marisa had only grown with time. This was not a phase; this was not a fling. This was something much deeper than he'd ever felt before.

After a couple of days, Dawson realized that all he wanted was to spend as much time as possible with Marisa. Surely his mother would eventually recover from the reality of his relationship with Marisa, but he knew that if he lost his chance with the lovely director, he believed that *recovery* wouldn't be possible.

Monday evening, after all of the performers had gone home for the night, Agnes let him into the locked theater before she switched off the lights and headed home.

"Don't leave any lights on, Dawson. You don't pay the light bill around here."

"Yes, ma'am."

He walked through the same door that he had walked through the first day he had met Marisa. It was only a couple of weeks ago but it felt to him like a lifetime. The seating area was dark while the only real light was coming from the stage where Marisa was sitting cross-legged, sifting through sheet music.

"Agnes let me in," he called out, not really knowing how to get her attention without scaring the wits out of her.

Marisa did start, but once she recognized his voice, she nodded her head and waved him over to the stage. He climbed up the steps and walked over to her.

She stood up, met him halfway and hugged him. Until that very moment, he had no idea how much he needed that hug.

"Are you okay?" she asked.

He leaned back to look down at her angelic face. "Are you?"

She nodded. "I think so. Agnes thinks free publicity is good publicity. The theater website has had a lot of traffic and ticket sales are up, so…" She shrugged. "Maybe she's right."

Dawson reached for the long, thick braid of her hair, so shiny and black and sexy on her. "That's one way to look at it."

"What's another way?" she asked, and he saw the sincere concern in her eyes.

"It's been a little rough around the Double J."

"I was afraid of that. Charity came in this morning looking like she hadn't gotten any sleep, and she left early."

"She takes it hard when our family gets to fighting."

"Fighting…about me?"

"Yes and no."

"Am I solving a riddle?" she asked him, and he could tell that Marisa had been feeling added pressure from the attention.

"It's not about you. It's about me," he told her honestly. "I've never fallen in line. I've always thought I'm the third son, why do I have to stay on any path other than the one I forge for myself? They have certain expectations for their children and I haven't been inclined to meet those expectations."

"They don't approve of me."

"It's complicated."

A flash of raw hurt swept across her face and she turned away from him. "Why don't you just tell them that I'm leaving at the end of November. I'm not a threat."

Dawson walked around to face her, took her hands in his and waited for her to look up in to his face.

"Hey," he said. "It hasn't been long since we first met but we have been honest with each other, haven't we?"

She nodded. "I have."

"And so have I," he said. "You mean something to me, Marisa. You *mean* something to *me*."

When she looked up at him, he saw tears streaming down her face; he wiped them away and for the second time in one week, kicked himself because he'd made one of the two most important women in his life cry.

"You mean something to me too, Dawson." Marisa stole her hands away to wipe the rest of the tears from her face. "I don't know what that something is, but it's there."

"Then don't build a wall up between us," he said, and then next words represented sentiments he had never felt before Marisa. "I need you."

Her eyes widened with both surprise and fear and it took her much longer than he would have liked to respond. When she did, she said, "I—feel," another pause, "that I may need you in my life right now."

Dawson furrowed his brow. "Not exactly the level of enthusiasm I was hoping for but I suppose it's a start."

MARISA COULD SEE that Dawson wanted to move on from the gossip column and the turmoil it had created in both of their lives, so she introduced a neutral topic that involved the pageant. Dawson, from the very beginning, had been a reliable sounding board for all things pageant.

"Did you hear about my drummer?"

"I did."

Marisa bent down to collect the sheet music she had strewn across the stage floor. "He has surgery tomorrow."

"Have you found a replacement?"

"Thankfully, yes," she said. "I'd hoped to get my drummer from Tenacity, but he's out of town until a day before our show."

"Figures."

"But one of my old bandmates…" She stopped and looked at him. "Do you even know that I was in a band?"

He nodded. "I follow you on all the social media platforms, we are Facebook friends and I subscribed to your YouTube channel. Row House Four was the name of your college band."

"Well, thank you. That wasn't stalkerish at all." She laughed and he felt gratified. There it was, that warm, tingling feeling that he got whenever he was with Marisa. It was a feeling he was beginning to wonder if he could manage to live without.

"My life took a different path but the band still gigs in Boston. My drummer, Shira Weiss, will be flying out to fill in at the show," she said. "I am so thankful to have such a good friend who also plays a mean tumbak."

"Definition needed."

She laughed again. "It's a hand drum that is played seated with the base between the thighs. It's one of the oldest instruments from India and it really adds a cool vibe to the songs."

He shook his head, fascinated with Marisa's appreciation for other cultures and finding ways to weave their dancing, their instruments into American classics.

After she put the sheet music away in a file cabinet just beyond the curtain, Marisa turned around and saw that Dawson was standing in the middle of the stage with a very peculiar look on his ridiculously handsome face.

"What's going on?"

"Come here," he said.

She walked over to him, curiously. "What do you have in your pocket? More marshmallows?"

"No." He patted the pocket in his shirt. "I keep those right here."

"You don't!" She laughed. "Do you?"

Dawson pulled a small bag of marshmallows out of his shirt

pocket and Marisa felt seen and appreciated and yes, loved. Such a simple gesture spoke more to her heart in a way that a thousand red roses and thousands of words could ever say.

"You're not all the way here yet," Dawson said, his feet slightly apart, his hands clasped in front of his body, waiting for her arrival.

"Well," she said, slowly walking on purpose now. "It's after hours, we are the only souls in this old, creaky building, the wind is howling outside and you are luring me—"

"Luring is a very strong word."

"*Luring* me over to you." She repeated the word with more conviction. "And you have something for me in your pocket. What do you have Dawson? Should I be worried?"

"You have taken this to a really dark place," he said with a smile. "Maybe I'm the one who sould be worried about you?"

"No. Ask anyone. I'm super sweet and totally harmless."

"Jury is still out on both counts."

She finally reached him and that was when he pulled a sprig of mistletoe out of his pocket.

Marisa put her hands up to her mouth, her eyes shining with surprise and delight. "Mistletoe, Dawson?"

"Mistletoe, Marisa." Then he said, "Do you believe in the magic of mistletoe?"

She put her hands on her lovely hips. "That's my line! You're stealing my lines, Dawson."

"And I'm trying to steal a kiss."

And then you'll try to steal my heart.

Dawson held the sprig over her head and then, giving her ample time to stop what was coming, he touched his lips to hers and that spark of energy sizzled between them. It was a quick, soft kiss, but for her, she could feel the vibration of his heart of gold when he touched his lips to hers.

Marisa still had her eyes shut and he took it as a direct invitation to kiss her again. Stuffing the mistletoe into his pocket, Dawson drew her into his arms, leaned down and kissed her how she had always imagined he would—deeply, passionately, and full of promise of good days yet to come. Marisa slowly opened her eyes and looked into his.

"Hmm," she murmured. "I wondered what that would be like."

"And?"

"Where's that mistletoe?" she asked in a languid, sexy voice she'd never used before.

"Right here." He pulled it out of his pocket.

Marisa took the sprig, grabbed his hand with her free one, and then led him over to the steps. She positioned him three steps down and facing her. Then, with a saucy, sassy expression on her face, she held the mistletoe over his head. Because he was several steps down, they stood eye to eye, lips to lips.

She kissed him as he had kissed her—with heat and passion—while they shared breath.

"You are full of surprises, Dawson John." Marisa touched the tips of her fingers to her lips.

He pulled her braid over her shoulder. "I can say the same about you."

Arm in arm, they walked down the steps together and Marisa picked up her backpack but Dawson lifted it off her shoulder and hooked it onto his, as he always did.

"Are you hungry?" he asked her.

"Famished," she admitted. "I love rehearsals, but they can be a real grind."

"Pizza?"

"Greasy?"

"No other way to eat it."

She stopped walking, so he stopped. "Are we sure we want to venture out into public again? One night at Wild Willa's Saloon and we made the gossip column three days in a row. And Charity was really upset. It hurt me to see *her* hurt so much. It must have been a bad scene at your house."

"I know. It was. And I'm sorry that Charity got caught up in it," Dawson said with an edge in his tone. "But I'm just living my life here. That's it. I like you and I want to buy you a slice of pizza. Do you want to eat pizza with me?"

She nodded.

"Then let's just do it, Marisa. Life's too damn short."

"Made shorter by eating cheesy, greasy pizza."

"I'm serious, Marisa."

"I know you are."

He held out his hand for her. "So?"

She took a moment, then slipped her hand into his. "So, okay."

He couldn't help but smile. "Well, okay then."

MARISA HAD WOLFED down three slices of pizza, and then she felt satisfied.

"Rate the pizza," Dawson said.

"Ten out of ten, for sure."

Dawson wasn't done so she felt content to sip her soda and enjoy looking at all of his handsomeness.

"I have a confession to make," she said, and heard shyness in her voice.

"Oh yeah?"

"I've spent more time than I'd like to admit surfing through your social media content."

He stopped chewing to smile a closed-mouth smile.

"Stop it!" She felt her cheeks flush.

He swallowed down his last piece of pizza with a long swig of soda. "So, did you like what you saw?"

"Honestly, it made me wonder if you own enough shirts. You were bare chested climbing mountains, bare chested BASE jumping off a bridge—illegal by the way—shirtless riding a horse, white water rafting, biking, hiking, zip lining, working out in the gym and paragliding. The only time you had a shirt on was for skydiving."

"They made me keep my shirt on."

"It's hard for me to believe that those abs are real," she said. "I mean who has abs like that?"

"Me."

"You're all muscled and tan and your abs are so defined that it looks like someone painted them on right before the pictures were taken."

"All natural, baby," he said, and wiggled his eyebrows up and down. "Want to cop a feel?"

"You quit it, Dawson!" She leaned forward and whispered harshly, "No more pictures in the paper!"

"Oh come on…be a sport." He laughed. "How about this caption—'Marisa Sanchez grabs more than a slice of pizza'?"

It was oddly easy with Dawson—they laughed, they challenged each other and they had been a shoulder for the other to lean on. And, as a total bonus, he was smoking hot and kissed like nothing she had ever experienced before. She would be reliving and replaying those mistletoe kisses for many years to come.

"Now, you are an adrenaline junkie," she said. "Charity was right about that. I can't believe how many places you have traveled just to put yourself in harm's way!"

"You could join me."

"Dawson, really? Do I look like an extreme sports enthusiast?"

He wiped his mouth with a napkin, then balled it up and dropped it onto his plate. "How do I know if I don't ask? You've got a wild side, I can sense it."

"Wishful thinking, more like it."

He smiled and winked at her again, leaning back in his seat, his body language open and confident. "How do you land on zip lining?"

She wrinkled her brow and her nose in thought. "I land on the side of 'no, not happening.' I will not let some stranger strap me into a safety harness when I have not personally investigated the safety and maintenance of that piece of equipment, and put my life in the hands of some dude—"

"Could be a chick. Sexist."

"Who is most likely high on skunk weed," she said, "while he pushes me off of a perfectly good platform and sends me hurling through the atmosphere on a tiny rope—"

"It's a very strong cable."

"Through trees! And what? I hope I make it to the other platform without smacking my head on a wayward tree limb or crash into the platform because this contraption they have put me on doesn't have brakes!"

Dawson listened to her, grinning from ear to ear. "Are you finished?"

She crossed her arms over her chest. "For now, yes."

"So, I'll put you down as a 'no' for zip lining?"

She nodded once. "Emphatic no. Hard pass."

"Where do you land on white water rafting?"

THE NEXT COUPLE of days after their first kiss, Marisa was grateful for her work so she could focus her attention on something other than missing Dawson. He had told her after he took her out for pizza that he would be helping Bronco set up for the Mistletoe Rodeo that always got started right after the Mistletoe Pageant. She hadn't expected to miss him as much as she did, and at weak moments she felt like crying. Of course, she was completely stressed out and exhausted—perhaps missing Dawson was that straw that broke the camel's back.

"Marisa!"

Marisa turned toward the door to the theater and saw her dear friend Shira Weiss running down the stairs toward her. Shira had shoulder length black hair with purple braids on either side of her head making her look like she was sporting a modified mohawk. Her eyebrows were black and they framed her light green and gold catlike eyes in the loveliest of ways. She had always been a slender, fit young woman who was bursting with positive energy and excitement for life in general.

Shira barreled over to her and threw her arms around her and rocked back and forth.

"Thank you so much for coming, Shira!"

"You bet," her friend said, her hands on her hips, surveying the environment. "This place is incredible."

"I think so too," Marisa agreed. "It can be drafty at times, but I really like it."

Marisa hugged Shira again; she felt so grateful that she would come all the way to Montana to help her pull off this job.

"You'll be staying at my aunt and uncle's house with me."

"Cool," Shira said.

"That way you won't feel so homesick for Thanksgiving."

Shira smiled at her, adjusting the Star of David necklace that she rarely took off.

"As long as I make it back in time for Hanukah, we're good."

Marisa gave Shira all of the music that she had provided to the Bronco-based band. The drummer knew many of these arrangements, so it wouldn't take her long to get up to speed for the show.

CHAPTER TEN

MARISA WAS WORKING furiously to pull all of the loose strings together as the town of Bronco anticipated the Mistletoe Pageant, which then led into the Mistletoe Rodeo. And even though she'd made changes based on the focus group and Dawson's insight, Marisa still felt out of her depth with this show. It was still a mystery who had ultimately recommended her for the job—not to mention hired her for this milestone event that was so steeped in Bronco tradition. But she was determined not to let anyone down—including herself.

"Hold up!" Marisa waved her hands at the dancers while she took the stairs up to the stage. "That's not the correct sequence for this song. Here, let me show you." Marisa nodded to Charity who had taken it upon herself to record the band's version of each song in the show so they could practice dancing and singing without needing the band at the theater. There would be rehearsals with the band coming up; for now, Marisa needed fewer people, not more, in the room.

Marisa worked with the dancers for a few minutes, demonstrating the steps then running the sequence a couple of times. Then she headed back down the steps so she could watch the dancers from the vantage of the audience.

"Yes!" Marisa clapped out the beat with her hands. "Yes! That's it! Now you're on track!"

Marisa gave Charity two thumbs-up. How would she have managed without her? So talented, so willing to pitch in. As much as her feelings had grown for Dawson, she loved Charity apart from him. And she hoped that no matter what, Charity and she would continue a friendship beyond this one show.

She turned away from the stage when her phone rang and she saw Dawson's name on the screen. "Hi!" she said as she walked to a more private spot. "I was just thinking about you."

"I was just thinking about you."

"How are the rodeo preps going?"

"Almost done."

"Wow! Already?"

"What can I say? Manpower, baby."

Marisa laughed, her mood buoyed by Dawson's phone call. Ever since he started helping with the rodeo, he didn't have as much time to stop by the theater as before. So, she was glad that he was wrapping up preparations.

"I'd like to see you tomorrow," he said, sending her heart racing. "What's your schedule look like?"

"Rehearsals in the morning, but I'm letting everyone off in the afternoon. Everyone is slaphappy. They need a break."

"I'm in luck, then."

"What did you have in mind?" Marisa began to imagine an intimate lunch for two, or sitting together in a movie theater sharing a big tub of popcorn, or even sitting close on a bench in the park across from city hall drinking hot chocolate and watching city employees set up the holiday decorations.

"Hiking."

"Hiking?" she asked as if he had suggested robbing a bank or stealing a car. "Are you crazy? Why do you think I would want to brave the cold, which will only get colder as we climb?" She shuddered. "Climb, what a horrible word."

"Have you ever gone hiking?" he asked. "It can be exhilarating. Out in the elements, back to nature, seeing wildlife up close and personal..."

"You are making a great case for why I don't like to hike. But for your information, yes, I've hiked with my brothers on Tenacity Trail."

"That's a really nice beginner trail."

"You've hiked it?"

"Of course," he said. "I've been to Tenacity too. I like your hometown."

"Well, if that trail is for beginners, I'm an infant. And I'm an infant that doesn't appreciate activities that involve no restaurants, or climate control, and offer a chance that I could fall on icy rocks and break my tailbone or be eaten alive by a hungry bear.

"In conclusion, why would I want to go hiking with you?" she asked him.

"Because I'll be there."

Marisa frowned and then after a couple of heartbeats, she said, "In that case, I'll go. But I get to pick our next adventure. Deal?"

"Deal."

THE NEXT DAY, Dawson picked Marisa up at the theater, and he drove them to an intermediate trail just outside of Bronco. He had chosen this trail because after seeing Marisa dance for hours without much effort, he believed that she had more stamina than she gave herself credit for.

"I'm glad to see you," he told her.

"I'm glad to see you!" Marisa agreed.

He had missed this woman more than he had ever missed anyone in his life. It had only been a couple of days that they hadn't seen each other in person but they had video chatted, talked on the phone and texted. It made him wonder if he was being an absolute fool to think that he could ever give her up. No, his parents were not on board and had told him without one shred of ambiguity that Marisa Sanchez was not John material. And that comment from his mother at brunch had so infuriated him that he'd spent the night on a friend's couch until he cooled off.

"Penny for your thoughts."

He could feel Marisa's gaze on his face, and it occurred to him that she could read him now in the same way he could read her. It had happened so quickly, this knowing each other, but wasn't that strong evidence to support their uncanny connection? Even if his parents never ceded this point, Dawson didn't care.

He reached over, squeezed her hand. "I was just thinking that I missed you."

Marisa made a sound of relief. "Okay, good. At least I wasn't the only one."

"You missed me?"

She nodded. "More than I should have, I think."

"How much is too much?"

"I don't know."

Neither did he and that was a fact. Now was the time to hike and have fun, and he certainly hoped to offer her his warm body as her own personal heater and he had every intention of kissing her when they reached the peak. Dawson had never wanted to create memories with any woman before. Most of his social media had been focused on extreme sports; in fact, his exes often complained that because he refused to post pictures of them that he wasn't serious about them. Maybe they were right; he'd already posted Marisa on his social media several times. If the *Bronco Bulletin* was going to keep putting them in the gossip column, why shouldn't he post?

"That's a long way up." Marisa put her hand on her forehead so she could block the light and gaze at the peak.

"It's not as bad as you think…"

She waved her hands at his body. "Says Adonis!"

Dawson smiled at her with a wink at being compared to a Greek god.

"Okay," she said with a grumpy tone of voice, "stop basking and let's go so I can make an immediate U-turn at the top and get back into this nice warm truck."

Dawson just grinned at her. He strapped on a backpack with supplies and led the way.

"I've never been allergic to bee stings, but just in case my body decides to go rogue on me, do you have an EpiPen?"

"Got it."

"There isn't a cloud in the sky, but I get sick whenever I get rained on…and if I get sick, there won't be any show…"

"I have ponchos."

"I didn't eat lunch. You picked me up right after rehearsals, and I didn't have a chance to even eat a granola bar. I tend to be hypoglycemic—I could get lightheaded and dizzy and then fall off of the side of the cliff..."

"I packed a picnic for us."

Dawson had never been on a hike with a person who complained that much but because it was Marisa and he thought she was adorable, he wasn't feeling irritated by it yet. Normally if someone was ruining his good time, he didn't wait—he dumped them and went on with his life. But Marisa was in a special category—a totally new category—so she was getting a lot of latitude from him.

"You are very prepared," Marisa grumbled.

He laughed and turned back to her, put her round face in his hands and kissed her. "You sound disappointed."

"Mmm, I feel less cranky now," she said. "Kiss me again!"

Five more kisses later, Marisa made it all the way to the half-way point before she couldn't continue. Her face was flushed from the cold air, but also from the exertion of hiking up an incline.

They sat down on one of the benches placed along the trail specifically for this reason. He handed her a bottle of water and a high energy, low sugar protein bar.

"How is it?" he asked.

"Tastes like Elmer's glue."

"I'm not even going to ask how you know that."

She chewed some more, washed down the last of the bar with water, put the cap back on, and then said, "I teach Bible school over the summer. I know what glue tastes like, trust me."

He smiled at her, put his arm around her, pulled her close and kissed the top of her head, which had been fortified with a very thick crocheted toboggan beanie.

"I think you're pretty amazing, Marisa."

When he gave her an unexpected compliment, Marisa actually turned shy for a split second, and her cheeks turned a deeper shade of pink. That blush on her cheeks was his reward. He found himself staring at her face, making a mental map of her petite nose, her dark eyelashes, tigress eyes and those full lips that made kissing her his favorite new pastime.

"Thank you, Dawson," she said quietly. "I think you're pretty amazing yourself."

"Then it's mutual."

She nodded. "Very much so."

He stood up, put the backpack on, then held out his hand for her. She took it and groaned when she stood up and had to straighten her back.

"I'm going to pay for this tomorrow, aren't I?"

"Maybe even tonight," he said easily. "Ready?"

While fielding many complaints about a slippery rock, a narrow trail, an industrious woodpecker that would surely attack her, and bears that would come out of hibernation just to eat her as a snack, Dawson managed to push Marisa to make it to the peak.

His companion stood near the edge of the rocky top of the mountain and looked back at the trail she had hiked to reach the peak. Her jacket was tied at her waist, and she drank down an entire bottle of water in seconds. Hands on her hips, her lovely chest rising and falling quickly, Marisa wiped the sweat from her brow.

"I can't believe you got me up here, Dawson."

He walked to stand beside her. "You got yourself up here, Marisa."

"You were so patient with me, encouraging, you knew when to let me have a break and when I needed to push through so I wouldn't lose momentum. You are an amazing coach. How did you learn to do that?"

"I don't know." He twisted the cap off of his water bottle. "I've never done it before."

Marisa looked over at him. "Never?"

"If someone doesn't want to go hiking, I leave them behind. If someone gets tired. I leave them behind."

"You never left me behind."

"No." He studied his companion's face—a face he had grown to love. "I didn't."

He was quiet for a moment and then he added, "I guess I

should take a hard look at what makes you so different from just about anyone else on the planet."

MARISA STOOD AT the peak and felt a sense of accomplishment that she hadn't expected. Dawson was right, she did feel a hiker's high and it lasted for a while. Then, the sweat on her skin began to make her feel chilled all over her body and she began to shiver. She untied her jacket from around her waist and put it on.

"Cold?" Dawson asked after he picked up the remnants of their picnic.

She nodded, her teeth chattering.

"Come here," he said. "Let me warm you up."

Dawson opened his jacket while she scooted closer to him. With his arm around her, Marisa felt cared for by this man who had turned her life upside down and every which way. It wasn't like her at all to play hooky to follow a cowboy, who also happened to be an adrenaline junkie, up to the top of a mountain! But this moment, cuddling with Dawson in a room with the best view nature could provide, was all the reward she needed for the challenging climb she had just completed.

"Better?" he asked.

She nodded, tilted her head back and looked into his eyes, which were filled with so much acceptance and dare she think... love? He cupped her face with his hands and kissed her sweetly. She leaned in, put her hand behind his head to offer him more and he took it. He deepened the kiss while his large hand slid into her jacket and cupped her breast. Every place on her body felt like it was on fire, her chill long forgotten, while warmth and tingling rushed from her toes, to her throat, to her fingers and her lips. It had been so long since she had let any man touch her like this; it had been such a long time since she had been kissed. But never in her life had she felt so desired, cherished, needed by any man. In both word and deed, Dawson was telling her that he cared.

"I think I'm warm enough now," she said, ending the lovers' embrace.

He gave her one final kiss on the lips. "I'm glad I could help. Ready to do the easiest part of this hike?"

"Yes, sir, I most certainly am!"

WHEN THEY ARRIVED back in Bronco, they were stopped by a police unit blocking the road including trucks for the local TV station KBTV.

"I wonder what's happening here," Marisa said, sitting forward in her seat.

"I don't know," Dawson said, "but at least they aren't trying to photograph us again."

Marisa looked at her phone to see if there were any real-time reports and her mood deflated. "Oh, no! This can't be."

"What?"

She showed him a link to the *Bronco Bulletin*'s home page. "Someone left a baby in a basket in the church vestibule!" This news hit Marisa hard. She had wanted to be a mother for so long but, so far, she hadn't met the father of her children. On the back end of her twenties, she was conscious that fertility declined significantly by thirty-five and she had truly begun to prepare herself to accept the idea that she might not have children. For someone to have a precious baby, a blessed gift from God above, and chose to leave it at a church, in the middle of winter, was very difficult for her to understand and even more challenging for her to forgive.

"Who would do such a thing?" she asked, upset.

"Someone desperate, I reckon."

She nodded but didn't speak for fear that she might start to cry.

He looked over at her, must have seen her pain, and reached for her hand. He took it in his and squeezed it to give her comfort.

"Do they say anything else?" he asked her.

"No. Nothing."

Once Dawson parked his truck in the theater parking lot, they both joined the gathering crowd. "I thought someone had left a doll," a church employee was saying when they got close enough to hear the ongoing press conference that had been set up in front of the church. "But then I realized it was a real baby! That's when I called the authorities and they're on the job now, so I feel like I've played my part in God's plan for this innocent child."

A reporter shouted a question. "Any idea who the mother might be?"

"No. No. I surely don't. I'll cooperate with the authorities, of course," the church worker said.

Another reporter asked, "What happens to the baby now?"

This time one of Bronco's police took the question. Marisa recognized Officer Lopez as he moved behind the mic and said, "The baby will be put in the care of social services until a suitable foster home can be located. And that's it for now, folks. We have work to do."

As the crowd dispersed, Marisa felt heartbroken for that little baby. "Marisa?" Dawson was steadfast by her side. "What's wrong?"

"I have always wanted to be a mom just like my mother. It's hard to believe that someone could be gifted with a child and then abandon it."

"The baby is in good hands now," he said. "This town comes together and helps each other out in a crisis or a pinch."

She hoped that was true. Her arms crossed over her chest, and her mind still with the baby, Marisa walked beside Dawson back to the theater.

"Are you going to be okay?" he asked her when they reached their destination.

"Yes." She nodded. "Of course. I just have a tender heart for children."

He reached for her braid and pulled it over her shoulder. This was something that Dawson just liked to do and she liked it. It made her feel connected to him.

"Well, get some rest tonight. Your big show is only two days away."

"Two days!" She gave a shake of her head. "So much to do! I've got to get my head back in the game. But—" she smiled up at him "—thank you for today. You got me to do something that

I didn't really think that I could do." She raised her arms up like Rocky after a prizefight. "I conquered the intermediate trail!"

"Yes, you did. Can I talk you in to the advanced trail after all of this holiday craziness settles down?"

This was the first time Dawson had ever spoken of a future between them after the show and after she had returned to Tenacity. In her mind, when she looked into the future, she still couldn't see Dawson there with her, living the quiet life of a family man. That was what she had dreamed of since she was a little girl helping her mother in the kitchen. It had been an old-fashioned model that wasn't really on-brand for her as the progressive game changer. But Marisa accepted that she was a whole, complicated person and she had a right to her own dreams.

"It's hard for me to even imagine life after this show!"

"I'm going to be in the front row supporting Charity and you both."

Instinctively, and not looking around to see if paparazzi were hiding in the bushes, Marisa hugged Dawson.

"Thank you, Dawson," she said. "You've helped me so much from beginning to end."

"All I did was help you change up your playlist, that's all."

"No," she told him. "You did much more than that."

Dawson had to leave to meet his brothers at the rodeo site while she headed back into the theater to wrap her mind around the next steps.

"Hi, sweetie." Agnes walked into the lounge that, at times, became her office.

"Hi, Agnes."

"We're in the home stretch."

"Yes, we are."

"How are you holding up?" Agnes said, putting on a fresh pot of coffee.

"Surprisingly well, really. I thought I would be a total mess. Maybe that will happen right after the curtain closes."

Agnes joined her at the table. "Did you hear about the baby in the church? Poor thing. I wish there was something we could do."

Marisa bit her lip. "I had an idea, but I'm not sure we would be allowed to do this. But…it might just help get more word out about the little one."

Agnes looked at her. "What idea?"

"Well," Marisa said, closing the lid of her computer. "What if we could shine a spotlight on his case by having him star as our baby in the manger? Of course we'd talk to all the proper channels for permission, and we'd make sure his guardian is there every step of the way. But really, you never know. Someone in the audience might just have some information."

"Do you know what, Marisa? I think that's an incredible idea!"

"Let's find out who we need to get approval!" Marisa said, excited. "We're going to do our best to help this little one find his family for Christmas gift!"

CHAPTER ELEVEN

THE DAY OF the Mistletoe Pageant, Marisa donned a dress that flattered her figure while the deep red displayed her Christmas cheer. She added the touch of wreath earrings and a matching wreath broach. She loved all of the holidays in her show, but her family celebrated Christmas in accordance with their faith, and Three Kings Day, in accordance with her Hispanic heritage.

"How's the house?" Agnes came up behind her while she was peeking out of the curtain.

"It's filling up, Agnes."

Marisa stepped back from the curtain and pressed her fingers into the corners of her eyes to stop tears of anxiety, stress, happiness and relief all balled up together.

"Oh, come here, baby doll." Agnes put her arms around her and hugged her. "You've done an amazing job, Marisa. I would tell you if you didn't."

"I know you would." Marisa laughed. And laughter was just what she needed.

The back of the stage was bustling and buzzing with excitement and nerves; Marisa pushed away her own feelings to focus on making sure every performer had a personal moment with her to discuss any last minute questions or concerns. Focusing on others had served her well in the past.

"All of the costumes are on point!" a singer called out to her. "Your mom is a genius!"

Marisa walked around a corner and found Sam Scott and Shira talking. By their body language, this wasn't the first time they had spoken alone. And the way Sam was smiling down at her friend and the way her friend was smiling up at the carpenter, Marisa was certain that some sparks would be flying while Shira was still in town.

"You did great!" Shira hugged her. "This is one of your best shows. I can feel it!"

"Are the sets up to your standards?" Sam asked her.

"You are a miracle worker, Sam. I came here with some props from Tenacity, but I'm bringing back art pieces you have created. Tenacity will be enjoying these beautiful creations for years to come."

Knowing that she could use the props for her regular gig as director and producer of the Tenacity holiday show, she had used money from her Tenacity budget to have Sam build the new props.

"I'm glad you're pleased."

"The manger? It is a masterpiece, Sam."

Marisa walked away, but she was still in earshot when her sassy friend said to Sam, "I love a man who is good with his hands."

Marisa kept right on walking, but said to herself with a smile, "Flirt!"

On her last round, she ran into a woman carrying a large arrangement of flowers. It was so large that Marisa couldn't see the entire top half of the woman's body—only legs down.

"Oh, Ms. Sanchez, I found you. These are for you. Where should I put them?"

"Is there a card?"

The bouquet was made of flowers that were a nod to her Mexican heritage while incorporating her favorite colors of yellow and purple. She plucked a daisy from the bouquet and tucked it behind her ear.

"Right here," the woman said.

"Thank you." She took the envelope. "Can you manage to get this to the lounge?"

"Yes, I can."

She opened the envelope and read the note. "Break a leg, Marisa. You've got this! Dawson."

She held the note to her chest and then tucked it into a side pocket of her dress. At that moment, Charity came full-tilt around a corner and barely had time to stop before running smack dab into her.

"Marisa!" Charity was bubbling over with performance day excitement. "Thank you so much for this opportunity! I love you. Is that okay for me to say? I love you. I hope we're friends forever."

Marisa hugged Charity and said, "We will be friends. Forever. Now go out there tonight and show this town just what a triple threat Charity John is!"

"I will!"

And then, just like a snap of the fingers, all of her worry, all of her work, all of her putting out fires, all of her questions and doubts and revising of plans disappeared. It was time to start the show.

Marisa walked out to the stage and stood in front of the closed curtain. The lights were lowered and a hush fell over the crowd. Right in the front row, Dawson was sitting with his parents, his siblings and their wives. She didn't look at him directly, but the daisy she wore tucked back behind her ear was a message just for him.

When the applause subsided, she continued. "Tonight we have a very special guest, Baby J, playing the role of baby Jesus in the manger. Please be very quiet when he is onstage and only clap after he has been taken backstage. Thank you so much, Bronco! Please enjoy the show!"

DAWSON SAT BESIDE his mother while they waited for the show to begin. They still weren't on the best of terms over the gossip column fiasco, but there was something upon which they always agreed—their love and support for Charity. As long as they stuck to the topic of Charity, things ran pretty smoothly between them.

When Marisa walked out onto the stage he immediately noticed behind her ear she wore a daisy from her bouquet, and he knew that she had not only done this as a thank you to him but it was a way to keep him close to her. Marisa looked spectacular in that red dress, but she was always pretty to him with her round face, her dark eyes, sexy curves and a smile that drew his attention time and again to her full, kiss-worthy lips that he taken to dreaming about.

He felt his mother's body tense next to him when Marisa appeared onstage, but to her credit, she pursed her lips and stifled even the tiniest of throat sounds. After Marisa took her seat behind the piano and the rest of the house lights dimmed, the band began to play and the curtain slowly opened. There on the stage was a vision the likes of which he had never seen: Charity standing alone with a spotlight on her. She was dressed in a modernized Mrs. Claus costume. Once Charity began to sing "White Christmas" acapella, a collective gasp could be heard from the audience. When he heard it, he closed his hand into a fist, hit his leg with it and thought to himself, *You did it, Marisa!* Right out of the gate, Marisa hit them with a beloved song that he'd told her was the most requested song at the local radio station.

Dawson had never felt as proud of anyone as he did of Marisa and Charity. They'd created a Mistletoe Pageant for the record books. Everything Marisa had done to marry her vision of bringing new musical styles and arrangements, with Bronco's usual pageant was masterful. And, every time Charity stepped out onto stage or sang a song or danced with the other performers, Mimi was clutching the arms of her chair so tightly that her knuckles went white.

Marisa had the audience in the palm of her hand. She played the piano, watched every move of the actors and dancers onstage and communicated with the live band. He could barely take his eyes off her.

When it came time for the traditional Nativity scene and Baby J was in the manger, surrounded by the three kings, Mary and Joseph, the audience was silent and respectful and Dawson believed that this would be the most talked about part of the most talked about show in the history of Bronco.

"I can't believe it's almost over," Mimi said to no one in particular.

Marisa played "Have Yourself a Merry Little Christmas" with her own arrangement while the cast made one last costume and set change. When Marisa finished the song, the audience clapped for her loudly and Dawson even heard some cheers. If this was a preview of what was to come after the last song, the cast would have to perform several encores.

The curtain opened and the entire cast was on the stage with Charity standing by herself in front of the others.

When Mimi made a sound in her throat, Dawson looked over at his mom, a woman whom he had never seen allow her social mask to slip in the slightest, and saw unshed tears in her eyes. He was at odds with both of his parents for the majority of his teenage and adult years and he supposed it always would be this way, but Mimi was still his mother. While the cast sang "We Wish You a Merry Christmas" with a classic arrangement, Dawson reached over to take his mother's hand. She held his hand tightly and even put her left hand on top of his.

"She's an angel, Dawson," she said in a wavering voice. "Do you see her?"

"I see her, Mom. I see her."

Mimi reached for her husband's hand and when Dawson leaned forward just a bit, he could see that his father was also stunned by his daughter. Charity was the youngest and the only daughter—it had been difficult for any of them, including him, to see her as a grown woman. After tonight, they were all going to have to rethink their relationship with Charity. Marisa saw in Charity what none of them really had before, and she had done her best to build up those raw gifts.

What Marisa had done for Charity only made him love her more. And it made him wonder—after everything Marisa had done for their daughter, would Randall and Mimi be open to the idea of her as a daughter-in-law?

MARISA SAT AT her piano and watched the final performance of the Bronco, Montana's, Mistletoe Pageant holiday show. She had deliberately omitted the piano from the last song so she could enjoy the performance. The night had been a triumph; it had and she knew it. Everything that she had wanted to accomplish—produce a show that would make Bronco feel at home in the theater, shine a light on Baby J, weave other cultural celebrations throughout while still maintaining the traditions that the town cherished—had been achieved, all with the hard work and support and dedication and talent that she had found in Bronco. As the last note of the last song was being sung, Marisa met Dawson's gaze and mouthed *thank you* to him. Dawson had saved this show for her, and if he hadn't cared about her and if he hadn't cared so much about Charity, this night would have surely turned out to be a disaster and might've just been a nuclear bomb on her career. She could easily imagine TikTok videos of her going viral, but this time for all the wrong reasons. Social media was, after all, a fickle lover.

When the curtain closed, Marisa was on her feet, clapping as hard as her hands would allow. She took the stairs and was there to continue clapping when the curtain reopened and the cast took another bow.

Marisa took a microphone, waited for the thunderous applause to die down and then she said, "Thank you, Bronco, for going on this incredible journey with me. I feel blessed and honored and all of the credit must go to the wonderful people standing behind me. Most of you know that I grew up not too far from here, in Tenacity. In my house, at Christmastime, there is a song that I sang with my family."

She turned her head to look at her cast. "We were hoping for an encore, and now that we have it this cast has kindly agreed to sing this song with me for all of you. Please sing along if you know the words."

Marisa returned to her spot behind the piano, a place that felt as comfortable to her as any other spot ever did. Right before she put fingers to keyboard, she closed her eyes and said a prayer. "This is 'How Great Thou Art.'"

She began to sing, and then the cast on the stage joined in on the harmony one layer at a time until the song sounded robust and round. Out of the corner of her eye, she saw the audience, a few at a time at first, stand up and they began to sing along. Marisa believed that this was a night she would never forget. And to end on a song that was a part of her own Christmas tradition brought her to tears, tears that she didn't try to wipe away, tears that she didn't try to hide. These were tears of exhaustion, relief, pride and love. And she deserved to have them!

After the song ended, there was an odd lull as if everyone in the building had breathed in at the exact same time. Then, the room erupted with clapping that reached the rafters. Marisa went onstage, hugged Charity, and then held Charity's hand as the cast took one final bow and the curtain closed before them.

She couldn't move. She couldn't think. She couldn't do anything really other than stand like an old tree rooted to its place. It was done and it had been done well. The entire cast circled around her, linking arms and singing her praises. There would never be enough words to express to them how much they meant to her.

"All I can say is you are amazing artists and it has been my absolute privilege to know you, work with you and learn from you. Now let's go celebrate at The Library! My cousin Camilla is the owner and she's got a spread ready for us! We have damn well earned it!"

DAWSON WAS STANDING next to his mom when Hannah Abernathy herself came to personally tell Mimi that Charity was the crown jewel of the show.

"Did you hear that, Randall?" Mimi whispered loudly enough that she really didn't need to attempt to whisper. "Our baby was the crown jewel!"

"Well," Randall said, his chest popped out with pride, "I think we already knew that."

"We did," Mimi agreed. "But it's nice to hear. Especially from an Abernathy!"

Once the curtain closed for the final time, all Dawson wanted to do was find Marisa and get her into his arms. That pretty red dress hugged her hourglass figure, and it had made all of his bells and whistles want to go off.

"Charity!" Mimi cried, reaching for her youngest child when she came off stage. "You were perfect. I've never been more proud of you."

Charity hugged her mom and then her dad and then worked her way down the sibling chain until she hugged Dawson.

"We had no idea you could sing like that, baby girl," Randall said, rocking back a bit on his heels.

"Well, all of the credit has to go to Marisa. She taught me so much in such a short amount of time."

Mimi's lips pursed and her body stiffened and she muttered something under her breath with a slight shake of the head.

Randall and Mimi wanted their triumphant daughter to join them at a party hosted by the Taylor family but Charity wanted to go to The Library with the rest of the cast to celebrate.

"Are you going to The Library with us?" she asked Dawson.

"That's a hell yes."

"Aren't you so proud of her?" She leaned over and asked for his ears only.

"Hell yes," he said again. "Do you know where she is?"

"She's outside speaking to a TV reporter. Everyone is hoping that after the extra publicity for Baby J his mother will come back to claim him."

After several more hugs from their parents, Charity and he finally made it outside while Marisa was wrapping up her interview.

"Dawson?"

"Yes, baby sis?"

"Do you love her?"

Blindsided, Dawson looked over at Charity. "What kind of a question is that?"

"Do you love her?"

"I think so," he said, annoyed at the question in the first place.

"She's my friend."

"She's my friend too."

Charity bit her lip before she said, "Marisa isn't a...casual kind of woman."

"I know that."

"So...treat her like you would treat me. Respectful like."

"Charity, Marisa is not my sister. Gosh darn why did you just put that thought in my head!"

"That wasn't my plan, but if what I just said keeps you an honest man, then my work here is done."

THE CAST AND crew of the Mistletoe Pageant, triumphant and high on good vibes and racing endorphins, gathered at The Library. They were loud and everyone seemed to be talking all at once. There was laughing, dancing, and there were times when groups of people began to sing, which prompted the rest of them to join in.

"You are amazing," Shira said as she found Marisa in the throng. "I've never seen anything like the show you just produced. TikTok is going to go crazy for you again."

Marisa hugged Shira tightly. Throughout the show, she relied on Shira to keep the beat and hold all of the instruments together.

"I can't thank you enough, Shira. You stopped your life to come to my rescue."

"That's what friends are for."

"Yes, but it's times like these that makes it crystal clear who are your friends and who are just acquaintances. And you, my dear, are the very best of friends."

"Same."

They linked arms together and walked in unison. "How do you like Bronco?" Marisa asked her friend.

"Handsome cowboys, bucolic views? What's not to love?"

"I've fallen in love with Bronco." Her personal truth? She had fallen in love with Bronco *and* Dawson John.

Shira linked arms with her. "Maybe we've both fallen in love with Bronco because we both fell in love with men *from* Bronco?"

"Maybe we shouldn't use the word *maybe*."

"That sounds like a song," Shira said. "Row House Four's

first single. Maybe I can lure you back to Boston to play with us? We miss you."

"I miss you guys too," Marisa said. "But…"

"Your life is here."

"Yes."

"And now your love is here."

Marisa nodded still coming to grips with the depth of her feelings for Dawson.

Shira hugged her again and whispered in her ear, "Now go take advantage of that handsome cowboy."

Marisa blushed and laughed and hugged her friend one last time before returning to Dawson's side. After the cast and crew sang "For she's a jolly good lady," Marisa felt loved, appreciated and accepted by the Bronco community of singers, dancers and musicians, and it was better than she had hoped for when she first took this job.

"Your cousin throws a damn good shindig," Dawson said, seeming happier now that she had returned to him.

"She really does," Marisa agreed, then said, "I'm a little overheated. Take a walk with me?"

Dawson finished his beer, and then they walked out into the frigid air. He put his arm around her, drew her close to him and did his best to keep her warm.

"What's on your mind?" he asked her. "You seem like you're a million miles away from me."

She smiled up at him. "I'm not a million miles away from you. I'm just thinking about how grateful I am for you."

"For me? What did I do?"

"Everything, Dawson," she said. "You challenged me, you supported me, and pushed me to reach higher than I had ever thought to reach. I have always had confidence in my abilities. But seeing myself through your eyes? Your unwavering faith, your unwavering support, lifted me up when I could have easily missed a step and faltered. So, I'm grateful for that."

"If I managed to do all that for you, Marisa, then I feel as proud as a puffed-up peacock." His words made her laugh. "I want you to know that I'm grateful for *you*. You trusted me to help guide you. You made me think that if a woman as special as Marisa trusts me, then maybe I'm not just the black sheep of my family. Maybe there's more to me."

"You are much more than that, Dawson. Much more."

Dawson took in a deep breath and then he said, "I've got some mighty strong feelings for you, Marisa. Feelings that I've never felt before in my life."

Marisa felt a swell of emotions rising to the surface. Even though she still couldn't see the road ahead that would bring them to the same place at the same time, Marisa wanted to savor every minute with Dawson she could.

"Do you remember when I told you that it was my turn to choose the next adventure?" she asked him.

"Yes," he said. "Lay it on me."

"Well, sex is considered to be a very good cardiovascular activity."

Dawson seemed to forget how to breathe and swallow. He started to cough and his eyes started to water.

"Are you okay?" she asked, patting him on the back.

"I don't know." He coughed a few more times. "That's really what you want to do?"

"You promised to do whatever I wanted."

Dawson grabbed her hand and started to head out for his truck. "Darlin', a deal is a deal. If sexy time is what you want, sexy time is what you're gonna get!"

CHAPTER TWELVE

DAWSON HELD HER hand all the way out to their family ranch, the Double J. Marisa had been exposed to wealth like the Johns' during her time at Berklee. Being in those fancy Boston houses had always made her feel out of place and uncomfortable regardless of how nice the people inside of the houses were to her. It was internal for her—an unwanted insecurity that she had been unable to overcome. So, pulling onto the main road to the Double J started her stomach to churning.

The cattle ranches in Tenacity looked like working ranches—there was a good bit of rusty barbed wire from four decades back when the fence was first built, the wood on the fences and other buildings had turned a grayish brown and had bowed so much that it popped off the nail and separated from the other piece of wood. The buildings were old, with plenty of moss growing on the roofs. Weeds weren't bothered with because it was all hands on deck just to keep the place afloat. But the Double J? Even at night, the place was so lit up that she could see that every fence was freshly painted, with no bowed planks. The grounds were pristine, which meant that the Johns had plenty of money to hire landscapers. A job like that for a place of this size? Dawson's parents probably spent more money on ground maintenance than her parents made a year. Every building was built with a similar color pallet, and the ones she could see on the long, paved drive were in top-notch condition. All of these things taken together read as "money, money, money."

"It's beautiful," Marisa said with an audible waver in her voice.

"It is," he agreed. "The folks run a tight ship."

Dawson must have detected her nervousness because he reached over for her hand and squeezed it. "Are you sure you want to do this *here*?"

"We can't go to my aunt and uncle's house."

"True," he said. "What about a hotel?"

"So the clerk can sneak a picture of us and send it to the gossip column?"

"Good point. I started to earn my bad reputation back in high school. But I don't want to tarnish your good name."

"Thank you."

Dawson had slowed down while they hashed out their options. When he reached the inner sanctum gate, he stopped and didn't punch the code to open it.

"It's your decision, Marisa. Do we go forward or do we turn around?"

Marisa chewed the side of her nail for a second or two. "Will we run into your family?"

"My parents typically go to our mountain cabin for the weekends, so we won't run into them. But you may run into my siblings." He looked over at her, still holding her hand. "Is the risk one you're willing to take?"

Marisa took another quick moment to mull it over and in the end she said, "One hundred percent."

He kissed the back of her hand before he rolled down his window, punched a code to open the gate so they could drive through.

Dawson parked his truck around the side where there was a side door to the farmhouse styled kitchen. Once inside the darkened kitchen, Dawson stopped at the refrigerator.

"Thirsty?" he asked.

"I could use a drink."

"Wine?"

"Yes, please. Red, sweet."

Dawson grabbed a bottle of wine and two glasses, then led her through the house to his room. A suite of rooms, actually.

Marisa walked around, taking it all in. "I think this bedroom is bigger than my childhood home!"

Dawson had stripped off his winter gear before he came over to help her out of her coat, hung it up next to his, and then gave her a bear hug. "Does that bother you?"

Marisa wished that it didn't but it did.

"I guess it does," she admitted.

Still hugging her from behind, Dawson kissed her cheek. "Is it a deal-breaker? Do I need to promise to give away every dime I have?"

Marisa pulled away. "Please don't make fun of me."

Dawson closed the distance she had put between them. He took her hands in his and looked deeply into her eyes so she could see his sincerity when he said, "Baby, I was teasing. I'm sorry if it came across that way. Forgive me?"

"Okay."

"Thank you." He kissed both of her hands, one right after the other. "Now, you said something about bed aerobics?"

That made her laugh, breaking the tension that had built up around them. "I did. Very good for our health."

Dawson got the party started by untucking his shirt, stripping it off and tossed it on a nearby chair.

"Holy cow," Marisa said. "It wasn't photoshop—your abs actually do look like that."

He smiled at her. "Why don't you come over here and inspect them. Touching is encouraged."

Marisa touched his six-pack abs, and she had never felt anything like that before. He was lean and muscular and so gosh darn beautiful that it took her breath away.

"I'm glad you finally took me up on my offer!" He laughed. "I was beginning to believe you'd never have the chance to inspect my best feature."

"Your abs are just one of many *best* features. Actually, let's just call your entire body your best feature!"

"So, you approve?"

"Me and the rest of the world."

"I don't give a damn about the rest of the world, Marisa. All I care about is you and me, in that bed, making love."

"Well, then, what are you waiting for, cowboy?"

"Not a damn thing," Dawson said. Then he swung her into his arms and carried her to bed.

DAWSON HELD MARISA in his arms. All that he had imagined about making love with her had come true and then some. How could he have known what making love with a woman that had stolen his heart would be like? What he'd felt for the other women he'd dated—and there were quite a few—wasn't love as he felt it now. He had enjoyed those women and they had enjoyed him in a casual, no real attachment agreement. He hadn't misled anyone; he had never made empty promises. There had been a handful of women that he'd thought might have been a love connection. He knew now he had been wrong about that.

"Are you comfortable?" Dawson had his arm around Marisa's shoulders while she rested her head on his chest and her hand over his heart.

She made a languid, relaxed, happy noise in the back of her throat and curled herself even closer to him.

Dawson closed his eyes, kissed her on the top of her head and continued to stare up at the ceiling, his mind focused on the sensation of having Marisa so close to him. The feel of her silky thick hair on his naked flesh, the scent of her skin, the curve of her hips and the roundness of her breasts were intoxicating. One time hadn't been enough. He needed more, and then more, and then more. Her silky skin pressed against his was an aphrodisiac. Having his hard body enveloped by her softness and her warmth took his mind to a place so high above the clouds that he wondered if it was all a dream.

Marisa ran her finger along the ridges of his abdomen, and that sensation aroused him. He captured her hand and guided it down to the part of his body that seemed to need her the most.

"Again?"

"Get on top of me," he commanded, and he was grateful that she was so generous with her sweet body.

And then they were connected as one, her beautiful large,

delectable breasts pressed against his hard chest, his hands holding her sumptuous hips as he rocked her back and forth. It was quiet this time, soft moans of pleasure, their breaths mingling. First was her pleasure and then it was his. Marisa's hands were on his shoulders, her hair was brushing over his arms and his chest, while she caught her breath. Dawson slowly rolled them both onto their sides as his body separated from hers.

"You're so beautiful," he whispered to her in the dark.

"*You* are so beautiful."

Marisa turned over so she could be the little spoon. Dawson listened while she fell asleep in his arms. And when her breathing was even and steady, he fell asleep, completely satiated from making love with an incredible woman who had just taught him the meaning, and the *feeling*, of genuine love.

MARISA AWAKENED ON the other side of the bed. Sometime during the night, she had turned and had cuddled with an amazingly fluffy pillow on Dawson's bed. It was nearly eight o'clock, and she couldn't believe she had made love to Dawson three times and then fallen asleep in his arms. No, she wasn't a virgin, but she wasn't a sex aficionado. Her experience was rather limited. Making love with Dawson, a man who had a very strong appetite, had made her feel incredibly sexy and desirable. But she wouldn't be honest with herself if she didn't have a small amount of regret. Not because she didn't want to make love with Dawson—she had and she did. What she regretted was the fact that she felt more connected and more attached to this incredible man. A connection that would make it very difficult to walk away from Dawson.

Maybe you don't have to walk away.

The tiny voice in her head gave her hope. Here, in the early morning hours, with Dawson sleeping beside her, she began to wonder if her negative assessment of their chances beyond this magical holiday season had been ill-conceived and a snap to judgment. Could she have a future with Dawson John? It seemed unlikely, but there was a sliver of hope now that hadn't been there before.

"Good morning," Dawson said in a sleepy voice as he reached for her.

"Good morning."

"How'd you sleep?"

"Like a baby." Marisa took her phone from the nightstand and saw that her aunt had responded to her text letting her know that she might be celebrating right through the night and into the early morning.

Dawson sat up. "I'm glad. Are you hungry?"

"I am," she said. "But I think I need to get to the theater, get my car, change out of these clothes so I can start packing up the props and costumes."

Dawson yawned, ruffled his hair, and then tossed the sheet off of his body and stood up, nude, without any self-consciousness at all. She pulled on her clothes from the night before that reminded her of the couple of times she had made the walk of shame. She hoped that Dawson had been right when he said that he doubted they would run into members of his family.

Dawson got dressed in jeans, T-shirt and boots. He walked over to Marisa, put his arms around her, kissed the top of her head and then kissed her lightly on the lips. "Are you sure you don't want me to scrounge up some breakfast for us here?"

"I am," she said. "I just don't want to—"

"I get it," he said. "I don't want to run into my family either."

Together they walked out of his suite of rooms and he took her back through the kitchen where he grabbed some fruit and small containers of orange juice for the road. Marisa followed him in her wrinkled dress.

They headed to his truck, got in, and when Dawson tried to turn over the engine, nothing happened.

"Damn." Dawson got out, lifted up the hood, fiddled with some wires and then tried to start it again.

"What's wrong?" she asked.

"I think it's the battery," he said. "Let's head over to the garage. We can borrow my mom's car."

Dawson typed in a code on a panel on the outside of the garage. The garage door opened and then it was too late. Inside, having just parked their Bentley in one of the bays, Randall and Mimi John were walking toward the door that would lead them into the house. Randall and Mimi stopped walking and so did they. Dawson cursed their luck under his breath, and all Marisa could do was stand there in broad daylight with "sex hair" and a disheveled dress that the Johns had seen her wear the night before.

"Dawson." Randall's one word held an encyclopedia of meaning.

"Dad," Dawson said. "Mom. You remember Marisa."

Mimi had a somewhat stiff in her eyes but she greeted Marisa and said, "You put on a lovely show, Marisa."

Feeling embarrassed, Marisa replied with a simple thank you.

But just when Marisa thought that this humiliating encounter was over, Mimi addressed her son. "Stop toying with her, Dawson. I don't believe this is a good match for either of you."

Having said that, Dawson's mother turned her back on them and disappeared into her mansion.

Randall shook his head back and forth, looking at the tips of his designer loafers. When he looked back up, he addressed Dawson only. "I'm not happy, Dawson. You're a man full grown, but as long as you live at the Double J, you need to abide by our wishes."

Marisa could feel the shift in Dawson's energy; she could see his jaw tighten, his eyes narrow, and every muscle in his body tense. But he remained quiet.

"I'm sorry it went this way, son, I really am." Randall gave a slight nod to her, and then he also went inside the house.

Dawson opened the passenger door of a forest green Jaguar and then got behind the driver's seat. He held his hands on the steering wheel with a tight grip and stared out of the windshield.

"I don't even know how to apologize to you about that."

It took Marisa a minute to gather her thoughts before she said, "I think that everything that needed to be said was said, Dawson."

Dawson had a grim look on his handsome face. "I don't know how I'm going to do it, Marisa. But somehow, someway, I'm going to make things right."

Even though she didn't blame Dawson for the rude, disrespectful, dismissive behavior of his parents, that didn't mean she wasn't taking an inventory of what their behavior meant for her relationship with Dawson. Perhaps this encounter with Randall and Mimi was a blessing in plain sight. This was a shot over the bow, and she couldn't stick her head in the sand and ignore the warning.

At the theater Dawson parked next to her car, which was covered in a dusting of snow from the night before. Dawson helped clean off her windshield and windows before he hugged her tightly and kissed her tenderly.

"What does this mean for us?" he asked her.

"Honestly, Dawson, I just don't know..."

"You don't know..." he repeated in a dull tone.

"I don't. I'm sorry. I still have to get myself packed up and on my way back to Tenacity. I'm the director and producer of our holiday show there, and I have a lot of work to do."

"When are you heading back?" he asked, his eyes shuttered, his arms crossed in front of his body.

"After Thanksgiving. I promised my aunt and uncle I'd help with the cooking. It's the least I can do."

"I'll let you go then," he said. "I'll call you later?"

She nodded. "Yes. Later."

"If you need my help packing up, I'm only a text away."

Marisa had the door open, one foot on the asphalt when she turned back to him, put her hand on his arm and said, "I don't blame you, Dawson. You aren't your parents' keeper."

"No, I'm not. But I'm sure as heck the one who's paying for their sins."

AFTER DAWSON DROPPED Marisa off at the theater, he drove back to the Double J without following any of the speed limit signs. He felt boxed in, controlled, like he wasn't his own man as long as he lived on the Double J and he couldn't stand it. It was their right to like or dislike whomever they wanted to, but to be so cold and rude to a woman he loved was his red line in the sand. And as far as following their rules while on Double J land, he could solve that problem right now. His parents wanted all of their children to marry and make a life at the Double J.

Dawson found his parents in the dining room having breakfast. He sat down at the table but didn't intend to break bread with his parents.

"Dawson, don't start," Randall said to him.

Mimi examined him. "I'm speechless Dawson. Is this some kind of adolescent rebellion?"

"The idea that you think it's okay to be rude to Marisa or anyone else I choose to spend my time with is crazy to me. What gives you the right?"

Randall's neck turned red. "I have every right. This is still my ranch, Dawson. And as long as I'm breathing, I can say whatever I want, in any way I want, to whomever I want."

"Then I think it's time for me to move on."

"Suit yourself," his father said, and then went back to his paper.

Mimi made an audible gasp. "Now wait a minute. Let's all calm down. You aren't moving out, Dawson."

"Let him go," Randall said from behind the paper.

"No. We have always planned to have our children settle down on the Double J and raise our grandchildren right here with us," Mimi said before she asked, "What kind of hold does this woman have on you, Dawson? Is she worth losing your family—your home—over?"

"I love all of you. But, she's important to me, Mom." He pointed to his chest where his heart was housed. "In fact, she's the *most* important thing to me. And you hurt her. It's a deep cut that I'm not so sure will heal over."

"It's better to rip that Band-Aid off, Dawson." Mimi's tone shifted from cajoling to cold. "You don't see that now but I did her a favor. And I did you a favor."

Dawson shook his head feeling defeated that he couldn't get his mother to see how much he loved Marisa. "No, Mom, you didn't."

Randall crumpled the paper, put it on the table and slammed his hand on top of it. "That's enough."

Dawson gave a nod, pushed his chair back and stood up. "That's actually something we can agree on, Dad."

He passed Charity on the way out.

"What's wrong?" his sister asked.

"Ask them," he said, giving her a quick hug.

He'd had disagreements with his parents, but he'd never come close to leaving the family ranch. The ranch was in his blood—he loved the land and he wanted to contribute to the family legacy. But he loved Marisa. He *loved* Marisa. And the fact that his parents wouldn't accept her was sending him to a place mentally he'd never experienced before. He didn't want to burn any bridges with his family—even though he believed that Randall and Mimi were always too focused on appearances and keeping up with the Taylors and the Abernathys. Dawson loved his parents. But if he had to choose between the woman he loved and his family? He'd light a match and burn down the bridge and the whole damn house. That was his bottom line.

THE DAY AFTER her encounter with Dawson's parents, Marisa did her best to focus on packing up the theater. She felt grateful for the distraction because as much as she had tried to shield herself from hurt, her heart ached. She figured she wouldn't be the Johns' first choice for their son, but the blank stare Mimi had given her was actually more hurtful to her than if Dawson's mother had exhibited outright anger. At least there would have been a feeling in there somewhere. But the cold stare had sliced her down to the core of her being.

"Thank you so much for helping, Sam," she said to the carpenter who was helping her pack all of the decorations and larger set pieces that he had built for her. The plan was to load up all of them into a rental truck and the day after Thanksgiving, he was going to drive it to Tenacity and unload it for her.

"No problem," Sam said. "Happy to help."

While Sam continued to pack up the truck, Shira pulled her aside. "Are you okay?"

Marisa turned her head away, pressed her fingers in the corner of her eyes to stop more tears from falling. She had cried the night before and her eyes were puffy as a result. The rejection stung, of course it did, but it also shattered the slim hope in her heart that things might work out for her and Dawson. Family was too important to her; she would never marry a man whose parents didn't approve of her. That would set them up for a lifetime of pain, and she wouldn't put either of them in that position. So, as she had always suspected, this thing with Dawson could only ever be a holiday affair.

"No," she said to her friend, "I'm not okay."

Shira hugged her tightly and said, "I can see that something happened…"

"Yes. Something did happen. But I just…*can't* talk about it."

"I'm here for you, Marisa. You know that," Shira said. "No matter what, I'm in your corner."

"Thank you," she said, still fighting back another round of tears. "You're the best friend I've ever had."

CHAPTER THIRTEEN

THE NEXT DAY Dawson attended the opening of the Mistletoe Rodeo with his family. Things with his parents were still shaky after the incident, but their family tradition was to attend the rodeo together and that was a tradition that Dawson didn't want to throw away. Randall and Mimi would always be his parents, no matter what. And when he did eventually have children—and ever since he met Marisa, he'd been giving a lot of thought to the idea of having a family of his own—they would be his children's grandparents. Ever since he saw how emotional and caring Marisa was about Baby J, he had begun to see her in the light of a mother; and he could easily imagine her as his wife and the mother of his children. And he had to believe that given enough time, his parents would grow to love Marisa the way he loved her.

Charity, who was sitting next to him, skimmed the program while they were awaiting the opening ceremony that would kick-off the rodeo. A newcomer to the country music industry would be singing the "Star Spangled Banner." Charity leaned over and said to him, "Brooks Langtree, the Hawkins Sisters and Geoff Burris and his brothers Jack and Ross are all appearing today."

Dawson was preoccupied with his phone. He had called Marisa several times and she didn't pick up; he had also texted her and even though he could tell that she had read the text, she hadn't replied. She was avoiding him. The encounter with his parents at the Double J had done more damage than he originally thought.

"Damn," Dawson said under his breath. Part of him wanted to go find her and hash things out between them. But as much as he didn't care about appearances when his parents were trying to keep up with the Taylors and Abernathys, he didn't want to give the gossip mill more material when it came to Marisa and him. Everyone knew their family's tradition of going to the rodeo together. If he suddenly disappeared, folks who liked to share tidbits with the local gossip columnist would notice.

"What's going on?" Charity leaned over and whispered the question.

He shook his head, refusing to speak about it. He sent Charity a text instead, and when she read it, she looked over at him and frowned. He knew that Charity would share in his concern that Marisa wasn't communicating with him. Charity loved Marisa too.

"Why don't you get off your phone, little brother?" Maddox said. "There are some mighty fine women here who would make you a very happy man if you would just give them the time of day."

Not wanting to draw any more attention to himself, Dawson turned his phone on vibrate and put in the left pocket of his shirt just in case Marisa got back to him. Charity saw a friend on the bleachers down several steps; when she left, the seat between him and the aisle opened up. Before he could think anything about it, one of the daughters of a cattle family in a neighboring town, Emma Lou, appeared next to him. She was exactly the type of woman his mom wanted him to marry—cattle family pedigree and a debutante to boot. And of course he could see that she was pretty—everyone with eyes could. She had long blond hair, pretty blue eyes, fair skin, and a lean body from years of riding and playing hard with her older brothers. She was beautiful, bubbly and sweet as sugar. And she was uncomplicated. Before Marisa, Emma Lou might've made it onto the the short list of potential wives when he was ready to go that route further down the line. Mimi would have some reservations about the cost-benefit to their family in that Emma Lou's folks had half the land holdings and head of cattle.

"Hi, Dawson." Emma Lou sat real close.

Dawson tried to put some distance between him and her, but on his other side Maddox wasn't budging. Emma Lou came from a family that had been in Bronco for many generations. They didn't have money like the Taylors or Abernathys, or even the money his family had, but she did come from a family who had enough money to pass Mimi's litmus test.

"Hello, Emma Lou." Mimi leaned forward so she could greet his unwanted companion.

"Hi, Mrs. John! I hope you have a happy Thanksgiving."

"You too, dear." Mimi said with a smile. "Please tell your parents 'hi' from Randall and me."

"I will," Emma Lou said. "My parents just think the world of your family."

"Well, isn't that sweet?" Mimi smiled, "Don't be a stranger. You have an open invitation. I bet Dawson would just love to take you for a ride on the Double J."

Emma Lou glanced shyly at Dawson, a pretty blush on her cheeks. "I'd really like that. Thank you."

When his mother finished, Dawson said, "It's good to see you, Emma Lou."

"I couldn't believe it when I saw you sitting here," she said rather shyly, dipping her head down and looking at him from that angle. "I was actually hoping to see you here today."

"Is that right?"

She nodded. "I'm riding today during intermission. My riding team is part of the entertainment."

"Well, I'll be sure to watch out for you."

There was a lull in the conversation during which Dawson felt that Emma Lou had been angling for him to ask her out on a date.

"We're having a barbecue tonight to celebrate opening day of the rodeo. My mom and dad would love for you to come."

"I appreciate the offer, Emma Lou, but I'll have to take a rain check on that. I already made plans for this evening."

Emma Lou's full, glossy lips turned down into a sexy pout

that Dawson was certain paved the way for her to get anything she wanted.

"He'd love to come," Maddox said as he leaned over.

Emma Lou looked between Maddox and him.

Dawson took his elbow and jammed it into Maddox's ribs. That made Maddox laugh while he rubbed his side.

"I'm sorry, Emma Lou," Dawson said, bent on saying the right thing to get Emma Lou off the bench and headed back to her seat. "I can't tonight, but maybe some other time."

Emma Lou brightened up, lost some of her shyness and she threw her arms around him, kissed him on the cheek, and then said, "I'd love a rain check! I'm going to hold you to it, Dawson John! And that ride on Double J."

After Emma Lou was out of earshot, Dawson snapped at his brother. "What the hell was that, Maddox?"

"Just helping you to move on."

"Well, damn well don't!"

Maddox held out his hands in surrender. "I hear you. I get it."

Dawson received a text, grabbed for his phone, looked at it and then shoved it back in his pocket. It was not Marisa.

"You're that hung up on this woman…"

"Marisa," Dawson said in exasperation. "Her name is Marisa."

"Okay," Maddox said, backtracking. "You're that hung up on Marisa."

"Yes. I am."

"You've picked a hard row to hoe, brother."

"That's my business, isn't it?"

Maddox nodded his head. "You're right. It is."

"Then back off."

"I'm just trying to help."

"If you want to help," Dawson said directly but not loud enough for their parents to hear over the din of the crowd, "when I do convince Marisa to marry me, accept her as I have accepted your wife."

Maddox looked stunned when he mentioned marrying Marisa in such stark terms. A moment later, he gave the slightest nod to let Dawson know he had heard him and had agreed to the terms.

He was tight with all of his siblings, but he wouldn't stand for their interference in his love life. His mood was dark and even the energy and excitement in the arena for the opening of the rodeo wasn't distraction enough. Why was Marisa refusing to answer his texts and voicemails? They had made love, and yes, had a horrible encounter with his parents, but he shouldn't have to pay for their sins. Marisa's behavior got him thinking— had his parents given her the out she needed to ghost him? Had this always been part of the equation for her? Have a holiday fling with a local cowboy and then move on? Had he misjudged Marisa that much?

To that last question, he answered "no." Marisa wasn't the type of woman who had one-night stands on the regular. This undeniable bond between them went both ways. Maybe she didn't want to show it, but he had no doubt that she felt it just the same as he did.

Charity returned to her seat just in time for the opening of the rodeo. Riders carrying American flags galloped around the arena, and then they halted in a line on either side of a podium. The crowd was on its feet, stomping and yelling and hooting and hollering. And for a quick minute, Dawson's mind focused on the opening ceremony instead of fixating on Marisa.

"Good afternoon!" The mayor of Bronco stood on the platform. "Welcome to the Mistletoe Rodeo!"

That got another loud cheer from the crowd.

"Please remain standing for the 'Star Spangled Banner,' which will be performed by Miss Marisa Sanchez!"

Dawson's heart seized and his eyes found Marisa, dressed in jeans, boots, a Christmas sweater with blinking lights and a cowgirl hat.

"Marisa?" Charity asked, looking back through her program.

Marisa walked up the steps to the platform and accepted the microphone from Mayor Smith. A hush fell over the crowd, which made the unhappy grumbling of some spectators more noticeable to Dawson.

Marisa bowed her head for a moment before she began to sing the national anthem acapella. Marisa's clear, razor-sharp tone filled the stadium as she navigated the tricky parts of the national anthem seemingly without much effort at all. When she finished, the stadium erupted with clapping and cheers.

Dawson looked over and even his parents were clapping. Perhaps not as enthusiastically as most of the crowd, but they *were* clapping. That was a baby step.

Marisa took a bow and then waved to the crowd before she left the podium. Dawson kept standing and said to his parents, "You're proud of Charity's performance in the Mistletoe Pageant, Mom. Right?" He pointed to Marisa. "Well, Marisa's the one who saw her talent and helped her sing like an angel. Look, Mom, I love you. But I need you to see how special she is because I love her."

He'd made a scene and he didn't much care. Dawson didn't wait around to hear his parents' response. He scooted past Charity to the aisle, raced down the stadium steps and then ran to the area where the performers waited for their turn. Dawson ran into Sam backstage.

"Have you seen Marisa?"

"She just left," Sam told him.

"Which way?"

Sam pointed to the exit for the parking lot on the right side of the arena. If he could catch her, she couldn't ignore him like she could with calls or texts. He just needed to talk to her face-to-face; he was sure he could make her understand his parents and their family dynamic. Dawson took off toward the parking lot and then searched the rows of cars hoping to catch her before she left. He couldn't find her Falcon anywhere. He stopped running and paced in a circle while he caught his breath.

"Damn it!" Dawson cursed loudly. "Damn my rotten luck!"

SHEET MUSIC. COSTUMES. A few odds and odds. They were all that was left in the Bronco Theater for Marisa to pack. Sam had already loaded the larger items into the rental truck, and Marisa was all alone in the theater. She tried to focus on the task at hand, but her thoughts were elsewhere. With Dawson John.

When Marisa had been asked by Mayor Smith to sing the national anthem after the scheduled performer had come down with the flu, she had been happy to help. Standing up on the small stage, Marisa had known, that Dawson would certainly be somewhere in the crowd. She'd never thought that she would be able to pick him out of the densely populated stadium seats. It had been standing room only. But sure enough, she'd found him, and seeing him had made it difficult to sing. Her heart had been racing, her legs had gone weak at the knees, and it had taken every ounce of her self-determination to keep her focus on the lyrics. When she finished, she'd walked as quickly as she could to the back area, literally bumped into Sam as she rounded a corner and then headed out to the parking lot. She had been avoiding Dawson and she still was.

She wasn't proud of it but she was in self-preservation mode. Not only her heart but her work was at risk. The town of Tenacity was counting on her, and she refused to let her winter romance with Dawson John interfere with the preparations for the annual holiday show in Tenacity.

"Hello, sweetness and light." At the sound of the voice, Marisa looked up and saw Agnes enter the theater.

"Hi, Agnes."

Agnes looked at her closely. "You look heartbroken, Marisa."

Marisa's face crumbled as she turned toward Agnes and flung herself into the woman's arms. She had cried more in the last couple of days than she had in several years. She had fallen in love with Bronco and one of its native sons.

Agnes held on to her for a good long while before she asked, "Dawson?"

Marisa wiped her tears off of her cheeks with a nod.

"What happened?"

"I..." She paused, then restarted. "I spent the night at the Double J."

"Oh, I see."

"His parents returned early from their trip to the lake house..."

Agnes looked at her with years of wisdom in her eyes. "And it didn't go so well."

"No," Marisa said. "It didn't."

Agnes hugged her again before she asked, "And how has Dawson reacted to all of this? Was he supportive of you?"

"I heard from Charity that Dawson had a major blow up with his parents over me."

Agnes's bushy eyebrows lowered. "Charity told you? Not Dawson?"

Marisa shook her head. "I haven't spoken to Dawson."

"I see." Agnes rocked back on the heels of her sensible shoes.

Marisa began boxing some more items. "It's for the best."

"Maybe it is, maybe it isn't," her elder said slowly.

"We are too different, Agnes. We want different things. How we see our future is worlds apart."

"Fiddle sticks," Agnes said. "Finding your soulmate is the tricky part. Most people live their whole lives looking for their other half and never find it."

Marisa paused from her job and looked over at Agnes. "Were you one of those people?"

For the first time, she saw deep sadness in the elder woman's eyes. "No. I did find my soulmate."

"I didn't know you're married, Agnes. You've never mentioned it."

"I never married."

Marisa sensed that the story Agnes seemed to want to tell her deserved her full attention. "Why not?"

"Because I was young and I thought I had life all figured out," Agnes said. "Ben and I disagreed on just about everything. If I said the sky was blue, he'd say it was orange. If he said the grass was green, I'd tell him it was purple. The only thing we could agree on was that we loved each other. We were crazy for each other, much like you and your cowboy."

Marisa couldn't dispute that. She was crazy about her cowboy. But did Dawson *really* feel the same way about her? Or was he mistaking infatuation for love?

Agnes continued. "His parents didn't approve of me and mine weren't too thrilled either." She paused, swallowed several times, and then said, "We let the opinions of others dictate our relationship. And little by little, brick by brick, our relationship crumbled. Not our love," Agnes said emphatically. "Never our love."

"What happened to Ben?"

"He married a woman who passed whatever parent test I had managed to fail. He had several children."

"Oh, Agnes, I'm so sorry." Marisa hugged Agnes. "And you never married."

"No. I didn't," she said. "And there isn't a day that goes by that I don't feel regret. I hope you won't walk that same path, Marisa. It's a lonely one."

DAWSON HAD ALMOST given up trying to get in touch with Marisa; he didn't mind giving up some of his pride but not all of it. But then he received a text from her and he felt like he had just hit the lottery. Instead of texting her back, he called her.

"Hello?" Her voice was thin as she answered.

"Howdy, stranger." He tried to add humor to a situation that held no humor for him.

"Sorry."

"I need to see you, Marisa," he said seriously. "We need to talk."

"I agree."

"When?"

"Maybe the day after Thanksgiving?" she suggested. "I plan on leaving around noon."

"I was actually hoping you would stop by the Double J for Thanksgiving dessert."

There was a very long pause on the other end of the line.

"Dawson, your parents have made their feelings about me very clear," she said.

"And I have made *my* feelings about you very clear as well, haven't I?"

Another lengthy pause and Dawson silently cursed the fact he was doing the exact thing he hadn't wanted to do—get into a debate with Marisa.

"I understand how you feel, Marisa," he said, breaking the silence, "and I can't say that I blame you. But don't just shut me out of your life like we don't mean something special to each other. Please don't do that."

In his short experience with Marisa, he knew that she had

a heart of gold—she was kind, considerate and did everything she could to make those around her feel good.

"Let's meet the day after Thanksgiving, say nine o'clock? At the theater?"

"Yes," she said. "Nine sharp. At the theater."

"Happy Thanksgiving, Marisa," he said, with a feeling of dread that Marisa may be trying to take then full circle and end their relationship exactly where it began.

"Happy Thanksgiving, Dawson."

THANKSGIVING MORNING, MARISA was up early to prep all of the ingredients needed for the day. In the Sanchez household, the Thanksgiving menu always included traditional American dishes—turkey, stuffing, mashed potatoes and apple pie for dessert. But they also cooked dishes inspired by their Mexican heritage. Marisa's mother had taught her how to make fried polenta with chorizo, galletas de suero, roasted chile corn bread, chili lime Broccolini, pumpkin empanadas, and tres leches pumpkin flan.

Once all of the prepping was done, Marisa called her mom, dad and siblings in Tenacity to wish them a happy Thanksgiving. It was odd to miss Thanksgiving with her Tenacity family, but it was also a blessing to be spending a holiday with her aunt Denise, uncle Aaron and her cousins Dylan, Dante, Camilla, Sofia, and Felix and their significant others. The house was small and tidy, and the delicious smells from the kitchen made the entire house smell wonderful.

"Why so sad, Marisa?" Her great uncle Stanley appeared beside her while she made the pumpkin empanadas.

"I'm not sad," she said, and then she met Stanley's gaze and she realized that he had been on this earth too long to believe her flimsy attempt to pretend all was right in her world.

"Okay," she corrected, "I'm sad. But I'm doing my best to not let it ruin this special day."

"Did I tell you that Winona's daughter Daisy received a note from her?"

Marisa stopped her hands for a moment to give her great uncle her full attention. "No, you didn't."

"Well, she did. It said that she's fine and she just needed some space."

"Oh, Uncle Stanley, I'm sorry."

"Thank you," he said, and she could tell that while he was still heartbroken, the note confirmed everything he had ever thought about Winona—she was too independent to settle down with him.

"I think it's time for me to move on," he said. "But I just can't. I just—" he paused to gather his emotions "—can't. I love her too much. And I know she loves me. She could change her mind and if she does, I want to be waiting for her. I'm always going to wait for Winona."

Marisa gave him a hug, careful not to touch his shirt with her doughy hands. "I think she will find her way back to you, Tio."

"Thank you. I am glad to have an ally in love." Stan said, doing his best to regain his composure. "Now! Don't look so sad, dear one," her uncle said. "You never know who might show up at your door."

BY NOONTIME, THE entire family, plus Shira and the carpenter, Sam, were migrating toward the tables. They were packed in tightly with card tables set up anywhere there was space, and Marisa absolutely loved it! The house was warm, redolent with the scent of Mexican spices, and there was loud laughter mixed with equally loud talking. The energy in the house was simply contagious, even for Marisa. She had awakened in a sad mood and missing Dawson, but the wonderful distraction of cooking for family had allowed her to feel joy in a holiday that had always symbolized the meaning of family for her.

A main table was set up, buffet style, and everyone got in line to take a turn. It made Marisa feel a sense of satisfaction to see her family and friends fill their plates full with the food she had helped to prepare. Marisa was ready to get into the line when she heard a knock at the door. Stanley answered it, and then she heard him say, "Dawson John! Happy Thanksgiving!"

Marisa's heart jumped into her throat, and she froze like a deer in headlights. She peeked around the corner, certain she hadn't heard what she thought she heard. There, standing in the doorway holding a pie in his hands, was Dawson. Now she understood the cryptic comment her great-uncle had said about someone showing up on their doorstep!

"Happy Thanksgiving, Mr. Sanchez. Thank you for inviting me," Dawson said. "I have this pie for you, but I didn't make it."

"Mr. Sanchez is my father," Stanley said. "Call me Stan."

"All right, Stan." Dawson crossed the threshold. "This pie was made by your neighbor. She caught me on the sidewalk and asked me to give it to you specifically. Seems to me she's trying to win your heart."

Stanley looked at the pie as if he was trying to offer him a poisonous snake. The elder gentleman simply refused to take it off his hands.

"Well, Dawson," Stanley said, "The quickest way to a man's heart is though the stomach. And, I did tell her that my favorite pie is cherry. I never get to eat cherry pie on Thanksgiving. Majority rules so it's apple pie or pumpkin pie for me."

"Not this year."

Stan gave him a brief smile and welcomed him inside, still refusing to physically take the pie. "You're correct young man! Not this year. Perhaps this pie is a sign that it *is* time for me to get back in the saddle."

"Well, Stan, that is a mighty fine looking pie."

When her great-uncle put his arm around Dawson's shoulders and patted him on the back like they were very old pals, Marisa felt all bent out of shape. She didn't even know that they two of them were acquainted at all much less her great-uncle inviting the man that she was currently trying to avoid to Thanksgiving dinner!

CHAPTER FOURTEEN

"MARISA!" GREAT-UNCLE STANLEY called out for her. "Look who I just found at the door! And he comes bearing a gift!"

Marisa met Dawson in the small foyer with a forced smile on her face and a cheerfulness in her voice while her family watched them curiously. "Well, Dawson John! What a surprise! Happy Thanksgiving."

He smiled at her like he had just pulled off the most amazing trick. "Why thank you, Marisa. Happy Thanksgiving to you too!"

"Let me take that pie off your hands," she said to avoid any attempt on his part to hug it out. But if she were being completely honest, she also needed an excuse to make use of her hands so she didn't leap into his very strong, very hard-muscled arms. She didn't think there was a chance for them to achieve long-term happiness together, but her body had a mind of its own. Her body wanted to find a private place ASAP so she could strip the cowboy out of his expensive clothing and take him for a nice long ride. She was blushing just thinking about it!

Her aunt came over to welcome Dawson. "What a wonderful surprise, Dawson."

Dawson smiled at Denise. "I was happy to get the invitation from Stan. I hope it isn't too much trouble."

"It's no trouble at all! Please make yourself comfortable."

Denise pointed to a laden down chair in the foyer. "Coat pile's over there." Then she turned to Marisa. "Let me take that pie off your hands so you can spend some time with your beau."

"He's not my beau," Marisa said in a harsh whisper.

"Well, I suppose that's an old-fashioned word." Denise seemed to miss the point. "Love interest? Boyfriend? Your plus-one?"

"Don't you have to get that pie to the dessert table?" she asked, praying to a higher power to make this conversation end.

"Yes! Lord if my head wasn't attached!" Aunt Denise said good-naturedly. "And you might sit down for a spell, Marisa. Your face is red as a hot coal in a firepit."

Marisa cringed and then glanced over her shoulder to see if Dawson had heard that. He had.

"Surprise?" he said with a sheepish expression on his face.

"What are you doing here?" she asked under her breath while she pressed her cool hands onto her neck and cheeks. "We agreed to see each other tomorrow…"

"Yes. Nine sharp. I'll be there with mistletoe." He smiled that smile of his that made it difficult to concentrate much less stay angry with him. "But I didn't want to be rude to Stan by turning him down. He's been through a lot lately what with the note Daisy received from her mother. So, when I ran into him at the hardware store—"

"The hardware store? Why were *you* there?"

"I'm a rancher, Marisa, which means that I do ranch work." He held out his hand for her to inspect. "Look here. These are the calluses of a man who works with his hands."

"Those could just as easily be from pulling handles of slot machines in Vegas," she said, resisting the urge to fold her arms in front of her body. "You aren't the only sleuth on social media."

He then leaned down to say for her ears only to hear, "Now I am kind of offended because I thought you would have felt these calluses when I touched every inch of your sweet, sexy, succulent—"

"Dawson!" She said his name while looking around for any prying ears.

"—body."

Marisa wanted to grab his overpriced designer cashmere coat off the pile on the couch, march back over to him, throw it at him and then escort him to the front door, push him out on the stoop and then laugh triumphantly as she slammed the door in his face.

But she did none of that. Instead, she led him into the living room where he knew Shira and Sam were talking with her cousins.

"Dawson!" The room erupted with good cheer when Dawson entered the room. With his height and those ridiculously broad shoulders, Dawson seemed to make the cozy room shrink. While everyone made a big fuss over him, she did her best to appear perfectly normal on the inside while she felt absolutely and positively *not* normal on the inside.

She entered the kitchen, ran the gauntlet of relatives looking at her with hopeful, romantic eyes before she reached her great-uncle, who she asked in the softest, most pleasant voice she could manage at that point in time, "May I have a word with you, Uncle Stanley?"

"Well, sure I have a minute for you!" Great-Uncle Stanley said in a booming voice that made everyone in the kitchen look over at them. "Is there something wrong?"

"No! No, no. Nothing's wrong," she was quick to say with an equally quick smile to her relatives. "I'd just like some advice."

Still with a smile on her face, which stayed in place until she was out of view, she led her great-uncle to the guest room she had been occupying. She waved him in before shutting the door.

"Why did you invite Dawson for Thanksgiving?" she asked in a frustrated, yet still respectful whisper.

"Well, I saw that you were looking a little down in the mouth and since today is all about gratitude and forgiveness, and since I figured the two of you must have had a lovers' spat when I ran into him at the hardware store, I invited him. Aren't you happy to see him?"

"It's a mixed bag," she said honestly. "Why didn't you ask me first? And how do you know Dawson anyway?"

"Well, I believe I met him at a town picnic. He's very

friendly," Stanley said. "And I didn't ask you because I thought that it would be a nice surprise for you."

Marisa closed her eyes tightly, working very hard to keep calm. In the interim, her great-uncle asked, "Are we all good? Dinner is about to begin and I want to get out there before the kids scrape all of the marshmallows off of the sweet potato casserole."

"Well, I can't blame you there. I've got a soft spot for marshmallows too," she said. "But just for future reference, Uncle Stanley, I loathe surprises!"

Stanley tapped the side of his head with his finger. "I've got that little tidbit locked in right up here."

"Okay." She couldn't stay mad at Uncle Stanley so she just gave up trying. He meant well, she knew that. And since she couldn't go back in time and stop the hardware store event, she was just going to enjoy the holiday. Dawson was, in fact, here so she had to believe it was simply meant to be.

When she walked into the kitchen, it was almost empty—only Aunt Denise was still there. In the living room, a crowd had gathered around Dawson as if he was a rock star or famous actor. The women were fawning and the men were laughing and slapping him on the back.

Hands on her hips, she asked, "What is it about that man?"

Aunt Denise kept on arranging the buffet but she looked over and asked her, "I think you might be able to answer your own question, *sobrinita*."

When Uncle Aaron announced, once again, that it was time to eat, everyone lined up to fill their plates with Great-Uncle Stanley first to the "sides" table.

"This is a plot twist," Shira said as she jumped the line with the blessing of those behind her. She came up close to Marisa.

"Isn't it though?"

Dawson, who had already managed to fill his plate, stopped chewing for a split second, smiled at her, gave her a thumbs-up and then went right back to chewing.

"Did you know...?" Shira asked.

"Uncle Stanley," she said. "He wanted to surprise me."

Shira laughed. "Mission accomplished."

Marisa narrowed her eyes in thought. "I've only known Dawson for a hot minute, but I think there is more to this invitation than meets the eye."

"Fishy." Shira nodded.

After they both scored their food, Shira and she took their seats at the card table where Sam and Dawson had already nearly cleaned their plates.

"Ladies." Dawson and Sam both stood up and held out the chairs for them.

"How's the food?" Marisa put her napkin in her lap.

"I've never tasted anything this good." Dawson stabbed at an empanada.

"I second that," Sam said, scooping up a big helping of garlic mashed potatoes.

"How did you manage to beat us to the table?" she asked.

"Everyone is so sweet here," Dawson said with a happy grin on his face. "They asked us what we wanted and they brought it to us."

"Of course they did," Marisa said in resignation.

"Now," Dawson said after cleaning his plate, "I didn't expect to see you here, Sam. That's been a nice surprise."

"Good food. Good company." Sam smiled at Shira before he hopped back in line for a second go-round.

Dawson pat his stomach. "Well, she isn't quite full yet. I think I can go for seconds myself. Can I get you anything while I'm up?"

"No. Thank you," she said with a small smile.

"Go in hot," Sam told him. "I had to fight for this last empanada. The Sanchezes don't play."

"Wish me luck." Dawson pushed back from the table.

"Godspeed, noble knight!" Sam held out his fork for Dawson to clink with his fork.

When Dawson came back with another full plate, Aunt Denise and Uncle Aaron began a time-honored tradition of having each guest saying what they were grateful for. This was one of her favorite parts of the holiday and when it was her turn, she knew exactly what she wanted to say.

"I am grateful for my faith and for my big, beautiful, Sanchez family. Thank you for all of the support you have given me over the years. I am thankful for Agnes Little and all of her guidance during the preparation for the Mistletoe Pageant. And I am thankful for my friends Shira and Sam who were pillars of strength when I was off my rocker. And I feel very thankful for Charity John who is an incredible talent, and I now feel very lucky to call her my friend."

She hadn't known until this very moment how she was going to handle the Dawson *situation* but then, after looking into his ocean blue eyes and seeing a part of him that was as trusting and hopeful as one of her students back in Tenacity, Marisa decided to just speak from her heart. "And last but certainly not least, I am thankful for you, Dawson. You helped me understand Bronco and pulled me out of a nosedive. You were the secret ingredient of my success."

One of her male cousins cupped his hands around his mouth and said, "I'll be grateful when Marisa is done being thankful!"

Everyone laughed and she said, "Whoever said that? No dessert!"

Dawson stood up and said, "I am thankful for friends, family, my health, and the Sanchez family for inviting me in and feeding me so well."

When he patted his stomach, her relatives laughed along with him. Dawson just waltzed in, as he always did, with his good looks and cowboy charm and just won everyone over!

"But what I am most thankful for is Marisa." Dawson caught her gaze and held it. "You taught me what true love is and what true love means to me. So thank you, Marisa. I love you."

While her family and friends burst out with clapping and hooting and making kissing noises to tease her, Marisa felt like her entire being got blown backward. Dawson confessed his love for her in front of her entire Bronco family! The room went quiet and fuzzy in her mind and there was an odd ringing in her ears and she felt just a bit nauseous. This was the "sickness" Agnes had said was going around the theater. Not the flu or the common cold—it was *love*! And she had been bitten by that bug and had come down with a very strong case of love for Dawson John.

AFTER CLEARING OFF the tables to make room for dessert, Marisa asked if her aunt Denise needed anything.

"Not at the moment, *sobrinita*," Denise said. "Why don't you keep Dawson company. It was such a nice surprise that he accepted Uncle Stanley's invitation! He's a good one."

Marisa decided that it would be helpful to have a private confab with Dawson and probe him about how this invitation came about.

"Dawson?" She found him in the living room sitting on the couch sandwiched in between two of her cousins while he watched the football game in Spanish.

"Yes, my love?"

"I'd like to take a stroll," she said. "Care to join me?"

"It'd be my pleasure and my honor."

They passed Shira on their way to the front door. "I'll save you some rugalach."

"Thank you," Dawson said. "I had my eye on that."

"Not for you dummy," Shira said.

Dawson exaggerated a hurt look. "It's Thanksgiving, Shira. Aren't you supposed to be extra nice to people?"

Shira turned around, her thick curls bouncing around her shoulders. "I'm sorry, Dawson. Let me try again and give you some friendly advice. If I were you, I'd consider wearing a helmet."

DAWSON'S CHANCE MEETING with Stanley wasn't by chance at all. He knew several people who worked in establishments along Commercial Street who knew Stanley's morning route. First, Stan grabbed a cup of coffee, black, and then he bought the newspaper, tucked it under his arm, and then right before he reached the hardware store, he threw his empty cup of coffee into the garbage can and then walked into the hardware store, newspaper still tucked tightly under his left arm. The owner of the hardware store, the father of one of the boys Dawson played high school football with, didn't mind giving him the 411 on Stanley's route and he "bumped" into Stanley, a man savvy to the ways of the heart and, after expressing his heartache about not sharing a special holiday with Marisa, he had managed to finagle an invite to the Sanchez Thanksgiving.

"I'm glad you enjoyed dinner with my family," Marisa said quietly.

He had offered her his arm and was heartened that she took it.

"It's the best Thanksgiving meal I've ever had," he said honestly. "Thank you for not tossing me out on my ear."

"Don't think I didn't consider it." She laughed, enjoying the smoke curls that appeared for a short time when she spoke.

"Oh, I bet you did," he said. "What changed your mind?"

"Thanksgiving." She paused, then said, "You."

Dawson stopped walking and looked down at Marisa's lovely face. "Hold up. Am I about to receive some sort of credit for something?"

"Pump the breaks, Dawson." She favored him with a small smile. "You won't be receiving a medal of honor anytime soon."

"Darn it."

"But I could see how much you wanted to be with my family…"

"You."

"My family and me. So I decided, in the spirit of Thanksgiving, to forgive you for whatever you did to get Great-Uncle Stanley to invite you."

He started walking again and tried to think of some rational way to explain the invitation but couldn't think of anything other than some version of the truth. "Well, I did bump into Stan in the hardware store. But I wouldn't be telling the whole truth if I said it was accidental."

"Go on…"

"I planned it," he admitted. "I had some folks help me figure out his routine and—" he shrugged "—I bumped into him on purpose."

Marisa looked up at him with a disapproving eye. "And how did you manage to get my great-uncle to invite you?"

"Actually, he kind of did it on his own."

Marisa shook her head.

"Hear me out," Dawson said. "I did plan the meetup, but I

was just hoping that he would put in a good word for me with you. But then he started to tell me that you were missing me…"

"He did not!"

"…and I told him how much I was missing you. And I think he took pity on me, Marisa. Stan is a man who understands how a broken heart feels."

Marisa turned around to head back to the house. "It wasn't his place to tell you that I was…missing you."

"He was just trying to be helpful," Dawson said. "Don't be mad at him."

"I'm not. How could I be? He's nursing a broken heart and he doesn't want anyone else to feel that pain."

Slowly, they walked together, and Dawson felt like a lucky man when Marisa moved closer as small flakes of snow fell from the sky.

"Was Stan right? Were you missing me?"

Marisa didn't answer right away; she took her time while he suffered in the silence.

"Of course I missed you," she finally admitted. "But I thought it was best if we spent some time apart to clear our heads and process what has happened…between us."

She looked up at him with those brown eyes that were soulful and sexy, eyes he wanted to look into for every single day of his life. There was no question. He was convinced that Marisa Sanchez was his one true love.

"It *has* been a whirlwind," she added after a step or two.

"Most epic love stories start that way," Dawson replied. "And as for time apart, I couldn't disagree more."

Marisa raised her eyebrows at him, doubting his words. "So are you now an expert on love, Dawson?"

"Now that I've met you? Yes," he said definitively. "You leave tomorrow, and I have no idea where we stand and that *not knowing* is driving me nuts. I love you and I believe in my heart that you love me too! We don't need less time, *mi corazon*." In the yellow light of the streetlamp, he could see it on her face that he had surprised her in a good way when he called her "my heart" in Spanish. "We need a lifetime of time."

CHAPTER FIFTEEN

DECLARING HIS LOVE for Marisa when he knew darn well that she might just reject him and leave him heartbroken for the first time in his life scared Dawson in a way that he couldn't possibly explain or express. All he knew was that climbing up rock faces at high altitude, BASE jumping off of bridges, skydiving, any other adrenaline-spiking things that he had done all of his life—*none* of those things compared to the fear he had at the thought that he might lose Marisa forever. Once she went home and got settled back into her life—a life she didn't think he could live with her—they would lose all momentum and he would become a small blip on Marisa's lifeline. Perhaps a fond memory eclipsed by this imaginary perfect man she had in her mind. He *had to* convince her to think with her heart, not her mind.

He stopped walking to take her hands into his as snowflakes swirled around them in a magical dance. "I never expected this, Marisa. I've felt more, said more, stood up for what *I* want more than I ever have in my life. I've grown leaps and bounds because of my love for you. I mean, heck, I declared my love for you in front of *everyone* like a love-sick puppy."

She smiled at him. "It was the highlight of the Thanksgiving *'What are you thankful for'* Sanchez family tradition."

"See there?" Dawson said. "Old Dawson…"

"Three-weeks-ago Dawson."

"...would never have done something like that. *Never!* That's got to count for something, don't you think?"

She didn't answer right away but finally said, "I don't know what to say..."

"I only want you to say what's in your heart, Marisa. Nothing more, nothing less."

Quietly, thoughtfully, Marisa said to him, "Dawson, you were a complete surprise for me."

"Yes, I know. And you for me!" he told her. "I sounded like a first-rate sap in front of your entire family! Ever since the day that I met you, I've been asking, *Who the heck are you, dude?*"

"You didn't come off any way other than sincere," Marisa said. "You spoke from your heart. That's what you want from me, which is no less than what you have given to me tonight."

Then she added, "And, *of course*, my family adores you!"

That made him smile because that was a major win in his column. "They do, don't they?"

"People cannot resist you," she said with a resigned sigh. "My friends, my family. Anyone with a pulse."

"How about you?" Dawson asked in a deliberately flirtatious manner. "Can *you* resist me?"

DAWSON SMILED AT her with his brilliant, charming smile, the smile that reached his blue eyes that changed from light blue-gray to an enigmatic ocean blue depending on the light. Factor in the perfect chin, strong nose and jawline that were sheer perfection no matter the angle, and Dawson became the stuff of photographers' dreams! Add to all of that his body by Greek gods and his confidence... Dawson was pushing the boundaries of what it meant to be human.

"Ugh," she said with an eye roll. "You're so annoying with all of those pretty boy good looks and cowboy charm."

"You are the very first complaint I have ever had," he countered.

"Nauseating."

Dawson laughed good-naturedly. "You look like you need a kiss."

"I'm not going to kiss you in front of God, my friends and my family."

"We could duck around the side of the house where it's dark. I've already spotted a couple of places where no one can to see us."

"First, you're giving of a stalker vibe," she said as they continued on the short walk to her aunt and uncle's house. "Second, I think we should steer clear of any *romantically driven* activities."

"Making love?"

She nodded and then shook her head and the sultry way he said "making love" made every fantasy come to life in her mind.

In a whisper, she said, "Yes. That. Keep your voice down..."

"So no kissing?"

"No! Absolutely not," she said as she pointed to the house. "We are going to go inside that house, act like civilized people..."

"No problem."

"*And* we are going to table any serious or potentially emotional topics until tomorrow."

"Don't worry," he said with a cavalier shrug. "We've already established that your family loves me."

She stopped and looked up at him when they reached the front door. "Dawson?"

"Yes, *mi corazón*?"

"Sometimes I feel like slugging you right in the arm!"

"Oooh." Dawson wiggled his eyebrows at her with a chuckle. "Foreplay."

"THIS WAS SUCH a wonderful Thanksgiving," Aunt Denise said.

The majority of the family had headed home while Marisa helped her aunt clean up the kitchen and put away the leftovers. And even though she had spent Thanksgiving in Bronco instead of Tenacity, it had been a memorable holiday. One full of surprises. She certainly hadn't expected to see Dawson at their front door. She'd been thinking of him ever since he'd left. While her heart rejoiced at seeing him, walking with him, wrapping her arm in his, her practical mind just could not piece together a long-term future with him. If she couldn't see a "forever" with Dawson, wouldn't it be easier on them to make a clean break when she left for Tenacity tomorrow?

She didn't know the answer to that question yet. All she knew was that she'd get no sleep tonight as she mulled it over.

She focused on her aunt. "Yes, it was a wonderful Thanksgiving," Marisa agreed.

Many of the family members would be back tomorrow to eat again—everyone knew the food was even better the next day. In fact, she planned on leaving Bronco at noon the next day so she could share Thanksgiving leftovers with her parents and siblings in Tenacity. But first she had to meet Dawson at the theater and Marisa was dreading it. She truly loved Dawson. They loved each other. But even though it was said in songs and repeated for generations of hopeless romantics, love couldn't conquer all. It just couldn't.

"I was so happy to have Dawson with us," Aunt Denise said. "He's such a nice young man. Polite. Considerate. And so handsome. It's hard to believe that any one person could be that handsome, but then there he is! Living proof."

"He is handsome."

"And just imagine! Dawson John in love with my niece." Aunt Denise beamed at her. "The two of you could make the most beautiful babies!"

Marisa froze. "Aunt Denise, we just met! I live in Tenacity and he lives in Bronco."

"Oh, please," her aunt said. "Those are molehills."

"By the way," Denise said, "did you hear that Dottie is fostering Baby J?"

Marisa stopped her work and looked at her aunt. "No. I didn't! I'm so glad you told me. Baby J broke my heart."

"I think he broke every heart in Bronco."

Still wired by too many cups of coffee, Marisa kept working on the stack of plates, and out of the corner of her eye, she saw Great-Uncle Stanley heading toward the front door spruced up with a button-down shirt and a tie.

"Where are you going all dressed up?" Marisa called to him.

With a sheepish look on his face, Stanley backed up, poked

his head in to the kitchen and said, "I thought I'd go next door and thank our nice neighbor for the delicious cherry pie."

"What a wonderful idea, Uncle Stanley!" Aunt Denise exclaimed. "Ask her if she'd like to come over tomorrow. Plenty of leftovers."

Stanley acted excited by the idea, but that excitement, Marisa noticed, did not reach his eyes. "You never know. I just might."

Marisa walked over to him and fiddled with the tie knot. "There you go. That's better."

"You are a dear," Stanley said.

"Tio," she said in a lowered voice for only their ears, "you haven't eaten one piece of that cherry pie."

"I didn't?" Stanley didn't make eye contact, fiddling with his tie. "Just an oversight, I'm sure."

Everyone in the family wanted to see Stanley happy again after his broken engagement with Winona. A nice neighbor who baked his favorite pie just might be a new love interest that would serve to heal Stanley's bruised heart. But, from Marisa's vantage, Stanley didn't look like a man ready to move on. In fact, Marisa was convinced that he never would be no matter how many well-meaning friends and relatives wanted him to.

As Stanley left, Shira appeared balancing a stack of plates and cups and balled-up napkins.

"I think the living room is in pretty good shape now," her friend said.

"Thank you!" Aunt Denise had taken a liking to Shira. "You didn't have to do that!"

"And you didn't have to feed me."

"Fair enough." Denise flashed a tired smile. "I'm about to call it quits with this mess."

"I'll finish washing," Marisa said.

Her aunt hugged her tightly with tears in her eyes. "I'm going to miss you, Marisa. I'm used to you being with us now."

"I'll be back," Marisa said. "I promise."

"I'm going to hold you to that," she said, and then hugged Shira. "You come back too, you hear?"

"Yes, ma'am."

Aunt Denise shuffled off to bed and in what seemed like

no time at all, Stanley returned and his head was down, and she could see tears on his cheeks. She went to him, "Tio, what happened?"

Stanley accepted her hug and whispered, "I went right up to her door and I stood there and stood there and," he paused, "I just couldn't do it. I couldn't. So I came home."

"I'm so sorry, Tio."

He wiped the tears for his love off his cheek with a handkerchief Marisa knew Winona had accidentally left with him. "I couldn't eat that pie, Marisa. Not one slice. If I did, I would feel disloyal to Winona."

"You don't have to eat the pie, Tio."

"I'm not going to." Stanley shook his head. He kissed her on the cheek and disappeared down the hallway. Feeling sad for her uncle, Marisa went back to her cleaning, and then her mind wandered as it often did to Dawson. She could see some of her uncle's traits in him; he loved quick, he loved hard, and he was hard to move once he had given a woman his heart. Could she learn from Uncle Stanley's and Winona's romance or was this, in truth, a cautionary tale.

MARISA PUSHED HERSELF to finish the kitchen chores with Shira's help. When they were done, the kitchen was back in order and all of the food was safely stored in the refrigerator for tomorrow's post-Thanksgiving meal.

"I'm beat," Shira said, slumping onto the couch with a glass of wine in her hand.

"Me too," Marisa said. "Exhausting and yet totally worth it."

Shira nodded and they stopped talking for a bit and enjoyed the silence. Marisa's mind was whirling. Tomorrow she would be leaving Bronco. And that meant she was leaving Dawson too.

"So, tell me." Shira turned her body toward Marisa. "What's going on? Dawson crashed Thanksgiving?"

"Yes, he did."

"Why?"

"He was afraid to let time pass after..." Marisa didn't like to think about the scene with Dawson's parents much less give voice to it.

"After what?"

Marisa recounted the scene at the Double J and Mimi's blatant rejection of her.

Shira stared at her for a moment before she shook her head in disbelief and wordlessly got up, sat down next to her and wrapped her arms around her.

"I am so sorry, Marisa," Shira said to her. "You didn't deserve that."

Shira didn't move back to her spot at the other end of the couch; instead, she stayed close, holding her hand.

"I've never felt that humiliated in my life," Marisa admitted. A long-term relationship always felt like a long shot at best, but after Mimi's rejection, that long shot became an impossible shot. She felt sure of it now.

Shira squeezed her hand to comfort her. "And what did Dawson say about it?"

"He was furious," Marisa said. "And from what I heard from his sister, Dawson had a heated argument with his parents."

"He's protective of you."

"Yes, he is. And I feel protective of him."

"What do you mean?"

"Family is everything to me," she said. "I will not be the reason Dawson cuts his parents out of his life."

"Would he actually do that?"

"Yes," Marisa said quietly, "I believe he would. He loves me."

"And you love him?"

"I do. And I would never marry a man whose family doesn't accept me. Even if we *could* work through our differences, Mimi John's disapproval is a deal-breaker for me. No matter what, those are his parents, his flesh and blood. Dawson will always be stuck in the middle, unable to choose between his mother and his wife and never be able to completely please either of us. And when the children come, and they would most certainly come, will Mimi John accept them? There are just too many *what-ifs*, and when I add them all up, it's…"

Shira nodded her understanding and filled in the last two words of that sentence. "Game over."

THE MORNING AFTER Thanksgiving was overcast, windy and cold, with a few snow flurries swirling around in the frosty air. Sam was on the road to Tenacity with the sets and props. Shira had left early to catch a flight back home and Marisa already missed her dear friend. She had just packed her suitcase and put it in the trunk of her car along with a container full of the last chocolate rugalach, before she said a final goodbye to her aunt, uncle, and great-uncle Stanley.

"Couldn't you stay longer?" Aunt Denise asked one last time.

"I wish I could, but I have to get back to Tenacity and begin to prepare for that holiday show."

"I understand." Aunt Denise gave her one final hug and a kiss on the cheek. "I love you."

"I love you."

Stanley took charge of her suitcase and walked out to the car with her, and then hoisted the suitcase into her truck.

"I hope you have a wonderful time on your date."

"I will! All I have to do is turn on that Sanchez charm," Stanley said with a wink.

"True," she said, walking to the driver's-side door.

But Stanley blocked the door and asked, "So, what happened with that beau of yours?"

"Nothing to report. He had a good time and we left it at that."

"Don't give up on him, Marisa. Don't do that," Stanley said with a direct gaze. "He has such a deep love for you. I can see it in his eyes as plain as day."

She really didn't want to dredge up things that she had been actively trying to bury and forget. But Stanley was her elder and she had to show him that respect. "Sometimes love isn't enough."

Stanley threw up his arms and exclaimed, "What do you mean love isn't enough!"

Marisa wanted to point out that he was currently nursing a wound to the heart from Winona, but she would never rub salt into a wound and kept that point to herself.

Instead, she replied, "Dawson and I are so different. I think if I tallied everything up, we would have more in the different column than in the in-common column."

"Well, that's your problem right there, *mi gran sobrina*! Don't tally! In fact, *never* tally! I had a very successful marriage to my beloved first wife, and do you know the secret of that marriage?"

"Don't tally?"

"*Never* tally!" Stanley hugged her again.

"Okay, *gran tio*, I will try," she said and then added, "Tio! Don't give up on Winona."

"I won't. No. I won't!" her uncle called after her. Just before she got behind the wheel, Stanley blew her a kiss and she blew on back and he caught it and put it on top of his heart.

ON HER WAY to the theater, Marisa was mulling over everything that had happened in the whirlwind that was her time in Bronco. She felt like she needed weeks to process the events, and she still had conflicting thoughts in her affair of the heart with Dawson. Halfway to the theater, Charity John called.

"Hi, Charity!" Marisa said, happy to hear from her new friend and also happy for the distraction.

"Did I catch you at a bad time?"

"No. I'm just heading to the theater to make sure I haven't left anything behind. I also have to say goodbye to Agnes. I hate goodbyes, and I've already had too many today."

"I'm not looking forward to you being back in Tenacity," Charity said. "I already miss you."

"I miss you too," Marisa said. "But we're only an hour and a half away. You're always welcome to visit me. My couch is a pullout."

"You might be sorry. I might just take you up on that."

"Please do!"

After a quick moment of silence, Charity said, "I feel terrible about how Mom has spoken to you. Dawson filled me in."

"Thank you, Charity. But you don't owe me an apology."

"I just don't want Dawson to lose you over something our mom said."

Marisa's mind whirled with thoughts that would end this conversation topic. Her future with Dawson was theirs to figure out.

"Your mom has a right to her own opinion, Charity," she said. "And I know that you and Dawson do not agree with her."

"Absolutely not! I don't want to hold you up, but even if you and Dawson don't work out, promise me that we will still be friends."

"Charity! Of course we will be. My relationship with Dawson is separate from our friendship."

"You're the sister I always wanted, Marisa." Charity sounded as if she was crying but doing her best to hide it.

"I love you, Charity. We are sisters of the heart, and we will be sisters of the heart forever and for always. Okay?"

"Okay."

"Do you believe me?"

"You wouldn't tell me a lie."

"No, I wouldn't."

"That's why I believe you."

They said their fifth *goodbye* as Marisa pulled into the parking lot of the theater. She put the car in park, turned off the engine, and stared at the old brick theater that had become a second home for her. Even though she was excited to get back home, it didn't change the fact that she would miss the Bronco Theater and every one of the artists who helped her pull off a pretty darn good Mistletoe Pageant.

Marisa was about to get out of the car when the phone rang. It was Charity again.

"I almost forgot to tell you!" Dawson's sister said in a rush. "If you see something in the gossip column that looks really bad, I was there and that picture isn't worth a thousand words. That picture is telling a thousand lies."

CHAPTER SIXTEEN

MARISA STOOD ON the stage and looked out onto the empty seats. Now that the pressure of putting on a show for Bronco was gone, she felt a deep sense of melancholy. If the mayor of Bronco asked her to put on the next Mistletoe Pageant, Marisa believed she would say "no." She had the right singers, the right musicians and all of the stars had aligned for her *this* time She couldn't imagine seeing Dawson with another woman on his arm, staring at her from the front row with the rest of John family as they watched Charity pull off another triumphant performance. It would be too painful to handle.

"There she is." Agnes walked out onto the stage. "I will miss you, Marisa."

"Thank you, Agnes. For everything." Marisa hugged the older woman. "I wouldn't have been able to put on a puppet show much less a Mistletoe Pageant without you."

"It does my old heart good to know that I could support someone as amazing as you," Agnes said. The older woman was not one for emotion so she turned away, took a moment to collect herself. When she turned back, she had successfully pushed down any sadness and she asked, "So you're all packed up?"

Marisa nodded. "Dawson is meeting me here and after that, I'll drive back to Tenacity."

"And another show."

"Yes. I'm actually exhausted, but I'll be running on adrenaline for the next couple of weeks," she said.

Agnes offered to make her one last pot of high octane coffee for the road; Marisa was grateful for the offer. She had tossed and turned all night thinking about the conversation she would have with Dawson. She intended to end their relationship, in part, to protect each of them from bigger heartbreak down the road.

Marisa followed Agnes to the lounge and while she was waiting on the coffee, she saw the *Bronco Bulletin* on the counter, picked it up and turned to the gossip column. There, she found a picture of Dawson cuddled up with a very pretty blonde, and then a picture of her singing the anthem at the rodeo. The caption read: "Dawson John's Tale of Two Women."

"Trash," Agnes said with disdain.

"Charity warned me about this."

"Junk, plain and simple. I heard this was a setup."

"Are you serious?"

"You know I always am."

Marisa sat down at the table and ran her hand over the photo of Dawson. "If I didn't know better, I would think Dawson was playing around on me."

Agnes poured her the first cup out of the pot.

"Everything I did here with Dawson, I always wondered if there was someone hiding somewhere just waiting to catch us doing something wrong."

"Or making it look like you were." Agnes joined her with a mug of coffee.

"What's the point?"

"To sell newspapers. That's it in a nutshell. Abernathys, Taylors and Johns sell papers. Build them up, tear them down, cha-ching."

"I won't miss the fishbowl that's for darn sure," Marisa said with a frown.

"No. I suspect not." They finished their last cup of coffee and Agnes hugged her for a long while before she said, "Well, let's get on with it. Can't get anything done if we're blubbering all day."

And that was the last words, for now, from her dear friend Agnes.

Marisa returned to the stage, grateful for the quiet time theater to say goodbye to the theater. While she was sitting on the edge of the stage, with her legs dangling, swinging back and forth, she could look back and imagine the first time she ever laid eyes on Dawson. She remembered her immediate reaction was one of annoyance and disbelief. *Annoyance* because he was being disruptive and *disbelief* that any person could be as downright perfect as Dawson. He had Hollywood bone structure that could rival George Clooney, Brad Pitt and any of the Hemsworth brothers. And, she thought, not for the first time, that he would make very pretty babies.

As if she had conjured him by thinking about him, Dawson walked through the door. He paused, stared at her and then he strode toward the stage in his easy manner, until he reached her, put his hands on her waist and swung her down to her feet. Without one word being spoken, Dawson took her face into his strong, capable hands and kissed her with all of the passion that he no doubt felt for her. It was the same passion that she felt for him and him alone.

"I miss you like no other." Dawson put his forehead against hers. "An hour feels like a week when I'm away from you."

"I…" She paused to consider what she was about to say, not wanting to lead him on. "I miss you too, Dawson."

"You don't have to miss me, *mi amor*!" Dawson caught her gaze and held on to it. "I'm right here. I've always been right here. Waiting for you. I know that now. All of the roads I have traveled were leading me to this moment with you."

Dawson took her by the hand and led her up to the seat where they had fallen in love at first sight.

Still holding her hand, he asked beseechingly, "Please talk to me, Marisa. Tell me what's going on in that brilliant mind of yours. If you meant what you said that you didn't blame me for the horrible ways my parents acted, then why have you pushed me away?"

She looked at their intertwined hands, wanting to say the right words that conveyed the right meaning.

"If your parents can't accept me, Dawson, there isn't any sense in continuing on. It's early yet. We can do the most loving thing and let each other go now before we involve anyone else."

"Like our children."

"Yes," she said. "Like our children. Innocent bystanders."

"And if I don't care what my parents want—"

"They will always be your parents, Dawson. I cannot be a part of you losing them. I couldn't live like that, *knowing* that."

Dawson looked away and he saw resignation in her eyes when he looked back at her. "So there's no way to win."

"Dawson," Marisa said, "I do love you."

"And I love you," he said. "My gut is telling me there is more to this, Marisa. There is something between us—or maybe it's *someone* else?"

He wasn't exactly wrong. Marisa breathed in and then let it out slowly. "I don't know if I can explain it."

"Please try."

She slipped her hand out of his and put both of her hands together in her lap. "Ever since I was a little girl, I always had a picture in my mind of the man I would marry."

Dawson waited with an intense look in his ocean-blue eyes,

"I thought I'd marry a man like my dad. Hardworking, focused on family and community."

"And that's not what you see when you look at me?"

"No."

"Maybe your husband will struggle to make a living…"

"He's a hard worker…"

"Maybe struggles financially," he countered. "And of course he doesn't spend his time rock climbing, skydiving…"

"Gambling…"

Marisa saw a cloud enter Dawson's eyes as he stood up, put his hands into his pockets and paced around a bit before he turned back to her. "So what you're saying—and stop me if I'm wrong—is this whole entire time I've been competing in a head-to-head battle with a fantasy man who only exists in your imagination and I'm *losing*?"

Dawson stood a few feet away from her but he felt a million miles away. His eyes turned stormy blue-gray as they filled with a deep sense of rejection.

"I knew there was something else, but I just couldn't put my finger on it," Dawson told her as much as he was telling himself. "Now it all makes sense. I was always going to lose you, Marisa, wasn't I? How can anyone win against a man who doesn't actually exist?"

She couldn't deny it because what he said was true.

"Let me ask you a question. If I gave all of my money away to whatever cause you want, could I win against that perfect man in your head? Or am I damaged goods because I was raised by wealthy parents?"

"The money isn't the issue," Marisa tried to explain, "It's about what someone does with the money that matters to me."

"No fun, just give to the community until there's nothing left."

"I'm sorry that I've hurt you, Dawson." Marisa stood up. "I didn't want us to end like this."

Dawson dragged his hands through his hair. "I didn't want us to end *ever*! But you are so damned stubborn, so damned determined to break things off for a figment of your imagination! A ghost! Has it ever occurred to you that you are discriminating against me?"

"Don't be ridiculous." She frowned at him, arms now folded protectively in front of her body.

"You have painted me with a broad brush, Marisa. All people with money are bad…"

"That's not true," she interjected defensively.

"…and all people without money are good. Black and white without any gray area," Dawson said angrily. "I could have met you where you are, Marisa. If you had only let me in! Instead, you're running away!"

"I'm going home, Dawson, not running away," she said. "I want you to answer this. Be honest. Brutally honest."

Dawson had his hands jammed into the front pockets of his jeans, his handsome face wracked with pain she knew that she had put there! And it hurt—it ached—and she just wanted it to stop for both of them.

"Could you live my life in Tenacity? It's a simple life but a good life. I'm a music teacher and a community organizer. I'm not going to jump out of airplanes or lose thousands of dollars in Vegas even if I had millions in the bank."

Dawson stared at her for several minutes before he said, "So no compromise, Marisa? No negotiation? Just your way or the highway."

Did he have a point? Was she too rigid, too focused on helping others—and doing it her way—that she was unwilling to compromise? And because he had made a point that hit home, she shook her head, trying to think of what to say next and coming to the conclusion that she couldn't find even one good word in her muddled brain.

And that's when Marisa felt like her head was spinning; suddenly she felt hot and sweaty and confused. Dawson crossed the short distance between them, pulled her into his arms, kissed her like a man who would kiss her, hold her and love her for the rest of his life. He buried his face in her neck, holding on to her a while longer while she held on to him.

"I love you, Marisa," Dawson said. "And I know without any doubt that I will love you for the rest of my life."

And then, Dawson turned on his heel and walked away from her, leaving her speechless and frozen in her spot. She waited for it, she watched for it, but Dawson never once looked back.

In the week after Marisa had ended their relationship and had returned to Tenacity, Dawson had avoided his parents and spent time with his brothers rotating their large herds of cattle to different pastures. His brothers didn't expect him to talk, and that suited him just fine. Several women who read the gossip column that had put one small kernel of truth in his breakup with Marisa approached him when he was in town, but he brushed them off as gently as he could. He didn't need another woman; he needed Marisa.

"Hey there, stranger." Charity found him in one of the smaller, less central, horse barns on the Double J.

"Hey, sis."

Charity rested her arms on the stall gate and watched him groom a lovely coal black mare with a long, thick raven mane and tail that he had recently purchased at an auction.

"She's gorgeous."

"Yes, she is."

"What did you name her?"

"La Bella Reina," he said. "The beautiful queen."

Charity didn't say anything about the name; it could remain unspoken. When he had named the new mare, Marisa, as she always was no matter how hard he tried, was in the forefront of his mind.

"Have you spoken to her?" Charity asked.

"Nope." Dawson brushed the mare's neck. "Don't expect to."

"So, that's it?" Charity started to pick at that scab. "Done deal?"

Dawson stopped brushing. "Don't go rewriting history, sis. She broke up with me, not the other way around!"

"I know that." Charity frowned at him with a deep wrinkle between her golden eyebrows. "But you're the man."

He started brushing again. "What are you driving at, Charity?"

"Marisa is a modern woman with some old-fashioned values. She would expect you to fight for her."

"Damn it, Charity! For the last time, she broke up with me! I've made a jackass out of myself trying to get her to accept me as her man and I'm done! I've suffered enough humiliation on that front and I'm not going to do it again."

There was a good long silence between them before Charity said in a less confrontational tone, "You haven't even tried to talk to Mom about Marisa."

"Why in the hell would I?"

"Because you are the only one who can bring Mom over to your side of things. If she changes sides, Dad will too."

"I've never gotten through to her, Charity. Not on the first time and not on time fifty."

"Dawson!" Charity's tone sharpened again. "If you love Marisa as much as you say that you do, you have to try! She doesn't want to lose *you* any more than *you* want to lose her. Have you noticed a common denominator, Dawson?"

"Yeah. I caught it."

After another silence, Charity asked, "Can I tell you something that must be taken to your grave?"

"What's that?"

Charity looked around and then whispered as if ears were everywhere, "I'm the one who sent an anonymous letter to the mayor about Marisa. I hyped up her credentials and suggested hiring her for the pageant."

Dawson stopped his work on the mare to look at her. "So, you're the one Mom has been trying to ferret out? Enemy number one?"

His sister had a very proud expression on her face. "Yep. I'm enemy number one."

Dawson hadn't laughed or smiled since Marisa left town but that made him laugh out loud.

"You're gutsy, baby sis. I'll give you that."

"So, in a way, I'm the one who brought you and Marisa together."

"I'll try not to hold that against you."

"Not my point, actually," Charity said with another frown. "I brought the two of you together, so I must insist that you make amends with Marisa. I want her to be my sister for real, which means that you need to marry her because my other brothers already have wives."

Dawson opened the stall door and joined Charity in the aisle. "We have spoiled you rotten, haven't we?"

"Not sure what your point is…"

"Charity, I'm getting pretty tired of explaining this to you, so this is the last time. She broke up with me. I'm not the man she wants. If you've got a problem with that, talk to Marisa."

"I have. And she misses you. I can hear it in her voice."

Dawson threw the brush into a bucket harder than was needed. "Well, I guess that makes one of us because she hasn't answered my texts or my calls."

"Absence makes the heart grow fonder," Charity said. "She misses you, Dawson. Call her."

"I'll think about it. Okay? But that's it. No more of this."

Charity flung herself into his arms and hugged him tightly. "Thank you, Dawson!"

"I'm not promising anything here," he called after her as she disappeared from view.

MARISA WAS BACK in Tenacity and she felt grateful to be back in her tiny two bedroom, one bath brick ranch and her comfy bed snuggling with Saint Nick, the kitten she had rescued from the Tenacity community center. Charity and she were in regular communication, but she was careful not to ask about Dawson and Charity never offered even the smallest glimpse into Dawson's life. They were both trying to navigate an emotional land mine without putting strain on their friendship. It was difficult to admit, but she shouldn't have promised Charity that their relationship would remain the same. How could it?

"All right! Let's start that dance sequence from the beginning! Step ball change, step ball change, stomp, stomp, clap once, clap twice, and then come back to your partner."

Marisa was teaching her Tenacity performers a new dance that she had developed for the Bronco show. Rehearsals for the Tenacity show had been a lifeline for her. When she wasn't at the theater, she spent time with her family and her friends, doing her best to not miss Dawson. But no matter how she tried to fix the gaping hole in her heart left by Dawson, it didn't work. At night, Marisa had plenty of time to mull over the valid points Dawson had made during their last conversation in the Bronco Theater. Perhaps she *was* painting him with a broad brush, judging him too harshly and denying his ability to grow to become her perfect match. After all, wouldn't she also need to grow no matter who she married?

"Beautiful!" Marisa clapped for her dancers. "Let's take a ten minute break."

While the performers moved to the side of the room to rest, Marisa worked through some new steps, eyes closed as she imagined how the movements would coincide with the lyrics of the songs. She took two steps back, spun around, and then once she felt she had worked out the sequence, she looked at herself in the wall of mirrors and then she froze her in her tracks.

"Merry Christmas, Marisa."

There stood Dawson John, in Tenacity, crashing another one of her rehearsals. Dawson was dressed in jet-black jeans, black cowboy boots and a black button-down shirt, tucked in. Instead of a Stetson, Dawson had donned a Santa hat, a thick white beard and carried a sack of presents flung over his shoulder.

"Merry Christmas." She took a step toward him. "I've missed you."

"Missing you has been my constant companion."

"I'm sorry." She took another step.

"I love you, Marisa," Dawson said, and that was met with cheers and whistles and clapping from her performers who were well aware of her breakup with Bronco's infamous Dawson John.

"I love you." Marisa walked toward him as tunnel vision took over and she forgot that anyone was in the room other than the man of her newly formed dreams. All she could see was him, and all she could hear was the rapid beating of her heart.

He met her halfway, as he had always told her that he wanted to do.

"Te amo, mi amor." She told him she loved him in Spanish when she reached him.

"Te amo, mi amor."

Dawson learning bits and pieces of Spanish only endeared him to her more. Knowing that Dawson was her destiny, she rose up onto her tiptoes and kissed him sweetly with a promise for more in a private setting.

"Your beard tickles, Santa." She teased him, her body buzzing with electricity that always happened when her cowboy was nearby.

"I was hoping you couldn't resist a sexy Santa," he said with a wink.

"I can't. And I won't! Not for one more minute!" Marisa said as she turned to her performers. "That's a wrap!"

That started another round of cheers and catcalls as she hooked her arm with Dawson's. "How long are you here for?"

"For as long as it takes," Dawson said, his blue eyes full of love for her to see so clearly. "I've taken a room at Tenacity Inn. You got to know Bronco, now it's my turn to get to know Tenacity. Any I fully intend to show you that I can be the man of your dreams."

Marisa smiled at that, moving closer to him. "And I'm going to show you that I can live a little and splurge on a trip to Vegas every once in a while."

"Damn I love you."

She laughed happily. "Damn I love you."

Happy to be reunited, arm in arm, Marisa asked him, "Would you like to come home with me? I have a present for you under my Christmas tree."

"Lead the way home, *mi amor*."

WHEN CHARITY HAD suggested that he go to Tenacity dressed as a modern sexy Santa, Dawson had thought she was nuts. But darn it if it hadn't worked. He had just pulled into Marisa's driveway, lined with cheerful candy canes, and the house, the windows, the doors, and all of the trees had been covered with lights. He parked his truck, eager to be alone with the woman he fully intended to marry.

"It's small." Marisa opened the front door. "But it's cozy."

"I like it," he said. "It holds your spirit."

He followed her into the house and was greeted with the scent of pine trees and cinnamon and vanilla that permeated the quaint living room. Marisa took his coat to hang up before she turned to him with a smile. "I kind of miss the beard."

"I'll wear it every Christmas, just for you."

Marisa got them some hot chocolate with marshmallows while he made friends with Saint Nick on her love seat. Then she knelt next to her cheerful, sparkly tree and searched for his present.

"I didn't know if I would have a chance to give this to you." She handed him a small box. "I hope you like it."

Dawson unwrapped the present, took the lid off of the box, and found a heavy, polished silver buckle that featured a lone cowboy on a horse out on the prairie. There was a small mine-cut diamond on the cowboy's neckerchief.

"It was my grandfather's. He was a vaquero. A Mexican cowboy," she told him. "Do you like it?"

"I love it," Dawson said, shocked at the content of the box. "But I can't accept this."

"I want you to have it," she said. "My grandfather, God rest his soul, gave it to me to pass down to my children."

Dawson then realized the magnitude of this gift. "So, let me get this straight…you are giving me this because you see me as your future husband and the father of your children?"

She put her hand on his. "Yes. I can. And… I want to say that I'm sorry for how things between us ended…"

He hugged her tightly and kissed her sweetly. "Let's leave that in the past and focus on the future."

With Marisa's help, he switched out his old buckle for her grandfather's. "How does it look?"

"Like it was meant for you."

He gave her another "thank you" kiss before he pulled a present out of his Santa bag and handed her a box that he had wrapped himself and it was, admittedly, a hot mess.

Marisa unwrapped the box and looked inside. Her eyes widened as she took an etched piece of glass.

"Is this the…"

"Bronco Theater."

"How did you do this, Dawson?"

"I found a place that could turn photographs into glass art," he said with a shrug. "I thought you'd like it."

She gave him a big hug. "I love it!"

Marisa took the glass art over to her mantel and put it in the center as a crown jewel.

"There's more," he said as he pulled the last present out of his Santa bag.

"I don't think anything can top that," she said told him.

"Let's just see about that." He put a small box wrapped beautifully in red sparkly paper topped with an ornate white-and-green-striped bow.

"It's so pretty," Marisa said.

She opened the box to find a necklace with a dainty piano charm. It was simple, unadorned and completely spoke to her heart.

"It's perfect," Marisa said before she kissed him. "Will you put it on me?"

"My pleasure."

Marisa lifted up her hair while Dawson brought the necklace around her neck and clasped it.

He then took the opportunity to kiss her, slow, long, with a promise of more.

"How does it look?"

"You make it beautiful."

The expression on Marisa's pretty face confirmed that he had bought the right gifts for his beloved.

"We were both thinking about each other," Marisa said, touching the charm on her neck. "We were both wishing for a Christmas miracle."

They embraced, holding on to each other, knowing that they had found their forever person. Marisa would be his only love, the mother of his children and the keeper of his heart. After some time holding Marisa tight in his arms, he said, "I want to tell you something, Marisa."

She waited, but her body tensed as she felt a shift in his tone to the more serious.

"My mother would like to come to Tenacity for lunch. She wants to spend time with you. To get to know you."

Marisa pushed herself up to look in his face and waited.

"She understands how much you mean to me, Marisa. How much I love you," he said, "and that I fully intend to marry you."

Marisa's eyes teared up as she reached for his hand. "I love you."

"She wants to make amends. Can you give her a chance?"

"Yes." She nodded. "If she is sincere, I can."

As the pain of weeks apart dissipated, Marisa went to the kitchen, with a promise for a speedy return, to get them some spiked eggnog. When she came back, Dawson was standing in her living room holding a sprig of mistletoe over his head.

"So, do you still believe in the magic of mistletoe?" he asked.

Marisa put down the mugs and stepped into his arms. "More now than I ever have in my life."

After three kisses beneath the mistletoe, Dawson took out his phone and snapped a selfie to capture the moment.

"We make a handsome couple," he told her, "do I have your permission to post this?"

Marisa laughed. "Feel free to post to any social media you please."

He touched a few buttons on his phone and then showed her. "Are you going to change your status to in a relationship?"

"Yes. Of course I will." His future wife hugged him tightly. "Will you?"

"Already did it," he said. "Just waiting on you to catch up."

Dawson gave his true love another Christmas kiss beneath the mistletoe. He kissed Marisa with all of the love in his heart and he knew without any doubt that theirs would be a lifetime of love and romance and children. And he would make darn sure that every doorway in their house would hold a sprig of mistletoe, no matter the time of year.

* * * * *

Don't miss the stories in this mini series!

MONTANA MAVERICKS: THE TRAIL TO TENACITY

Welcome to Big Sky Country! Where spirited men and women discover love on the range.

The Maverick's Christmas Kiss
JOANNA SIMS
October 2024

The Maverick's Christmas Countdown
HEATHERLY BELL
November 2024

The Maverick's Resolution
BRENDA HARLEN
December 2024

MILLS & BOON

A Proposal For Her Cowboy
Cari Lynn Webb

MILLS & BOON

Cari Lynn Webb lives in South Carolina with her husband, daughters and assorted four-legged family members. She's been blessed to see the power of true love in her grandparents' seventy-year marriage and her parents' marriage of over fifty years. She knows love isn't always sweet and perfect—it can be challenging, complicated and risky. But she believes happily-ever-afters are worth fighting for. She loves to connect with readers.

Books by Cari Lynn Webb

Harlequin Heartwarming

Three Springs, Texas

The Rancher's Secret Crush
Falling for the Cowboy Doc
Her Cowboy Wedding Date
Trusting the Rancher with Christmas
The Texas SEAL's Surprise
His Christmas Cowgirl

Return of the Blackwell Brothers

The Rancher's Rescue

The Blackwell Sisters

Montana Wedding

The Blackwells of Eagle Springs

Her Favorite Wyoming Sheriff

Visit the Author Profile page
at millsandboon.com.au for more titles.

Dear Reader,

I relocated often growing up, and that trend continues. It doesn't matter whether you're moving from one apartment to another in the same building or venturing across country, relocating is hard work. It's also exciting, exhausting, fun and frustrating. But that's change—a bundle of mixed emotions that are best when acknowledged and trouble when ignored.

In *A Proposal for Her Cowboy*, Lacey Nash returns home and finds herself boots deep in change. Lacey wants to prove herself at her new job and with her family, no matter how challenging. When Lacey runs into a cowboy from her past, she realizes the biggest change might be heart-sized. If this adventure-first cowboy and strong-minded cowgirl can trust their hearts, they might find love is a journey best taken together.

It's summer in Three Springs, Texas, where swimming isn't reserved only for the townsfolk, the social calendars are full, and there's always room on the porch. So grab a glass of lemonade and join the fun.

Happy Reading!

Cari Lynn Webb

To my grandparents,
whose love story continues to inspire me.
I miss you.

Special thanks to my editor, Kathryn Lye.
To my husband and daughters for always being
ready with a hug and a laugh. To my writing gang,
who doesn't hesitate to answer my calls and texts.
My stories are better thanks to all of you.

CHAPTER ONE

BABYMOON. BEFORE LACEY NASH could translate her ex-husband's early-morning text, the two-way radio clipped to her shoulder chirped.

Static scratched across the speaker, followed by the timid but sweetly high-pitched voice of Gertie Tiller. The long-time dispatcher for Three Springs County Sheriff's Department. "Deputy Nash. You copy? C-o-p-y."

Lacey waited for Gertie to finish stretching out the *y* in *copy* like the final note in a solo stage performance. Silence was her cue. She pressed the button on her radio and said, "Ten-two." Then a quick, "Copy."

"Copy that," Gertie singsonged. "Over."

Lacey grabbed her newly issued camel-colored deputy's hat from the hook in the mudroom and walked outside.

More static. A distinct throat clearing, then Gertie said, "Code ten-fifty-three at Clearwind Lake."

The road was blocked at Clearwind Lake. Lacey locked the door to her stepdad and late mom's ranch house, which was serving as Lacey's residence, and reached for her radio.

But Gertie was back. Her words expanded her vocal range into a squeaky high pitch. "Correction. Code ten-ninety-two at Clearwind Lake."

Parking complaint. Lacey unlocked the dark blue SUV

parked in the driveway and climbed inside the latest addition to the fleet of vehicles for the Three Springs County Sheriff's Department.

Another throat clearing crossed the speaker and Gertie's overly excited words peeled out. "Code ten-fifty-four. Clearwind Lake. That's the one."

Livestock on the roadway. Lacey buckled her seat belt, started the SUV, and pulled out of the driveway. Given the continued stretch of silence across the two-way, Lacey finally took her chance. She activated the radio speaker and said, "I'm en route to Clearwind Lake."

A long sigh pushed across the two-way. Censure filled Gertie's suddenly bland words. "I know you are new, Deputy Nash, but we prefer to use codes on this frequency."

Lacey laughed, then sobered before she spoke. Gertie was part of her team now, and Lacey wanted the woman to like her. She pressed the radio button for a succinct "ten-four."

Sunglasses on, Lacey watched a hawk soar above the endless open plains of the Texas Panhandle that stretched out on either side of the road. The land was broken only by fence lines marking off ranches, cattle farms, and recently harvested wheat fields. Not another person was in sight. Only her and the hawk. Her shoulders loosened as they'd been steadily doing since her arrival stateside six months earlier. Now she was back home for good. No more active-duty deployments overseas. No more putting service before family. She'd made promises, and it was past time to keep them.

Her phone chimed a new text alert. No doubt from her ex-husband. *Again.* He was one of a handful of people who had her personal phone number and used it regularly. Lacey ignored it. She had time to deal with her ex-husband and his babymoon situation—whatever that was—after her shift ended.

She might have moved home to reconnect with family, but she still had a job to do. One she took quite seriously, even if she was patrolling sleepy country roads, instead of being part of an active military police force stationed on a massive base in South Korea or Germany.

Lacey turned onto the road leading to Clearwind Lake and

pulled in behind a familiar deep blue Three Springs County Sheriff's Department truck. Her stepdad, Sheriff Wells Hopson, was already on the scene. No surprise there. *Swells*, as she'd affectionately called him when she was a kid, was more dedicated to his job than anyone Lacey knew. Her superstep—her other nickname for him—was the reason she'd chosen a career in law enforcement.

But right now, he was Sheriff Hopson, her superior and her boss. He stood in the middle of the road with his back to her. Two men stood beside him. The taller was a classic cowboy, from his worn brown hat and his plaid shirt and fit-just-right jeans to his dust-covered boots.

Oversize camo-colored waders swallowed the shorter man. Still, she recognized the shock of white in the man's otherwise short dark hair. Mayor Paul Molina had been at her swearing-in ceremony for Three Springs County Sheriff's Department. Mayor Molina had a firm handshake, a thick accent, and a rumbling, good-natured laugh not easily forgotten.

"Gentlemen." Lacey approached the trio, followed the direction of their focus, and finally got to the source of their standoff. *A turtle.* Albeit a very large one. And if she wasn't mistaken, a turtle of the snapping breed. No wonder Gertie had trouble with the correct code. Lacey shook her head. "Don't tell me you three are scared of a turtle."

"It's not exactly little," Mayor Molina mused and switched his fishing pole to his other hand.

Lacey eyed the turtle, guesstimating he weighed in at close to forty pounds.

"And they aren't called snapping turtles for nothing," Sheriff Hopson offered.

"Remember when Gus Ranford lost his toe to a snapper?" Mayor Molina rocked in his rubber boots as if checking that his toes were still attached.

Lacey winced. Her gaze tracked to the cowboy, and her own toes curled in her black patrol boots. Her heart snapped to full attention. *Caleb Sloan.* The cowboy was no stranger. *And* he was no longer a boy she'd once known in high school. He was inches taller than her towering stepdad, unfairly handsome, and watching her like he knew the secret to life and wasn't willing to share.

One corner of his mouth tipped into his cheek, and he touched the brim of his hat. Just a flick of his fingers in acknowledgment. Amusement washed through his slow Texas drawl. "Where exactly was Gus when this snapper got him?"

Lacey knew exactly where she was when she'd first been hooked by Caleb Sloan, his daredevil charisma, and thrill-seeking ways. On a date with one of his best friends. That hadn't stopped her from recklessly accepting Caleb's dare that night and the many others that soon followed.

But the days of carefree nights, reckless abandon, and teenage adrenaline rushes were long gone. Her mother's cancer diagnosis had reined Lacey into being responsible and pragmatic. Later, an unexpected pregnancy had extinguished the last of the impulsive nature still kindling inside Lacey. She'd outgrown cowboys like Caleb Sloan and was surely better for it.

"Gus was walking barefoot in Eagle Run River." Sheriff Hopson rubbed his fingers across his upper lip hidden inside his well-groomed beard. "Got him good. Wouldn't let go until he'd gotten what he wanted."

"Never did find that turtle." Mayor Molina eyed the turtle blocking the road as if he might be the toe-snatching culprit.

"I'm sure Gus always put his boots on before going into the river after that incident," Lacey said.

"Don't reckon that he did." Mayor Molina chuckled. "Rather, he walked on the other bank of the river. Used to say if he lost his other little toe, he'd be back in balance."

Caleb's laughter spilled out, unchecked and unabashed.

And entirely too distracting. Lacey's lips twitched. She tugged her attention from the much-too-good-looking cowboy and focused on the issue at hand. "Well, this turtle can't be left here. Someone will run him over."

"How do you tell a male from a female turtle?" Mayor Molina knocked his bucket hat askew.

"Tail size." Lacey waved toward the turtle. "Males have longer tails than the females." The guys blinked blandly at her. She shrugged. "Aspen got an A on her school project about turtles and sent it to me."

Caleb stuck his hands in the back pockets of his jeans and considered her. "Then you know the proper way to handle a turtle, Deputy."

She knew the proper way to handle more than a turtle, including how to handle a disarming cowboy like him. *Don't.* She added a challenge to her words. "Do you?"

His close-lipped grin and his hooded gaze were pure mischief, as if riling her was the only game he wanted to play. But Lacey dealt with lawbreakers and avoided heartbreakers at all costs.

He nodded.

She set her hands on her hips. "Then why haven't you moved the turtle?"

"We like our toes and our fingers." Sheriff Hopson held his arms out in front of him and wiggled his fingers.

"We can't stand here all day, watching this turtle to make sure he crosses safely." Lacey didn't try to hide her exasperation.

"I suppose we could draw straws," her stepdad offered. "Shortest one moves the turtle."

Lacey glanced at her watch. Thirty minutes until the park officially opened. They could be sorting straws for the next hour. She walked to her vehicle and grabbed a pair of gloves from the passenger seat. Passing by the men, she tossed over her shoulder, "Watch and learn, boys."

Lacey circled the turtle from the back and picked him up. Quick and efficient. She wasted no time releasing him into the grass and backing away with her hands up. Like most wild animals, turtles preferred not to be handled. The turtle poked his head out, considered her for a brief second, then started ambling through the grass. Lacey turned to gloat, but the men were focused on Sheriff Hopson. *Huh?*

Her stepdad tapped his phone screen, cleared his throat, and announced the time.

A triumphant grin spread across Caleb's face, and he extended his hand, palm up. "Pay up. I called that one almost to the minute."

"She always had a big soft spot for wildlife." Her stepdad passed Caleb a twenty-dollar bill and added, "Even the mean ones."

Mayor Molina placed another twenty dollars on Caleb's palm and said, "I suppose you knew that little fact too, Caleb Sloan."

"I used to know that." Caleb smiled and stuffed the cash in his back pocket. "But it has been years since Lacey and I have seen each other. People change."

Caleb had changed. His shoulders were broader. The beginning of a dark beard covered his cheeks as if he'd woken up eager to take on the day and skipped shaving. And there was a confidence in the well-built man before her that she found more than a little appealing.

But clearly the boy she'd known hadn't grown up. *The devil-may-care is rooted deep in that boy, Lace. Take care not to get tangled up too.* Those had been her mother's words after meeting a teenage Caleb Sloan.

Lacey hooked her thumbs on her utility belt, jabbed her elbows out to expand her space, and bumped her unwanted thoughts about the handsome cowboy aside. "This was a bet? Don't you have real work to be doing somewhere else?"

"It's my day off." Mayor Molina snapped the suspenders on his waders and waggled his eyebrows. "Only work I intend to do today is fish."

"Well, now that the livestock is no longer blocking the roadway—" Lacey peeled off her gloves and turned toward her vehicle "—I think I'll get back to work."

"The turtle isn't the livestock, Deputy Nash," Caleb drawled and then chuckled. His gaze gleamed before he pointed to the lake nearby. "Walter is."

Lacey gasped, then sputtered, "That's a bull."

CHAPTER TWO

ONE OF THE largest bulls Lacey had ever seen was standing serenely in the lake, within splashing distance of the area roped off for public swimming. The same area families would soon be arriving to use while they enjoyed their last days of summer vacation. She'd been so focused on the snapping turtle she'd never even glanced at the water. Not exactly the attention to detail she prided herself on in her line of work.

"That's a Beefmaster bull to be exact," her stepdad offered mildly.

"What's he doing here?" Lacey asked.

"Don't look at me." Caleb held up both hands, grinning. "I didn't invite him."

"Clearly, Walter believes the lake is his own personal watering hole." Mayor Molina waved his arms and brandished his fishing pole as if preparing for a joust. "He charged me something good earlier. I dropped my tackle box, and now my best lures are scattered all over the shore."

Lacey spun and eyed the rust-colored bull. "Who does Walter belong to?"

"Murphy." That reply came in unison from the trio.

"Where's Murphy?" Lacey prodded.

"Boise." Again, the reply came in unison.

"As in Boise, Idaho?" Lacey clarified.

The trio nodded.

"Well, Walter can't stay here." Lacey crossed her arms over her chest. "Allyson Loret is having her tenth birthday party here in just over an hour." Gertie had shown Lacey the parks and rec calendar yesterday after they'd gone through the fish and game handbook.

"Sort of takes pin-the-tail-on-the-bull to a whole other level, doesn't it?" Caleb quipped.

Her stepdad and the mayor chuckled.

"This isn't really a time for jokes," Lacey said. "Walter needs to be moved. We can't very well throw a rope around him and walk him home."

"Why not?" Caleb dusted his hands on his jeans. "You said it yourself, Deputy Nash, we can't have Walter crashing the birthday party, even though he's quite tame."

Tame. "That's a two-thousand-pound animal," Lacey said. With a battering ram for a head, amazing agility, and nothing meek in his massive, muscular body. She glanced at Caleb. "What? Are you going to stroll over there and just lasso Walter?"

"Something like that." Caleb lifted one shoulder.

"Be serious, Caleb." Lacey moved to block him. "This isn't a game."

Caleb eyed her from beneath the brim of his cowboy hat. "This isn't my first rodeo, Deputy."

Lacey shot him a look. "This isn't a rodeo either." There was no arena. No fences. No precautions. No first aid. Nothing but him and a bull. The odds heavily favored the bull.

A teasing tone matched his broad grin. "Why, Deputy Nash, I do believe you might be worried about me."

"Of course I am." Lacey leaned toward him. "It's my second day on the job, Caleb Sloan. I can't have a citizen I'm supposed to protect be trampled by a bull. Not. On. My. Second. Day."

"No one is getting trampled today." Caleb knocked his cowboy hat lower on his head. "Your record will remain unblemished."

He sounded disappointed in her, as if she'd somehow let him

down. Lacey narrowed her eyes and searched his face. *Impossible.* This was Caleb here-for-the-entertainment-only Sloan.

"Relax, Deputy." Caleb's smile thinned. "Reinforcements have arrived."

The reinforcements were two trucks with attached trailers and a pair of tall cowboys. After handshakes with the newcomers, Lacey was introduced to Evan Bishop, one of the largest local cattle ranchers in the area. The other cowboy was none other than Ryan Sloan, Caleb's champion bronc-riding older brother.

Lacey's stepdad and the mayor jumped into the sheriff's truck and drove it to block the park entrance until Walter was contained.

"What's the plan?" Ryan opened the doors of the horse trailer hitched to his truck. Evan went inside and guided a sleek bay out.

"I figure I'm going in." Caleb handed his cell phone to his brother. "Unless either of you want to test the waters?"

"My Mischief doesn't appreciate the water like your horse." Ryan led a gray-dun mustang into the parking lot, then worked on saddling the powerful horse. Evan seconded Ryan's claims.

"You aren't seriously going into the water, are you?" Lacey watched Caleb head inside the trailer. "That's your plan? Swim with Walter?"

"There's a little more to it than that." Caleb guided a stunning dark gold Palomino horse out of the trailer.

"A cowboy, a bull, and a lake." Lacey shifted her gaze from one cowboy to the next. "Does anyone else think that sounds like the start of a bad joke?"

Evan ducked his head, hiding his grin, and escaped inside the trailer.

"We need to stop and think." Lacey squeezed her fingers to her temple. She was known for being levelheaded in any situation, even the most stressful. She was also notoriously hard to ruffle, according to her former captain. Yet she felt flustered. And wasn't that more irritating than a swarm of horseflies? She widened her stance as if to prove her cowboy couldn't knock her completely off-balance. "We need to talk this through."

"There's no time. The kids are coming soon. Walter has got to go." Caleb tapped his wrist. "Tick. Tock. Tick. Tock."

Still, she hesitated and rounded on Caleb's older brother for backup. "You have to agree there's nothing reasonable about swimming with a bull."

"There's nothing particularly sensible about Walter preferring this lake," Ryan countered.

"But here we are." Caleb motioned toward the bull still standing hip-high in the water, seemingly bored by the commotion he was causing.

Lacey knew better than to believe a bull had found his inner zen in a public lake. Even one with a fetching white mottled face and a sleepy look about him.

"My daughter is coming to the birthday party." Evan carried a saddle from the trailer and set it on his bay horse. "Riley will be more than mad if Walter ruins her afternoon swim with her friends."

"Nothing for it, Lacey." Caleb laughed, easy and upbeat. "Walter's pool time is up." He paused and tipped his head at her. His grin came slowly. "Now, Deputy, as luck would have it, we have an extra horse who appreciates the water. You're welcome to join me for a morning dip."

Join him.

Lacey blinked and watched his smile lift into his cheeks, all white teeth, charm, and challenge.

"I seem to recall a time when you couldn't stay out of the water. Always goading me and our horses to join you for a swim." He leaned toward her. "Think of it like old times." With that, he walked away, whistling a happy tune, and then disappeared inside the trailer.

Oh, her cowboy wasn't wrong. That was back when they were teens and she spent endless summer days doing exactly what she wanted. Indulging her love of horses, the water, and whatever brought her joy. But this wasn't a vacation. And one persuasive yet provoking cowboy wasn't going to make her forget herself or her duty. Lacey crossed her arms over her chest.

Ryan said quietly, "Believe it or not, Caleb knows what he's doing even if he seems less than serious."

Serious. Caleb looked absolutely thrilled. Lacey muttered and reached down to untie her boot. "He looks like he's headed to a water balloon fight with the birthday party kids."

"Caleb treats everything like a good time." Ryan met her gaze over his horse's back. "This should not surprise you. Didn't you two spend a lot of time together in high school?"

"That was high school." Lacey loosened the shoelaces on her other boot. "It was all about having a good time back then."

"True." Ryan made a final adjustment to his horse's saddle. "Gran Claire always admired what she called Caleb's extra ounce of giddyup in his get-up-and-go."

"I'm also certain your gran Claire wished for a little less giddyup more than once," Lacey countered.

"It's good to have you back, Lacey." Ryan laughed. "Maybe you could hang out with my little brother more. Your down-to-earth sensibilities might rub off on him."

Hang out with Caleb Sloan? Not happening. Lacey wasn't a teen looking for adventure. These days she was looking for routine and stability. Things Caleb wasn't known for. Her gaze landed on her barefooted cowboy. Caleb had swapped his jeans for swim trunks and ditched his plaid shirt for a plain T-shirt. But his cowboy hat remained firmly in place along with his confidence.

He watched her slide her boots off and headed toward her. "Change your mind, Deputy?"

About being tempted by a certain daredevil cowboy? Not likely. Lacey shook her head.

"Are you scared you might enjoy this, Deputy?" Caleb rubbed his chin, his words casual.

"There's nothing to enjoy here. And you certainly shouldn't be treating it like some big game either." Lacey unfastened her utility belt and walked to her car. She dropped the belt, two-way radio, and her cell phone onto the seat and rearmed the vehicle. Then she went back to Caleb. "And I'm not scared."

"I don't believe you," he challenged.

"I'm a mom now, Caleb." She stripped off her socks and tossed them on her boots. "I don't have time for fear or fun."

He tapped the rim of his hat higher and eyed her. "Then what are you doing?"

"My duty." Lacey took the reins of the chestnut Arabian horse with four white socks from Ryan. She led the horse toward a rock, stepped on the stone, and mounted bareback in one fluid motion.

Admiration flashed across Caleb's face before he turned and mounted his horse bareback.

Lacey guided the horse to stand beside Caleb's, close enough that her knee brushed his bare leg, and her words reached his ears only. "Seems not much has changed. You still need a cowgirl to protect you from yourself, don't you?"

"A lot has changed since high school, Deputy. That I can promise you." There was a glint in his blue eyes. "But one thing remains the same."

"What's that?" She adjusted her horse's reins.

His lips twitched. "Once a cowboy, always a cowboy."

And once a fool... But she promised herself never again. Her failed marriage had taught her the perils of losing her heart to the wrong man. And this cowboy was all kinds of wrong for her.

"Time to wrangle Walter," Caleb announced and handed Lacey a rope. "Do you remember what I taught you about roping a steer?"

"Some lessons are hard to forget." Lacey coiled the rope to her liking and gripped it in one hand.

"That's good to know." Caleb chuckled. "And if you have fun, Deputy, I promise not to say: *I told you so*." He winked and turned for the shoreline.

Lacey followed him. He looked relaxed, his horse equally untroubled by the bull staring them down.

Walter appeared unimpressed by their arrival and, more important, not the least bit riled. But even Lacey knew that could all turn on a dime. She kept Walter in her sight line.

"Fortunately for us, Walter is motivated by food," Caleb explained. "This will help get him into the trailer once he's out of the water. Unfortunately, Walter has indulged his love of wandering during his retirement at the farm. When he gets out beyond the dock, like he is now, he gets stuck and freezes on the sandbar."

"This has happened before." Lacey considered the supposedly scared bull.

"Took us a while last time as I was the only one in the water." Caleb adjusted his position on his horse. "Now I have you to assist."

"What are we doing exactly?" Lacey asked.

"Wading into the water, roping Walter, and encouraging him to leave the sandbar." Caleb worked his rope through his fingers. "When we get him to shore, we bribe him with a trail of his favorite snacks that will lead him right into the trailer."

Lacey twisted around and saw Ryan scattering carrots and potatoes on the ground. "Can't we throw apples to Walter to get him to move?"

"Tried that. Walter didn't appreciate bobbing for snacks. Can't say I blame him." Caleb rolled his shoulders. "Now we leave the apples inside the trailer as his final reward."

"You make it sound simple." Lacey flexed her fingers around her rope.

"What could go wrong?" Caleb smiled. At her frown, he reached over and touched her leg. "You don't have to do this," he said and clearly meant it.

Lacey lifted her chin. She meant to pull her own weight, professionally at the sheriff's department and personally as a parent. She would settle for nothing less. And if it meant wrangling a bull out of a lake, so be it. "Here's hoping Walter is famished from his swim and wants his snacks more than he wants to trample us."

"I'm willing to bet on it," Caleb replied.

Lacey wasn't taking that bet.

"Follow my directions from Walter's other side." Caleb pointed to where he wanted Lacey.

Lacey and her horse splashed into the lake. When the water swirled around her calves, Caleb halted her. His rope glided around Walter's neck on the first try. Lacey finally hit her mark on her fourth attempt.

Turned out the roping was the easiest part. Coaxing Walter off the sandbar took patience and persistence and a bit of a soaking.

There was an ongoing loosening and tightening of the slack in their ropes in tandem with the backward and forward movement of their tolerant and well-trained horses. It was a war of wills until Walter shook his massive head, gave in with a snort, and stepped forward. Lacey cheered and called encouragement to the bull, promising him all sorts of delicious delights if he just came to shore.

Finally, Walter reached his first onshore snacks, devoured them quickly, and lumbered along the makeshift path of tasty goodness. Lacey and Caleb kept pace beside the bull, guiding him gently toward the open trailer.

Ryan and Evan waited on their horses, their ropes ready in case Walter decided on a detour. In the end, Walter's appetite won out, and the fresh produce captured the old bull's full attention. Soon, Walter was inside Evan's trailer, noshing on a bushel of fresh apples, none the worse for his swim.

The horses were praised, rubbed down, and in Ryan's trailer in no time. Minutes later, Ryan and Evan jumped back in their trucks and pulled out of the parking lot. Lacey waved goodbye and headed to her vehicle.

"It's only you and me." Caleb followed her. "You can admit it now, Deputy."

"Admit what?" Lacey unrolled her pant legs and squeezed more water out of her uniform.

Caleb lifted his cowboy hat and brushed his hand through his thick brown hair. His damp T-shirt stuck to his chest. He still wore his shorts, but he'd slipped on his cowboy boots. His wide grin suggested he'd been mastering the art of the proper cannonball at the lake all day, not roping a bull. "You can admit you had fun just now. I promise not to tell."

And I promise not to be charmed. By him or the diversions he lived for. The same ones she used to crave. Once upon a lifetime ago. Lacey opened her car door and glanced at him. "There's nothing to tell. I was doing my job."

"Fine, Deputy Nash, welcome home," he drawled, his eyebrows lifted. "If you change your mind and decide to start chasing fun like you used to, come and find me."

"I can't," she said simply but decisively. "I'm a mom now."

"Last I checked moms aren't exempt from enjoying life," Caleb said, amusement in his words.

"And cowboys aren't exempt from growing up," she countered.

His smile never wavered. He touched the brim of his hat and dipped his chin. "Hope to see you around, Deputy."

Lacey watched Caleb walk over to her stepdad and the mayor near the shore where the pair had been collecting the mayor's lost fishing lures. Laughter soon erupted from the men. Lacey shook her head and got into her vehicle.

Fun wasn't her priority. Her eight-year-old daughter was. She'd missed the last five years of Aspen's life while serving overseas. Now she was home to rebuild their relationship. To do that, Lacey had to become as perfect a mom as her ex-husband's current wife. Aspen's stepmom quite possibly held the title for best mom ever. At the very least, the woman had set a very high parenting standard.

Chasing after adventure with a handsome, heartbreaker cowboy like Caleb Sloan would be misguided and unwise. Nothing about that sounded the least bit perfect.

CHAPTER THREE

CALEB SLOAN WAS the last Sloan brother still single. His older brothers had all found love with their life partners and a golden future. Caleb had never given the future much consideration. He preferred to live in the moment, never tied down to anything or anyone.

But he couldn't deny the restlessness he felt recently or the nagging suspicion that his current lifestyle wasn't sustainable. Maybe "the moment" wasn't everything it was cracked up to be.

Not to mention, he wanted to be his family's first call in a crisis, not the one they called only for a fun time. Case in point, Josh had contacted their oldest brother for help after his recent wedding setback, leaving Caleb, Josh's very own twin, to find out last.

Now, Josh and his fiancée were headed to Alaska to help Vivian's parents, who'd been in a rafting accident, and the rest of the family had rallied, thanks to Carter, and kept the couple's nuptials on track in their absence. Everyone except Caleb.

Worse, a pretty cowgirl Caleb hadn't seen since high school had accused him of not yet growing up. Just that morning. As if Caleb hadn't changed since their teenage years. But Lacey Nash only knew the boy Caleb had been, not the person he was today. Proving the bold deputy wrong was going to be immensely amusing and extremely satisfying.

Caleb parked his truck in front of Misty Grove Distillery and climbed out. He ran his palms over his clean button-down dress shirt and newest pair of jeans. He waved a greeting to the distillery's maintenance manager driving a UTV through the parking lot and headed toward the most recent addition to the property: a two-story building that housed a tasting room on the first floor and the main offices on the second.

No, Caleb wasn't satisfied any longer. And it was clearly time for a change. He walked into his oldest brother's corner office and handed a folder to Carter.

Carter opened the folder and scanned the paperwork inside. "What's this?"

"Job application for Misty Grove." Caleb sat in one of the twin high-back chairs in front of his brother's massive desk.

"I know that." Carter dropped the folder and frowned. "Why is your name on it?"

Caleb met his brother's unflinching stare and aimed for a serious and professional tone. "I'm applying to work here."

"You already work here." Carter crossed his arms over his chest and rocked back in his leather office chair. "We all work here. We own the business."

"No. I fill in here," Caleb corrected. He helped out whenever Carter was short-staffed in the warehouse or when he needed a last-minute tour guide. Caleb leaned forward and tapped the papers. "This is for the marketing director position."

"That's a full-time job, little brother." Carter arched an eyebrow.

Carter had skipped over the unqualified argument and struck right at the perceived problem. Caleb's work history was rooted in part-time. More often seasonal and temporary.

Caleb notched his chin higher. "I know what it is."

"You don't do anything full-time," Carter said and quickly held up his hand when Caleb opened his mouth to argue. "Those were your words, not mine. That's just the way you are, little brother. The way you've always been."

But not the way he intended to continue being. The problem was proving he could change—to himself and his family. He eyed his older brother. "I want the rehearsal dinner and the reception."

Carter scrubbed his hands over his cheeks. He hadn't shaved in days, and his eyes were red-rimmed. He wore the look of a sleep-deprived new father well, thanks to the arrival of his twins. Carter sighed. "What?"

"Give me Josh's rehearsal dinner and reception to organize," Caleb jumped in as was often his way. All in and no second thoughts. "Give me full control. We'll host the reception here at the distillery. No interference from anyone else."

Carter closed his mouth and studied Caleb.

Not receiving an outright refusal, Caleb rushed on, "It'll be a preview of the types of events we could hold here. And it will provide a glimpse into what I can do in terms of marketing as well." He paused, then added, "Also, it's one less thing you have to deal with."

Carter steepled his fingers under his chin, seemingly unmoved by the weight of what he had to deal with. He asked carefully, "What about the firehouse? The rodeo?"

Caleb volunteered at the fire station and worked as a pickup rider at the rodeo for the local stock contractor. He mostly picked up shifts when he wanted, where he wanted. He argued, "That won't get in the way."

"What happens when a more tempting offer catches your attention?" Carter pressed.

Caleb wasn't offended. The old Caleb lived by such whims. But not now. "Come on, Carter. Josh is my twin. I'm his best man. I will get this done." He inhaled. *If you want something different, Caleb, you have to do something different. Otherwise, all you've got is the same.* This strategy was certainly different enough to make his late gran Claire cheer. "Everyone is going to love both events. I guarantee it. And you will want to hire me."

"But will you be happy, little brother?" Carter asked and waved his arm at the stacks of documents and the open laptop on his desk. "Committing to an office forty hours a week. Tied to a chair and desk day in and day out."

Caleb blocked out the image of riding beside his deputy at the lake that morning. Like old times and yet somehow better. More appealing in a new sort of way. His interest in Lacey Nash was not the point though. He countered, "You're happy. In fact, this is the happiest you've ever been, big brother. Your words, not mine."

"I am happy. More than I thought possible." Carter twisted the wedding ring on his finger and smiled. "But that's more to do with Tess, the life we're building together, and now our kids." Affection softened his features as if he still hadn't quite adjusted to having his own children.

Caleb was impressed by his brother's easy acceptance of his new parental role. And he still marveled at watching Carter turn from tough-as-nails into a soft marshmallow whenever he held his daughter and son.

While Caleb loved his niece and nephew, that wasn't the change he wanted.

"Let's be clear, big brother," Caleb said. "I'm thrilled for you and Tess. I'm delighted my twin is getting married. And that Ryan and Grant are both hopelessly in love. I even love each of my sisters-in-law."

"*But,*" Carter pressed. Amusement flashed in his gaze.

"But I'm more than happy with my current relationship status set to single," he explained. A certain fiery-haired, brown-eyed deputy notwithstanding. Still, falling in love was one adventure too far for him. After all, hearts were not to be trusted.

Carter arched an eyebrow at him.

Caleb straightened in the chair and refused to back down. "This is about you recognizing me as more than filler around here." Not Caleb recognizing his heart.

"You got it." Carter nodded. "The rehearsal dinner and reception are all yours. Show me what you've got, then we'll talk about marketing director."

"You won't regret this." Caleb pushed out of the chair and headed for the door.

"Just make sure you won't regret this." Carter's words stopped Caleb in his tracks. There was a hint of caution in his tone and expression. "You have to be certain this is really what you want, little brother."

"I wouldn't be here otherwise." Caleb walked out of the office, confident that a career pivot was all he needed to bring his life back into balance.

CHAPTER FOUR

LACEY HAD BEEN stateside for only six months and living in Three Springs for less than a week. She'd been meticulous about her transition from active duty to civilian life. She'd worked with a counselor at the army's VA office to transfer her skill set from the military police to a deputy sheriff's role. Not once, while completing her classes and the sheriff training academy, did she second-guess her decision. Not once did she question her abilities.

Yet standing on the quaint front porch of her ex-husband's newly built house in Belleridge, she was doubting herself. Was she too late? Too late to make up for the years she'd missed with her daughter.

How she'd love to drive to her stepdad's ranch and claim one of her mother's encouraging hugs. Unfortunately, her mom had passed away five years ago. Lacey was on her own, with her regrets and her decisions and her promises. She inhaled and pressed the doorbell.

Her ex-husband opened the door, wearing a polo shirt, slacks, and his typical half smile. The one that softened the calculation in his gaze and enhanced his features. Jeffrey Furth was one of the youngest partners at his law firm, dedicated to his career in contract law while always managing to look after his family.

Jeffrey folded Lacey into a quick hug and said, "You never answered my texts."

Her ex-husband had a talent for wrapping any criticism inside kindness, as if to soften the rebuke. Still, Lacey had always sensed she fell short with him when they were together, and it seemed she felt the same even now. She released him and stepped inside. "Sorry, I was working."

"Well, there's no time to explain that now." Jeffrey shut the front door and touched his ear. "I can hear the oven timer going off in the kitchen."

As if on cue, Sarah-Beth, Jeffrey's wife of four years, appeared in the great room with an enthusiastic welcome. Her smile was as sunshine-bright as her sunflower-yellow dress that fell delicately over her pregnant belly. Her embrace was all-encompassing despite her petite stature. Sarah-Beth was polite, warmhearted, and impossible not to like.

"Dinner is ready. It's best while hot." Sarah-Beth turned without releasing Lacey's arm and called up the stairs for Aspen, then added, "Aspen, your mom is here."

Mom. That was Lacey. A simple word over text and quick video chats. But to *be* a mom. Not so easy. Lacey hadn't been hands-on in five years. And she'd misstepped a time or two when she'd had the role full-time. But tonight wasn't about dwelling on the past.

Footsteps sounded on the hidden staircase, and her daughter appeared. Taller, as expected. She was a burst of color in a lilac cotton tank dress and floral-print platform high-tops—just like her stepmom. Lacey ran her hand over her neutral-colored T-shirt and plain jeans. She'd never been one for bold colors. She and her daughter were different that way.

Aspen's dark blond hair was the exact shade of her dad's. One more difference. Lacey tucked her red hair behind her ear. Anyone would think Aspen was Sarah-Beth and Jeffrey's daughter, not Lacey's. Until they looked into Aspen's deep brown eyes. Those were an exact match to Lacey's. The hesitancy—the wariness—in Aspen's gaze mirrored how Lacey felt.

Lacey forced a smile around her uncertainty and held out a

paper shopping bag. "I brought banana pudding from Lemon Moon Diner for dessert."

Delight filled Aspen's face. "That's my favorite."

Lacey gave Aspen a slightly awkward one-armed hug and slanted a grateful glance to Sarah-Beth for the dessert suggestion. There was so much to learn about her daughter, but it wasn't a race.

"Aspen, please put the banana pudding in the refrigerator." Sarah-Beth led Lacey into a modern country kitchen with butcher-block countertops, white Shaker cabinets, and just the right number of vintage knickknacks to be whimsical, not over-the-top. A scented candle invited guests to breathe deeply, relax, and stay for a spell.

Lacey inhaled and lowered her shoulders. This was the first of many evenings. The awkwardness would fade in time. *Practice patience.* Apt advice from her transition adviser.

"Lacey, what would you like to drink? We have wine and beer." Sarah-Beth motioned to the built-in wine refrigerator. "As well as sparkling water and pink lemonade."

"Pink lemonade please." Lacey took in the wall of framed artwork. Each piece was signed in block letters by Aspen and provided a visual timeline of kindergarten through third grade. Studio portraits and vacation snapshots filled the adjoining wall. The imprint of a happy family was stamped in every corner, shelf, and niche in the homey house. She added absently, "Pink lemonade is my favorite."

Aspen shut the refrigerator and spun around. There was accusation and wonder in her words. "It's my favorite too."

Common ground. That was a good start. Lacey exhaled. They would find even more.

"Mama-Beth puts strawberries in hers to make it pink," Aspen explained. "And she uses secret ingredients to make it sparkly like a unicorn's magic."

Lacey used the artificial pink lemonade mix from a can. She wasn't surprised Sarah-Beth leveled up simple lemonade and stirred it into something magical. Lacey smiled. "I can't wait to try it."

"It's nothing but a splash of cranberry juice and sparkling

water," Sarah-Beth whispered and pressed a tall glass into Lacey's hand. Her expression was compassionate, her words understanding. "I'll text you the recipe. Comes together in a snap."

Nothing for the talented Sarah-Beth who seemed to excel at culinary endeavors and family management. Lacey lived to protect and serve. But kitchens needed to be protected from her.

"I've been craving cranberry juice since I found out I was pregnant." Sarah-Beth laughed, scooped a heaping serving of pasta from the casserole dish on the stovetop, and handed the plate to Lacey. "This is my three-cheese chicken parmesan pasta." Sarah-Beth served Jeffrey and earned a sweet kiss from her husband.

Lacey and Jeffrey had never shared such easy affection. Lacey's mom and Swells had. Lacey had always wanted that. Back when she still wanted a life partner and a relationship. Now the only relationship that mattered was the one with her daughter.

"This is my favorite meal." Aspen took her plate from Sarah-Beth, headed to the rustic kitchen table, and tipped her head. "Guests sit there."

Lacey slid into the chair at one end of the table. Jeffrey sat at the other end.

Aspen settled on the left side of her dad and smiled. "Mama-Beth lets me help make the noodles."

"We've been experimenting and making our own home-made pasta." Sarah-Beth took the chair on Jeffrey's right and smoothed a napkin over her lap. "Tonight is our first attempt at bow tie noodles."

"I think they're perfect." Jeffrey speared a noodle on his fork and grinned at Aspen, then his wife. "Just like you two."

The perfect family. The trio was that. With their homemade pasta, homemade lemonade, and homegrown connection. Lacey didn't begrudge them any of it. She would be forever grateful Jeffrey and Sarah-Beth were there for Aspen when Lacey wasn't. Lacey simply wanted her own special connection with her daughter. She just wasn't certain how to build one. Or even where to start. Still, she'd never backed away from a difficult mission before. And this was the most important one yet. "So, Aspen, when does school start?"

"In two weeks. Then I'll be an official fourth grader." Aspen sprinkled more parmesan cheese over her pasta. "There's lots to do before my first day. Lots."

Her daughter stretched out *lots* into several syllables. Lacey detected a hint of warning. As if Aspen was cautioning Lacey that she might be too busy to spend time with her. But Lacey wasn't there to interfere. *Patience.*

"Speaking of a lot going on." Jeffrey set his fork down, wiped his napkin across his mouth, and revealed a wide grin. "I have an announcement now that we're all together. It's a surprise really."

Aspen rubbed her hands together. "Dad always has the best surprises, right, Mama-Beth?"

"He's certainly surprised us more than a time or two." Sarah-Beth chuckled. "We've enjoyed every one so far."

That her ex-husband had never organized a good surprise of the birthday sort or any other for Lacey during their time together was not the point. Although, getting served divorce papers while Lacey had been deployed overseas had been quite surprising. That was part of the past Lacey wasn't here to revisit. She held on to her smile.

"Surprise, honey," Jeffrey announced. "We're going on a babymoon."

"A babymoon. Really?" Sara-Beth pressed her fingers against her cheeks. "But I thought there wasn't time. That we couldn't…" Her words drifted off as her tears slipped free.

"You're happy, right?" Worry stretched across Jeffrey's face. He reached for his wife. "This is what you wanted."

"I'm thrilled." Sarah-Beth accepted the napkin Lacey handed her and patted her damp cheeks. "When is this happening?"

"That's the thing," Jeffrey cast a quick glance at Lacey before smiling at his wife. "We leave this weekend. Saturday actually. I know it's soon."

Two days soon. The surprises kept coming. Lacey sat back. She should not be shocked. This was her ex-husband's way. He did things his way. He was usually well-intentioned, not purposely inconsiderate. He simply assumed he knew best. As for fallout, that was for everyone else to clean up.

"Where am I staying?" Aspen asked quietly.

There was that fallout. Written all over her daughter's pale face.

Jeffrey reached across the table and squeezed Aspen's arm. "With your mom at the ranch, of course."

Lacey was speechless. She really should've answered his text this morning.

"It'll be good for you two. To reconnect." There was an insistence in Jeffrey's words. "That's what you want, isn't it, Lace?"

Absolutely, but on her terms and Aspen's. Not his. Lacey figured Aspen and she would get to know each other at their own pace. No rush. No forcing. No pushing. Lacey inhaled, searching for the serenity Sarah-Beth's scented candle promised. "How long will you be gone?"

"Three weeks." Jeffrey eyed her, not looking the least bit apologetic.

Three weeks. Twenty-one days. Just her and Aspen. Lacey kept her expression neutral, despite her racing thoughts outpacing her racing pulse.

Aspen had been three years old when Lacey was last on full-time parenting duty. She'd been scribbling outside the lines and playing in the sandbox. That was a far cry from the almost nine-year-old girl seated at the table. The girl with stronger opinions and more complex feelings. Lacey and Aspen knew nothing about each other on the daily. What did Aspen like for breakfast? Or lunch? Was she early to bed and late to rise like her mother? Or smiling at the sunrise like her father?

"I've got a client in Florida," Jeffrey explained. "The timing worked out brilliantly where I'll be able to combine work and pleasure in the Florida Keys. It just aligned and came together seamlessly."

For you. Lacey nodded.

"What about the Junior Royal Rodeo Contest?" Aspen looked at her stepmom. Her words were imploring. "We were supposed to go shopping, Mama-Beth." Aspen aimed her displeasure at her dad. "You promised me I could enter this year."

"I promised I'd think about it," Jeffrey corrected. "It's not really a good time."

How many times had Lacey heard that in their brief marriage? *It's not a good time, Lace. I've got to concentrate on law school. Or my internship. Or anything else. Can't we talk about this later?*

"Maybe next year, honey," Jeffrey offered.

"That's what you said last year." Aspen's eyebrows smashed together. "What about my riding lessons? I only just started."

"I put those on hold." Jeffrey's words were calm yet resolved. "With the baby coming soon and the new school year, and now your mom is finally home. This is for the best."

Lacey slipped her hands under her legs to keep from raising her arm and asking who it was best for. But she'd been home less than a week. Surely it was too soon to toss her mom-card on the table. It wouldn't be fair to anyone. But the defeated expression on her daughter's face made her chest ache.

"When school begins in two weeks, you'll be too busy for horses and all that anyway," Jeffrey stated. "Surely you'll want to take piano lessons this year and more art classes."

"Until you change your mind on that too." Aspen frowned and eyed Lacey. "I suppose you don't want me to have any fun either."

I want you to like me. Not look at me like I'm the enemy. I never wanted to be that. Lacey opened her mouth.

Jeffrey cut her off, "Aspen Carole Furth, we do not use that tone in this house." Jeffrey's frown matched Aspen's. "You need to apologize."

"I'm not sorry." Aspen shoved her chair back and shouted, "You are all ruining my life." Then she raced across the great room and up the stairs.

Definitely not the reunion Lacey had imagined. She started to stand. Jeffrey touched her arm. "Let Sarah-Beth go check on her. Sarah-Beth has a way with Aspen's unfortunate outbursts."

Unfortunate outbursts. He'd accused Lacey of having similar reactions. *Lace, there's no need for so much emotion. This is solving nothing.* At that time, her mother had been battling cancer again. Her husband had been withdrawn and distant, except when he was with their daughter. Lacey had been struggling to balance the demands of work and parenting and a marriage that was unraveling. Then she'd gotten notice about her deployment. There'd been every need for emotion.

Jeffrey pressed on, "We have things to discuss, and now is a good time."

Lacey sat back down. Sarah-Beth gave Lacey's shoulder an encouraging squeeze and slipped out of the kitchen.

Lacey watched Sarah-Beth until she disappeared up the stairs and glanced at her ex-husband. "Don't you think this news warranted a phone call?"

"You wouldn't have answered," he countered. "You were working."

Lacey started to argue.

"Don't deny it, Lace. Your job has your full focus. As it should, by the way," he said. "I'm not blaming you. It is what it is. Besides, I did text, if you will recall."

He stopped short of blaming her for being unprepared. If only she'd replied to his text. Too late now for if only's.

"I won't apologize. My wife wants a babymoon." Jeffrey pushed away from the table and refilled his plate with more pasta, clearly undisturbed by the commotion he'd caused. "The timing works, and I'm taking full advantage. I'm doing this for Sarah-Beth."

Lacey had seen how much it meant to Sarah-Beth. But she'd also seen the devastation on her daughter's face. That was difficult to overlook. "I'm happy to have Aspen even if she's less than thrilled to stay with me."

"Aspen will come around," he said gently. "Give her time."

That was exactly what Lacey was trying to do. "I'll need her doctor's contact information and every detail about school." What was the protocol for the first day of school? Were moms still cool in the fourth grade? Did she drop off and leave or walk her in?

"Sarah-Beth has everything organized. School supplies are already bought." Jeffrey returned to his chair. "She'll fill you in on everything you need to know for the first day of school and anything else in regard to Aspen's care."

Ready or not, Lacey needed to get her mom act together. Yet Lacey had no idea how she would ever measure up to Sarah-

Beth's practically perfect stepmom status. Lacey knew she was far from flawless; still that wouldn't stop her. "Aspen will stay with me." Lacey paused, then added, "And it's going to be wonderful." She'd make it so.

"That's good to know." Jeffrey polished off his second helping and leaned his elbows on the table. "Now that you're home permanently, it might be time to revisit our custody agreement."

"Seriously?" Lacey searched Jeffrey's face. She'd considered it but only in passing. It was nothing she had wanted to hope too hard for, especially this soon.

"You've got three weeks to prove that you can be the parent you need to be with our daughter." He eyed her.

"I came home for Aspen." Lacey had no intention of leaving and letting her daughter down again. She picked up her lemonade and kept her words casual. "What's this about the Junior Royal Rodeo Contest?"

"Let it alone, Lace." Jeffrey waved his hand. "It's better this way. Don't take on more than you can handle."

"But Aspen seemed pretty upset," Lacey said.

"It won't be the last time she's disappointed in not getting what she wants." Jeffrey sighed. "Besides, the decision has been made."

"You already decided not to let her enter before you even booked the babymoon," she guessed.

"Does it matter when I decided?" He frowned. "Horses and all that, it's just a phase. She'll move on in a month anyway. That's the way kids are."

"What if she doesn't?" Lacey pressed.

"She will," he insisted. "Besides, we aren't exactly horse people."

Lacey hadn't been either. Until her mom had married Swells and her new stepdad had taken her riding. She'd fallen in love with the sweet mare and never looked back. And today at the lake, on Caleb's horse, she'd felt a rush of those feelings all over again. "I wasn't either, but I learned and loved it."

"And you were reckless and careless when you rode." He arched an eyebrow at her. "I remember the stories you told me."

True, she'd ridden too fast, jumped things she shouldn't have, in hindsight. Been fearless. But she'd never purposefully put a horse in danger. The horses had been well trained, well-conditioned, and Lacey had trusted them completely. As if her horses had understood that riding had been her escape. In those daring moments, she'd been truly free. Truly happy. It was hard to explain. Even harder for people who didn't ride to understand.

"Aspen and horses aren't a good fit." There was a decisiveness to his words. "Trust me."

Lacey trusted that her ex was a good father and meant well. But she wanted to talk to Aspen. Hear from her daughter what she wanted. And perhaps be the one to make it happen for her.

Jeffrey paused. "I know that look."

Lacey blinked at him.

"Promise me you'll let it go, Lace." Jeffrey held her stare. "One reformed daredevil in the family is more than enough. Aspen isn't like you."

"What does that mean?" Lacey asked.

"Nothing." Jeffrey pulled back. "Just promise me you won't encourage her. Aspen is talented at the piano and art. That suits her."

"She could do all that and ride horses too," Lacey argued.

"To what gain?" he asked.

"Why can't it simply be for the pure joy of it?" Despite the bull and her claims about duty, Lacey had felt a bit of that former joy at the lake. And she'd welcomed it.

"That's not the lifestyle we've built for our family." Jeffrey stacked the empty plates and stood up. "Rodeos and horses are not the world Aspen is being raised in. It's not for her."

It wasn't for him. Never had been. But that didn't mean Aspen should be excluded.

"It's not what you do anymore either." Jeffrey walked into the kitchen and set the dishes in the sink. "You're a deputy now and a mom. What more could you need?"

An image of a certain cowboy with mischievously tempting blue eyes and an unshakable smile came to mind. Quickly, Lacey tried to regain her focus. "We aren't talking about me. We're discussing our daughter."

"Horse riding lessons. The Junior Royal Rodeo Contest.

Where does it end?" Jeffrey asked. "We've got college to fund, not a horse to buy and a stable to build."

"Isn't being a kid about being exposed to all sorts of things? Trying new things?" Lacey carried over the last of the dinner dishes. "Shouldn't we encourage that as her parents?"

"Parenting is also about guiding our kids in the direction we know is best for them." Jeffrey dried his hands. "Same as our parents did for us."

Lacey crossed her arms over her chest.

"You gave up horses, Lace," he said. "And haven't suffered."

There hadn't been a choice. Her mother had been diagnosed with cancer. Her parents had sold her horses to cover the mounting medical bills. Lacey had gotten an after-school job and wanted to keep her parents from worrying about her. But she'd suffered. They all had. "The situation is entirely different."

"No." Jeffrey set his hands on her shoulders and looked into her eyes. "If we're going to coparent, we need to be on the same page, Lace. Same as our parents were."

"What that means is, I need to be on the same page as you," she clarified.

"I know our daughter." There was absolute certainty in his expression and words.

Lacey met his gaze. "I'm still going to talk to her about it."

"Go right ahead." His eyes softened at the corners. "Then you'll see I'm right."

"What happens if you're wrong?"

"We can discuss it when I get back." He squeezed her shoulders, then chuckled. "But you know better than anyone I don't change my mind."

Lacey's mind was set too. Her daughter's opinion mattered. She wanted to listen to Aspen's side. But honoring her daughter's wishes could throw a wrench in Jeffrey's vision of ideal coparenting. And like it or not, her ex-husband was in control of their custody arrangement.

But Lacey could tread softly. After all, her daughter's happiness was at stake. And if it edged Lacey out of enemy territory in her daughter's mind wasn't that worth it?

CHAPTER FIVE

"LAST CALL!" Caleb shouted to the few remaining customers inside The Feisty Owl Bar and Grill, where he was filling in as bartender. The main dining room and kitchen had closed several hours ago. The staff were most likely already asleep in their beds. Caleb had sent Wes Tanner, the bar owner, home earlier to check on his wife, Abby, who was pregnant with their third child.

He placed several used wineglasses into the mini dishwasher below the counter and glanced up when the front doors opened. Surprise shot through him at the late arrival. But his smile spread slowly as if he wanted to keep the happiness to himself.

The intriguing woman walking toward the bar had always stirred something inside him. Back when he first met her, she'd been willowy and tall for her age. He'd never minded much when she looked him in the eye with her bold gaze and accepted his dares. Same as she hadn't backed down at the lake just that morning.

If he'd been of a mind to challenge for hearts, he'd consider hers a worthy prize. Even though his own heart had never been up for the taking. Still, he couldn't deny that the cowboy who claimed her heart would be the luckiest person around. And Caleb hated him already.

He scrubbed at a stain on the bar and tried to rescue his suddenly deflating smile. "Evening, Deputy Nash."

"I'm off the clock." She dropped her purse on a barstool. "I'm just Lacey right now."

There was nothing *just* about this particular cowgirl, even now with her chin-length red hair, striking dark brown eyes, and a certain poise that came from losing and winning life's battles. Not that he was noticing as anything more than an impartial former-friend-turned-temporary-bartender. "Well, *Just Lacey*, what can I get you?"

"There's no root beer at the ranch house." She sat on a stool. "And everything is closed."

"We've got you covered." It looked like he had something to offer her after all. Caleb grinned. "Want a scoop of ice cream in it? We've got that too."

"Don't make fun of my root beer craving." Lacey rested her elbows on the bar top. "Weren't animal crackers your late-night go-to snack?"

"Still are." And he refused to feel anything about the fact that she remembered such an insignificant detail about him. He filled a tall glass with ice and soda and considered the troubled glint in her gaze. "I was serious about the ice cream. Gran Claire always told me a scoop made everything sweeter, even your worries."

"Your gran Claire made everything sweeter," Lacey mused. "And better."

"That she did." Caleb set the root beer on a coaster in front of Lacey, then leaned down to brace his arms on the bar. He'd been the last Sloan sibling to find his height. In college, he'd finally topped out at six feet five inches, making him the tallest Sloan brother by a good inch and a half. Gran Claire had called him a special sort of late bloomer.

Late bloomer or not, Caleb had always been compelled to meet this cowgirl eye to eye. "I'm not even in the same league as Gran Claire when it comes to dealing with problems, but I'm here. What's keeping you awake tonight, Just Lacey?"

"I don't think you can help with this one." She dropped a

straw into her glass and chuckled. Yet the sound lacked any real pleasure.

"Try me. I might surprise you." He spread his arms wide as if to prove he had nothing to hide. "If it's relationship advice you need, I've got that. I'm practically a wedding coordinator now. Although wedding consultant has a certain ring to it."

Whatever the title, wedding and Caleb Sloan were more apt to clash than harmonize. Lacey gaped at him. "You? A wedding coordinator?"

"Technically, I'm not coordinating the ceremony. My brother Josh and his fiancée, Vivian, have that handled." Caleb watched closely for her reaction to his next admission. "I'm organizing the rehearsal dinner and the reception."

"But you know nothing about romance." Lacey leaned in as if imparting a long-held secret. "Word around town is that you haven't even been on a second date. Just a series of first dates."

She'd been asking around town about him? He liked that idea more than was prudent, even if she was pointing out his flaws. "My dating history doesn't mean I don't know about romance." *I could show you.* He straightened before that thought took root and quickly said, "Besides, I've been to my fair share of weddings."

"As a guest." Lacey pinched her straw and stirred her soda. The ice swirled around in her glass like the amusement curving across her face. "I bet you spent most of your time at the bar too."

"Don't forget the dance floor." Caleb lifted his eyebrows. "Can't resist a line dance." Or a slow dance with the right partner. Someone like her if he was choosing.

Her hair slipped from behind her ear, swept forward, and brushed against her jawline. Right where he wanted to slide his fingers to test for himself just how smooth her skin really was. If she was in his arms, he could do exactly that. Yeah, he would definitely pause for a dance-floor slowdown with Deputy Nash. Not that he would be asking her anytime soon.

Lacey straightened and secured her hair back behind her ear. "Caleb, be serious."

He was serious. He'd dance with her. Just about anywhere,

he supposed. He grabbed the bar towel from under the counter and got a firm hold on his foolish thoughts. This was supposed to be about her troubles, not his.

"What do you remember about the food at those weddings you attended?" Lacey ticked reception details off on her fingers. "What about the theme? The colors. The decor. The centerpieces. The table favors."

"I do remember the cake at Jodie Hayes and Harris Newton's wedding last summer." Caleb shrugged and frowned. "For the record, I don't recommend a kiwi and matcha cake. Unless you like the taste of freshly mowed lawn."

Lacey shook her head and stared at him. Amazement filled her words. "You really intend to put together an entire wedding reception for your brother."

"I do." Caleb crumpled a paper napkin and shot it into the wastebasket. He raised his arms in victory and said, "Just wait. You're going to be speechless when you see it."

"I don't think I'm on the guest list." She sipped her soda.

"You are now." Did the wedding coordinator have guest list privileges? Too late now. He wasn't rescinding the invitation. Still, he rushed on, "That means you'll need a plus-one of course."

Her eyebrows pulled together. "Why?"

"Because you need romance in your life, Just Lacey." And if she was dating someone, then he wouldn't want to dance with her. Wouldn't be tempted to sweep her off her feet himself. As if he was suddenly into things like that. But the only thing he was into was his career change idea and securing that full-time job at the distillery.

"How do you know I don't have a life of romance already?" she countered.

"Simple." Caleb gestured toward the unoccupied barstools on either side of her. "You're sitting all alone on a fine evening like tonight."

"I'm here because I wanted root beer." Lacey toasted him with her glass and finished her drink. "And if you'll recall, this is the only place open at this hour."

"If you had romance, you wouldn't be thinking about root

beer at this hour." Even more, she wouldn't be here with him. And he wouldn't be thinking about slow dances and impractical entanglements either.

"Romance is the furthest thing from my mind," she countered.

He wanted it out of his mind too, immediately, in fact. Dating led to a relationship, and what followed were expectations like forever love and long-term commitment. And that, for him, was where things fell apart and hearts got permanently bruised. He refilled her glass. "What is on your mind then?"

She took another deep sip, then tipped her head at him, sending her hair swaying against her cheek again.

He refilled the straws to keep from securing her hair behind her ear himself.

She asked, "Have you ever heard of a babymoon?"

Definitely not the conversation detour he'd expected. "That's what parents-to-be go on for a few days before their baby arrives."

She looked startled. "How do you know that?"

"My sister-in-law, Tess, had twins this past June," Caleb explained. "Carter took Tess on a babymoon to a luxury resort in Sedona. Apparently, the spa specializes in mother-to-be wellness. But both Tess and Carter got a weekend of private pampering."

They'd both returned blissful and practically glowing, prompting Caleb to do a quick internet search on the resort and their offerings. But a cowboy like him didn't need to glow. As for bliss, he would find that on his own terms.

Lacey's smile was soft. "A spa in Sedona sounds romantic and relaxing."

"That's what I hear." Caleb folded his arms and went back to leaning on the bar top. "Now Tess is convincing Maggie that she needs to take a babymoon. Maggie married Grant last year."

"Have all your brothers married?" Lacey smeared the water droplets on the outside of her glass.

Caleb lifted his hand, waving good night to Trey Ramsey and Keith Bauer, the last of the late-night bar patrons. And then there were two. He returned his attention to Lacey. "Once Josh and Vivian exchange their wedding vows, I'll be the last single Sloan brother in the family."

She considered him. "That doesn't bother you?"

"Not even a little." There was pride and conviction in his words. Once more, they'd detoured back to him. He aimed his grin at her and flipped the conversation. "But back to this baby-moon—are you organizing one?"

"My ex-husband and his wife are going on one," she explained. "So Aspen is coming to live with me for the next three weeks."

One more reason Lacey Nash was all wrong for him. She was part of a package deal. There were two hearts at stake, not one. That was double the heartbreak…and nothing Caleb wanted to be responsible for. He took in Lacey's less-than-delighted expression. "That should be a good thing, right?"

"Aspen isn't exactly happy about it." She wrinkled her nose. "She even claimed her dad and I were ruining her life."

Caleb winced. "Ouch."

"But I didn't even know about the Junior Royal Rodeo Contest until this evening. Jeffrey had already decided not to let Aspen enter. He only just told her at dinner." Lacey lifted her hands. Irritation crossed her face. "My ex-husband can take all the credit for ruining his daughter's life this round."

"Are you talking about the contest that's part of Three Springs's Rodeo Reunion over Labor Day weekend?" Here was ground he knew quite well. He'd spent a large portion of his time growing up inside a rodeo arena competing with his brothers and now as part of the rodeo's auxiliary staff. He loved every part of the rodeo, considered it a second home.

"What are you, Caleb Sloan? Like the town busybody or something?" Lacey stabbed her straw into the ice in her glass. "How do you know about that too?"

"Maggie, my sister-in-law, is the rodeo director. I guess you could say I have an inside scoop." He laughed and shrugged. "You do remember that this is a small town, right?"

Lacey's laughter blended with his. "Where everyone knows everything."

"More than that, everyone shares everything they think they

know with everyone else." He leaned toward her and pressed his finger against the bar top. "Fortunately for me, most of that sharing goes on right here."

"Do you work here full-time?" She glanced around the empty bar.

He shook his head. "Only when needed." And lucky for Caleb, Wes Tanner, the owner and his oldest brother's best friend, had needed Caleb's bartending skills tonight, or Caleb would have missed Lacey. He rubbed his chin. "You know, I can talk to Maggie. I'm sure it's not too late to enter Aspen in the Junior Royal Rodeo Contest."

Lacey was silent.

"You would definitely earn points with your daughter," Caleb suggested.

"Tempting," she admitted and set her palms flat on the bar top. "But it doesn't matter. I know nothing about rodeo contests like that. I wouldn't even have the first clue to help her get ready."

"Well, the offer stands," he said.

"Thanks." She sipped her root beer and seemed to be studying him over the rim of the glass. "So, you're a volunteer firefighter and EMT. Bartender. Rodeo pickup rider. Wedding coordinator. Have I missed anything?" Before he could respond, she added, "I make sure to listen well when those locals share what they know."

Soon he'd be down to one job. One job title. Once he impressed his older brother. As for his deputy, he wondered what it would take to impress her.

Not the direction he wanted to go. He rinsed his hands off in the sink and tossed that idle thought aside. "The locals forgot tour guide at the distillery."

"When do you sleep?" She chuckled.

He liked the carefree sound. A bit too much. He plucked up an empty bin and stepped from behind the bar before he decided to make her laugh more. Just for his enjoyment. "Why would I sleep? I might miss something good."

"You've been on the go since we met." She slipped off her

stool and followed him over to the section of tall round tables. "When are you going to slow down?"

Now that teetered very close to a common topic among his family. Their questions, however casual, always circled around the same theme. Caleb frowned. "Do you mean settle down?" Same as his family.

She hesitated, not fully committing.

"I'm working on a few things for the future." He stacked empty beer glasses inside the tub.

"Care to share what exactly?" She picked up two wineglasses from a nearby table and placed them into the bin.

"Not quite yet," he hedged and avoided meeting her gaze, not wanting to see the same doubt in her expression that his own family had been unable to hide earlier. After he'd announced his decision to work full-time at the distillery.

"Tell me about your plus-one for the wedding." She trailed after him, collecting more empty bottles and glasses from nearby tables. "Is she urging you to slow down too?"

"I don't have a plus-one." He couldn't quite pull the bewilderment from his words. "I'm the event coordinator. I'm exempt." That sounded reasonable enough to him.

Yet her frown indicated her displeasure. "But you need a date. As the wedding consultant, you should have a plus-one to prove you know all about romance."

"I don't need a plus-one to prove anything." Caleb lifted the tub and headed toward the kitchen.

"Wait. You've already dated all the single women in the county, haven't you? And at the rodeo." Amazement and amusement blended around her words. "You can't get a date, can you?"

"Of course I can get a date, if I choose to." Which he did not. Thank you very much. There'd been a time he'd gone on those first dates she'd accused him of. But recently, he'd given up those as well, preferring to avoid that trouble entirely.

"Prove it," she charged.

Oh, he recognized that forthright tone. The one that challenged and always intrigued him. He turned around, not surprised to find her less than a step behind him. "This is starting to feel like a wager."

Her smile turned knowing. "You never could turn one down."

"You never did back away." Then again, neither had he. And now he stayed right where he was. Close enough to tuck her hair behind her ear if he was of a mind to test the strength of those friendship bonds.

"Admit it, Caleb. You don't know what you want in a woman, same as you don't know what you want out of life. I do know what you need and that's a woman as dedicated to freedom as you." She stepped closer and braced her hands on the bin he held. "I bet I could find that woman quicker than you ever could."

"That's as confused as me saying I could help your daughter win the Junior Royal Rodeo Contest because I know cowgirls so well." He spun toward the kitchen before he was tempted to set the bin down and reach for her instead to prove what sort of cowgirl he could want. Needing the last word, he added, "Which I do, by the way. Know cowgirls well." With that, he let the door swing shut behind him.

"Like I said, prove it, cowboy." She pushed through the door right after him and stood in the kitchen, hands on hips. "Coach my daughter to win the contest, and I'll find you the perfect wedding date."

He set the tub on the stainless steel counter and opened the large commercial dishwasher. "What happens when you don't find my perfect date?"

She crossed her arms over her chest and lifted her chin. "I'll… I'll…get onstage and sing."

He glanced over his shoulder and considered her. "You vowed never to get on another stage after that one audition in ninth grade." Afterward he'd found her crying outside the auditorium, inconsolable. Lacey Nash, for all her bravado, had a serious case of stage fright. But she also had a voice that could soothe the crankiest infant or the most fly-by-night cowboy like him.

She eyed him. "I confess. I haven't been onstage since the day of that horrible audition."

He nodded. "So if you find my ideal date, what do you get?"

"You crochet three scarves and donate them to Three Springs's Rodeo Reunion silent auction." Her satisfied smile spread wide. "I know your gran Claire taught you. Remember when I caught you in the yarn aisle at the old craft store in Belleridge after school?"

Caleb nodded. He remembered more about her than was probably wise. That afternoon he'd been testing the gauge of different crochet needles for a difficult stitch he'd been trying to master to surprise his gran Claire. It had been impossible to pretend he was in the wrong aisle when Lacey had ambushed him, then refused to leave. Still, Lacey was the only one outside his family who knew about his favorite hobby. He'd been surprised she'd kept his confidence. Then again, he'd kept hers.

He'd kept other confidences too. Like how much he'd missed her when she ended things with his friend and they stopped hanging out so often in high school.

Lacey watched him. Her expression was thoughtful. "You aren't scared to accept this bet, are you?"

"Not exactly."

"Then we're doing this," she said.

"Unless you'd rather admit defeat now and skip straight to the singing." He hitched his thumb over his shoulder. "There's a microphone already set up on the stage out there. All we need to decide is whether it's a slow or fast song."

She laughed and flexed her fingers. "Maybe instead you should start warming up your hands for all that crocheting you're going to be doing."

Caleb grinned. He'd always liked that about her. She gave as good as she got. "I'm partial to an old-school country song."

"Remember neutral colors tend to be very calming for babies." One eyebrow flexed. Her tone was patient and knowing as if they were standing in the paint aisle at Rivers Family Hardware. "Think pale yellow. Or soft gray or even sage green."

"Are those your favorite colors?" he asked.

"Pale lavender," she said. "Wisteria are my favorite flowers."

That was information he might consider useful if he ever wanted to gather a list of his deputy's likes and dislikes. He dried his hands and headed for the swinging door. "Country classics are my favorite."

"Noted." She never hesitated. Her retort was far too cheerful. "I'll make you a playlist, and you can listen to it while you crochet."

"Do you prefer traditional or infinity for a style of scarf?" He watched the confusion register on her face. His smile stretched wider. He held the front door of the bar open for her. "I thought you might want a scarf to keep your vocal cords warm before your performance."

She stopped in the doorway and considered him. Her gaze was steady. "You know I always play to win. That hasn't changed."

But his awareness of her *had* changed. It was deeper. Stronger. It tugged on those elusive heartstrings. Good thing he'd clipped those years ago. "I'd be disappointed if you just gave in." Same as he would be hurt if he gave in to what his heart was saying. He skimmed a gaze over her face. "About that scarf..."

"Save it for the auction." She laughed and pulled her car keys from her purse. "My vocal cords won't be needing it. That much I can assure you."

He stepped back, watched her make her way to an old compact truck and climb inside. The truck's engine rumbled in the silent night.

One thing was certain. She was going to lose their bet. Because he feared he was watching his ideal cowgirl drive away right now. The cowgirl he could want if he was a different sort of cowboy.

Lacey Nash was made for settling down and the long-haul kind of love that only strengthened over time. She deserved a cowboy built for the same. Caleb lived only for the moment. And the only long haul for him was the lockdown on his heart. After all, love would surely trip him up if he stuck around to let it.

So he would keep his cowboy boots in motion like always and his destination in sight. And let nothing tempt him to change direction, not even his bold, brown-eyed deputy and her unwavering affinity for wagers.

Caleb turned, pointing his cowboy boots toward the bar and away from Lacey's fading taillights.

Less than an hour later, his checklist for closing was complete, the cash register receipts balanced, and the money secured in the safe. One more circuit through the main dining room and perimeter of the bar ensured the patio doors and windows were locked. He switched off the LED Open sign in the front window, armed the security system, and walked outside to his truck. The only place to go now was home.

He should be tired, worn out from the long day that had started at sunrise. But that restlessness rolled through him. It'd become something of a norm recently, like a chatty shotgun passenger he couldn't quite ignore. Only with Lacey, he'd felt a different sort of energy. A caring, more welcome kind. But still, they had shared nothing more than a friendly chat between a bartender and a customer.

As for their wager, well, he wasn't certain what that was other than a bout of nostalgia and an easy slide back to their old friendship. There'd been no official handshake to finalize the wager like they'd always done before.

Just as well because taking Lacey's hand in his tonight would've been a temptation too far.

Back on Sloan land, Caleb parked outside the detached garage beside the large farmhouse. The same one generations of Sloans had grown up in. The same one Caleb and his brothers had called home since they were little kids. What was supposed to be a short summer visit with their grandparents became something long-term and permanent. Thanks to his parents' divorce and his mom choosing to pursue her medical degree over raising her kids.

Now Carter and Caleb were the only two Sloan brothers left living on the property along with their grandpa Sam and uncle Roy. Although his other brothers and their wives hadn't gone far. Their properties each connected to the original Sloan land by way of an adjacent pasture, a patch of forest, and a stream.

Caleb climbed out and frowned at the brand-new ice-blue convertible angled a short distance away.

A movement near the stables caught his attention. He shifted as the owner of the stylish, statement-making sports car stepped from the shadows.

Lilian Sloan.

What was his mother doing here? She lived all the way over in Belleridge. Caleb checked his surprise.

She lifted a hand in greeting, her smile tentative.

That was to be expected. Mother and sons had been estranged until recently, when Lilian had abruptly shown up in town, intent on making up for past mistakes. Caleb supposed he was the last holdout with respect to forging a new relationship with his mom, same as he was the last single Sloan brother. But that common ground his older brothers seemed to have found with Lilian Sloan seemed to be just out of reach for him.

He shut his truck door and approached her, noticing she held a swaddled bundle in her arms. That the renowned heart surgeon had turned into a doting grandmother was almost unfathomable, given Lilian Sloan had skipped the parental stage for the most part with her sons. Caleb's frown deepened. "Mom."

"You're thinking it must really be desperate times if your brother and Tess called me to babysit Beck." Her words were hushed and lulling.

He was thinking he seriously needed to reconsider his night-owl tendencies. If he'd gone to bed at a reasonable hour like a normal person, he wouldn't have run into the only two women who seemed to possess the unique ability to stir up feelings inside him. As if he hadn't spent his entire life figuring out how not to free-fall into those so-called *feels*. "Mom, what are you doing here?"

"Giving the new parents some much-needed sleep." She made a cooing sound against his nephew's forehead.

"Where's Sadie?" he asked, referring to his niece and Beck's fraternal twin.

"Sleeping like an angel." His mom tapped the baby monitor clipped at her waist. "I've been listening. Not a peep out of her. But Beck seems to be having an out-of-sorts evening. Neither Tess nor Carter could get him to settle down after he ate."

Settle down. There was that phrase again. Caleb knew how his nephew felt. Out-of-sorts was his personal theme of late. Except when he'd been with Lacey, then he'd felt... He cut off that thought before it gained traction. Definitely not the time for that. He wanted to keep his head clear for this conversation.

"Your gran told me she used to walk you outside when you were fussy. She claimed she clocked several miles walking circles around the barns holding you at night." A pensive hopefulness circled through his mom's words. "Thought I'd try that with Beck."

Did you ever do the same for me? Caleb knocked that aside. He already knew the answer.

Caleb had barely passed his first birthday when his mother had dropped him and his brothers at their grandparents' ranch and never looked back. Her professional goals were noble perhaps to an outsider, but to someone who'd counted on her and trusted her to be there when he needed her, she'd failed badly at the time. He'd been too little to remember whether his mother had held him or his twin, Josh. But Caleb had decided somewhere along the way that she most likely hadn't. Certainly mothers who held and comforted their kids didn't turn their backs on them like she had. But that was the past. Nothing to see there. He crossed his arms over his chest. "Is it working?"

Beck's face pinched. His tiny body squirmed.

His mom's sigh held no heat. "It seemed to be. I think we might need another brisk walk around the barns." His mom peered at him. Her expression and tone were neutral. "Care to join us?"

So he could see even more how comfortable she looked holding his three-month-old nephew? How her caring seemed natural and genuine? It made no sense. This wasn't the woman he believed her to be. Yet watching her now made him reconsider. And that set him back. It was unexpected. Yet not in the let's-dive-right-in-and-explore sort of way he liked.

Caleb tucked the blanket under his nephew's chin. "You two seemed to be doing fine before I interrupted."

"I believe it has more to do with the lack of motion than your presence." She swayed from side to side.

"All the same, I'm going to call it a night." He watched Beck's face release. At least his nephew seemed to be relaxing. Caleb felt even more on edge now. "I've got to be up early for work."

His mother's eyebrows lifted. "I would've thought this late night would earn you a morning to sleep in and relax."

"Lazy mornings aren't really my thing," he said. Downtime offered more opportunities to think than Caleb cared for.

Reflecting is not something you avoid, Caleb. It's something you cherish.

But, Gran, if I don't go do things, I'll have nothing to reflect on.

Caleb would've sworn he heard his gran Claire's laugher in the rustle of the trees lining the driveway. He glanced at his mom. "There's no time. I'm taking over Vivian and Josh's reception and rehearsal dinner. And soon, the marketing job at the distillery."

She looked puzzled as she kept up the slow rocking motion. "And that's what you want?"

Her reservation about his announcement was not a surprise. His family hadn't hidden their doubt or skepticism. "Why does it feel like you don't agree?"

"If you're happy, that's all that matters." She swayed on.

Beck pouted as if he too doubted all that would lead to Caleb's happiness. His mother quickly adjusted her hold on Beck.

Lilian barely knew her youngest son. Caleb hardly wanted her to worry about him now. Besides, he was fine. He cleared his throat. "I know what I'm doing. What I want."

"That's good to hear." She cradled Beck up against her shoulder and cooed at him again, a series of *there-there*'s and gibberish. Her grin was wry. "Now I need to give my grandson what he wants."

For the first time since his mother's return, he wondered what she wanted. Caleb tugged the cotton hat decorated with teddy bears lower on Beck's forehead, then touched Beck's cheek. "Let your dreams take flight, little one."

His mother added quietly, "And tomorrow you can wake up and chase them."

Startled, Caleb lifted his gaze, took in his mom's wistful smile and tender expression. Searched again for that calculating career-minded stranger who'd left her family behind, but he came up blank. Again. He tucked his hands into his jeans pockets. "Gran Claire told me that when she tucked me in."

"That was my favorite good-night wish," his mom whispered

and pressed her cheek against Beck's head. "She said it to me every night growing up too. She was a wise woman."

Caleb nodded and noted Beck's nose wrinkling. "Beck however is looking less than pleased with such sage advice."

"He certainly is." His mother chuckled. "We'd best get moving. Good night, Caleb."

"Night." He started for the spacious two-bedroom apartment over the garage. The one he'd moved into after Josh and Vivian had moved into the farmhouse that had once belonged to Gran Claire's family on the adjacent property.

"Oh, Caleb, if you need help with the reception or rehearsal dinner, please don't hesitate to ask," his mother offered before she disappeared around the barn.

Caleb rubbed his forehead, made his way upstairs, and skipped turning on the lamp. Light certainly wasn't going to chase away his confusion. Not an hour ago, he would've dismissed his mother's offer out of hand. Now he appreciated her for making it. Not that he was accepting it.

It was certainly a night full of curveballs. Those never bothered him much. Just hit 'em out of the park had been Grandpa Sam's long-standing advice. But for the first time ever, Caleb hesitated.

His phone screen lit up in the dark. Caleb opened the new text from his deputy. It was a crocheting tutorial video that she'd captioned with one word: Inspiration.

His smile slipped slowly into place. Followed by that familiar rush of energy.

He knew he had to win their wager. How could he not? Otherwise, he feared he just might lose a lot more than having to crochet a few colorful scarves.

CHAPTER SIX

LILIAN SLOAN EYED the dark apartment windows over the garage and cuddled her grandson closer. She picked up her pace. "It's you and me, Beck. Surely, we can figure this out together."

Beck yawned against her shoulder.

"We need to get back to deciding on a name for me," Lilian murmured.

She hadn't quite adjusted to her new status as grandmother. Having passed on most of the "mothering" part, now she seemed to have jumped feetfirst into the "grand" part of parenting, intent on not missing this phase. She was retired, starting a new life chapter, and terrified.

Still, she was determined not to let the fear stop her. She'd been scared before—alone after her divorce from her sons' father. She'd pulled herself together then, graduated from medical school, and built quite a career for herself. A career she had been determined would mend her broken heart and outshine the memory of her cheating ex-husband.

As the years passed, the hurt and anger from the divorce faded. Fortunately, she'd excelled in the operating room and discovered who she was meant to be. Now she was adrift again, no longer holding a scalpel but instead an infant.

She fixed the blanket around Beck's tiny chin. "I will find my footing with you and my family." She'd made good progress so far and was committed to going the distance this time. She kept her steps brisk. "It all needs to start with a name. I do believe we've tossed out the standard Grandma, Grams, Granny."

Beck yawned again.

"Right, uninspiring." Lilian circled the stables. "Do we consider Gigi or Glamma or GamGam then?"

Beck sighed, his little body going lax in her arms.

"Right. Nothing worth waking for." She stroked his cheek, then reached to tuck his hand under the blanket. "How about Nana or Nan?"

Beck's tiny fingers curled around her finger and squeezed.

"I think we're getting close," Lilian whispered, trying to swallow the emotion from her words. "But if it's all the same to you, let's not decide tonight. We both know I'm still finding my footing. I don't want to trip myself up."

Three loops around the barns complete, Lilian made her way back inside the silent farmhouse. She tucked her soundly sleeping grandson in his crib beside his twin sister's crib and mentally congratulated herself. She crept out of the second-floor nursery, tiptoed downstairs, and felt her grin expanding.

The last time she'd sneaked down these stairs she'd been a teenager, trying to meet her boyfriend for a late-night swim at the Sloan family pond. She'd been celebrating how stealthy she was when she reached the mudroom undetected. Then the light had switched on in the kitchen, revealing her mother and highlighting Lilian's failed escape. She vowed that night that she'd be leaving Three Springs after graduation with no intention of ever looking back. She'd mostly stuck to that vow.

She turned the corner and pulled up short at the soft glow of the kitchen light. Only it wasn't her mother waiting for her. It was her oldest son, Carter. He was setting clean bottles and formula containers out on the kitchen island.

"Carter, you should be sleeping," she chided quietly.

"As should you." He opened the refrigerator, pulled out a bowl of grapes, and offered her some. "And I just slept four hours straight thanks to you. I feel ready to take on the world."

She noted the exhaustion under his eyes but refrained from

challenging him. "I predict Beck will sleep for another few hours before he wakes up hungry and ready to alert the world."

"He doesn't seem to enjoy sleeping, but he certainly likes eating." Carter's shoulders shook with laughter.

"If you scoot back to bed, you can have a few more hours of sleep too." Lilian took the fruit bowl from her son and set it back inside the refrigerator. "Imagine how you'll feel then."

"You might be right." Carter covered his yawn and grinned. "Tess made sure the guest room is all prepared for you."

"I told her not to do that." Lilian picked up her purse from the side counter and searched for her car keys in the outside pocket. "But I appreciate it."

"You're not staying?" He frowned through another yawn.

"I want to drive my new convertible with the top down at night." She peered at her son. "Silly, isn't it?"

Carter's expression softened. "Not even a little bit."

"I sound like a teenager." Perhaps it was being back in her family home. Wistfulness or something like that. When she left New York, her medical degrees packed into moving boxes and her hospital badge deactivated, she'd decided to free her emotions. She would feel what she felt and work through it all on her terms. Right now, she was feeling like a midnight drive.

"Be careful, okay? No speeding and watch out for other cars." Carter paused and rubbed his jaw. "And I sound like an overprotective father."

"That's not a bad thing. Your children will be better for it." She walked toward the mudroom, Carter following her. "Besides, driving home in the morning, there won't be any stars to appreciate."

"Text me when you get home." Carter held open the back door for her, stepped onto the porch, and pulled her into his affectionate embrace.

An unsolicited hug from her son, who insisted on watching over her. There was surprise and gratitude. Regret too. Regret for all that she had missed of her sons growing up. *Stay in the moment, Lilian.*

She reached up and touched Carter's cheek. "Get some

sleep. My grandchildren will need you wide awake and ready in the morning."

Once again, she was thankful for her parents. They'd raised her sons to become honorable men. She couldn't have asked for anything more.

Fifteen minutes into her drive back to her small cottage in Belleridge, Lilian eased her car over to the side of the deserted bypass and stepped out. She walked to the hood of her car, sat on top, and fixed her gaze on the stars lighting the entire sky. It was a view she hadn't realized she missed until now.

She spotted the truck approaching from the opposite direction, noted the law enforcement lights on the roof, and read the bold white Three Springs County Sheriff's Department lettering on the door when the vehicle slowed to idle beside her.

The window rolled down and revealed a weathered yet very handsome face beneath a buckskin hat. "Evening, ma'am. I'm Sheriff Hopson."

"Evening, Sheriff," Lilian said and introduced herself.

Sheriff Hopson cut the truck engine. "Do you need help?"

"I do." She took in the silver tinting his well-groomed beard and the laugh lines fanning around his eyes. Felt a quick hit of attraction when he stepped from his truck, revealing a lean, fit frame and a height she appreciated. She pointed toward the sky. "I can't seem to find the Big Dipper or the Little One for that matter." She slanted her gaze back toward him.

His eyebrows notched into his forehead. "If it's stargazing you're wanting to do, ma'am, the best place for that is at Silent Rise Canyon. There's a bluff out there."

"Is that so?" She shifted on the hood and considered him. "This spot right here doesn't seem so bad."

He scratched his cheek. Those laugh lines deepened. "But out at Silent Rise, you can almost touch the stars."

"Now you've captured my interest." In more ways than one. She slipped off the hood of her car and skimmed her hands over her pants. "How do I get there?"

"Afraid I can't tell you that." His expression was reserved, but there was a noticeable glint in his gaze.

Lilian frowned.

"But I could show you," he offered. "If you had a mind to spend the evening with an old-time cowboy."

There was nothing old about the man. He looked fine from his shoulders to his boots. Oh, she noticed the cowboy in his stance and in his confidence. She smiled. "Only if you have a mind to spend time with a retired doctor past her prime."

"Well, Doc, if you don't mind my saying, I happen to think experience looks quite fetching on you."

Lilian's cheeks warmed. No, she didn't mind in the least.

He opened her car door for her and tipped his hat. "How's Saturday night work for you?"

"That'll be fine." She slid into the leather seat and glanced up at him. "Where should I meet you?"

"Oh no, Doc, we're gonna do this proper." He shut her door and kept his attention fixed on her. "Dinner, stargazin', and maybe even a kiss on the cheek good night under the porch light, if we're both of a similar mindset."

"That sounds like a date, Sheriff Hopson." She buckled her seat belt and tried to clip her sudden excitement. She was a renowned heart surgeon, known for her steady resolve and even stricter discipline.

"Got something against a date?" he asked, sending those laugh lines crinkling.

"I'm a grandparent," she blurted.

"Welcome to the club. Between you and me, it's one of the best titles you can have." Amusement and pride flashed in his gaze. "But we're more than a title, aren't we? And we've certainly earned the right to have our own brand of excitement."

"What brand of excitement is that exactly?" she asked.

"You will have to join me for our date to find out." He tapped the brim of his sheriff's hat. "See you Saturday night, Doc."

Just like that, Dr. Lilian Sloan felt all those free, fanciful emotions from her teenage years spilling through her. And instantly, Lilian was knocked off-balance but in a perfectly good, perfectly wonderful way.

CHAPTER SEVEN

GAME ON.

Lacey closed the email confirming that Aspen's application to enter the Junior Royal Rodeo Contest had been received. The very one she'd filled out and submitted while sipping her morning iced expresso, thanks to Caleb's sunrise text. He'd forwarded the Junior Royal Rodeo Contest website link and a last-chance offer for her to concede.

An offer Lacey had not accepted. She started her truck and put it in Drive.

It was purely selfish, but Lacey wanted the next three weeks to start with a check mark in the win column. That meant giving her daughter something she wanted and going against her ex-husband's wishes. There would be fallout, but Lacey hoped to deal with that after Jeffrey and Sarah-Beth returned from their babymoon.

In the meantime, Lacey intended to do everything to help her daughter succeed in the Junior Royal Rodeo Contest. That included accepting Caleb Sloan's assistance and taking advantage of his connections.

Lacey had researched Caleb's very talented sisters-in-law last night after sleep eluded her. She was hopeful that with their rodeo background and achievements in the arena, they could offer some much-needed guidance and advice. After all, she wasn't going to leave her daughter's chances in the Junior Royal Rodeo Contest solely in the hands of one unpredictable cowboy and a spur-of-the-moment wager.

Her phone chimed as she stood outside the headquarters for Three Springs County Sheriff's Department. She opened a new text from Caleb and chuckled at the attached country music video links and his caption: Inspiration. The cheerful emojis he'd added confirmed her suspicion that her cowboy might be one of those exasperatingly chipper morning types.

She tapped on her phone screen. One quick internet search, and she texted her response to Caleb, complete with her own collection of emojis and hashtag: #cowboycrochet.

Smiling, Lacey entered the two-story office building that housed the department, a small jail, and the courthouse. She was early for her shift, and she had a cowboy match to make. Apparently, one of her favorite things was still besting Caleb Sloan. Time to get started.

"Good morning, Gertie." Lacey walked over to the modern curved desk that served as reception and dispatch. Lacey hoped her words sounded conversationally casual as she asked, "You wouldn't happen to have any single relatives living in the area, would you?"

"Only ones here are several decades outside your age bracket." Gertie lowered the microphone on her headset and revealed her slow blooming grin. "If you're wanting a hookup, it's Breezy and Gayle Baker we need to be calling."

Hookup? For me? Definitely not what Lacey wanted. "No." That word came out with unintended force. Lacey flapped her hands, trying to lower Gertie's indoor voice.

"Well, you can't turn your eye on the married ones," Gertie whispered. Disapproval punctuated her hushed tone. "That's frowned upon around here."

"I'm not turning my eye on anyone, married or otherwise," Lacey argued and lessened the urgency from her words. "I only just moved here."

"No time like the present to get started." Gertie's attitude gained more gusto.

"What are we starting?" asked Lacey's stepdad as he crossed

the threshold, his sheriff's hat propped on his gray-tinged hair and his uniform precisely pressed.

"Lacey's social life, Sheriff Hopson," Gertie supplied, with even more zeal. "Seems she's getting it going."

"Nothing like jumping right in with both feet." Her stepdad stopped at the end of the long reception desk. Approval creased the edges of his smile. "I've been telling Lacey for months it's past time she gets back out there."

Gertie nodded sagely, like she'd been offering the same advice to Lacey for even longer. Her shrewd gaze fell on Lacey. "Can't let a divorce sour your enjoyment of life."

"It didn't," Lacey said weakly. "I was working overseas." And feeling a lot of satisfaction with her career as a military police officer.

"Can't let work interfere either." Her stepdad rubbed his beard. "It's all about balance."

Gertie gave another sage dip of her chin. "My first marriage only lasted three years. I worked hard, and he played even harder. I never much cared for the seesaw on the playground, and my marriage felt the same. Second marriage was just as teeter-tottery."

Lacey was feeling slightly off-kilter herself…and uncertain how to veer the conversation away from her personal life. That there was no "social" in her personal life was entirely on purpose. A preference she had no interest in changing anytime soon.

Gertie shook herself as if dusting off that sand from the playground. "But the third time, well now, it has sure proven to be the charm." Gertie twitched her penciled-in eyebrows at Lacey. "My Joe and I been married going on twenty-three years. Finding the right partner is the key."

Her stepdad nodded. "Gertie, I take it you have leads on a partner for our Lacey."

"Already connected with my network." Gertie tapped a nail on her phone screen and plucked at her spiky platinum blond hair. "I'm proficient in multitasking."

Lacey smoothed the wince from her expression.

Gertie's phone chimed. "Look at that Gayle Baker's fast response time. She's especially spry when it comes to our bowling league and matters of the heart."

There were more of them. Women like Gertie. Right in town. Lacey grimaced and mentally flipped through a list of excuses that might halt this runaway train. *My single-mom plate is full. I've only just recently got back to town. I'm fine just as I am, on my own two feet.* Lacey rocked in her black lace-up boots. *Look. Steady. No fixing or mending required.*

Gertie's phone chimed again. Then again.

Lacey swayed.

Her stepdad set his arm around Lacey's shoulders and squeezed. Amusement threaded through his words. "Looks like the news is spreading about you, Deputy Nash."

"Best buckle up, dear." At the sixth chime, Gertie cackled. "Your social life is on speed dial now."

Speed dial. Lacey swallowed her groan. No one to blame but herself for this snag. Nothing to do now except retreat. Lacey pointed toward the clock on the wall. "Looks like my shift is starting. Better get to work."

Gertie set her phone down and scooted her chair along her desk like a train on its tracks. "Deputy Nash, I've got a ten-ninety-two on Fortune Street outside Three Springs's town hall."

Lacey nodded. "Improperly parked car."

Gertie glanced at her, and her glossy lips pursed.

"Ten-four," Lacey added.

Gertie's mouth relaxed. Yet a challenge glinted in her sharp gaze. "And we've got a ten-forty-nine at 412 Wildflower Court."

"That's Harvey Engell's house." Her stepdad frowned.

Lacey was confused. "Drag racing?" Wildflower Court was a cul-de-sac less than a mile from downtown Three Springs.

Gertie frowned. "Sheriff, you certain you don't want me to take that constable training after all?"

A sworn position would grant Gertie the right to carry a badge and a gun and arrest folks. The woman was already a force to be reckoned with.

"You're needed too much right here, Gertie." Her stepdad nudged Lacey in the ribs. "Keeping our deputies in line."

Gertie's shoulders straightened. She opened a drawer, took

out a booklet, and slid it across the desk. "Deputy Nash, I'll be charging for your next codebook. See that you don't misplace this one. Paper isn't cheap."

Lacey accepted the booklet and tucked it into the wide pocket on her cargo pants. "About that ten-forty-nine."

"That's a barking dog," her stepdad offered and held open the door for her that led to the deputy's desk and his corner office. His eyebrows raised. "Drag racing is ten-ninety-four, Deputy."

Gertie beamed at him. "That's why he's been elected sheriff for four straight terms. Follow his lead, Deputy."

"I will," Lacey promised. Although in truth, she'd been following her stepdad's lead for years now. Ever since her mother's cancer diagnosis days before Lacey's sixteenth birthday. She had no intention of stopping now.

Her stepdad turned in the open doorway of his office. "Deputy Nash, that dispute between the Buckner family and the Engells on Wildflower Court started before I was born. Stick to today's dispute only and try not to get sideswiped by their age-old feud."

"Understood." Lacey pulled her keys from her pocket and stopped at her desk to pick up a court summons and the wage garnishment documents she needed to serve on her way to Wildflower Court.

"Don't forget, I'll be over to the house with the new toilet and showerhead for Aspen's bathroom," her stepdad called out. "We can replace them both tonight."

"You didn't have to do that." Lacey tucked her lunch into a desk drawer. "Aspen and I could've shared the master bathroom."

"You both need your space," her stepdad said. "That's what your mom told me when you were living with us. That's why we put in that second bathroom."

That was Wells's doing. He'd gone above and beyond to make sure Lacey had felt at home in the large ranch house. He hadn't stopped at a bathroom installation. He'd taught her to ride a horse as well as any cowboy. And he'd taught her to drive both on the road and off in everything from a riding lawnmower to a tractor to a truck. But mostly Wells had taught her what it meant to serve and protect. "Thanks. I'm sure Aspen will appreciate it."

"Once we get the toilet and shower working again, she will appreciate it," he corrected. "Has to be perfect for my granddaughter."

Comments like that explained why Wells had a piece of Lacey's heart. She'd been his daughter from the beginning. Never a step-anything. Never an inconvenience. Never a bother. Despite already having three biological children to call his own. And Aspen, well, she'd been his granddaughter from the first call Lacey had made to tell her mom and Wells of her surprise pregnancy. When Lacey had emailed about moving back stateside, Wells let her know he'd meet her at the airport with the keys to the ranch house, claiming he'd been ready to welcome her home for far too long.

Her mom and Wells had bought the ranch house and land together as their wedding present to each other. The fifteen-acre property had been a dream realized for Lacey's mom and the foundation for the couple's retirement goals. But after Lacey's mom passed and that future collapsed, the dream had become more of an upkeep nightmare for Wells. He'd moved to a town house in Belleridge but hadn't sold the ranch. He claimed it was Lacey's legacy and hers to keep or sell.

Lacey headed out. "Well, I've got my tool belt ready and White Olive Pizza Shop saved to my contact list. Dinner is on me."

"Looking forward to it." He glanced at his phone and laughed. "And, Deputy, you might want to avoid checking your phone."

Lacey frowned, already reaching for her cell. "Why?"

"Seems Gertie included the rest of the team in your social life start-up." Her stepdad's deep laugh spilled free. "Deputy Frew and Deputy Byatt already have suggestions. And Deputy Trevino wants to know if you would consider dating navy or air force? He's got cousins serving in both military branches."

Lacey left her phone untouched and jammed her hat lower on her forehead. No choice now. She was going *no reply*. To her stepdad and her peers. And avoiding Gertie for the foreseeable future. She beelined for the door, lengthening her strides to outpace her stepdad's laughter.

All because she'd challenged a charismatic cowboy, then refused to back down. Surely one day she'd learn to curb her impulses around her cowboy and walk away before trouble found her. If only for her own peace of mind.

CHAPTER EIGHT

CALEB FLIPPED A pancake on the griddle in the Sloan farm-house kitchen, then placed it on the growing stack filling a plate nearby. More salt and pepper for the scrambled eggs cooking in the large frying pan on the stove. Followed by a quick check of the bacon sizzling in the oven. Caleb wiped his hands on the dish towel he'd tucked into his waistband, satisfied all was as it should be.

It was Friday morning. His day to cook breakfast for his family. Even though three of his brothers and their wives lived in different houses now, the Sloan farmhouse remained the gathering place for family meals. If they were in town, the Sloans made it to the farmhouse dining table for breakfast and dinner.

It was precisely how Caleb envisioned the entire day proceeding: as usual.

Not a curveball in sight.

Today he intended to get back to his normal routine. No wrangling a bull with a pretty and tenacious cowgirl at his side. No late-night root beer chats that tempted him to slow down and linger with said cowgirl. And most definitely no *feels* today.

Today was all about focusing. He had things to prove after all. And standing around accomplished nothing.

Carter wandered into the kitchen, cradling baby Sadie in

his arms. His hair was uncombed, his T-shirt wrinkled, yet his gaze was clear and alert.

"You look rested." Caleb slipped on an oven mitt, pulled the pan of bacon from the oven, and set it on the cool side of the eight-burner stove.

"Thanks to Mom." Carter handed Sadie to Caleb, then went to work preparing two baby bottles.

Caleb tucked the pink blanket around the baby and swayed like his mother had in the driveway. Sadie sighed contentedly, and Caleb offered his mom silent kudos. "I thought Mom would be here for breakfast, but her car is gone."

"She left last night." Carter filled a bowl with hot water and dropped both filled bottles inside to warm. "With her top down for some late-night stargazing."

"And you let her go?" Caleb turned off the burner for the eggs and returned to his slow side-to-side sway. "That hardly seems safe."

"How was I supposed to stop her?" Carter fixed two cups of coffee and set them on the table where he and Tess usually sat. He frowned at Caleb. "I can't take her keys. She's an adult."

Caleb said, "Doesn't mean we shouldn't look out for her."

"What is happening here?" Carter scooped Sadie back into his arms and eyed Caleb. His words were as bemused as his expression. "We are talking about Lilian Sloan."

"Our mom," Caleb corrected and grabbed shredded cheese from the refrigerator.

"Exactly." Carter stayed close by, following Caleb back to the stove. "This is the same person you've treated with less warmth than an ice bath since she moved back permanently."

"Can you *not* make this a thing please?" Caleb scooped scrambled eggs into a folded pancake to assemble his popular pancake breakfast tacos.

"But it is a thing," Carter stressed. "You and Mom don't…" Carter's face pulled in. "You two just don't."

His brother wasn't wrong. But today wasn't about reflecting on his messed-up dynamic with his mother. "Look, Mom and I ran into each other last night when she was here taking care of Beck." Caleb crumbled bacon over his pancake tacos. "We talked. Not a big deal."

"And the next time Mom wants to go stargazing alone after midnight…" Carter said.

"Call me. I'll go with her," Caleb said. "I'm usually up late anyway."

"You're right." Carter ran his hand through his hair, tousling it even more. "This is *so* not a big deal."

Caleb couldn't let it *be* a big deal. Otherwise, he might be tripping too close to those *feels* he wanted to avoid. Caleb ignored the heavy sarcasm in his older brother's words and thrust the plate at him. "That's the last of the maple pork sausage. If you want it, you better eat now before Ryan gets here."

"I'm already here." Ryan strolled inside, leaned around Carter, swiped a piece of sausage off Carter's plate, and plopped it in his mouth.

Caleb laughed. "I warned you."

"No more. The rest is mine." Carter lifted his plate out of Ryan's reach and frowned at his brother. "I thought Elsie would've taught you manners by now, Ryan."

"My wife loves me with or without manners. Besides, I thought you were greeting me with that plate like a good host, big brother." Ryan motioned toward Carter. "In fact, you look like you've got your hands full, I can take it for you."

Carter grinned and transferred baby Sadie into Ryan's arms. "My daughter wants to see her uncle."

"Favorite uncle." Ryan gathered Sadie close against his chest and cooed at her. "Isn't that right, little Sadie?"

"You can't be the favorite." Caleb went back to assembling his pancake tacos with the precision of a short-order cook filling a backlog of open tickets. "You didn't bring any gifts."

Ryan picked up a piece of bacon from the cookie sheet and took a bite. "And you did?"

Caleb aimed his spatula at the collection of large plush stuffed animals propped up on the couch in the family room. "There's even one for Maggie and my unborn niece or nephew she's currently carrying."

"I'll give you this round, little brother." Ryan fist-bumped Caleb. "But we've got years to settle the score for favorite uncle."

"Caleb, you really need to stop buying things for the twins." Tess walked in carrying baby Beck, picked up a blue-eared stuffed cow, and snuggled it tight. "But this is seriously cute and super soft, so thank you."

"Anything for my niece and nephew." Caleb set a plate on the table for Tess and motioned her to sit.

"Sure smells good in here." Grandpa Sam touched his stomach and paused in the archway. "Caleb, I'm glad you're here. Thought maybe you'd be too busy for sitting down with us."

"Breakfast is the most important meal of the day." And not letting down his family was even more important. That started by not skipping out on his usual responsibilities, even the simple ones like cooking family breakfast. Caleb fixed another plate for his grandpa.

Uncle Roy came in, finished tucking in his button-down shirt into his jeans, and greeted Caleb with a request for double the bacon.

The back door opened and slammed, then Maggie hurried in. "Please tell me I didn't miss breakfast. The hospital called early. They needed Grant for an emergency surgery on an incoming patient, and I fell back to sleep."

"You're right on time." Caleb piled pancakes onto a plate for his sister-in-law. "Plain pancakes. No eggs. And everything your stomach and the baby likes."

"Caleb, move in with Grant and me please." Maggie wrapped her arm around his waist and squeezed. "Our new place is less than a ten-minute drive away. It's even faster on horseback since Grant and Ryan carved out that new trail through the woods."

"He can't move in with you guys," Tess called out and lifted her coffee cup in a toast. "We need him here at the farmhouse more. No one makes coffee like Caleb does."

"And everyone needs their coffee in this house," Grandpa Sam chimed in. "Puts us in the right frame of mind to start our day."

"And deal appropriately with each other." Ryan grinned and tapped his glass against Carter's.

"That's why I perfected the art of coffee years ago." Caleb fixed his own plate and joined his family at the table. "Otherwise, mornings would have been unbearable around here."

"That's because Caleb is a morning person." Ryan waved his fork at everyone around the table. "And the rest of us are not."

"Just doing what I need to for my family." Caleb polished off his breakfast taco.

"Speaking of helping out family." Ryan stood up, piled more bacon on his plate, then added several slices to Uncle Roy's plate. "Caleb, Elsie had to bring her nieces to camp this morning. But my wife wanted me to tell you that she can help you with the rehearsal dinner and reception. Just call her."

He thought of his mother's very same offer. Caleb set his fork on his plate and sat back.

"Count me in." Maggie brushed her hand over her pregnant belly. "I just need a little advance notice. I'm ironing out a few hiccups with the Rodeo Reunion schedule."

"I can help you, Maggie," Caleb offered. "Just say the word."

"Caleb, your plate is already spilling over," Maggie chided.

That was intentional. His choice. Downtime had never been much to his liking.

Tess picked up a bottle from the bowl of water, tested the temperature on her arm, then returned to the table. Her words were gentle. "It's okay to say no once in a while, Caleb."

And risk letting someone down? Not happening if Caleb could help it.

"Tess isn't wrong." Carter accepted a bottle from Tess and repositioned baby Sadie for her breakfast. "Remember, I've got the event tent ready as a backup for the reception if you need it."

"Nothing wrong with a solid backup plan," Grandpa Sam mused.

"I appreciate it, but I've got it handled." Or he would soon enough. He couldn't afford to doubt himself if everyone around him already was. Before anyone else could offer their assistance, Caleb continued, "In the interest of taking Tess's advice, I'm going to say no to everyone here. Thank you, but I don't need your help." He couldn't very well take them to work with him when he got the full-time marketing job, so he needed to start as he meant to go on: on his own.

"That settles that." Tess laughed and pointed toward the hallway. "This is the last thing I'll say about it. Vivian mailed her wedding notebook overnight to the house. It's in the office for you, Caleb."

Caleb lowered his shoulders slightly, yet his suspicions lingered. It wasn't like his family to back off so swiftly. "I'll be sure to grab it before I leave."

Ryan dropped his hand on Caleb's shoulder and squeezed. "If you won't accept our help, then let's talk about something else interesting that I heard about a certain deputy."

Deputy. Caleb worked to remain relaxed. Any flinch, and his brother would pounce.

"Is this about Lacey Nash being at the bar late last night with Caleb?" Maggie took a bite of her pancakes and grinned around the mouthful. "I heard about that."

Uncle Roy gave a murmur of agreement and a head bob.

Grandpa Sam refilled his mug with the coffee carafe Caleb had placed on the table earlier, then tapped a heaping spoonful of sugar in. His words were as slow as the spoon he swished in the dark steaming liquid. "Seems we've all heard something about Caleb and a certain deputy."

Except it was nothing. Even if Caleb had lain awake entirely too long last night wondering about his deputy. But that was what happened when Caleb was idle too long. His mind ventured places his heart wished him to go. But that only led to bruised hearts. And that took the joy out of everything. No one wanted that, least of all Caleb, who prided himself on sticking to a life of fun and adventure.

"I was bartending." Caleb braced his elbows on the table, kept his words indifferent. "Should I tell you who else was at the bar with me last night?"

Ryan scoffed. "But Lacey was one of the last to leave."

"I'm not sure what that has to do with anything," Caleb said. Other than how having his deputy entirely to himself had been energizing and refreshing and not the least bit disagreeable.

"It's more like an observation," Ryan mused. "To do with what you will."

"In that case, I'll clear the table and tidy up the kitchen." Caleb gathered the empty plates around him. "I've got a meeting with the caterer later this morning."

"Come on, Caleb." Ryan jumped up and chased after him. "I'm sure everyone would like to know what you thought about Lacey in action yesterday at the lake. She never hesitated with Walter. It was quite incredible."

He thought his deputy had looked magnificent riding bareback on Denny, his Arabian. Lacey always had a natural affinity and grace on a horse. And she hadn't lost that, not even a little. He'd been impressed by her absolute steadiness and control, as if she'd been riding every single day since high school. He shrugged. "You already said it. She did well yesterday."

"Better than that." Ryan huffed. He accepted the empty plates from Grandpa Sam and Uncle Roy and paused for the round of goodbyes from the older cowboys. Then Ryan came right back to the conversation. "I would want Lacey riding with me in any situation. Any day."

You can't have her. She's... Caleb clenched his jaw hard and beelined for the kitchen sink. He could end his brother's prying by announcing that Lacey was setting him up with his perfect match. Thus proving there was nothing between him and Lacey.

Why had he even agreed to that?

"Ryan, leave your brother alone," Maggie scolded, then nudged Ryan back toward the dining table.

"Thanks, Mags." Caleb poured soap over the dishes in the sink.

"I owed you for the pancakes." Maggie chuckled and pulled a clean towel out of the drawer. "Which were excellent by the way. That offer to move in still stands."

Caleb laughed and handed her the frying pan to dry. "Hey, Mags, what can you tell me about the Junior Royal Rodeo Contest?"

"Not much," Maggie admitted. "I only ever competed in the arena."

"But you're the director for Three Springs's Rodeo Reunion," Caleb argued. "The contest falls under your jurisdiction."

"Isn't that like a conflict of interest if Mags tells you insider secrets about the contest?" Ryan suddenly reappeared, took the frying pan from Maggie, and put it away. "And why do you want to know?"

"Lacey mentioned it last night," Caleb hedged. "I was curious." Mostly about how to win the bet with Lacey. That part he left out. His family most likely wouldn't consider the wager the most responsible thing, and he was trying to prove he could change.

"I do know there's a lot involved for each contestant," Maggie said.

Caleb thought she was exaggerating but refrained from calling his sister-in-law out. Then he'd have to admit he was helping Aspen prepare for the contest. And his family would surely read too much into that. Those inevitable questions he didn't know how to answer would surely follow. "Okay, if you think of anything I can pass on to Lacey, let me know."

Maggie tipped her head and considered him. "Are you sure there's nothing going on between you and Lacey?"

Nothing he would ever admit to. "I thought we already went over this."

"Right." Maggie smiled and leaned in close. "If I tell you how to win the contest, will you tell me the truth?"

"You really are relentless, Mags." Caleb's shoulders shook. "The truth is we're friends."

Maggie's lips formed a fake pout before she grinned. "It was worth a try. I can't tell you how to win other than to get the highest scores from the judges."

Caleb nodded and concentrated on washing the dishes. One more thing he'd figure out for himself.

Thanks to Ryan and Maggie's assistance, the kitchen was back to rights in record time. He was just thankful the conversation never veered back to a certain deputy.

Caleb gently rubbed Beck's back and kissed Sadie's forehead, then picked up Vivian's wedding notebook from the home office. He skimmed the pages on his walk to his apartment.

Unfortunately, there were few notes and a rather excessive number of cutout magazine pictures. The photos featured everything from color choices to flowers to bridal gowns. There was enough to fill several bridal magazines in fact. The random collection of images and uplifting quotes was a bit dizzying. Caleb carefully closed the notebook to keep the pictures contained and left it on his kitchen table.

He was rinsing the shampoo from his hair in the shower when his phone started ringing. No sooner had he turned off the water than his voicemail chimed and his text message alert sounded.

Caleb dressed quickly, toweled off his hair, and skimmed his half dozen new text messages.

Maggie had sent the links to several websites on how best to prepare your junior cowgirls and cowboys for competition. Those would be very useful.

The caterer from The Jamming Fig texted to confirm Caleb's late-morning tasting. He checked his watch and grinned. He would be right on time.

The organizer of Belleridge's Last Dog Day of Summer, happening the following week, wanted to run through his emcee responsibilities at his earliest convenience. The dog event was one of his favorites. He looked forward to it every year.

And Wes Tanner wanted to know about his availability to bartend through the end of the month. Well, that depended on his success as a wedding coordinator and his pending full-time job offer. He kept his response to a simple I'll get back to you. Still, he might be able to fill in on the weekends and an occasional evening.

Lots to do. Even more to consider. Just the way Caleb liked it. On-the-go was his preferred setting. Had been since he was a child.

The voicemail came from the head of Three Springs County Fire Department. Chief Franson needed Caleb on call that afternoon. Kellie Pratt, one of the full-time firefighters, had to take her seven-year-old son to the ER for a possible broken wrist after he fell that morning. Caleb texted Kellie to check on her son and then responded to the fire chief before quickly changing into his fire-department-issued navy pants, navy short-sleeved shirt, and steel-toed boots. He grabbed his go bag with extra clothes and supplies, then headed out the door, humming the whole way.

It was shaping up to be a good day indeed.

CHAPTER NINE

FEET AWAY FROM his truck, the first curveball of the day hit Caleb.

He stopped humming mid-verse and took in the two older cowboys already seated inside his vehicle. He opened the rear passenger door and tossed his bag on the floor mat. Then he climbed into the driver's seat and glanced over at his front-seat passenger. "Grandpa Sam." A quick tilt of his head, and Caleb met the alert gaze of his uncle from the bench in the back. "Uncle Roy. Who wants to explain what you two are doing?"

"What does it look like?" Uncle Roy grumbled and buckled his seat belt with a decided click. "We are going to the tasting with you."

Click. Caleb shifted and regarded his grandfather.

Grandpa Sam snapped his seat belt strap against his chest. "Listen here, Caleb Sloan. We were invited to the tasting by Vivian and Josh."

"And you're not stopping us," Uncle Roy stated.

"Fine." Caleb started his truck, turned around in the drive-way, and drove down the long private road. "But let's go over the ground rules."

"There's only one rule we need to cover." Grandpa Sam tapped his finger against the console. "Roy and I have got opinions about food. We'll be voicing them to you and the chef. Like it or not."

Roy leaned between the front seats and shook his head. "We did not like those fancy finger foods and gourmet dinner choices at Carter and Tess's wedding. No, siree."

"My stomach ached for days after that so-called fish and vegetable burger," Grandpa Sam lamented and rubbed his stomach. "I want Josh and Vivian's guests to talk about the wedding, not suffer some form of food poisoning."

Caleb wiped his hand over his mouth and caught his laughter. His grandpa and uncle's antics made it impossible to hold on to his irritation. Not that he was surprised. Grandpa Sam had always spun the sour from Caleb's mood since Caleb was a child. The two older cowboys had hearts dipped in gold and intentions just as pure, even if their methods could be problematic at times.

Caleb straightened and cleared his throat. "Okay, my turn. We are only going to the restaurant and home. No detours of any kind." He paused for a beat, then continued, "I'm on call this afternoon and need to get you home."

"Kellie Pratt's son broke his wrist something good." Grandpa Sam stroked his beard, his words pensive.

"Got his foot caught on the last step off the school bus," Uncle Roy added.

"How do you know about that?" Caleb slanted his gaze toward his grandpa. "I only just heard."

"We've got our sources." Grandpa Sam's fingers sank into his thick beard, and his chin lifted. "Don't ask who either. We like to keep things confidential."

Uncle Roy warned, "Good ones too."

"I've nothing to hide," Caleb announced, aside from a bet with a pretty deputy and feelings he didn't want to encourage. "So your sources have nothing to report about me."

"You'd be surprised," Grandpa Sam mused, then swiftly diverted the conversation. "Now, what's on the menu? I'm getting hungry."

"You just ate breakfast a little while ago," Caleb said. "I made it. I watched you eat it."

Grandpa Sam dismissed Caleb's comment. "That was only a snack to hold us over."

"I'd like steak," Uncle Roy suggested. "And potatoes. Skip the green vegetables."

"We're sampling," Caleb said. At least that was what he assumed. He'd never actually tasted food options for a wedding reception before. "Not sitting down for a four-course dining experience."

"How will we know if we like all the courses if we don't try them?" Grandpa Sam countered.

"Can't have three good courses and a bad one," Uncle Roy said, his voice raised an octave. "It's the bad one everyone will be talking about the next day."

Caleb parked behind The Jamming Fig restaurant in Belleridge and cut the engine. "How about we head on inside and let the restaurant staff guide us?"

"Speaking of a guide." Grandpa Sam opened his truck door and peered back at Caleb. "Don't forget to grab Vivian's wedding notebook. If it's anything like Tess's and Maggie's, it'll tell you everything you need to know."

Caleb winced.

"You forgot it, didn't you?" Grandpa Sam accused.

"I left it at my apartment for safekeeping," Caleb hedged. He climbed out of his truck, pocketed his keys, and pretended all was exactly as he'd intended. "But I glanced over Vivian's catering notes."

"Great. Then there's nothing to worry about." Grandpa Sam followed Uncle Roy inside.

It was more like Caleb had flipped through the various pictures in the section marked Catering. Not that the stills of assorted fruit bowls, gardens, and candlesticks offered much direction for the menu. Still, Caleb refused to be concerned.

Surely, the caterer already had the couple's wishes. Vivian and Josh had booked The Jamming Fig months ago. It was their favorite date night restaurant. And according to Maggie, popular for local weddings. The caterer was the one with the culinary experience.

Sticking with that logic, Caleb stepped inside the trendy restaurant, took in the familiar face behind the reservation desk, and promptly forgot any worries. "KC Delvy."

"Caleb Sloan." KC reached out, gripped Caleb's hand in a firm shake, and pulled him in for a hearty pat on the back. KC's southern accent was unmistakable. "Haven't seen you since I tackled you in Amarillo at that rodeo roundup a few years back."

Caleb chuckled and introduced KC, short for Kurt Cash, to his grandpa and uncle. "KC is a saddle bronc rider. Few seasons ago, I went to assist KC off his bronc in the arena. Turned out that bronc had more bucking left to do after the buzzer. KC got sprung off, caught me around the neck and took us both to the dirt."

"Bruised my ribs something fierce that day. Could've been worse if Caleb and his first aid skills hadn't been there." KC rubbed his side. "I'm retired from the rodeo now. These days I'm slow cooking ribs on my smoker and taking risks with my spice blends."

"You're the chef here?" Caleb took in KC's white chef's jacket with The Jamming Fig logo embroidered on it. "Does Josh know?"

"I was promoted to head chef five days ago." KC tugged on his jacket as if the fit was suddenly uncomfortable. "I've been trying to reach Josh and Vivian. No luck."

"They're in the Alaskan backcountry," Grandpa Sam offered. "Josh's almost-in-laws had a bit of an accident."

"There's no cell reception where they're staying," Caleb explained. "But we're here to finalize the menu."

"That's good." Relief spread across KC's face. "I was worried about an anxious bride."

"Vivian will like you," Caleb assured his friend. "Vivian likes everyone."

"I'm more concerned about her liking my food." KC motioned them farther into the restaurant, which wouldn't open to the public for several more hours. "The former chef, who Vivian originally worked with, was offered an executive chef position at a five-star establishment in Dallas last weekend.

He left immediately. He was talented in the kitchen but terrible at paperwork."

Worry pinched the back of Caleb's neck. "What does that mean?"

"I've got nothing about Josh and Vivian's wedding," KC explained. "Not even a theme."

"Right. The theme." The photo collection that was Vivian's wedding notebook came to mind. Caleb blurted, "Whimsical."

KC slipped his fingers beneath the collar of his jacket. "That's a start."

Caleb pictured his intended venue: a former rackhouse at the distillery. "Rustic too." He squeezed his neck. Swore he could see Lacey's gloating smile. She'd mentioned something about theme and romance last night right before he invited her to the wedding. The worry spread. "And romantic."

"It's more than what we had," KC said, yet he sounded less than positive.

Silence settled between the men.

Grandpa Sam hooked his thumbs around his large belt buckle. "When do we get to the tasting part?"

"That's what we really came for." Uncle Roy rocked forward in his boots. Certainty in his words. "Food doesn't need a theme if it tastes good."

There. Good common sense. What more did they need? Caleb stopped short of hugging his uncle and grinned wide. "I agree. Let's get to the sampling."

KC tipped his head back and laughed. "Can't tell you how glad I am that you're my first wedding."

"You've never cooked for a wedding reception before?" Grandpa Sam's mouth thinned inside his thick beard.

Caleb's enthusiasm dimmed.

"I've never been a head chef until now." KC headed for a swinging door marked Kitchen. Resolve was there in the stiff set of his wide shoulders. "But I do know how to cook, and I can prove it to you."

Caleb knew a thing or two about wanting to prove himself. He owed his friend that chance. After all, this was about the food.

Intent on maximizing his time, Caleb tugged his phone from his pocket and clicked on the first link for the contest that Maggie had texted him. Any interrogation of flavors and food combos, he knew he could leave to his partners here.

Grandpa Sam and Uncle Roy trailed after KC as if newly appointed sous-chefs.

"There are sample menus on the counter you're welcome to look over." KC tied an apron around his waist, and finally appeared more at ease. "If you have any other wedding details, feel free to share those."

Right. Details. About the whimsically rustic but romantic wedding Caleb hoped Vivian would like. Of course, there was no rustic without the rackhouse. He opened the email app on his phone, typed a message to the administrator at Three Springs's town hall inquiring about any health and business permits that might be required for the rackhouse to be deemed an event space, and hit Send. As for the romantic angle, he had time to figure that out later. He hoped KC was too busy cooking to notice Caleb wasn't exactly forthcoming with wedding details.

Uncle Roy picked up a menu and held it close to his face. "Don't see a gourmet fish veggie burger."

KC fired up a gas burner and tossed herbs and spices into a small sauté pan. "I prefer to keep the meat in my burgers and the fish and vegetables on their own plate."

"I knew I liked you." Uncle Roy beamed. "You can keep those fancy vegetables off my plate altogether."

"Yes, sir." KC laughed and moved around the commercial kitchen with the competence and professionalism one would expect from a well-seasoned chef.

Caleb grinned, propped his hip against the stainless steel counter, and scanned the Junior Royal Rodeo Contest guidelines. So much for simple. His unease jumped several levels. "Listen to this. A junior rodeo contestant must be knowledgeable about horse breeds. Skills in horsemanship to include but not limited to tack, saddling, and the completion of a set pattern in the arena. The contestant must give a two-minute speech on a Western topic and complete a one-on-one interview with a judge."

KC whistled and shook his head. "How old are these contestants?"

"Between the ages of seven and twelve." Caleb squeezed his forehead. That was a tall order for an adult, let alone a kid. The more he read, the more he realized Maggie had seriously downplayed the work involved.

"I'd rather ride a bucking bronc." KC tossed potato slices into a fryer basket. "And at that age, I wasn't speaking on a stage."

"Caleb was on the baseball field when he was eight," Grandpa Sam quipped. "Striking out more times than not. But he wasn't half bad as catcher."

"I liked the action behind home plate," Caleb said and mentally ran through his calendar.

Teaching Aspen was going to take more than one afternoon. He didn't even know her level of horsemanship. The last person he'd taught anything to had been Lacey. That had been roping and jumping back when they were kids and too fearless to pull themselves back.

Grandpa Sam wandered over to check the contents in the pan on the stove. Caleb heard his grandfather inquire about hot chilies and pimento but paid little attention to KC's response.

The risks of horseback riding were front of mind. Especially the potential injuries. He'd experienced plenty of them firsthand and had seen people he knew get hurt. How was he supposed to ensure Aspen's safety? He had to protect her; she was Lacey's daughter. Suddenly a wager placed in an empty bar looked much different in the daylight. Felt much different too.

Uncle Roy lowered the menu he'd been studying and asked offhand, "What types of glasses do you have for wine, Chef?"

Caleb paced around the kitchen, trying to walk off his growing nerves. He could teach Aspen just fine if he cleared away any distractions.

"Red or white wine?" KC took his knife skills to a piece of steak.

"Dandelion," Grandpa Sam replied.

Dandelion. Caleb froze near the double-door commercial

freezer. This was what happened when he got distracted. His grandpa and uncle took advantage. He winced and took a step forward. Time to enter the fray. "We are not serving dandelion wine at the wedding reception."

"Why not?" Uncle Roy tugged on his salt-and-pepper curls. "The first batch is ready for sipping. The reception will be the perfect place."

Caleb set his hands on his hips. "For what?"

"For the introduction of our dandelion wine to the masses," Grandpa Sam stated, both his expression and words tinged with exasperation that it wasn't already obvious. "Where better to start building the buzz for our dandelion wine than the wedding?"

"Buzz," Caleb repeated.

"You know what buzz is, Caleb. It's what all the people want these days." Uncle Roy's thick eyebrows burrowed together. "To have a buzz. That builds a following, you know. And a following is what they say we need."

"You really should be up on all this already, Caleb, if you're going to be the big marketing executive at Misty Grove." Grandpa Sam's gaze narrowed on Caleb. "It's basic marketing for every great product."

But they had no product. Caleb smashed his lips together and glanced at KC. The chef's knife cuts gained speed as he shifted from the steak on the cooking island to dicing a tomato on the prep area in the corner. It seemed Caleb was on his own to deal with his grandpa and uncle. "How many bottles of dandelion wine do you have?"

"We've premeasured the servings," Uncle Roy said, a challenge in his voice. "We've got enough for at least one hundred people."

Caleb had finally caught a break. "Well, Josh mentioned the guest count was over one hundred and fifty before he left for Alaska." He spread his arms wide and tried to sound sympathetic. "Can't serve your wine if you can't serve everyone. Don't want to leave anybody out. That would build bad buzz. And that's the last thing you want."

Grandpa Sam pointed at Caleb. "This isn't over."

But it had to be. Offering their dandelion wine at the wedding, not to mention selling it later, would require following regulations, filing paperwork, and acquiring licenses. And the distillery wasn't licensed for dandelion wine.

Not to mention Caleb had a little girl to give horse-riding lessons to, as well as a long list of other commitments he'd made. He couldn't be introducing dandelion wine to the public. *No. Not happening.*

Caleb took in his grandpa and uncle, noted their earnest expressions and the determination in their gazes, and caved. He sighed, long and loud, more exasperated with himself than the duo. "What if I put together a separate tasting party specifically for your dandelion wine?"

Grandpa Sam's gaze switched to assessing. "What kind of tasting party?"

"An exclusive one that will build buzz," Caleb said, using their words to sway the wily pair. He appealed to his uncle. "It will be all about you and your product. What could be better than that to build buzz?"

Uncle Roy shared a looked with his brother, gave a barely-there nod, then said, "We want it booked on the calendar, Caleb, so it's official."

"And soon," Grandpa Sam said.

Crisis averted without disappointing his grandfather and uncle, Caleb agreed, "Fine." He motioned toward KC and asked, "Now can we please get back to the menu for the wedding reception?"

Uncle Roy wandered closer to the plates KC had set on the serving area. "Chef, there's something wrong with these French fries. They're stuck inside the meat."

Grandpa Sam joined his brother. "Nothing natural about that."

"Those are steak frites." KC chuckled, wiped his hands on a towel, and moved to stand next to the pair. "Just steak-wrapped French fries that you can pick up with your hands and eat in several bites. No utensils required." KC gestured with his arm out. "It's time, gentlemen, to sample."

Uncle Roy plucked a French fry bundle from a plate and took

a large bite. He was reaching for a second fry bundle while still finishing off the first one.

Delight filled Grandpa Sam's face. "The wedding needs these. Add them to the menu."

"Glad you like them." KC pulled a tray from beneath a heat lamp. "But we need to start with the type of dinner I should prepare."

"Okay, Caleb, I reckon this is where you come in." Uncle Roy lifted a bacon-wrapped meatball from another platter. "We came for the tasting."

Dinner type sounded strangely close to theme. Caleb shifted from one booted foot to the other and stalled. "Maybe you should give us a rundown of our options."

"A plated, sit-down dinner," KC offered. "That's the most formal. I would need to know plate counts. Meal restrictions. Two course selections, single or double entrée, tableside dessert or not. Appetizers for the cocktail hour." KC set an empty frying pan in the industrial-looking sink. "I'm sure I'm missing something."

Caleb was missing the answers to everything KC had said after *formal*.

"Linen color." KC snapped his fingers and gave a satisfied nod. "For the tables and bar."

Grandpa Sam frowned. "Fancy silverware and all that is too fussy."

And confusing. Caleb stuffed a meatball in his mouth and sighed happily over the spicy flavor. When had this stopped being about good food?

"Buffet then." KC returned to the cooking island. "Table count and linen color is still needed."

What color was whimsical, rustic, and romantic? Caleb reached for another meatball.

"Never much liked standing in line for food," Uncle Roy mused.

"Stations are a new trend." KC set a plate of stuffed mushrooms on the counter. "They allow for the guests to move around throughout the evening. Each station has specific foods like small bites, pasta, carving roasts, fresh produce. Almost anything you can imagine."

Caleb was quickly warming to the idea. "So, it's like a pick-your-own-food adventure for the guests."

KC nodded.

"That's sounds fun." Caleb took out his buzzing phone and swiped on the screen. "Very on theme too. We want stations." A text from the fire chief about two feuding neighbors in Three Springs caught his attention. He opened it and frowned. "Okay, we need to wrap this up and get on the road."

"But we barely got to our sampling." Uncle Roy frowned.

Caleb glanced up. "Any chance we can take some of this to go?"

"Sure," KC said. "I can pack it up."

"Great," Caleb said. "I've got a call I need to get to."

"But we still have to decide on the foods at the stations." KC stacked steak frites into a to-go container.

Caleb did what came naturally. He improvised. "I like the stations you listed."

"But…" KC started.

"I trust you," Caleb said and threw out the culinary buzz-words he'd heard tossed around. "Locally sourced. Farm to table. We want that at the stations."

"How about I put together a full menu and email it to you?" KC asked.

"Yes." Caleb shoved his phone in his pocket.

"Don't forget the steak bites. We want these for our exclusive tasting party too." Grandpa Sam arched an eyebrow at Caleb. "We are having food to go with our wine, aren't we?"

"Isn't a proper party without good food," Uncle Roy chimed in.

Caleb looked at KC. "Can you fit in a dandelion wine tasting party?"

"I'll send you my available dates." KC grinned. "Don't forget I need the color for the linens."

"Right." *Color.* Caleb made a mental note, took the to-go containers from KC, and hustled his grandfather and uncle outside.

Once they were in his truck and heading to Three Springs,

he realized it would be out of his way to drop off his uncle and grandfather back home. The fire chief's instructions had been clear, yet also confusing. He evidently wanted Caleb at Wildflower Court before there was a problem between the Buckner family and the Engell family.

"Never been on an actual emergency call before," Uncle Roy said, his words upbeat. "What's the protocol when we get there?"

"The only protocol is for you two to stay in the truck," Caleb said. "And there isn't an actual emergency yet."

"There will be if we have to sit in the truck," Uncle Roy countered. "It's too hot this afternoon."

"I'll leave it running," Caleb argued.

"That's bad for the engine," Grandpa Sam said.

But it was worse for the crafty pair to get involved in a neighborly dispute. Caleb wasn't even certain what was going on with the feuding families. "I really need you to remain in the truck."

Grandpa Sam tapped on his phone screen. A satisfied grin on his face. "Breezy and Gayle are less than five minutes from Wildflower Court. Seems they're heading there on official business for the *Herald*."

"Tell 'em we're on our way," Uncle Roy ordered, suddenly cheerful again. "We'll be getting out of the truck now, Caleb. On account of needing to check on our friends."

"Fine." Caleb ground his teeth together and knew he wouldn't win this round. "You can wait with Breezy and Gayle but please try not to interfere."

"I stopped interfering in the feud between Harvey Engell and Jack Buckner years ago," Grandpa Sam declared. "More stubborn cowboys than those two, I never met."

Caleb refrained from correcting his grandfather, who happened to be the most stubborn cowboy in the entire Panhandle, aside from his brother, Roy.

"But, Caleb," Grandpa Sam said.

"Yeah?" Caleb glanced over.

Grandpa Sam looked up from his phone. "You're for sure going to be interfering."

"Why is that?" Caleb asked.

"Seems your deputy is smack in the middle of what's sure to become a skirmish between Harvey and Jack." Grandpa Sam frowned. "Don't you remember the last time those two old goats quarreled?"

Caleb shook his head.

Grandpa Sam's words were earnest. "They started a fire."

Caleb stepped on the gas.

CHAPTER TEN

A DUEL WITH water hoses.

What was the code for that? Lacey parked at the end of the cul-de-sac on Wildflower Court, climbed out of the SUV, and quickly assessed the situation.

Four large truck tires hung from an oak tree in the center of an immaculate lawn that looked like it belonged on a private golf course. Underneath the oak tree's thick branches sat a riding lawnmower also missing its wheels. And somewhere inside one of the houses, a dog barked. But it was the two older gentlemen in a standoff at the single-lane gravel drive dividing the two properties that had Lacey's attention.

One guy held a garden hose and garden shears and wore clogs with white socks that extended to mid-calf. The other gripped his own garden hose with a commercial-grade brass nozzle and adjusted his canvas tool belt stuffed with every piece of inventory from the garden section at Country Time Farm & Ranch Supply.

Lacey approached the pair, completed introductions, and asked, "What seems to be the problem?"

Mr. Engell reached down, unclipped a steering wheel from a carabiner on his tool belt, then waved it at Lacey. "He's holding my lawnmower for ransom."

"You have the lawnmower, Harvey." The morning sun highlighted the silver in Mr. Buckner's black hair and the glee in his grin. "Just not the wheels. No more mowing before the rooster crows now."

"Well, Jack, it sure seems like you have a similar dilemma," Mr. Engell retorted. His sand-colored beard was longer than the hair left on his partially bald head. He rushed on, "Now your namesake grandson can't speed around, run over my lawn, and bust my sprinkler heads."

"This is a shared driveway." Mr. Buckner aimed his nozzle toward the gravel. His words were terse. "Could be anyone in *your* house who keeps busting your precious sprinklers. Pay your family more mind than you do your precious grass, and I bet you don't have any more breaks."

Mr. Engell clenched the steering wheel. "The tread marks in the grass match Jack Jr.'s truck tires."

"Those tread marks match every truck on the street, even yours parked in your garage." Mr. Buckner started forward, his tone determined. "I'm getting those tires back right now."

"Not another step." Mr. Engell flipped his hose on and blasted Mr. Buckner's bare knees and socks. "Step on my lawn, and I'll have this nice deputy arrest you for trespassing."

"I'll have you arrested for vandalism." Mr. Buckner tossed his shears aside, adjusted his hold on his garden hose, and doused his adversary from his bald head to his army-green rubber gardening boots.

"And I'll have you both arrested for disorderly conduct," Lacey cut in. "Hoses off! Now." Lacey eyed both men and waited until the water slowed to a trickle from both nozzles. "Just so we are all clear. If I take you both in, and I will, I'll have you stay in the same cell for the entire weekend."

Mr. Engell's bald head glistened.

Mr. Buckner rolled forward in his squishy shoes but held his silence.

Satisfied that she had their full attention, Lacey said pleasantly, "And your stay might get extended into next week since Judge Rawlins is in New Mexico taking a hot-air balloon ride. And you do not want to ruin number eight on the honorable judge's bucket list. Do we all understand each other?"

Mr. Engell gave a curt nod and ran his palm over his damp head. "Jack can't prove nothing."

"The tires from my grandson's truck are dangling from your tree, Harvey." Mr. Buckner's face reddened. "In your front yard."

"I was asleep in my room all night. Ask my wife." Mr. Engell's sarcasm was hard to miss. "I woke up and found new lawn ornaments. Imagine my surprise." Mr. Engell pointed to the tree in question. "You know I'm growing fonder of the industrial art look the longer I'm out here."

Mr. Buckner proved his reflexes hadn't dulled with age. Once again, his hose was back to full blast and soaking Mr. Engell from head to toe. But in a deft move, Mr. Engell dropped and rolled like a trained firefighter, sprang back up behind Lacey, and caught Mr. Buckner in the chest with the precision aim of his heavy-duty brass nozzle. Peels of delight filled the air, along with a cackling "gotcha!"

That was when the duel turned into an all-out water war.

Lacey lunged toward Mr. Buckner. He swung wide. Water doused her hair, splashed across her face. Mr. Buckner danced backward in his rubber clogs and wielded his hose, sweeping it in rapid arcs. He soaked everything in his path, including Lacey and Mr. Engell, all the while hurling taunts to his foe.

Lacey changed tactics and spun around, intent on Mr. Engell instead. He dodged to the right, soaked her entire front in his effort to keep Mr. Buckner in his spray line. At his adversary's shout about a low blow and his electronic hearing aids, Mr. Engell chuckled and slowed only to shimmy in celebration.

Lacey doubled down and leaped forward, reaching for the brass nozzle. Mr. Engell yelped and yanked back. Something hard knocked against her forehead. Water sprayed across her eyes. Lacey remained undaunted. Her fingers finally connected. She tightened her grip around the metal extension and wrenched the garden hose from Mr. Engell. Shoving the flow lever to the off position, she rounded on Mr. Buckner and ignored the water dripping down her face. "Turn it off! Now!"

Mr. Buckner's eyes flared, then his eyebrows zoomed up into his hairline.

"Not a word." Lacey held up her hand, palm out. Mr. Buckner opened his mouth, Lacey cut him off. "Do. Not. Talk."

"But…" Mr. Engell stepped toward her.

"Don't anyone move either." That order from a new male voice boomed across the gravel drive.

The two older gentlemen stilled instantly.

Lacey peered through the wet strands of hair stuck to her face.

Caleb.

He never bellowed. Never roared. Never lost his temper. Yet she knew from the impatience in his long, determined stride that carried him toward her and the firm set of his jaw that the command had come from him.

She noticed that witnesses had gathered—two older women were standing beside a bright green SUV with Sam and Roy Sloan. The taller of the white-haired women aimed a phone at them as if she was recording the scene. The other lady waved and kept her digital camera in front of her face.

Caleb reached Lacey and drew her full attention. He tipped her chin up and peeled her hair away, clearing the left side of her face in seconds. His touch was tender, efficient, and at complete odds with the irritation in his clenched jaw.

Lacey tried to swat his hands away. "Caleb. Stop."

"Hold on." He ignored her and tilted her head back farther. "I need to see how deep the cut is."

"Cut?" Lacey stopped fighting him. "What cut?"

"The one above your eyebrow." He blocked her arm when she reached up to touch her face. "The one bleeding down your cheek."

Lacey swiped her fingers across her damp cheek, then groaned at the blood staining her skin. "It can't be that bad. I hardly felt it."

His gaze narrowed. His mouth thinned. His words were stiff. "Just missed your eye. And you need stitches. I'd guess at least a dozen."

She heard the quick gasps of the two men behind her and frowned. "Don't exaggerate, Caleb."

"I'm not." Caleb reached into his pocket and pressed gauze against the cut. "It's deep and on the face."

"Can't you sew it up?" she asked.

"No. It's bleeding way too much." He lifted the bandage, cursed under his breath, and added more gauze. His gaze collided with hers. Frustration coated his words. "I'm too mad. And my hands are far from steady right now."

But his touch was gentle. Looking at him so closely, she could see there was no trace of the boy who would've encouraged her to laugh this off and teased her until she smiled. Examining her wound was a grown man, protective and concerned and undeniably appealing. This cowboy she wanted to know from the inside out.

"Stop," she sputtered. *Stop looking after me. Stop making me feel cared for. Protected. I do that for myself.* His gaze held hers. "Make it stop bleeding, please, so I can deal with this." *And you. I have to deal with you. Otherwise, my heart will start bargaining for more again. But those bargains never work in my favor.*

"You need to get this treated now," he insisted.

"I can do that after this situation is handled." She wanted to sound firm, decisive, despite the ache building in her temple.

"You can't drive and apply pressure to your wound." Caleb frowned and slipped more gauze underneath his palm. "You can't stop applying the pressure either."

"I'll take her," Mr. Buckner offered.

"I'll drive her," Mr. Engell said at the same time.

"I'll call the ambulance first." Caleb's expression darkened again. "Deputy Nash wouldn't need to go to the hospital if you gentlemen..."

Lacey pressed her hand flat against Caleb's chest, pulling his gaze back to her. "I got this. Let me handle it, and then I'll go to the hospital but not in an ambulance." That was the last thing she needed.

He inhaled and exhaled slowly. She felt him relax. Finally, he nodded but didn't move from her side or release his hand from her forehead.

Lacey reached for the radio clipped on her shoulder and gave Gertie a ten-thirty-three, requesting immediate assistance from

Sheriff Hopson at Wildflower Court. Then she pulled Caleb's hand away and pressed her own palm to her wound.

At Gertie's acknowledgment over the two-way radio, Mr. Buckner said, "You don't need to be calling the sheriff to come out here."

"It was just a water fight." Mr. Engell's forehead wrinkled.

"I'm going to the hospital thanks to you two and just your water fight," Lacey said, displeased to her core. She'd always hated needles. "Now you get the sheriff. Congratulations, gentlemen."

"If you hadn't stepped between us, you would've been fine," Mr. Engell said.

Caleb stiffened beside her.

"Here's what's going to happen," Lacey jumped in. "It's called a truce, fellas."

Both men gaped at her.

Lacey might've laughed at their shared indignation, but the throb in her head was building with an insistence she couldn't quite quell. She spoke around the pain. "You're going to put the wheels back on the lawn mower and the truck together."

Both men started to argue.

Lacey's patience stretched thin. She pushed on, "Together, gentlemen. Or you will go to jail for the weekend. Same cell. Where you will stay until you've worked out your differences."

"I can't go to jail." Mr. Engell shifted from one rubber boot to the other. "I've got a Roots and Shoots garden club meeting tomorrow. I'm treasurer. They need me."

"My granddaughter has her first soccer game of the season." Mr. Buckner set his hands on his hips. "I promised I'd be there."

Lacey worked her mouth into a stiff smile. "Uh-huh. So what's it going to be? Truce or jail."

"Temporary truce," Mr. Buckner stated, then extended his hand toward his adversary.

"Temporary," Mr. Engell agreed and shook his neighbor's hand.

Lacey started to correct the two men.

"Take the win, Lace," Caleb whispered. "They haven't shook on anything in years."

"He's not wrong, dear." That statement came from behind her. Lacey turned to see that the amateur film crew stood within hearing distance. The taller of the pair tucked her phone into the zippered pocket on the bib of her ladybug-red overalls and introduced herself as Gayle Baker. "You can't end a feud that deep in one day, sweetie."

It turned out the other lady was Gayle's sister, Breezy, who nodded, then pointed to the quarrelsome neighbors. "All you can do is hope to fill it in. Cover it up layer by layer. Until one day it's no longer a tripping hazard and no one hardly gives it a second thought."

"Besides you're starting to leak again, dear." Gayle's thin brows lowered as if to hide beneath her moon-round eyeglass frames. She tapped a pale pink nail against her forehead.

Lacey scrunched her nose at the trickle she felt near the edge of her eye.

Breezy pressed a microfiber towel into Lacey's other hand. "This one's clean. Keep a package in our console for spills and such."

Lacey pressed the towel over the already soaked-through gauze and tried not to think about the stitches she needed.

"Come with us, Deputy Nash, we'll get you to the hospital right quick." Gayle slipped a thin arm around Lacey's waist.

"But I need to…" Lacey started.

"Get to the hospital," Caleb finished for her. "I can hear the sirens on the sheriff's car approaching now."

Sure enough, the sirens blared louder. Lacey watched the truck stop and her stepdad climb out. One sweep of the cul-de-sac, and his demeanor soured. "Someone needs to tell me why my deputy is bleeding."

Everyone started talking at once. The sheriff raised his hands and called for silence.

Gayle patted her zippered pocket. "I've got it all on record-ing, Sheriff Hopson. I'll send you the video on our way to the hospital."

Her stepdad's frown deepened.

"I just need a few stitches," Lacey offered. "I'm fine."

"You will be fine when you get a doctor to examine you," Caleb added, his words a mix of concern and exasperation.

"I have a job to do," Lacey countered.

"Deputy Nash, the Baker sisters will drive you to the hospital," her stepdad stated, his words succinct. "Caleb will fill me in."

No sooner had her stepdad spoken than Lacey found herself bustled into the back seat of the Bakers' cheery green SUV. Breezy was behind the wheel, and Gayle buckled in beside Lacey in the back. For support, the petite woman claimed.

Lacey leaned back against the headrest and switched hands, giving her left arm a rest from applying pressure.

Breezy handed her camera to Gayle and started the car. "It's a good time to look through the pictures and see which ones are worth uploading."

"Uploading." Lacey met Breezy's clever gaze in the rearview mirror.

Breezy's eyebrows twitched upward before she slipped on a pair of teal-framed, blue-lensed sunglasses. "Gayle and I were at the scene today on official *Three Springs County Herald* business."

"Our great niece, Reyna Boland, is a reporter for the *Herald.*" Breezy swiped through photographs on the digital camera. "The paper covers Three Springs, Belleridge, and Llyne and anything happening between our three towns."

"Reyna is up in Llyne today." Breezy lowered her voice to a confidential tone and turned onto the main highway. "She's investigating some cattle rustling claims up there."

"Not the first time cattle have gone missing up in those parts," Gayle mused, then grinned at Lacey. "When we called Reyna about the feud being reignited, we assured her we'd get all the details." She patted her zippered pocket. "And we certainly did that. What with me filming and Breeze taking pictures, we didn't miss a second."

"Now we need to get those photographs to Reyna," Breezy declared. "Can't keep the news waiting."

The spry pair was nothing if not efficient. Although it was not lost on Lacey that neither one mentioned Reyna specifically requesting their assistance at the scene. Yet to be fair, the ladies hadn't intervened and, for the most part, had done their spectating from a safe distance. Still, Lacey should deter them from sending anything to a news reporter. If only her head wasn't pounding.

It was as if Breezy scored extra points for every pothole she hit. Every thump of the tires seemed to throb double-time between Lacey's temples.

Gayle nudged her bony elbow into Lacey's ribs. "Do you have a favorite side or angle, dear? What with your rather stunning red hair and high cheekbones, it is hard to imagine you have a bad angle."

The compliment set Lacey back. She ran her fingers through her damp hair, knowing the water had drawn out the waviness and the humidity, the inevitable frizz. Her hair had always been too red to be truly auburn, yet not quite red enough for her to be a classic redhead. Growing up, her height had been a talking point, her indecisive hair a curiosity, and her impulsive nature a concern. But *stunning*, well, that had never been attached to her before.

"My sister is right," Breezy added. "Your hair is like a kaleidoscope of spectacular shades. It's sure to capture a cowboy's interest from the get-go."

A cowboy's interest. A cowboy like Caleb, perhaps? Lacey stopped smoothing out her hair. She'd let it frizz and watch those cowboys pass on by. After all, capturing a cowboy wasn't top of mind. Or even bottom of mind for that matter. As for Caleb, she only ever challenged him. Instead, his perfect cowgirl would do nothing less than captivate him.

"Speaking of angles," Breezy started and chuckled. "We once knew the most charming cowgirl, Darlene Berry. Everyone called her darlin' Darlene, and well, she believed all her angles were perfect."

"It wasn't true." Gayle shook her head forlornly. "But we didn't have the heart to tell the sweet woman. Darlene tried, but she always looked rather queasy in photographs." Satisfaction curved Gayle's smile up into her papery cheeks. "But you don't seem to have that problem."

"That's a relief," Breezy chimed and drove straight for another pothole. "We don't want the launch of your social life to start out poorly."

Launch of my social life. Lacey's stomach bounced. Her head pulsed.

"That means we've got to put your best face forward in the newspaper," Gayle explained.

"Although your wound could draw those caring cowboy types right to you." Breezy's words were thoughtful.

Her wound had certainly drawn out a side of Caleb that Lacey hadn't seen before. She couldn't remember the last time she'd been looked after like that. Lacey stopped her full-body sigh. She didn't need looking after or any such thing. She wiggled in her seat and pressed her own very capable shoulders into the soft leather.

Gayle's chin dipped. "Now, a compassionate cowboy is certainly worth catching."

Lacey straightened even more. "I think there's been a misunderstanding." A heart-size one.

Caleb was a well-trained EMT. Of course he was compassionate and skilled at looking after the injured. He'd done nothing more than his job with Lacey. It was so easy for her heart to read too much into it. But it was a quality that would certainly appeal to his perfect cowgirl—the one Lacey promised to find for him.

"You've a different cowboy type in mind, don't you, dear?" Breezy said, her expression understanding.

"Why don't you tell us about the cowboy partner you would like?" Gayle took Lacey's free hand. "We've got ideas, of course. But it would be good to hear from you."

Lacey jumped right to the point. "I don't want a cowboy." *Compassionate or otherwise.* Because she was home to mend the wounds she'd caused in her daughter's heart, not open her own to new ones. The only heart that really mattered was Aspen's.

"I fear it's the blood loss, Breeze." Gayle patted Lacey's hand and kept her voice low. "I think there's been more than we suspected."

Breezy gave a *hmm* sound of agreement.

"I didn't come back for a cowboy," Lacey said, adding resolve to her words, wanting these two sweetly misguided and oh-so-persistent retirees to understand. "I'm here for my daughter, Aspen."

"Right." Gayle squeezed Lacey's fingers with decided vigor. "We need to add a cowboy with an affinity for family to the deputy's ideal partner list."

The only list Lacey needed was a grocery shopping list. And perhaps Caleb's ideal cowgirl list if he even had one.

Lacey winced at Breezy's bull's-eye hit of another pothole and argued, "All of this is really unnecessary. My social life is fine as is." No jump start required.

"You should rest now," Gayle said gently. "Once we get your wound cleaned and fixed up, you'll see things much clearer."

Lacey closed her eyes and gave in. In truth, the throbbing had escalated to what felt like a viselike clamp around her head. All from one seemingly small cut. Fortunately, the conversation ceased. Not that it mattered.

Things were already perfectly clear for Lacey. Nowhere in her future did she see a cowboy. After all, falling for a cowboy would only mean giving her daughter less. And Lacey had vowed to give her daughter all she had.

If that meant keeping blinders on her heart to protect herself and Aspen, that was exactly what she would do.

CHAPTER ELEVEN

JUST HOW LONG did it take an almost nine-year-old to get settled? Lacey checked the time on the microwave clock the next morning. Aspen had arrived exactly twenty-eight minutes ago. Exactly three minutes after that, Lacey had shown her daughter to her bedroom and told her she'd let her get settled in. Now Lacey wondered what to do next.

Wait her daughter out? Another minute clicked by on the clock.

Check on her? Was that hovering too much? Ask her if she needed anything? Wanted anything? Was that too soon? It was well past breakfast time yet much too early for lunch.

Lacey paced around the small kitchen in her ranch house. Watched another minute tick by.

The debate in her head raged on.

Lacey started down the hallway, but the doorbell had her spinning around and heading for that instead. The cowboy standing on the other side of her screen door had her grinning. Seeing a familiar face grounded her. She picked up her pace. "Caleb. What are you doing here?" *Whatever the reason, I'm grateful.*

"I wanted to check on you." He smiled and held up the shopping bags he was holding. "And I brought you gifts. But if this is a bad time, I can go."

"No," Lacey blurted, then rushed on, "Please come on in." *And tell me what to do. Help me get this right.* She propped open the screen door and motioned him inside. "What is all this?"

He stopped in the foyer and faced her. "First, tell me how you are."

Scattered. Panicked. Fearful I'm gonna mess up being a mom. Take your pick. She reached up and glided her fingers lightly over the bandage above her eye. "Twelve stitches. You were right."

He hardly looked relieved by that news. He prodded, "Concussion? Headache? Tenderness?"

"No concussion. Mild headache and tenderness, yes." She lowered her arm. "And I'm sure there's going to be bruising." She smiled, hoping his frown would stop deepening. "But I was introduced to a lovely and extremely meticulous plastic surgeon. We bonded over the fact that we both don't like needles. She claims the scar will be minimal."

"You never much cared about scars." His frown finally softened. "But you always hated needles."

"And you always hated horror movies," she said.

"Still do," he admitted and adjusted the bags he held. A bright gleam took over the seriousness in his gaze. "And I still like gifts, giving and getting them. But these are for you."

There was the Caleb she wanted. The carefree, nothing-to-stress-about-here cowboy. Lacey took the purple paper shopping bag stuffed with glittery tissue that he handed to her.

"That is chocolate from Tess, my sister-in-law," he explained. "If you like it, you can find more at Silver Penny. Tess owns the general store, and her award-winning chocolate is known from the Panhandle to the Gulf."

Lacey started to peek inside the bag, but Caleb presented her with another larger shopping bag.

"Elsie, my other sister-in-law, sent chicken and dumplings with homemade biscuits and homemade honey butter," he said. "The honey is from her and Ryan's bee farm."

Her stomach rumbled, and she laughed. "Great, we know what we're having for dinner tonight."

"Maggie, my third sister-in-law, wanted you to know Aspen

is cleared for the contest," Caleb continued. "Mags plans to find a way to help her that isn't a conflict of interest since she's the rodeo director." His grin shifted into mischievous.

This was what she needed. A light and easy distraction to allow her to get her parenting feet under her.

"Carter sent this from his private bourbon collection." He lifted a bottle from the last bag he clasped. "But considering you have a head injury at the moment, I'll be more than happy to hold on to it for you."

"You will not keep that." Lacey tipped her head toward the kitchen. "We can put everything on the table, including the bourbon."

Caleb swept up the bags and carried them into the kitchen.

Lacey put the casserole dish in the refrigerator, then sneaked a bite of Elsie's homemade biscuits—and discovered one bite wasn't enough. "These are delicious, and I'm afraid I won't be sharing." She took out the whole biscuit and proceeded to devour it without guilt. To Caleb's clear amusement. Savoring the last bit, she said, "This is all too much."

"It is the town's way of telling you that we look after our own," Caleb said and turned toward the door. "I'll get the rest."

"There's more?" Lacey trailed after him.

The rest included a vegetable basket with selections from Mr. Engell's backyard garden. A red velvet ice-cream cake from Mrs. Buckner and a handwritten apology. Cookie tins, homemade candies, and jars of nuts. A fruit basket from the neighbors next door to the Buckners and a note requesting that Deputy Nash please not judge the entire Wildflower Court by the stubborn ways of two cantankerous old men.

Lacey propped the note card on the table and took in the array of goodies. The house had been full of baskets and food when her mom was first diagnosed with cancer. It had seemed like the entire town had rallied around them. No questions, just support. Over a decade later, and that support was being extended to Lacey. It was more than she'd expected and made her especially determined to look after her hometown and the locals living there.

"Mom, the new shower is even better than the one at Dad's

house." Aspen skipped into the kitchen, her twin braids swinging over her shoulders.

Score one for Lacey. She had to thank Wells again for his handiwork last night. Her daughter seemed comfortable. At home even. The tension in Lacey's shoulders released.

"Whoa." Aspen gaped at the kitchen table. "That's a lot of stuff. Is it for us?"

"Housewarming presents," Caleb said and introduced himself to Aspen. "You might want to hide the chocolate chip peanut butter cookies from your mom. Those are the best, and you won't want to share them."

Aspen pressed her hands over her mouth to muffle her giggle.

Genuine amusement. They were on the right track. "Hey," Lacey objected. "I'm right here."

"Fine." Caleb sighed and sorted through one of the baskets. He found a robin's-egg blue jar with the word *Sweets* on it, twisted off the top, and handed a cookie to Lacey. "You can have one." He pressed the jar into Aspen's hands. "But the rest are for Aspen. They'll be a good treat after her riding lesson."

"What riding lesson?" Aspen sobered and glanced from Caleb to Lacey.

Time to take a side: her daughter's or ex-husband's. Lacey lowered her cookie to a napkin on the table.

"Can't win a spot on the Junior Royal Rodeo Court if you can't complete the pattern in the arena properly," Caleb quipped.

"But I'm not competing." Aspen folded her arms around the cookie jar. Her bottom lip jutted out. "Dad said no."

"I don't recall giving my answer. I'm your parent too." Lacey brushed her hands together, wiping off the cookie crumbs and smiled at her daughter. She'd chosen her side the minute she began the paperwork to retire from the army. "And as it turns out, I'm here, and your dad is not."

Aspen's eyes widened. Hope filled her face. "Can I enter the Junior Royal Rodeo Contest?"

"Well, you can't enter twice." Lacey chuckled and stood up. "I submitted your application yesterday, which was accepted by the way."

Aspen's smile was pure joy. She lunged at Lacey and hugged her tight, despite not letting go of the cookie jar. "Thanks, Mom."

Lacey took in the moment, embraced her daughter, and told herself whatever the fallout, it would be worth it. Her gaze connected with Caleb's over her daughter's head. His expression was tender, affectionate, and unguarded. She could've hugged him. Instead, she mouthed a silent *thank you*.

He tipped his chin in acknowledgment, then seemed to distance himself.

Most likely her imagination. She was the one feeling emotional after all. Lacey concentrated on her daughter. "You're in the contest." She released Aspen and held her shoulders. "That means you need to work hard to get prepared, and Caleb is going to help us with that."

"I'll do whatever he tells me," Aspen promised and looked at Caleb. "I'm a real good listener. That's what Mama-Beth tells me. She also says I catch on real quick." She tossed one braid over her shoulder. "What do we do first?"

"That's for Caleb to tell us." Lacey broke her cookie in half and handed a section to Caleb.

He took a bite of the cookie and said, "First, you need a horse."

Aspen's face scrunched together. "I don't have one."

"Lucky for you, I know where to find one." Caleb pulled his car keys from his pocket. "Ready to go meet your new teammate?"

Aspen glanced at her mom.

Caleb smiled. "Don't worry. Your mom will be right there with us." His tone relayed understanding and patience. "Although, she will be watching from the sidelines and not riding with us today because of her head wound."

Lacey finished her cookie and pointed at her temple. "It's a small cut."

"Head wound," Caleb countered and started for the front door. Aspen chased after him as if afraid he might leave without her. His words were gratingly pleasant. "And it hasn't even been twenty-four hours since you suffered your injury, Lace. You need to take it easy."

"Caleb Sloan, you are not my doctor." Lacey grabbed her purse from the kitchen chair and two jars of snack mix from the Baker sisters' basket and rushed after the pair. "I will decide if I ride or not. Not you."

"Your mom doesn't like it when people tell her what to do," Caleb said to Aspen on the porch, his words secret-sharing low. "But I do it anyway. When she's riled, her cheeks turn a shade almost as pretty as her hair."

Caleb thought her hair was pretty. *He thinks I'm pretty.* Lacey fumbled with the key in the front door. It seemed cowboy compliments rattled her.

"Come on, Lace," Caleb called out. "We want to see what color your cheeks are."

Her daughter giggled.

Lacey's cheeks warmed, but she refused to call it a blush. Her cowboy might get her riled up. But he would not be the cause of her blush. After all, it was those blinders on her heart that made her resistant to cowboy compliments. Lacey inhaled and turned toward the pair.

Caleb's one-sided grin came slow, same as the spark of appreciation in his blue eyes. "Told you she was pretty."

The heat beneath Lacey's skin flared. She battened down her heart, sweeping aside her sigh.

Aspen nodded, her grin enthusiastic. "She sure is."

Caleb's grin stretched farther into his cheeks, compelling and captivating.

Again, she was tempted to get to know this cowboy. But his side wasn't the one she wanted to be on. And it wasn't her heart's turn this time around. It was about her daughter.

Lacey tipped her chin up and strode past the pair. "Stop trying to distract me, Caleb. I know my own mind, and you won't be telling me what to do."

"We will see about that," Caleb muttered behind her. "Especially if Aspen and I just want to keep you safe."

Lacey turned to see her daughter tucked up against Caleb. If he lifted his arm, Aspen would be sealed against his side. They'd bonded already. How easy he made it look. Lacey wanted to know Caleb's secret. She took in their earnest expressions and said, "Well, I appreciate you both wanting to look after me."

Pleasure washed over Aspen's face.

"You're welcome." Caleb stepped around Lacey and opened the passenger door for her. When she climbed into the front seat, he leaned in and whispered, "And I wasn't distracting you. I was serious. You've always been pretty to me, riled or not. That's just a fact."

Lacey's throat went dry. Her pulse picked up. And all because her cowboy just got to her and she had no idea what to do about it.

Caleb turned to open the door for Aspen and waited until they were both settled, then made his way to the driver's side. The truck started, and he pulled out of the long driveway.

Aspen buckled her seat belt and said, "I've been learning all about horses, Caleb. Mom sent me a book for Christmas. Remember that, Mom?"

"I do." Lacey shifted in the leather seat, avoided looking at her cowboy, and smiled at her daughter, loving her excitement.

"Dad said I should be reading what he calls the classics instead of horse books," Aspen announced.

Lacey heard the frown in Aspen's voice and found herself frowning too. Perhaps she shouldn't have told Jeffrey all about her horse adventures growing up. Perhaps his dislike for the equestrian world was her fault somehow. Lacey had just wanted her ex to understand her passion. She'd wanted to share something about herself that had meant so much to her. If she had shared her joy for singing, things might have been different. Yet her self-assured ex would have most likely considered her stage fright an unfortunate weakness. Looking back, Jeffrey and she hadn't shared much in common, aside from a chemistry that had fizzled out too soon.

Lacey's gaze slanted toward Caleb. That hit of awareness sparked instantly. True, her cowboy captivated her. But she couldn't afford to bargain her heart away only to have it broken. She needed it whole for her daughter. "Aspen, I think you should read what makes you happy."

"That's what Mama-Beth says too. Horses make me happy."

Aspen popped her head between the front seats. "What makes you happy, Caleb?"

Being with her daughter made Lacey happy. Her gaze returned to Caleb. *And you. You make me happy, cowboy.* And that was trouble. Good thing it would all be resolved with that perfect cowgirl match Lacey had promised him. His cowboy compliments and blue-eyed charm would be for someone else. Just as Lacey wanted. No, she told herself, that certainly wasn't a pinch of envy or even unhappiness inside her. How could it be? Lacey had given up trouble a long time ago.

"A lot of things make me happy." Caleb pulled up to a stop sign. He tipped his head, skimmed those daringly perceptive blue eyes over her face.

Lacey searched his gaze. Felt that awareness flare through her again. Still, she held his stare for a beat. Then another. *You feel it too, don't you? Stop it. Shut me out.* She blinked. Retreated. *I can't...*

Finally, he slipped on a pair of tinted sunglasses, blocking her out just as she wanted.

Lacey exhaled and faced forward in her seat. "I can answer what makes Caleb happy."

"Is that so?" he asked, his words a challenge filled with curiosity and amusement. And suggested affection between more than friends.

That way led to trouble. *Turn around. He's not your happy.* Lacey blurted, "Super spicy food makes Caleb happy." His eyebrows lifted, and Lacey rushed on, "You were always daring me to eat peppers and hot sauce and ordering everything extra spicy."

"I still prefer that extra spice on my food," he admitted.

Aspen wrinkled her nose. "Hot spices don't make my stomach happy."

"I also like lima beans and spray cheese from a can." Caleb grinned. "Those aren't spicy. Your stomach should like them, Aspen."

"But, Caleb, that's gross." Aspen giggled.

"Well, you don't eat them together." Caleb's laughter joined Aspen's and filled the truck cab.

Lacey added one more thing to her happy list: the sound of her daughter's joy. That was it. She would make her happy list so crowded that there would not be enough room for her cowboy on it.

"Aspen, there are two boxes next to you." Caleb turned onto the bypass. "One is for you. One's for your mom."

Lacey pressed her lips together, tried not to shout *no more gifts. You're not mine. I'm not yours.* Clearly, she had to find that cowgirl for him and fast.

"We got more gifts." Wonder spread through Aspen's features. She handed the box with Lacey's name on it to her, then asked, "Can we open them now?"

"Sure can." Caleb chuckled.

Lacey spread her fingers over the box resting in her lap and willed her pulse to slow.

There was a rustling sound from the back seat, followed by, "It's a real cowboy hat." Aspen sounded awestruck. "I never had one before. Thanks, Caleb."

"I already checked, and it's approved attire for the contest," Caleb explained and touched his own cowboy hat. "Figured you can't be a cowgirl without the hat."

"Awesome." Aspen stretched the word out with even more amazement. "I love it. Do you love yours, Mom?"

Lacey lifted the lid of the box and ran her fingertips over the classic felt cowboy hat inside. It was the color of desert sand with a simple silver buckle on the matching felt hatband. Simple. Understated. And exactly what she would've picked for herself. As if her cowboy already knew her so well. "I do like it a lot." *And you, cowboy. I like you too. But I can't let myself. You have to understand.* "Thank you, Caleb."

"Wait." Aspen shifted and leaned forward again to peer into Lacey's hat box. Aspen said, "Mom, our hats match."

Lacey glanced over the seat to take in her daughter. Her cowboy hat was propped expertly on her head as if she'd always been wearing one. Lacey asked, "Is that okay?"

"Yeah." Aspen adjusted her hat and grinned. "I think it's cool."

Now she was cool. Score another one for Lacey. All thanks

to Caleb. She owed him. Lacey lifted her hat out of the box and set it on her head.

Caleb glanced over and said softly, "There's the cowgirl I remember. I knew she was still in there."

Cowgirl. No, she wasn't that. Hadn't been one in longer than she could remember. Couldn't be one now. Because then her heart just might get confused and make a bargain to become *his* cowgirl.

CHAPTER TWELVE

ARRIVING AT THE Sloan stables, Lacey remembered to take her cowboy hat off. She was returning it carefully to the box when Aspen caught her. "Mom, you gotta wear your hat too. Today, we're cowgirls."

"Right." Lacey propped the hat back on her head and climbed out of the truck. "Do we look like cowgirls?"

Aspen's mouth pinched toward the side. Her head shook. "We're gonna need real cowboy boots like Caleb's." She pointed at Caleb's weathered square-toed cowboy boots.

Lacey nodded and wiggled her toes in her old but reliable running shoes, concentrating on her daughter rather than the cowboy standing too close. "Anything else?"

"Jeans too," Aspen said decisively. "Like Caleb's."

Lacey patted the pockets of her olive green cargo pants, then tugged on her ivory tank top. "Let me guess, we need shirts like Caleb's too?" Making Lacey the cowgirl to his cowboy.

Aspen nodded solemnly, then brightened. "But purple plaid. That's my favorite color."

"Looks like we've got some shopping to do." Lacey held her hand out to Aspen. "How about today we just keep our hats on, be ourselves, and act like cowgirls?"

Aspen slipped her hand into Lacey's. "How do cowgirls act?"

"The cowgirls I know are brave, hardworking, and look after their families." Caleb walked with them toward the stables.

"Like we're looking after Mom by not letting her ride today, right, Caleb?" Aspen asked.

Caleb opened the door to the stable and grinned. "Now you're thinking like a cowgirl."

"Now I just need to be brave and work hard just like Mom." Aspen squeezed Lacey's hand, then released her and walked inside the stable barn.

Lacey's chest tightened. She hadn't known what her daughter thought about her until now. Aspen's words strengthened her in the best possible way. Sharpened her focus back onto her daughter where it belonged.

A cowboy with a pure white beard, white hair, and a sparkle in his gaze waited in the center aisle of the stable barn.

Caleb stopped inside the door, set his hands on his hips, and said, "Grandpa, what are you doing?"

"Lacey Nash." Sam Sloan ignored his grandson and opened his arms wide to Lacey. Sam was older but still the considerate, gentlemanly cowboy she'd known as a kid. Sam added, "Breezy and Gayle whisked you away yesterday before I could give you a proper welcome home. Hope your head's not paining you too much today."

"Hurts less now." Lacey smiled and stepped into Sam's embrace, then gently squeezed the older cowboy she'd always adored. "It's good to see you, Sam."

"Your mom sure would be proud of you. A decorated career in the army. Now a deputy sheriff." Approval was there in his words, fondness in his soft smile. "I sure know how proud Wells is of you. And I'm proud of you too."

"That's kind," Lacey said. And so very appreciated. His words settled deep inside her, filled her like her daughter's had. "It's good to be home."

Sam gave Lacey another quick hug, then released her and turned to Aspen. "And this must be Aspen, our Junior Royal Rodeo cowgirl."

Aspen beamed.

Sam extended his arm toward Aspen. "Pleasure to meet you."

Aspen slipped around his arm and hugged him instead. "Mom said I can be myself. And I usually get to hug Santa. And you look an awful lot like Santa except skinnier."

"Well, I'll take that as a compliment." Sam laughed, embraced Aspen cheerfully, then frowned at Caleb. "Did you see that, Caleb? That's a proper greeting for an old cowboy like me."

Lacey swallowed her laughter.

Caleb grinned wide and opened his arms. "Hello, Santa Sam."

Aspen giggled.

Caleb hugged his grandfather and hung on for an extra-long moment. His grandfather stepped back, and Caleb's grin stretched even farther.

"We don't have time for your foolery, Caleb Sloan," Sam admonished and set his hand on Aspen's shoulder. "We've got to get our young cowgirl ready."

Caleb nodded, his words dry. "I was trying to greet you properly like you requested."

"I already got the best hugs of the day from these two cowgirls," Sam retorted. "Now, I've saddled a horse for you, Caleb, in case you want to ride too. And I set everything out for Aspen. She'll need to do that herself in the contest. It's best to practice now."

Caleb scratched his cheek. "Let me guess, you read the rules, didn't you?"

"This morning in fact." Sam wrapped his fingers around his large belt buckle and smiled. "Can't help her win if we don't know what it takes. Of course, you could've told me yesterday about helping Aspen, so I had more time to prepare." Sam frowned. "Instead, I had to hear it from Maggie at breakfast, which you skipped."

Lacey peered at Caleb to see how he was taking Sam's scolding.

"I had gifts to deliver, but I'm glad you missed me, Grandpa." Caleb chuckled.

"We made some decisions this morning I reckon you'll be wanting to know about," Sam said. He spoke with a casual attitude, but his gaze was shrewd.

"What were those?" There was a reserve to Caleb's words and expression.

"Glad you asked." Sam's grin disappeared inside his thick beard. "We've booked our private dandelion wine tasting event. It's on the calendar for next weekend."

"That sounds fun." Lacey smiled.

Caleb frowned. "And soon."

"Your uncle and I told you we weren't waiting," Sam warned. Then he adjusted the silver clasp on his bolo tie, cleared his throat, and said, "Lacey, I'll make sure you receive a formal invite, of course." His lips twitched, and his eyebrows waggled, returning him to his good-natured ways. "Caleb is organizing our private affair. It'll be an evening you won't want to miss. I can promise you that, right, Caleb?"

Caleb looked like he wanted to miss it. He scrubbed a hand over his face. "Grandpa, we can talk about this later."

"The date is set," Sam insisted. "There's no bowling league or garden club that night. Everyone has already marked their calendars for the tasting. That means it's officially booked." Sam preened at Lacey. "Around here, we prefer full calendars. Being social keeps us young."

"Or it keeps them merrily mixed up in everyone's business," Caleb whispered to Lacey.

Lacey tried not to laugh, but it was hard work.

"What about me?" Aspen thrust both her arms out.

"Don't you worry, we'll do something just as fun." Sam smoothed his fingers through his beard, his words reassuring. "What if we set a date for ice cream?"

"Can we have root beer floats?" Hope seemed to rise behind Aspen's eyes. "I like those so much."

"Now you sound like your mom. If she wasn't riding, I'd catch her down at Frosty Dreamer's Parlor, sipping on a root beer float." Sam chuckled, then turned to Caleb, his words firm. "Mark your calendar, Caleb. We need to take Aspen for root beers floats and soon."

"I'll get right on that." Caleb rubbed his hands together. "But right now, we need to get back to the horses."

"Sam, I see the stunning Arabian I rode the other day at the lake." Lacey pointed toward the far end of the barn. The sleek Arabian had his head extended over the stall as if he wanted to be included.

"You won't be riding Denny today." Sam shook his head and crossed his arms over his chest. "What with your head all banged up like that."

Not Sam too. Lacey adjusted the brim of her hat to hide the bandage. "It's just a slow ride around the arena with Aspen."

"Sure it is," Caleb mumbled, then coughed, covering the rest of his words.

Lacey began to confront Caleb and defend herself, but Sam stopped her.

"Don't think I'm gonna fall for that one, my dear." Sam tapped his forehead and rattled on, "Age has only made me wiser. I haven't forgotten what you used to tell me way back when." Sam's eyebrows hitched up underneath his cowboy hat. "You'd look me right in the eye and say: *we're just going to take it easy today, Mr. Sloan. Enjoy the grounds with the horses.*"

Lacey tried not to wince. Those had been her exact words to Sam every time she and Caleb had been caught leading horses from the Sloan stables. Lacey glanced at Caleb.

He smoothed his hand over his mouth, but his smile remained. He shrugged. "He's not wrong. We used to say that all the time."

Aspen flicked her attention from one to the other as if not wanting to miss a word.

"Now don't go denying it. It's much too late for that." Sam swished his finger between Lacey and Caleb. "In truth, it was too late when you two were kids. Don't think we didn't know what you were up to."

Lacey clasped her hands behind her back as if she'd been caught sneaking in after curfew.

"We?" Caleb pressed.

His grandfather chuckled. "We as in me and your gran Claire. Lacey's darling mama." Sam ticked the names off on his fingers. "Wells too."

Sam made it sound like Lacey and Caleb were up to more

than riding. Back then they'd been friends only. But now. Now, she wanted…

One side of Caleb's mouth lifted. That private grin hooked her, hinted at shared secrets and heated her cheeks. Lacey slapped her palms over her face and willed her sudden blush to subside.

"What did they do?" Aspen asked.

"Jumping," Sam replied. "The kind on horseback."

"No way." Aspen rounded on Lacey. "You actually did jumps and stuff?"

"Oh, yeah. Couldn't hardly get your mom out of the saddle once your grandpa Wells plopped her in it," Sam explained all too cheerfully. "She was jumping everything from hay bales to fences to streams on her horse."

"Whoa." Aspen looked Lacey up and down like she was trying to imagine it but couldn't.

"Your mom was a highflier." Sam raised his arm. "Graceful like an angel as she and her horse soared over whatever was in her path. A real natural."

"I wouldn't go that far," Lacey said, although Sam's praise wasn't entirely unwelcome. Her two passions had been singing and horseback riding. Her horses had been her most loyal listeners.

"You were that good, Lacey," Sam countered. "Otherwise, I wouldn't have let you go and ride on our property. Especially after your gentle-hearted mama would call and blister my ears something good." Sam touched his ear. "My ears are still ringing from her phone calls."

Aspen giggled softly, her shoulders shaking.

Her mom had known what Lacey had been up to? Here Lacey had thought they'd been so clever all those times. She looked at Caleb. He seemed as surprised by Sam's admission as Lacey.

"It's true," Sam insisted and eyed Aspen. "Your late grandma was a force to be reckoned with. She'd call and tell me: *Sam Sloan, those kids are at it again. You'd best make sure my girl gets nothing more than a scratch. You hear me?*"

Aspen pressed her hands against her mouth. "What did you do?"

"Listened, of course," Sam said, wisdom crinkling the skin around his clever eyes. "You don't interrupt moms when they are giving you a piece of their mind. Remember that."

Aspen nodded. "Yes, sir."

"No sooner had Dana blistered my ears than my own sweet Claire would come out to tell me those two were are it again. And I'd best watch over 'em," Sam lamented, then pointed his finger at Caleb and Lacey again. "If one was jumping, the other was jumping higher."

Aspen spun toward them. Hands on her hips, eyebrows arched. Accusation was written all over her face. "You *both* jumped."

Caleb rubbed the back of his neck.

Lacey started to deflect, then glanced at Sam. "Sam helped us. More than once too."

"That he did." Caleb chuckled and edged closer to Lacey as if to make a united front. "Grandpa stacked more than a few hay bales for us to jump."

"I had to look after you somehow, didn't I?" Sam turned but not fast enough to hide the twinkle in his eyes. For all his bluff, he'd enjoyed himself.

"When do I get to jump?" Aspen hopped up and down and clasped her hands together. "Who's going to teach me? Mom. Caleb. Santa Sam."

The stables quieted as if even the horses were anxious to find out.

"Best to leave these sorts of decisions to the grown-ups." Sam cleared his throat. "Think I'll just head on over to the arena and get it opened up for you all." With that, he scooted silently and rather spryly out a side door.

Lacey's first instinct was to put her foot down and declare no jumping. Not ever. She'd lose a point for sure with that decision. But Aspen was a child. *My child.* Jumping was dangerous. The idea of Aspen getting injured was like a full-blown nightmare. Lacey managed a calm, "We can talk about jumping when you get older."

"Now you sound like Dad." Aspen crossed her arms over her chest.

Lacey understood Jeffrey's point of view a bit better. Kids didn't always have to get what they wanted. It was just that looking at her defeated daughter made all the guilt for the years Lacey had missed well up inside her. Disappointing Aspen was the last thing Lacey wanted. Talk about a parenting rock and a hard place. She touched her forehead.

Caleb moved to her side, set his hand on Lacey's lower back. His words and touch were gentle. "My gran Claire was a real deal cowgirl, and she loved her horses more than anything."

Lacey managed not to lean into Caleb, yet she stayed still and right beside him, grateful for his steady touch and quick assist.

Aspen's frown softened. "I bet your gran did lots and lots of jumping."

"She sure did," Caleb said, a smile in his words. "But she also did lots and lots of learning first."

"I already learned lots of stuff in my horse books," Aspen said, her frown returning. "Every night in my bed I read and read."

"But I'm talking about a different type of learning," Caleb continued, unruffled. "This is learning about your horse. What she likes to eat. Her favorite treats. If she likes a blanket at night or not. Where she likes to ride. What scares her."

That was the type of learning Lacey wanted to do with her cowboy. Or would want to do if she wasn't finding Caleb his one true cowgirl. Lacey eased away from his side.

"Spiders scare me." Aspen slipped her hand into Caleb's and walked with him past the stalls. "And mean snakes. Are your horses afraid of snakes?"

"That depends on the horse." Caleb slowed by a stall and stroked his hand between the ears of a brown quarter horse. "Denny over there is too curious for his own good. While Winston here is too lazy to be bothered by much of anything. And the farm cats sleep with Catnip down in the first stall, so she hasn't had to worry about critters of any variety bothering her."

"Catnip is lucky. I want to sleep with a cat," Aspen admitted and reached up to touch Winston's face. "Or a dog. Then I wouldn't ever get scared at night. Do you get scared, Caleb?"

"Sometimes," he confessed. "But I think you're right. I should get a pet too."

Lacey was scared she was already learning so much about her cowboy the longer she watched him with her daughter. She was even more scared that when he moved on with his cowgirl match, not even a pet of her own would be enough to fill the loneliness. But that was impossible. This was Caleb. And she was Lacey. And they were not... They were just *not*.

Aspen grinned and swung their joined hands between them. "When I learn about my horse, can I jump then?"

"So you start with having to learn all about your horse," Caleb explained. "Then you become friends. After that, partners. And that's when you trust each other."

"And then we jump," Aspen announced.

No. Lacey shook her head. There would be no jumping on horses for Aspen. And certainly no other kind for Lacey that included leaping from friends to something more.

"Gran Claire always told me you can't move straight to jumping. That's just poor planning. And nothing good ever comes from that," Caleb said. "And I'm going to add, you can't jump without trust."

Right. Lacey couldn't trust. Not her cowboy. Not herself. She'd keep her feet planted right where she was, and friends was how they would stay.

Caleb stopped at the stall with a striking tan-and-white Paint inside. "Ready to meet your teammate and get to know her?" He handed an apple to Aspen. "Her name is Biscuit. She's calm, friendly, and one of my favorite horses."

Aspen gripped the apple and leaned toward Caleb. Her whisper was heavy with worry. "What if Biscuit doesn't like me?"

Caleb lowered to a knee in front of Aspen. "Biscuit will like you because you have what my gran Claire would call heart."

"How do I know if I have heart?" Aspen's gaze never left Caleb's.

"You're here, aren't you?" Caleb countered. "Can't get where you want to be without taking that first step, right?"

But if Lacey didn't let her heart take any step, then she would stay where she wanted to be. Here, with her heart intact and all for her daughter.

Aspen pursed her lips, then finally nodded.

"Come on." Caleb opened the door to Biscuit's stall and led Aspen inside. "Biscuit is waiting."

The pair moved from treats to grooming to finally braiding Biscuit's mane together. The conversation never paused, switching from horse breed facts to horse care to horse tack and its specific uses as they saddled the patient mare. Aspen listened, followed directions, and kept up her own steady stream of praise for Biscuit.

All the while, Lacey watched the pair and feared her own heart was showing. Yet she couldn't move away and wanted to be closer. To join in. Fortunately, the closed stall door reminded her to keep to her side.

Finally, Aspen ran her hand down the length of Biscuit's neck, complimented the mare's light blue eyes, and declared, "Biscuit likes her mane braided. Now we match." Aspen leaned in, whispered to the mare, then grinned at Caleb. "We're ready to ride now."

Caleb put the brushes away and led Biscuit out of the stall. Outside, he handed the reins to Aspen and let her guide Biscuit into the covered arena. Caleb, Aspen, and Biscuit moved into the soft, sandy arena.

Lacey paced in front of the metal gates, trying to walk off her sudden apprehension. She caught sight of Sam strolling toward her and joined him at the curve of the arena. "I'm a little more anxious than I thought I would be. She's ridden before but not much. I just want her to…" *Love it as much I did. Not fall. Have fun. Not get hurt. Enjoy herself. Not get defeated. Get back up.*

Sam set his hand on Lacey's arm, drawing her gaze to him. "Worry is what comes with loving someone the way you love your daughter. There's no getting around it."

Lacey considered Sam. "What do you do about it?"

"You make sure when it can't be you watching over her that the right people are doing it for you." Sam tipped his chin, and Lacey followed his gaze toward the center of the arena. Caleb was now seated behind Aspen on the mare.

Their heads were bent together as Caleb talked to her daughter and guided Aspen's hands around the reins. Lacey's shoulders loosened. "Wells taught me to ride the same way."

"Your mom knew Wells was one of the good ones." Sam propped his arms on the metal gate. "My Claire would've called Wells a cowboy worth keeping."

Wells was certainly that. Her stepdad had always looked out for Lacey and her mom.

Lacey watched Caleb and Aspen circle the arena. Aspen waved as they passed, pure delight on her face. Joy was in her gaze. Lacey had felt all that when she'd first learned to ride all those years ago. And those feelings had only grown the more time she spent with her horses.

Her gaze landed on her cowboy and stuck. She needed to find his cowgirl match soon, before she decided he might be her cowboy worth keeping.

CHAPTER THIRTEEN

CONGRATULATIONS WERE DEFINITELY in order.

It was after lunch, and Caleb was driving Lacey and Aspen home. That Aspen's practice had gone better than he'd imagined wasn't his cause for celebration.

Rather it was the fact that he could finally look at the bandage on Lacey's forehead and not get irritated all over again. Finally, he was not thinking about what could've happened if the nozzle had struck an inch lower or an inch to the right. True, her cowboy hat covered part of the bandage, and she was staring straight ahead, but Caleb meant to take small successes where he could.

"Can we stop at Cider Mill Orchard?" Lacey asked. "Breezy and Gayle told me about the farmers market there. And I wanted to pick up some fruit and vegetables. Breezy said the owner has a selection of homemade baked goods featuring her fruit that are not to be missed."

Caleb glanced at Lacey and got distracted by that bandage again.

"I promise I'll be fast," Lacey said, misreading his frown.

"Have you ever been to Cider Mill Orchard?" Caleb switched on his blinker and pulled into the left turn lane.

"No," Lacey said.

"Well, I can promise you it won't be a quick stop," Caleb said.

"Wanna bet?" She leaned on the console, her grin teasing.

"I'm not going to accept." Because a new wager would mean higher stakes. And for things that changed friendships. Things he should not be considering. Caleb concentrated on the road.

"You're going to thank me later." Meanwhile, he would be grateful he'd stayed inside those long-standing friendship boundaries.

Lacey laughed. "We shall see about that."

And he would see that he friend-zoned Lacey. Caleb pulled into the parking lot and glanced into the rearview mirror. "Ready to get lost sampling apple cotton candy and apple cider in the biggest farmers market you've ever been to?"

"Yes!" Aspen cheered and climbed out of the truck.

Caleb guided the pair through the entrance to the outdoor market.

Aspen came to a halt. "Whoa. This place is huge."

Lacey nodded.

Caleb leaned in and whispered, "You can thank me now."

Lacey shook her head, but her shoulders quivered. Her amusement was obvious. "We never really defined quick, did we?"

"Nice try." Caleb lifted his hand and waved to a woman carrying a bushel of apples. "Come on and meet Whitney Carson. She owns the place. And then you can shop."

"I can come back another time if you're in a hurry," Lacey said.

He wasn't in a hurry to leave her. That thought should have him running back to his truck. Caleb was never one for lingering. But that was exactly what he did. "Take your time. Aspen and I have sample tables to find." He grinned at Aspen. "It's like a treasure hunt."

"Uncle Caleb," a familiar voice shouted. "Uncle Caleb!"

Caleb turned and caught the two young girls careening into his arms. Autumn and Gemma Parks were energetic and animated and his sister-in-law Elsie's nieces. Caleb wasn't quite sure how the family tree worked regarding Elsie's nieces. Elsie and Ryan had officially married in a small private ceremony in June. And Caleb had suddenly earned the uncle title. He'd been too thrilled and honored to make a correction or worry about the bloodline details.

He lifted them both and spun around in several circles to their collective delight. Then he asked the adorable pair, "Who are you here with?"

"Auntie Elsie and Uncle Ryan are picking out onions." Gemma Parks pointed to the vegetable sign, then grabbed his hand and twirled around underneath his arm.

Autumn said, "Dad needed to work today and Uncle Ryan said we could help with exercising Midnight Rose and Sundancer when we get back."

"Can you come over and ride horses with us too, Uncle Caleb?" Gemma asked. "We get to go visit the dandelion fields."

"I can't think of anything better that I have planned. I'm sure I can find a horse in our stables who would enjoy some exercise." Caleb accepted their excited hugs and introduced the lively pair to Lacey and Aspen.

"Can we show Aspen the apple sweets section, Uncle Caleb?" Autumn asked.

"With the candy apples and fudge and apple ice cream." Gemma sang the words and wiggled her hips.

"Can I go with them, Mom?" Aspen asked.

Elsie and Ryan joined them. The girls barely lasted through another round of introductions; their collective excitement was ready to burst free.

"I'll take these three to the candy cottage." Ryan kissed Elsie and added, "And you can shop at your leisure."

"I'm going to show Lacey the scented soap and candles Whitney just started selling." Elsie linked her arm around Lacey's. "We'll catch up with you guys later."

Caleb shook his head at his sister-in-law. "It's not what you think, Elsie."

"You have no idea what I think, Caleb Sloan," Elsie countered. "And if you're worried about what I might ask Lacey, then it is exactly what I think."

Caleb frowned.

"Come on, little brother." Ryan's hand landed on Caleb's

shoulder. "My wife is not going to let up until she talks to Lacey alone."

"But it's not what she thinks," Caleb called out, ensuring his words reached Elsie and Lacey.

Elsie laughed and tugged Lacey down an aisle of potted plants until they were out of sight.

"So what is it?" Ryan bumped his elbow into Caleb's side, then clarified, "Between you and Lacey."

"Why does it have to be something?" Caleb nudged his brother away.

"It doesn't," Ryan said. "It just feels like there's something. You know?"

No. He didn't know. Or rather didn't want to know. That would only blur things between him and Lacey. And he wanted to be clear where they stood for his heart's sake and hers. "Look, I'm really happy for you and Elsie and what you've found together." Caleb nodded vigorously at his older brother. "Love looks good on you."

Ryan pressed his hands over his chest and gave an exaggerated sigh. "That's the sweetest compliment you've ever given me."

Caleb chuckled. "Just because you like love and wear it well that doesn't mean everyone around you wants to try it on too."

"You've never tried on love, little brother." Ryan lifted his arm and flashed his wedding ring at Caleb. "How do you know it won't fit you?"

Because that meant opening his heart fully. Without restraint. Without restrictions. That was opening himself to things that hurt. And nothing about that fit him well. "Trust me, I know."

"That's the thing about love," Ryan said, his words wise, his expression sincere. "It's like those new trend-setting boots in the store window. The ones that look impractical and stiff and entirely unsuitable. But then one day those same boots show up in your favorite color, and you finally try them on. And you discover they're a perfect fit, and you never want to take them off."

"Do you hear yourself? You're talking about love and boots as if they are the same." Talking to his love-sunk brother was testing his patience. Caleb picked up his pace to catch up with the kids. "I already have enough pairs of boots that fit perfectly fine. So how about we agree to disagree on this thing you call love?"

"Only if you agree to admit I'm right," Ryan said. "When the time comes, of course."

Caleb crossed his arms over his chest. "You're serious?"

"I like to be right," Ryan said, with too much satisfaction. "I like it even more when my brothers publicly admit I was right and they were wrong."

"Fine," Caleb said. "Now can we talk about the dandelion wine tasting party?"

"You mean event," Ryan corrected. "Grandpa Sam and Uncle Roy were very specific about the name this morning. It's not a private wine tasting party. It's an *event*. Apparently, that sounds more exclusive. And exclusivity builds buzz."

Caleb's head was starting to buzz. He yanked off his cowboy hat as if that was the cause of his tension and ran his hand through his hair. "Why did you and Elsie agree to let them use the greenhouses for their *event*?"

"Why did you agree to put together the *event* in the first place?" Ryan countered and set his hands on his hips.

"To keep them from interfering with the wedding reception," Caleb admitted. "And I didn't want to disappoint them."

"We didn't either." Ryan nodded and sighed in solidarity. "I'll get the wine bottles moved from the barn to the greenhouse."

"I'll take care of the rest," Caleb said. "Shouldn't be that complicated."

"Don't look at me for more help." Ryan lifted his hands. "I'd tell you to plead with Elsie to lend a hand, but I'm taking her to Arkansas this coming week to pick up two more retired bucking broncs. We're making an extended road trip out of it and leaving tomorrow."

"You're not going to be here?" Caleb asked.

"We'll be back in time for the tasting event," Ryan said, sounding far from reassuring. "But I'm sure you're right—it can't be all that complicated to organize. Send out invites. Get some good food, and you're done."

"Except Grandpa and Uncle Roy expect an exclusive event."

Caleb smashed his hat back on his head, wondering when it'd gotten so complicated.

"Yeah, I don't even know what that means." Ryan chuckled and tapped his fist lightly on Caleb's shoulder. "Good luck with that one, little brother."

The girls raced up, grabbed their hands, and started pulling them across the farmers market.

Caleb laughed and asked, "What's the rush?"

"Dogs." The reply came simultaneously from the spirited trio.

Elsie and Lacey suddenly appeared in the aisle. Elsie lifted her arm, blocked their path like a crossing guard at the elementary school, and said, "We are leaving now. Ryan cannot go see any dog."

There were grumbles of discontent from the trio.

Elsie continued, "Ryan cannot get attached to another dog. Smarty Marty and Butter-Belle won't like it."

"Are those your dogs?" Lacey asked.

"Those are the goats," Gemma announced.

Elsie chuckled. "Goats who think they are dogs. If they aren't following me around the farm, they are attached to Ryan. Of course, he gives them treats and picks them up as if they are baby kittens."

"So you're a rancher too?" Lacey asked.

"I'm a transplanted event planner," Elsie said. "Learning my way around a farm with a few more mishaps than grace."

"Don't let her fool you." Ryan swept Elsie into his arms. "My wife is amazing and can do anything she sets her mind to."

Elsie wrapped her arms around his neck and kissed him. "And my husband is one of the good ones."

Gemma groaned and lamented, "They are always doing this."

Autumn nudged herself between them. "You both promised, not here."

"Fine. I'll kiss my wife later." Ryan laughed and bent down near Autumn. "Climb on. It's a free ride back to the truck."

"No fair. It was my turn." Gemma set her hands on her hips.

Ryan swept the little girl up into his arms before her pout could fully form. "Hang on tight, Autumn. I've got to shake Princess Gemma's smile free."

"Hold on." Caleb motioned for Ryan to prop Gemma on his back, then he glanced at Lacey. "I'll meet you and Aspen over at the dog adoption tent." He grinned at his brother. "Race you to the truck. Last ones buy ice cream at Frosty Dreamer's after our ride later."

Gemma cheered on Caleb, and the race was on with Elsie following close behind. Minutes later, Caleb found Lacey at the edge of the dog adoption tent. She was biting her lower lip and watching Aspen peer into one kennel after another.

He moved to stand beside Lacey and said, "Looks like maybe it wasn't Ryan we needed to worry about getting attached."

"Caleb, tell Mom she needs a dog," Aspen pleaded and rushed on, "'Cause then she won't be alone when I'm with Dad and Mama-Beth."

"I'm not sure it's a good time," Lacey hedged.

"But, Mom, it's a dog," Aspen argued. "She can sleep in your bed. Protect you. Give you kisses when you're sad." An excited brown terrier licked Aspen's face through his cage. Aspen's laughter peeled out around her.

"She makes a good case," Caleb said. He could make a similar case as a cowboy. One who could kiss Lacey when she was sad or happy or simply standing beside him. *Lacey and kisses.* That was dangerous territory. Caleb moved closer to Aspen and the dog kennels, but those unwise thoughts nipped at his boot heels.

Aspen spun around and pointed at a blond Labrador retriever curled up at the back of a kennel. "We need to adopt her, Mom."

Lacey joined them. "Why this one?"

"All her puppies got adopted." Aspen tapped the laminated card attached to the dog's kennel. "And now she's a mom with no family. We need to be her family."

Caleb had no argument. No counter for Aspen. Family was everything to him. Always had been. He noted Lacey opened her mouth, tucked her hair behind her ear, then closed her lips together softly. As if she too struggled for a sound rebuttal. Family meant something to her. It was good common ground for friends—like they were. Even more important for that "something more" that he was starting to think about more than he should.

"Her name is Butterscotch, Mom." Aspen clasped her hands together in front of her and heightened the imploring plea in her words. "She's so sad. And alone. Look at her. We gotta help her. Give her a family."

The struggle was there in Lacey's unblinking brown eyes. The indecision in the seal of her lips, not firmly set, yet still holding back. Caleb searched for a way to help. But Aspen had already swayed him. He wanted to adopt Butterscotch, gather up Aspen and Lacey, and call them his own. What he needed to do was turn around and walk away. Fast and far. What he actually did was stay put.

"Please, Mom." Aspen stretched her words out, clearly not ready to concede.

Lacey collected herself. "I suppose it doesn't hurt to meet her."

Caleb supposed it wouldn't hurt for him to greet the dog either. It wasn't like he was adopting her. Or claiming a family. He already had one.

The dog rose and slowly inched toward the front of the kennel. Her tail barely twitched, but she sniffed Aspen's fingers wrapped around the wire door. "Can she come out?" Aspen asked.

One of the adoption workers was there in an instant, clipping a leash onto Butterscotch's collar, and leading them all into a portable pen. Aspen sat on the grass and patted her legs. The sweet dog dropped into Aspen's lap without hesitation. Aspen's arms wound around the dog's body.

"She likes me," Aspen said, her grin stretching from cheek to cheek. "Come meet her, Mom."

Lacey had no sooner sat down than Butterscotch was wiggling to get to her, her tail whipping back and forth in excitement. Lacey laughed and moved, allowing Butterscotch to press right up against her.

"Look, Caleb," Aspen called out. "Butterscotch likes Mom the most."

"I think you're right." He knew someone else who was starting to like Lacey more and more. Maybe even the most.

Aspen hugged her mom and Butterscotch. "I told you she needed us."

He was starting to think he might need them too. Caleb bent down in front of them and greeted the dog.

"I think I'm getting a dog," Lacey whispered and touched his arm. "Tell me this is a bad idea."

Caleb considered her hand on his arm for a beat. It was a bad idea of colossal proportions. Caleb only needed a career pivot, not a relationship upgrade. Yet when he looked into Lacey's enchanting brown eyes, he tended to lose himself and forget. "I want to, but I can't." *I'm not good with people's hearts, even my own.* He leaned in and said, "I think Butterscotch is smiling right now."

Lacey shifted, and her fingers flexed around his arm. "It's hard to tell who's smiling more, Butterscotch or Aspen."

"Or you." He reached up and tucked her hair behind her ear. Just the smallest shift, and he could brush his lips against hers. Just a light caress. But those heartstrings tugged. And he guessed one brief kiss wouldn't be nearly enough. He pulled his hand away.

"I think I'm getting a dog." Lacey's eyes sparkled at him, then she waved to the volunteer. Her grin was sunshine bright and everything he could want aimed his way. She spoke to the volunteer. "What paperwork do I need to sign? We choose her."

I could choose you. But that means choosing my heart first. And that was not something Caleb had ever done. He wiped his hands on his jeans and stood up. "Guess we better get some dog supplies as well."

It wasn't long before the paperwork was completed and submitted. And the dog supplies, conveniently available for purchase at the adoption event, were stashed in the truck. Butterscotch leaned against Aspen on the back bench, the pair already content and looking inseparable.

Caleb turned onto the street that led to Lacey's ranch.

"I almost forgot the best news in all the excitement of meeting Butterscotch." Lacey lowered the volume on the radio and grinned at him. "You have a date tonight."

"I have a date," Caleb said carefully. *Please let it be with a deputy, her daughter, and their new dog.*

"Yes. Her name is Eryn. She is Whitney Carson's cousin, and she's free tonight." Lacey fumbled with her phone. "I told her you would text her about meeting up for movie night tonight downtown."

Caleb flexed his fingers around the steering wheel and hoped his expression was neutral.

"Elsie mentioned that movie night is really popular." Lacey tapped on her phone screen. "I thought it would be good to have a first date in a crowded place. Elsie and I both really liked Eryn, and Whitney vouched for her."

"You've thought of everything." *Except asking me what date I really want.* Caleb was pleased his words sounded almost indifferent.

"You can't back out," Lacey warned. "I heard you tell Ryan and Elsie's nieces that you had no plans tonight."

"I'm not backing out," he assured her and pulled to a stop in Lacey's driveway.

In fact, he was leaning into a date. All the way in. Just to prove that there was nothing between him and Lacey. That Ryan was completely wrong about there being something between them. And that Caleb had just gotten caught up in the moment earlier. His boots had taken a bit of a detour at the farmers market, but he was back on the right path now.

"Look, I'll text her right now." He put the truck in Park and picked up his phone from the console. "Happy?"

"Very," she said, albeit a little too quickly and a bit too briskly.

Caleb eyed her, then decided that was only his ears deceiving him. After all, she'd orchestrated the whole date thing. The wager was entirely her idea. And she'd vowed to win. Of course, she was happy about finding him a date. Same as he would be. He would be thrilled in fact. As soon as he got over that annoying bit of disappointment that his date wasn't with his deputy. Surely that would happen any minute now.

He typed his text and hit Send. Eryn's response came immediately. Caleb worked his best smile into place. "We're meeting at six in the square. Looks like I have a movie night date."

"Great." Lacey gathered her purse. "It's a triple feature. Should be good weather too."

"What more could I ask for?" Other than more time with a certain trio.

Lacey glanced into the back seat. "Come on, Aspen. We've already taken up enough of Caleb's time. He's got a date to get ready for."

"Can we go to movie night too, Mom?" Aspen opened her door. "Autumn told me that Riley would be there. She says I gotta meet Riley 'cause she's in the Junior Royal Rodeo Contest too."

"Riley Bishop is the daughter of Evan Bishop, the cattle rancher you met at the lake the other morning with Walter," Caleb explained to Lacey. At her nod, Caleb added, "Evan is married to Paige, who happens to be Tess's sister."

Lacey chuckled. "I think I got it straight."

"And Ms. Paige is a veterinarian. That's what I want to be when I grow up," Aspen announced. "I gotta meet her too. So does Butterscotch. In case she needs a doctor."

"Can't argue with a proper vet meet and greet," Caleb said cheerfully.

"Okay, looks like we'll be heading to movie night as well." Lacey climbed out of the truck and waited for Aspen and Butterscotch to jump out.

Aspen led the dog around the front yard, then straight into the house.

Lacey smiled at him. "Thanks again for today. Maybe we'll see you tonight."

He wanted to tell her she could count on that. But he had a date. Although not with her. He started the truck and touched the brim of his cowboy hat. "Hope you enjoy your evening, Deputy."

And he hoped that the notion of being friends with his deputy would start to fit right again. And soon. Because it was the only thing between them.

CHAPTER FOURTEEN

THE OUTDOOR MOVIE night was as popular as Elsie claimed. Lacey took in the bustling crowd filling the square, sitting in chairs, stretched out on blankets. Friends and neighbors mingled. The kids played. The laughter swirled with its own melody. All while a popular children's movie about a collection of animated toys played on the jumbo movie screen at one end of the square.

Lacey watched Aspen with her new friend, Riley Bishop, as the pair chatted nonstop and walked Butterscotch around a small group of trees. Riley's stepmom, Paige, had set up a collection of chairs and blankets for friends and family nearby. Lacey had promised to come back after she returned her ex-husband's call about an urgent situation.

Wanting to make sure Sarah-Beth and the baby were well, Lacey walked across the street, seeking a quieter location. She moved under the dim awning of Rivers Family Hardware and dialed Jeffrey.

Her ex-husband answered on the second ring, gave a curt greeting, followed by, "This is not what we agreed, Lacey."

"Jeffrey, what are you talking about?" Lacey wandered down the sidewalk.

Her ex-husband's sigh rolled across the speaker. "I overheard

Aspen and Sarah-Beth talking earlier. I know Aspen went riding today."

Lacey stopped abruptly. "First, is everything okay with Sarah-Beth and the baby? They are fine, aren't they?"

"Couldn't be better," Jeffrey quipped. "But could we please stay on topic?"

Lacey was trying to. "You texted me about an urgent situation." She gripped her phone tighter. "I thought something was seriously wrong."

"Something is wrong," Jeffrey stated flatly. "You entered Aspen in that contest, and we agreed not to."

That was his urgent situation? Lacey inhaled and worked to keep control of her growing frustration. "No, we didn't agree." She turned back toward the crowded downtown square. "You told me. Same as you told Aspen."

"We discussed this, Lacey," Jeffrey retorted. "This isn't how we coparent correctly or effectively."

"We didn't discuss anything," Lacey countered. Discussions and the right conversations had never been their specialty. Perhaps if they had, Jeffrey and she might've worked out differently. But debating the past was hardly productive. It was over. Her gaze skimmed the sea of happy smiling faces. "But I did talk to Aspen like I told you I would. She wants to do this, and I'm going to help her."

"This is not a good idea," Jeffrey stressed. "You're making me look like the bad parent."

"Jeffrey, this isn't about you," Lacey said. Her gaze landed on a familiar cowboy who wasn't so far away that she couldn't get to him. Or see that he was completely alone. But that wasn't right. "Look, this is about Aspen. She needs to be our focus."

"Well, make sure this is not about you either, Lacey," he challenged. "Aspen is not you."

He said it as if being like her was a bad thing somehow. Lacey fought the urge to apologize. Her gaze returned to her cowboy and stuck. She kept her cool. "What does that mean exactly?"

"Look, this conversation is better in person," Jeffrey said, his words yielding slightly. "I've been trying to do what's best for Aspen since you deployed. It's not too much to ask that you follow my lead now, is it?"

There it was. That guilt surged again. Along with the urge to apologize. It took a minute, but she managed to unclench her jaw and loosen her grip on the phone. "You're right, Jeffrey. This is a conversation best had face-to-face."

"We'll meet as soon as Sarah-Beth and I get back to Three Springs," he stated.

With that, he ended the call. No good night. No sleep well. Just silence, doubt, and second-guessing herself.

But Lacey had watched Aspen with Caleb in the Sloan stables and the arena. She knew in her gut that horses were more than a phase for her daughter. Aspen had a passion and a natural affinity for them. And that elusive *heart* that Sam and Caleb referenced.

Aspen is not you.

Surely, she wasn't just wanting to see herself in her daughter, was she? Grasping for common ground that wasn't there. Misreading everything. She caught sight of her cowboy, still alone on that blanket.

Lacey tucked her phone into the pocket of her denim shorts and started across the street. She should head back to Paige and sit with the veterinarian's family. Keep the evening entirely about Aspen.

But her gaze was fixed elsewhere, and her feet followed, leading Lacey toward her cowboy. As if he'd called her. It was more that she felt drawn to him, wanting him to help her feel something other than uncertain.

Lacey navigated around several blankets and finally reached her cowboy. "Where did your date go?"

Caleb grabbed her hand and tugged her onto the blanket. "If you keep standing there, the people behind you are going to start hollering because you're blocking the screen."

Lacey waved an apology to the family behind them and settled beside Caleb. "Well, where is Eryn?"

"She left halfway through the first movie to find mosquito spray," he said, his words bland and unbothered.

Lacey looked around. "But the second movie just started playing."

"Yeah, well, it seems Eryn ran into Matt Molina, the mayor's son, inside Goodstart Pharmacy," Caleb explained. "Eryn and Matt got to talking. And they decided to grab banana splits and watch the movie from inside the ice-cream parlor."

Lacey gaped at him. "Eryn bailed on you for the mayor's son."

"Don't underestimate the power of a banana split," he said, laughter coming from his lips.

"It's not a root beer float with homemade ice cream," she countered.

"No, it sure isn't." He dropped his hat on the blanket, tousled his hair, and grinned at her.

She studied him. "You're not mad."

"Not really." He stretched out on the blanket and stacked his hands behind his head. "It wouldn't have worked out between us anyway."

"You don't know that," she argued. She needed to argue. Otherwise, she would give in to her pleasure that his date had sputtered and failed. And that was entirely the wrong kind of thinking.

"Eryn wanted a banana split." He tipped his head toward her. His expression was serious, yet there was an undercurrent of his usual good humor in his words. "And I don't like to mix my fruit or my ice-cream flavors. I like to keep things simple and uncomplicated."

He'd always been straightforward, never pretending to be anything he wasn't. Never apologizing either. She'd always admired that about him. She stretched her legs out and leaned back on her arms. "What now?"

"We watch the next movie." He motioned to the screen. "Enjoy the evening. Let Aspen have fun with her new friends. The same way we used to have fun while the adults sat around."

"I never much thought about my mom and Wells having fun together when I was a kid," she confessed.

"I think most kids are too busy thinking about their own entertainment." Caleb stared up at the night sky, his words wistful. "I know I was."

Lacey drew her legs up and rested her arms on her knees.

"What's on your mind, Lace?" He shifted beside her and sat up. "Something tells me it's not about the fun we had as kids."

"We did, didn't we?" she said. "Have fun."

"Why do you sound surprised?" he asked and propped his arms on his raised legs, mimicking her position. "You were there for our adventures. Heck, you came up with most of them."

"Not after my mom was diagnosed with cancer." She set her cheek on her knees and looked at him. "And everything stopped being fun."

He scooted toward her as if he wanted to block out everyone around them. As if he wanted to be certain she heard his next words. His gaze drifted over her face, part stunned and part alarmed. His eyebrows lifted slightly. "That's why you broke up with Grady Welton and stopped coming around?"

Did you miss me? She nodded. *I missed you.* "I had to be there for my mom. I had to be responsible, do whatever I could to help her and Wells."

"I would've helped you," he said softly. "If you'd asked."

She believed him. "Your gran Claire dropped off meals. The Baker sisters and neighbors did too. I'm not sure Swells and Mom knew what to do. There was so much food."

His gaze searched hers. "I would've…"

She reached out and set her hand on his arm, stopping him. "I know."

But she hadn't wanted his pity. Caleb had been the one she turned to for excitement and adventure. An escape. A good time. He'd always made her laugh. She hadn't wanted him to see her cry. She'd never wanted to be the one to ruin his fun.

He covered her fingers with his hand as if wanting to stay connected. "You gave up fun in high school." She opened her mouth to object, he rushed on, "For good reason. When did you start having fun again?"

"That's just it." Her fingers tightened around his arm. She felt his strength and his warmth underneath her palm. Felt it inside her chest. She exhaled and admitted, "I never really did."

He didn't pull back. Didn't let go. Simply studied her, questions in his intensely appealing eyes. "You even went into the army. Wells and your mom would fill me in when they got your letters. They were always so proud, they'd tell everyone who'd listen to them about you."

She smiled. "I enlisted because the army paid for my college degree. There were so many medical bills, I couldn't burden Wells and Mom with paying for college."

He pressed his lips together.

"I don't regret a minute of the time I served," she said, wanting him to understand. "The military made me a better person. Don't get me wrong, I liked serving. I would do it again."

"But," he pressed.

"But it was lonely most of the time." Her fingers flexed around his arm again as if he was her anchor while she spilled her unspoken truths. "Then I married Jeffrey." Her words swept around her sigh. "And I was still lonely."

Caleb edged even closer until their knees and shoulders touched and kept his hand covering hers.

"You asked what was on my mind before, and it was just that." She bumped her shoulder against his, but it didn't lighten the mood. Instead, she leaned right into him as if she needed another connection with him. Or perhaps she just wanted to feel steady. "I realized Jeffrey and I never had fun together."

"You dated and got married." His fingers caressed her wrist. A back-and-forth slide. His gaze searched hers. "There had to be good in there."

"We had a baby and responsibilities and more important things to always think about," she said. His fingers continued that slow slide, his touch so light against her skin, yet so very soothing. "It all happened too fast. In the wrong order."

"Why did you get married?" he asked.

"It was the responsible thing to do," she admitted. A surprise pregnancy had fast-tracked them past dating and straight into parenthood. And she'd been so certain what they felt for each other would be enough. "We needed to come together as parents for our child."

"But you weren't truly happy," he guessed.

"That shouldn't have mattered," she countered. "It was the right thing to do for us."

"You made the best decision in the moment, and according to Gran Claire, that's all any of us can hope to do," he said, his expression pensive.

Would Gran Claire think it wise or foolish if Lacey twisted her wrist and linked her fingers with Caleb's? Was the best decision moving her hand out from underneath his or holding on tighter? Lacey kept her arm in place, afraid to make a choice. And perhaps that was for the best. In this moment.

"What now?" he asked.

"What do you mean?"

"You are home," he said. "Isn't it past time to find that fun again?"

With you? That idea was entirely too tempting. "I'm home to prove I can be the parent Jeffrey needs me to be." Although, on that front, she was falling short already. Her ex had made that clear during their phone call.

"I'm not going to offer parenting advice. That wouldn't be right." Caleb squeezed her hand. "But I don't think it's wrong to want to be happy too, Lace. You shouldn't have to apologize for that."

I could be happy with you. But would you keep my heart safe? Not just in this moment, but always? Because she vowed not to bargain for temporary ever again. Her heart wasn't up for a trial run. Not this time around.

She slid her hand from beneath his, eased away from his side and back into that easygoing banter shared between friends. "Hey, I owe you an apology for Eryn. I wouldn't have suggested this date if I knew mosquitoes would chase her away and straight to Matt Molina."

Caleb chuckled. "That's okay." He reached into a picnic basket nearby and handed her several frosted animal cookies. "Now there's more snacks for us."

"You brought animal cookies." Lacey plopped a bite-size

unicorn cookie into her mouth and savored the crunch of the colorful sprinkles and sweet frosting. "I never did like sharing the good snacks anyway." She swallowed and examined the cookies in her hand. "Wait. These aren't store-bought. Did you make these?"

"Of course. I made them earlier with Gemma and Autumn for their princess tea party." He grinned. "Gran Claire taught all her grandsons the basics. How to cook, how to dance. Some of us are better than others."

She laughed and shook her head. "Smug is not a good look on you."

His grin tipped farther into one cheek. "But it's true. Ask my brothers."

"I just might," she challenged, then finished off her other animal cookies. "Now tell me, why is it Gran Claire taught you to crochet and none of your brothers?"

He stuck his animal cookie into his mouth and grinned. "Weren't you listening? I'm the best. Gran Claire knew it."

Lacey shoved him playfully. "What's the real reason?"

He brushed his hands together and eyed her. "I never sat still. Gran Claire used to say: *if that child doesn't learn to sit still once in a blue moon, his run is going to run out before he turns eighteen.*"

Lacey chuckled.

"It's true," Caleb said, not looking the least bit put out. "She'd say it to anyone who came to the house. I was apparently an ongoing topic in her weekly crochet group."

Lacey smothered her laughter, trying not to be too loud.

"Someone—and I'm fairly certain it was Breezy Baker—suggested Gran Claire give me something to do while I was sitting." Caleb opened a bottle of root beer and held it out to her. "Turns out I can sit still if my hands are occupied."

If I held your hand, would that be enough to keep you beside me? Just for a moment? Just for right now? Because I'm happy. And I know it won't last. She sipped her root beer and gathered her words. Now wasn't the time to go chasing after her heart. "I'm quite certain the rodeo's auction will be more than pleased with your handiwork. Word around the station is that they are short on donations this year."

Before he could respond, Aspen came and plopped down on the blanket. Butterscotch stretched out beside her. "We came to watch the movie with you. Our feet and paws are tired." Aspen rolled over onto her stomach and eyed the picnic basket. "And we sure could use a snack."

"Help yourself." Caleb chuckled and slid the basket closer to Aspen. "I'm sure there is something in there that Butterscotch will like too. But keep the grapes to yourself."

"Those are bad for dogs." Aspen sorted through the basket. "Onions and chocolate too. I read about it."

"Is there an animal you haven't read about?" Caleb teased.

Aspen opened a bag of peanut-butter-filled pretzels. Her expression was thoughtful. "I like all animals. Farm animals especially."

"Why is that?" Caleb reached into the basket, took out a bag of popcorn, and tossed Butterscotch several pieces.

"I want to be a veterinarian like Riley's bonus mom, Ms. Paige, so I gotta know all about farm animals." Aspen sighed like it should have been obvious.

"Are you sure you want to be a veterinarian?" Lacey reached into the popcorn bag and scooped out a handful.

Suspicion crossed Aspen's face. "Dad told you, didn't he? Then he also told you it was just a phase."

Seemed everything with their daughter was a phase. When did it stop being a phase? Lacey feared it might be when Aspen chose something Jeffrey approved of. Lacey frowned. "Why would your dad say that?"

"'Cause we aren't farmers." Aspen tossed another pretzel into her mouth and crunched down on it.

"Doesn't mean you can't become a veterinarian and treat animals, even ones on farms," Lacey said, unless Jeffrey already had a vision for his daughter's future.

"That's what Mama-Beth told me." Aspen smiled and rolled back over to watch the movie. "I love this part of the movie. It's so funny. You gotta watch."

Lacey was too busy looking at her contented daughter and

trying not to look at the cowboy beside her. The one who made her feel pretty content herself. She warned herself not to read too much into it.

Yet the movie ended all too soon for Lacey. She stood and took in her daughter who was trying to cover up yet another yawn.

Aspen frowned. "But there's another movie."

"It's getting late, and we have lots to do tomorrow," Lacey said. "And I see Grandpa Swells headed this way. He's our ride home."

"Can't we stay a little longer?" Aspen pleaded and fought off another yawn.

Lacey saw her stepdad wave and waved back. Lacey noticed his other hand was clasped around that of a tall, elegant woman.

"Who's that with Grandpa?" Aspen jumped up and waved both arms at Wells.

Caleb stiffened beside Lacey. His words were bleak. "That's my mother."

Caleb's mother. She was there and with Wells. Not just walking beside Lacey's stepdad but appearing to be very much *with* her stepdad. But this was the woman Caleb never talked about—not even in passing when they were growing up.

Lacey turned to Caleb. "Wells mentioned he was going out to dinner when he dropped us off here. He never told me who he was going with."

Caleb nodded, plucked his hat off his head, and finger combed his hair.

"This is awkward." Lacey knocked the loose grass from her shorts.

"Awkward doesn't even begin to cover it." Caleb tapped his cowboy hat against his thigh and slanted his gaze toward Lacey. "Guess it's time to meet the parents."

CHAPTER FIFTEEN

HER FIRST DATE in more decades than she wanted to count, and Lilian Sloan felt as if she was a teenager already breaking the rules. She took in the guarded expression on her youngest son's face and slowed her steps. She'd wanted more than a cool indifference from Caleb. Well, she had Caleb's attention now. For good or ill was still to be seen.

Perhaps Caleb's obvious reservations were valid. She had no business holding hands with the handsome sheriff and strolling through the park like they did this every evening. The heavens knew Lilian had gotten relationships and love wrong before. She was supposed to be older and wiser.

"Too late for second thoughts, Doc." Wells squeezed her fingers and drew her gaze to his. "We're all but caught." He looked rather delighted, sounded rather pleased with the outcome. "If our kids hadn't seen us, well, I reckon most of Three Springs has, and word would've reached 'em soon enough."

"You don't mind?" She searched his gray eyes. The ones she had decided over dinner were steel-colored and wonderfully expressive. "You don't think we're moving a little fast?"

"At our age, we don't have the luxury of taking it slow." His gaze gleamed. "And I'm feeling things I thought I left behind long ago."

She'd always preferred a straight talker. "You're not alone

in those feelings." Lilian tightened her grip around his hand. "And this is nice. Quite nice."

"I'll take that," he said, his smile tender. "But just so you know, I'd like to see this become something special and quite lasting, if you're of a mind to agree." He raised their joined hands and pressed a soft kiss against her fingers. "But for now let's enjoy nice."

Lilian's smile sank deep inside her. "I'd like that."

"Since that's settled, it's time to quit stalling." Amusement curved across his face. "Can't leave the kids waiting."

Lilian laughed and walked with him to meet his stepdaughter and granddaughter. Her son was civil yet cautious.

Introductions concluded, Wells grinned and said, "We've decided to switch cars and take Lilian's instead. We put the top down and let the night right in beside us." Wells dropped his arm around Aspen's shoulders. "We figured Aspen would enjoy a ride in the convertible."

Aspen grinned. "Can we ride with Ms. Lilian, Mom? Please?"

"Sure." Lacey tucked her hair behind her ear. Her gaze slanted toward Caleb as if she was waiting on him for something.

But Lilian's son remained quiet and seemed far from enthusiastic about a top-down drive home.

Lilian took in a stoic Caleb, then Lacey and decided there was a definite undercurrent there. Her gaze shifted to the bandage on Lacey's forehead. Her inner doctor might be retired, but she was still alive and active. "Lacey, how is your head? No pain? Lingering side effects?"

That question snapped her son from his complacence. His focus shifted to Lacey and locked on the deputy as if she was his only concern. And that undercurrent stirred.

"It's fine. I'm fine." Lacey barely touched her bandage. "It hardly bothered me at all today."

Lilian nodded and smiled.

"Never did thank you properly for looking after Lacey yesterday." Wells turned to Caleb and extended his arm. "Sure do appreciate it."

Caleb and Lacey's stepdad shook hands. Then Lacey stepped

toward Caleb and thrust her arm out too. She said, "I never thanked you either."

Caleb considered her hand, then wrapped his fingers around hers.

Lilian was convinced she'd never seen a simple handshake look more like a promise of something more. Perhaps it was how her son held on to Lacey's hand for a beat longer than necessary. Or perhaps it was the catch of their fingertips on the release. Whatever it was, that undercurrent swelled.

Her son was back to looking guarded. And poor Lacey looked plain perplexed. Lilian supposed it didn't matter if one was young, old, or in-between, love was simply hard to get right.

Lilian smiled wide and held her arm out to Aspen. "Ready to feel the night wind in your hair?"

Aspen chewed on her bottom lip. "What about Butterscotch?"

"Butterscotch will fit perfectly between you and your mom in the back seat." Lilian reached down and rubbed the friendly dog's ears.

Wells stepped up beside Aspen and the dog. "I think Butterscotch just might love the car ride more than any of us."

Aspen took Lilian's hand and kept her grip on Butterscotch's leash. "Hear that, Butterscotch? You won't have to put your head out the window. Just put your nose in the air."

They waited for Lacey and Caleb to settle on a practice time at the Sloan stables for the next morning, then they were off. Their pace slowed to allow Butterscotch the appropriate sniffing of the fire hydrant and stop signs and whatever else caught the dog's interest. As for Lacey, with every pause, she glanced back toward the downtown square.

Stopping at a tall pine tree, Aspen asked, "Mom, can Ms. Lilian and Grandpa Swells come shopping with us tomorrow? Grandpa knows cowboys, and Lilian dresses pretty. We gotta be cowgirls, Mom."

Lacey pulled herself back to the conversation. "If they are free, they're welcome to join us." She set her hand on Aspen's shoulder. "Aspen is in the Junior Royal Rodeo Contest and wants to look her best."

"And we gotta be cowgirls," Aspen stressed, then added more emphatically, "'Cause cowboys and cowgirls go together, right?"

Lacey nodded absently and again glanced back to where a certain cowboy was standing.

Lilian considered her own hand clasped securely in the sheriff's and smiled. "I could use a pair of cowboy boots myself. I've been thinking it's time to expand my wardrobe."

Wells grinned. "I was going to stop in at the station tomorrow, but I'd be willing to meet you three for a bite to eat between stores."

"Then it's settled," Lacey stated, although still looking distracted.

"It's a shopping day for us," Lilian said. And if the topic of Caleb and Lacey as a couple came up, well, she'd take that conversation one store at a time. Surely that was good listening, not meddling. After all, she'd vowed not to interfere in her sons' lives when she moved back, and she intended on keeping her word. Still, she couldn't help but ask, "Is something wrong, dear?"

Lacey wrung her hands together, then pointed toward the square. "I forgot something."

More like someone, Lilian was willing to bet.

"I can run back and get it," Wells offered. "What'd you leave behind?"

Lacey tapped her mouth and looked away.

Lilian chuckled softly. "I think Lacey needs to find it herself."

Lacey's cheeks warmed.

"Wells and I can take Aspen and Butterscotch home." Lilian touched Wells's arm, drawing his attention to her. "And we're happy to stay until you get home, Lacey, aren't we?"

Wells scratched his cheek, considered Lilian. Then his eyebrows lifted, and his eyes widened as if reading into Lilian's unspoken words. "Absolutely. Aspen and I can show Lilian how to make our special yogurt smoothies."

"Yes!" Aspen cheered. "Those are the best."

"No need to rush, dear." Lilian squeezed Lacey's shoulder lightly and said, "Often things like these can't be found in one night. But the more time you spend together looking, you realize it was always right there in front of you."

Lilian hustled Aspen and Wells away before Lacey could disagree.

Wells leaned in and whispered, "I've got my eye on you, Doc. I know what you're up to."

"I haven't the faintest idea what you're referring to." Lilian kept her tone bland.

"And after all that talk at dinner about not messing in our kids' lives." Wells chuckled and squeezed her hand. "My doc... the matchmaker."

"I always fancied myself more of a big-city career-minded girl," Lilian replied lightly.

"I always fancied a woman who knows her mind and exactly who she is," Wells said, appreciation clear in his expression.

Lilian used to know who she was. Now, she wasn't so sure. She tucked herself closer into the sheriff's side.

But for the first time, in a long while, she thought maybe she was starting to find herself again.

CHAPTER SIXTEEN

ALONE. JUST LIKE he preferred.

Caleb watched the opening credits scroll across the giant movie screen. He pulled out his cell phone but kept the screen on lock. All that waited there was the email from the county detailing his permitting problems for the rackhouse. Nothing that could be solved until Monday when the town hall was open.

The night stretched out before him. Though the solitude that had once appealed was now oddly off-putting and slightly uncomfortable.

Of course, all he had to do was pack it up, ditch the musical rom-com movie about to play, and skip into The Feisty Owl. Then he would be far from alone among the Saturday night singles and the weekend merrymakers. They would welcome him. They always did.

He looked across the street at the brightly lit Feisty Owl sign. All he needed was a few hours inside. Then the night wouldn't seem quite so endless. And surely a line dance or two would cure him of whatever strange melancholy seized him now.

Caleb packed up the picnic basket and fastened the lid.

A pair of sandals, revealing bare toes and a thin silver ankle bracelet, stepped into his line of sight. Caleb lifted his head, skimmed his gaze over white jean shorts and a flowy light purple shirt to a pair of deep brown eyes. His grin came as easy as the anticipation inside him.

Caleb suddenly reevaluated his evening plans. "Thought you were headed home, Deputy."

"You seemed a little taken aback about your mom and Wells," she explained. "I came to check on you."

Check on you. Not to be confused with *I wanted to be with you.* Caleb's smile dimmed. He folded up the blanket. "I don't want to talk about whatever that was between Wells and my mother."

"We don't need to talk." Lacey grabbed the other end of the blanket and walked the ends to him. "But we are getting out of here."

Caleb took her ends of the blanket, being careful not to touch her. Otherwise, he might be tempted to hold her hand, same as Wells had clasped his mother's. Like a cowboy who'd found his partner and had no intention of letting go. But Caleb was more of a go-it-alone cowboy. He buried his hands in the blanket. "Where are we going?"

"I know a place." She extended her arm and flexed her fingers. "Give me your keys. I'll drive."

There was a playfulness to her soft smile. A challenge in her brown eyes. A confidence in her stance. And it was all so very appealing. *She* was so very appealing. He doubted she even knew how much.

She was asking for more time with him. He wanted the same with her. What was the harm? It wasn't any sort of permanent detour. Just a way to spend the rest of the evening. Besides, she'd piqued his curiosity. And his curiosity always got the better of him. He reached into his pocket and set his truck keys against her palm.

Lacey accepted the keys, then pressed the picnic basket into his arms. "Come on. Let's go."

Twenty minutes later, Lacey steered his truck onto a barely visible side road covered in brush and cut the engine.

Caleb glanced out the window and rubbed his chin. "This is Clearwind Lake. And the front gate is closed and locked."

"That never stopped us before." Lacey opened the truck door. "You coming or waiting here so you can hear all about it later?"

That had been their taunt to each other years ago. *You can sit back and hear about it later. Or you can join in and experience it. The choice is yours, but get a move on.*

Caleb grinned. "Do you remember where the back trail is, or do I need to show you?"

"Grab a flashlight, cowboy, and follow me." With that, Lacey hopped out.

Caleb took two flashlights from the toolbox underneath his back seat and joined Lacey on the dirt road that narrowed to a single-file trail. Soon enough they wound their way down to the shore of Clearwind Lake and then onto the dock.

At the end of the dock, Lacey slipped off her sandals, sat, and dipped her feet into the cool water. "I used to come out here a lot and wait for a shooting star to fall into the lake on the horizon."

"Gran Claire used to tell me that those shooting stars were the ones that granted wishes." Caleb sat, leaned against the last post on the dock, and propped his arm on his raised knee.

"The wish granters, she called them." Lacey swirled her bare feet in the water. "And to cover all my bases, I wished on all the stars in the sky, just in case one fell while I wasn't here."

"That was very thorough," he said.

"I was a desperate teenager."

"What were you wishing for?"

"For my mom to get better," she confessed, then lifted one shoulder. "For more time with her."

He felt himself tense and tossed a small pebble into the lake. "I didn't ever wish to be with my mom. Not once." Strange how his body relaxed at the admission. The words somehow freed him. "That's bad, isn't it?"

Lacey reached over and set her hand on his leg, just above his knee.

He considered her touch, gentle yet solid enough to tether him to the moment while the past swept around him. He set his head back against the post and stared at the stars. "I should've wished for her. Kids should want to be with their moms."

"But you had your gran Claire, your grandfather, and your

four brothers," she said, a sincerity to her words that suggested he let himself off the hook.

"All my memories start and end with them," he said. "They've always been there for me. Whenever I needed them." For so long, his brothers and grandparents had been all he ever needed. Yet now, when he looked at Lacey, he needed…

He lifted his gaze out over the dark lake waters. But he couldn't quite ignore the feel of her hand on his leg. A simple show of support. A connection he shouldn't want to encourage. "Now my mother is back in my life, and I don't know what I'm supposed to feel."

"Maybe it's not about deciding how you're supposed to feel." She shifted to face him, drawing one leg out of the water so her thigh touched his. One more link between them. Her hand never moved. "Maybe instead it's just honoring how you feel."

Like accepting that he felt more at ease right now with her than he had in years. Here, completely surrounded by the stillness of the night, which he usually avoided, but wanting nothing more than for this moment to last. "I'm starting to think my mom isn't the person I made her out to be."

"I would be surprised if she was," Lacey said, her smile brief. Her expression was all compassion and tenderness. "We all have sides we show and others we hide."

I'm hiding now. From you. Because I can't—won't—show you my heart. He searched those stars, then shifted his gaze back to hers, not surprised to find her watching him. "I need to get to know my mom and the person she is now, don't I?"

"That's a good place to start." She nodded. The motion made her hair sweep across her cheek. "Then you can decide how you really feel as the person you are, not the boy you once were."

The boy he once was had liked the girl who challenged him to keep up. But the cowboy he was felt something more than simple affection for the cowgirl sitting beside him. Yeah, he knew full well what he felt; he just wasn't certain he liked it. "What do we do about your stepdad and my mom?"

She blinked and brushed her hair off her cheek. "Nothing."

Could he do that with Lacey? Nothing?

"If they are happy, then we should let it play out," she said, sounding certain. "Not interfere."

Happy. He was perfectly happy with the way things were between him and his deputy, wasn't he? He shouldn't let something like his heart interfere with that. He pressed, "Then it doesn't bother you? Them dating."

The corners of her mouth dipped down. "It bothers me more to think of Wells unhappy and alone."

But Caleb was alone. And not unhappy. Although, he supposed, he hadn't really given his happiness much thought... until recently. He nodded. "We will let it play out then." Same as he would with his deputy.

"I don't know what's worse, how skeptical you sound or how bleak you look," Lacey said, her words teasing. She dipped her fingers in the lake and splashed him. "They're grown-ups. They can date."

He liked the sound of her laugh. The playful tilt of her head. Her candid smile. "What about you?"

"What about me?" She trailed her fingers in the water.

"You're grown up," he said. "You could date too." *Would you say yes if I asked?*

She dried her fingers on her shorts and shook her head. "I've got to concentrate on Aspen. She is my priority. I don't want anything to interfere with that."

He understood her position yet wanted to disagree.

"In fact, I should probably get home to my daughter." She picked up her sandals and put them on. "It's her first night at the ranch. Wells and your mom will want to be getting home too."

Caleb pushed away from the post and stood. Lacey was on her feet before he could offer her any assistance. He switched the flashlights on and handed her one, then they made their way back to the fence and the trail.

Inside the truck, Lacey asked, "Mind if we roll the windows down?"

Caleb obliged, lowered all the windows, and reversed out of the dirt road.

"Usually if I'm not asleep at this hour, I'm working." She

buckled her seat belt and rested her elbow on the doorframe. "But now I can enjoy the night a little while longer."

And Caleb could enjoy the picture she made. Her arm out the window, her fingers floating on the night breeze. Her head rested against the seat back. Her eyes were closed. Her face was peaceful, her barely there smile blissful. Sitting next to her inside his truck, catching glimpses of her, he realized how much he wanted to make her happy. For more than this one moment.

But he feared she wouldn't be happy with what he offered— a heart more locked down than open. Caleb concentrated on the road and left Lacey free to appreciate the night on her own terms.

Too soon, he was pulling into her driveway. Walking her to the front door. Preparing to end the moment.

Only two steps onto her front porch, she turned and thrust her arm out to him. "Good night, Caleb."

He stared at her hand for a beat, then slipped his fingers around hers. If he'd been a different cowboy, he might've eased her arm up and pressed the softest kiss against her knuckles.

Or perhaps he might've tugged gently until he could gather her up into his arms and simply hold her close.

Instead, he skimmed his thumb across her palm, watched her eyes flare slightly and her breath catch. And he wondered again what it would take to be her cowboy. But he already knew. It would cost him more than he could give.

One more caress against her skin, as if he needed the memory, and he released her. He touched his hat and retreated. Back behind those friendship barriers where hearts were safe and happiness guaranteed. "Night, Deputy."

She slipped inside without a backward glance. And then he was alone again. Just like he wanted.

He kept the truck windows down on his drive home, willing the midnight breeze to carry away his foolish thoughts. Then he turned up the radio to crowd out his sudden discontent.

He drove up the driveway, noted the dim light over the back porch of the farmhouse and the two figures waving to him. And his discontent doubled. So much for being alone.

What was it with coming home late and running into his

family? Didn't his family sleep anymore? Caleb walked around his truck and up onto the back porch where his older brothers, Carter and Grant, were sipping bourbon and talking.

"Glad you're here." Grant transferred baby Sadie into Caleb's arms and shook out his own arms from his shoulders to his wrists. "Your niece missed you."

Caleb adjusted the blanket with stars and moons and unicorns around his niece. "What are you two doing exactly?"

"Maggie fell asleep, and I didn't want to wake her," Grant explained and stretched his arms over his head as if he was warming up for a midnight jog. "So we're having a sleepover." Grant tapped Sadie softly on her nose. "Only this little one refuses to sleep."

"She's been rather insistent about being held however," Carter added, trying to sound vexed. But his doting-dad smile gave him away. "We came out here so she wouldn't wake the rest of the house."

"How long have you been out here?" Caleb asked. Sadie gave a full body yawn.

"Long enough for a glass of bourbon." Carter lifted his tumbler.

"And two servings of Tess's Black Forest cake," Grant added, not looking the least bit regretful about overindulging. "If you want any, you better get in there quick. It'll be gone by morning."

Carter touched his stomach. "We were just discussing another slice when you pulled in."

"Don't let me stop you." Caleb tipped his chin toward the back door.

"We've moved on," Grant said and considered him. "We decided we'd much rather hear about your evening. Tell us about all the fun you've been having."

What could he tell them? The venue was questionable, the reception in jeopardy unless he secured the necessary permits. Not going there. He could tell them that he hated handshakes. Or more specifically, handshakes with a certain deputy. That would ignite too many questions.

Caleb paced around the porch, then turned back to them. "Did either of you know Mom was seeing Sheriff Hopson?"

"Mom is dating…" Grant dropped into a chair beside Carter and stared into his tumbler as if searching for his response. Finally, he nodded. "I always liked Wells Hopson."

"I don't think Mom is looking for your approval." Caleb frowned.

"She has my support." Carter sipped his bourbon. "I always liked Wells too."

"This is not about liking Wells Hopson," Caleb charged, then lowered his voice at the baby's wrinkled brow.

"What is it about then?" Grant asked and exchanged a look with Carter. Grant set his elbows on his knees and studied Caleb as if he was one of his brother's patients withholding information. His grin finally came. "You don't like the idea of Mom with Wells because of Lacey."

Carter nodded and murmured his agreement. "That makes sense."

"What does Lacey have to do with this?" Caleb asked and rocked Sadie.

Grant and Carter exchanged another silent look. Grant shrugged, his words simple and direct to better emphasize the obvious. "You like her. That's what Lacey has to do with this."

"And I suppose it's weird to have your mother dating your girlfriend's stepdad," Carter mused and swirled the single ice cube in his tumbler.

Girlfriend. Caleb looked at the baby in his arms as if she could rescue him. She gurgled and kicked her legs and fisted her tiny fingers. *Good advice, little one. I need to fight.* "Lacey and I aren't dating. The only label we have is friends."

His brothers completely ignored him. Grant tapped his tumbler against Carter's glass and said, "I suppose it could be weird, but it is not a deal-breaker."

"Definitely not a deal-breaker," Carter agreed.

The deal-breaker was his two older brothers and their misconceptions. Caleb thrust his hand through his hair and kept swaying for Sadie's benefit. "I'm not dating. But thinking about Mom dating doesn't feel right."

"Why not?" Carter shook his head. "It's not like we're kids and wanting Mom and Dad to reconcile."

"Yeah, that ship sailed decades ago," Grant said flatly.

"More like sank," Carter quipped. "When they divorced."

"It's not that," Caleb argued. "I don't know how to explain it." Other than he thought of his mother as perpetually single, like himself. Determined to prove they could face the world on their own—no partner required. Because a closed heart was better than a broken one.

Grant made one of those annoying *hmm* sounds as if that summed up everything.

Caleb narrowed his gaze on his brother yet tried to relax his body for Sadie's sake. "What does that mean?"

"It's simple." Grant waved his hand toward Caleb, a satisfied gleam in his gaze. "If Mom finds someone, you really will be the last single Sloan."

"But he has Lacey," Carter offered as if suddenly eager to help.

"I don't have Lacey," Caleb countered. "And I don't mind being single. The last one *or* the only one." Was that a crack he heard in his voice? Like he lacked conviction? Impossible.

Grant steepled his fingers under his chin and looked thoughtful. "Little brother, who exactly are you trying to fool?"

"I'm serious," Caleb said. He had Lacey's friendship, and if he wanted more, well, that was only a momentary lapse, wasn't it? In the morning, the moment would have passed, and he'd be on to the next thing. Without his deputy. "If I was with Lacey, why would I let her set me up with someone else?"

"Wait." Carter held up his hand and blinked at Caleb as if clearing his head. "Lacey is setting you up?"

"She claims she can find me the perfect cowgirl." As if she existed. Okay, she might. And she could very well be his deputy. But that wasn't the point. Caleb winced. "It was all part of a wager we made."

"And you agreed to be matched up?" Grant smoothed his fingers over his mouth, but the dismay was there on his face.

"It's not like she's going to succeed." Tonight's movie date fiasco was a prime example. Caleb had been more than a little relieved when Eryn had texted him about running into Matt. So relieved he'd encouraged her to go enjoy her evening. Caleb asked, "Why do you think I took the bet in the first place?"

Grant's words bordered on grim. "You never bet against love, little brother."

"Love," Caleb sputtered. "This has nothing to do with love."

"It's always about love, even when it's not." Carter stretched out his legs and yawned.

Now the two of them sounded like Ryan. Caleb should *not* be surprised.

"He's right." Grant was solemn.

"This from two cowboys who are so blinded by love all you see are rainbows and unicorns," Caleb said. Same as Ryan. And his twin, Josh.

"I'm not complaining." Grant shrugged a second time. "I always liked rainbows."

Caleb swallowed his groan.

"I like my view. It suits me." Carter propped his boots on the coffee table as if he wanted to get even more comfortable and eyed Caleb. "But you, little brother, seem to be the only one all riled up tonight. Maybe you should try on our love-tinted lenses."

"It's impossible to have a conversation with you two," Caleb muttered.

"You just don't like what you're hearing." Grant sipped his bourbon and considered Caleb over the rim of his glass. "But being the very supportive older brothers that we are, we feel it's our duty to say it anyway."

"You've made your point." Caleb frowned and sped up his rocking for his niece.

Carter and Grant chuckled, then toasted each other again as if pleased with their results.

"Speaking of things I don't like hearing," Carter started. "What is this about a dandelion wine tasting party?"

"You mean the dandelion wine event," Caleb said, glad for the change in topic. "It's nothing. It's for Grandpa and Uncle. I've spoken to Ryan. We're hosting it out at the greenhouses on Elsie and Ryan's farm."

Carter paused. "You really think you have time for that with everything else?"

"It's a simple party," Caleb said, working that missing conviction back into his words. "Nothing to it. Besides, if I don't do it, Grandpa Sam and Uncle Roy plan to serve dandelion wine at Josh and Vivian's reception."

Carter frowned.

Grant laughed. "Nice save, little brother."

"That's what I do well—improvise and think on my feet." Caleb grinned. "Now that my niece is back to sleep, my work here is done too." Caleb handed a snoozing Sadie back to her dad and said, "Believe it or not, Carter, I've got this."

Carter nodded and said, "And I still have a tent ready as the wedding reception backup plan. Let me know when you need it."

"I won't," Caleb assured him. "Like I keep telling you, I have everything in hand."

With that, Caleb walked into the farmhouse, picked up the last of the Black Forest cake from the counter, and strolled back outside. He was off the porch, cake container in hand, before Grant and Carter caught on. Wishing his brothers sweet dreams, after assuring them he was only looking after their health, he headed to his apartment.

He was confident he had the wedding reception and rehearsal in hand. Or he would as soon as he solved the permit problem. The very one he'd discovered when he checked his email after Eryn ditched him during the first movie. Turned out the rackhouse needed to meet fire codes and other building restrictions to be fully permitted as a multi-use venue space. Caleb needed that muti-use venue space at the distillery to prove to his brother he had both vision and the ability to handle the marketing director position. He'd been working through possible solutions for the rackhouse when his deputy showed up and he chose to be distracted.

Now all he knew for sure was that if his deputy offered him one more handshake, he just might kiss her instead. But he feared there would be no walking away after that.

CHAPTER SEVENTEEN

LACEY LIFTED HER face toward the summer sun beaming down on her inside Lilian Sloan's stylish convertible. She let the wind tangle her hair and soaked in Aspen's enthusiastic back-seat radio sing-along. She even joined in for a verse or two, earning Aspen and Lilian's approval.

If only Caleb could see her now—having fun, finding her happy. Like he'd suggested she do last night.

Well, it was a new day. Aspen had ridden alone with Caleb beside her on his horse during their morning practice. Lacey had watched her daughter's confidence grow with every turn around the indoor arena. That feeling of contentment from the night before filled Lacey all over again.

"Everyone ready to shop until they drop?" Lilian parked her car in the public parking lot in downtown Belleridge and pressed a button on the dashboard to lift the convertible top back in place. "What does a cowgirl wear for the Junior Royal Rodeo Contest?"

"I gotta have a white shirt, jeans, and boots." Aspen unbuckled her seat belt. "Caleb already got Mom and me hats."

"She also needs to dress up her jeans for the speech and group interview portion of the contest," Lacey explained.

Aspen wrinkled her nose at the mention of the speech.

"I scouted the boutiques and boot store online last night." Lilian dropped her key fob into her purse and climbed out. "Several should have Aspen's size."

Aspen scooted along the back seat. "Mom needs stuff too."

"I'm good." Lacey helped Aspen out of the two-door car and smiled at her daughter. "Today is about you."

"But you told Caleb you were gonna ride next time. No matter what he said." Aspen set her hands on her hips. "And you told Grandpa Swells you could use new boots. I heard you."

Lacey met Lilian on the sidewalk. "Steel-toe boots seem to be all I own." Along with a pair of old sandals and worn running shoes. Khaki uniforms and monotone colors rounded out her closet. Nothing overly fun there.

"I understand." Lilian pointed at her feet and wiggled her toes inside her strappy sandals. "I've been discovering the joy of a flirty sundress and sassy sandals now that I've traded in the scrubs and white coat."

"I've been in neutrals so long I can't remember what my style is," Lacey admitted.

"I suggest a little of everything," Lilian said. "Then you put on whatever fits your mood and makes you feel your best."

Feel my best. She wanted that. More, she wanted her mood to stay right where it was now. She linked one arm around Lilian's and the other around her daughter's. "Ladies, it's time to let our inner cowgirls shine."

Aspen cheered, and the shopping spree was on.

Successfully finding all the required clothing and a few extra outfits was relatively easy, thankfully, and eventually, they made their way to the final store of the afternoon, Horseshoes and Boots. Just inside the entrance, Aspen promised to find Lacey the prettiest boots and sprinted down an aisle to begin her quest.

Lacey watched Lilian act demurely again when another local stopped to greet her and mentioned that she had seen Lilian with the sheriff the other night. It had happened in practically every store. Someone commenting on what a charming couple Lilian and the sheriff made. Or how nice it was to see the sheriff out with Lilian. And Lilian, for her part, was gracious if slightly flustered. But Lilian Sloan didn't strike Lacey as a woman who flustered easily.

"I could use your advice on boots," Lacey said and earned a grateful glance from Lilian, who wished the woman a good day and walked beside Lacey down the wide aisle. The shelves were filled with boots from top to bottom.

"Wells tells me that you and he are an item," Lacey said casually.

"We haven't labeled things between us." Lilian held up a pair of pink cowboy boots. "Too much?"

Lacey nodded yet refused to be diverted. "Does Wells know you aren't at the labeling stage?"

"We're taking it slow," Lilian hedged, then showed off a pair of vivid teal boots.

Lacey shook her head. "It's funny because just this morning, Wells told me you've been texting and doing that video call thing every day." Lacey picked up a plain brown boot. "Rather late into the night, in fact."

A blush colored Lilian's cheeks. She took the boot from Lacey and set it back on the shelf. "One would think he and I were teenagers all over again."

"I can tell you that he's really happy." Lacey stopped and met Lilian's gaze. "And Wells hasn't been happy for a long time. I think that happiness is thanks to you."

"I'm sure it's having you home again," Lilian countered, yet her small smile hinted that Lacey's words pleased her. "Now you and Wells are working together."

"It's perhaps partly from my return," Lacey conceded. "But you've put a certain twinkle into his gaze."

Lilian touched her cheek and laughed. "I'm not sure I've been accused of that before."

"Does it bother you?" Lacey asked, searching Lilian's face. She could see why Dr. Sloan had captured her stepdad's attention. Lilian was not only attractive, she had poise and confidence too. Not to mention a warmth that Lacey herself seemed to be getting accustomed to.

"This is nothing I expected to find when I moved back," Lilian confessed.

"What did you come back for?" Lacey asked.

"I suspect the very same thing as you." Lilian dipped her

head toward Aspen down at the end of the aisle. "Family called me home. It was past time to make amends."

Lacey nodded. She knew all about making amends. She accepted two boot boxes from Aspen with instructions to try them on. She waited until Aspen was out of earshot before asking, "How is that going? You being home and making amends."

"There have been speed bumps," Lilian said. "That's to be expected. My sons aren't the boys I walked away from."

"Aspen isn't that same little girl anymore either." Lacey watched her daughter run her fingertips over one pair of sample boots after another. "I'm worried I'm giving in too much. Giving her everything she wants to make those amends. Worried it's too easy. Worried I'm getting it wrong, that I'm going to mess it up all over again."

Lilian chuckled. "I can guarantee you'll mess it up again."

"That's not very reassuring." Lacey hugged the boot boxes.

"I prefer to deal in facts." Lilian tugged a boot box from the shelf and placed it on top of Lacey's. "None of us are perfect. At best, we get perfect moments that add up to something special."

Lacey had spent perfect moments with Caleb and Aspen recently. In the arena together. In the truck, laughing and teasing. Then alone at the lake with Caleb. She sat down on a chair. "What if I can't trust in those moments?"

"Then I'd say we have even more in common than I first thought." Lilian dropped into the chair beside Lacey and kicked off her sandals. She leaned her shoulder against Lacey's and said, "Perhaps we can figure it out together."

"I'd like that," Lacey said and picked up the first boot box from Aspen.

Lacey missed her mom. It had been more than a minute since she had opened up to anyone. Now she had shared with not one but two Sloans in a matter of days. Still, she appreciated Lilian for her candor and support. Same as she appreciated Caleb for his friendship.

And that was what she wanted—his friendship. Despite feeling like those handshakes she'd shared with him recently had been somehow "less than." They had left her wanting more. Like a kiss. Unrushed and under the stars. *Foolish thought, that.*

Lacey lifted the lid on the box and quickly swallowed her laughter. "But first we need to figure out how to tell my daughter that sparkles and rhinestones are not quite the style upgrade I had in mind."

"It glitters brighter than a disco ball." Lilian lifted one of the red rhinestone high-heeled boots from the box. "*You* may want less sparkle, but I do believe I just might need more. May I?"

Lacey smiled and handed the box to Lilian. "Aspen will be thrilled."

As it turned out, Lacey kept to a traditional cowboy boot but chose a rich indigo color. The intricate stitching covering the deep blue suede shaft that reached mid-calf added extra flair according to the salesperson. And Aspen and Lilian convinced her the denim color would go with her new dresses.

As for Lilian and Aspen, they both opted for more flare in their step. Lilian kept her pearl bedecked and rose gold metallic trimmed boots in the box. Aspen wore her new boots right out of the store. After she excitedly declared the glittery gold starbursts on the boot shafts were good luck and the deep pink on the stitching her favorite color ever.

Outside on the sidewalk, Lilian checked the time on her phone. "We can do one more stop before we have to meet Wells at the All-Day Corner Diner for an early dinner."

"I don't think my hands can carry any more shopping bags." Aspen kept her arms down at her sides.

"We're done shopping," Lilian announced and started down the sidewalk. "It's time for some pampering. I can't think of a better way to celebrate our success than manicures and pedicures."

Lacey checked her fingernails. "I can't remember the last time I put nail polish on."

"Put clear on if you'd prefer." Lilian held open the door to the nail salon. "But this is my treat for letting me tag along today."

"Mama-Beth goes to a place like this." Aspen walked inside, her eyes wide. "Mama-Beth says it puts a spring back in her toes."

"We could all use more spring in our step." Lilian checked

in with the receptionist who led Aspen and Lilian to the nail booth together.

Lacey followed a friendly nail technician to the only vacant spot in the row of pedicure chairs. Within minutes, Lacey's feet were soaking in the warm whirlpool bath and her entire body was relaxing. She was starting to see the appeal.

Lacey was about to doze off when the doors to the salon opened and a pair of lively and familiar retirees swept in. The Baker sisters exchanged hugs with the staff and complimented the customers on their fashionable looks.

Gayle Baker caught sight of Lacey and bustled over. "Nice to see you sprucing yourself up, Deputy."

"We have the perfect event to supercharge your social life." Breezy handed Lacey a colorful flyer. "Mark your calendar, dear, for this Wednesday. We've already tapped several cowboys for you."

"Simple meet and greets." Gayle's eyebrow lifted over her glasses, revealing her light purple eye shadow. "Nothing formal. Bring your new dog, and everything will feel even more natural."

Lacey glanced at the flyer for the Last Dog Day of Summer. An annual event for dogs to show off their agility and style, make new four-legged friends, and win prizes. In the corner, she noted that the special emcee was none other than Caleb Sloan.

The woman beside Lacey lifted the flyer Breezy gave her and whispered, "They remind me of my own grandmother." The flyer flickered as the woman peeked around it to track the Baker sisters in action. "I wonder if they are in cahoots with my grandmother."

Lacey laughed. The Baker sisters did a circuit around the haircutting stations, passing out flyers like free candy before sashaying back to Lacey's chair.

Gayle tapped a metallic yellow fingernail against her lips and grinned. "I do like your color choice for nail polish, dear." The woman beside Lacey chuckled and wiggled her fingers polished with a similar sunflower yellow. Gayle continued, "I'm quite sure there will be a cowboy at the dog festival to catch your fancy too."

"Do you have a dog, dear?" Breezy plucked at her short, bold white hair.

"It's not a requirement." Gayle rocked back and forth in her rubber clogs. "You could simply tell 'em you're just shopping."

"For a cowboy and a canine companion." Breezy nudged Gayle and burst into laughter. "Best kind of two-for-one around if you ask me."

Lacey laughed too. She couldn't help it.

The woman beside Lacey chuckled and said, "I do have a dog that I was planning on bringing."

"Then you'll be there." Gayle beamed and squeezed in between the two chairs. "What's your name, dear?"

The woman shook the Baker sisters' hands and said, "I'm Georgia Moure."

Lacey lowered the flyer and shifted to take in the woman beside her. "Georgia Moure from Three Springs High School, home of the Prairie Dogs?"

The woman tipped her head and studied Lacey. "Oh my. Lacey Nash." Georgia gasped, then laughed. "I can't believe we've been sitting here for this long and didn't recognize each other."

"It's all that foil in Georgia's hair." Breezy peered at Georgia and shook her head. "Can't even tell what color her hair really is."

"Still, we should've recognized each other," Lacey said. "We spent our junior and senior years working together at Double Dutch Donut Shop, glazing and topping dozens and dozens of donuts."

"I haven't eaten a donut since high school." Georgia chuckled. "I think my clothes and my hair just stopped smelling like burnt donuts last year."

"I thought the same." Lacey laughed. "What have you been doing?"

Lacey and Georgia spent the next hour getting caught up. Georgia was a local general contractor with a list of adventures under her belt longer than Caleb's. She dabbled in breakaway roping when time allowed. And from the hilarious stories she shared, she didn't take herself too seriously.

The more they talked, the more Lacey realized Georgia was Caleb's ideal cowgirl. Georgia could help him with the building permitting issues he'd told Lacey about earlier. Even more, Georgia practically *was* Caleb, from their shared nature to their carefree outlook to their mutual love of the rodeo. Georgia was *the* cowgirl to his cowboy.

Excited, Lacey pulled out her phone and texted Caleb to see if he was still in town. He'd mentioned needing to meet with the caterer and run a few errands for his grandfather's event.

His reply came quickly. He was around the corner, just finishing with the caterer. Luck was on her side.

Lacey paid, checked on Aspen and Lilian who were still drying their toenails, and stepped outside to meet Caleb to give him her news.

When he rounded the corner and caught sight of her, that slow half grin lifting into his cheek—the one she thought of as for her only—she wanted nothing more than to launch herself into his arms. And claim him as her cowboy. Lacey blanched.

Her cowboy kept coming toward her. His gaze fixed on her.

Her heart raced. *He's mine.* No, that was wrong. All wrong.

He closed the distance. Almost in launching range. Two quick steps and one leap. He would catch her. She knew it. But catching a cowboy had never been her goal.

He finally reached her.

Lacey tempered herself, tucked her arms at her sides, and kept a friendly space between them. "I have good news. I found a solution to your permit issues for the rackhouse reception space and located your perfect cowgirl." *It's not me.* Her heart pounded. *But we already knew that.*

"Wow." He crossed his arms over his chest. "That's quite the productive day."

"It was," she said.

Something like disappointment flashed in his gaze.

Lacey shut down her imagination and adjusted those blinders back over her heart. Then rolled on, "Anyway, I ran into a friend from high school. Georgia Moure is a contractor with experience at getting town hall officials to permit old buildings."

"That is good news." Caleb nodded, his expression guarded.

The salon door opened, and Georgia stepped outside. Her blond hair floated around her shoulders before she propped a cowboy hat on her head, shadowing her pretty face.

No turning back now. Lacey smiled wider. "And here she is now." Lacey drew Georgia over for introductions.

"If you are free now, I'd be happy to discuss converting your rackhouse into an event venue and see if I can help." Georgia oozed authenticity and genuine kindness that only made her more attractive.

Lacey tried not to fidget and fix her own hair.

Before Caleb could respond, Lilian and Aspen were there. Aspen rushed to hug Caleb and show off her nails.

Lilian flashed her phone. "Wells just texted that our table is ready at the diner."

"Perfect timing," Lacey said, making sure her smile was perfect. Her words perfect. Because it was all so very perfect. Caleb and his perfect cowgirl. Just like she'd imagined. "We'll just be going and leave you two to get to know each other."

Caleb held Lacey's gaze for a beat, rubbed his hand over his cheek, then he grinned at Georgia. "I happen to have some time now. The Four Fiddlers shouldn't be too loud this early."

"Great." Georgia hugged Lacey with a promise to see her at the Dog Day event on Wednesday.

And like that, the perfect cowboy pair walked away.

Lacey tried to stay upbeat. "Ladies, I am starving, and I'm suddenly in the mood for a triple chocolate fudge brownie milkshake."

Aspen glanced over her shoulder. Her frown puckered her eyebrows. "Why didn't you invite Caleb to come with us? He likes milkshakes. He told me so."

"Caleb has work he needs to do." Lacey took a step in the direction of the diner, hoping the others would do the same. "And my friend Georgia is going to help him."

Aspen cast one more glance over her shoulder. "You shoulda worn your cowboy hat and boots, Mom."

"Why is that?" Lacey asked.

"'Cause cowboys and cowgirls go together," Aspen said.

Yes, they certainly did. Cowboys like Caleb belonged with

perfect cowgirls like Georgia. And if her own heart hurt just a little at that thought, well, that was nothing for a onetime cowgirl like Lacey to simply dust off.

CHAPTER EIGHTEEN

CALEB'S MOOD WAS SOUR. It had started to turn three days ago when his deputy thrust his perfect cowgirl at him on the sidewalk in Belleridge and strolled away without a backward glance—or, it seemed, even a second thought. And his mood had been on a steady decline ever since.

The wine tasting event was proving more labor-intensive than he'd assumed. He still couldn't reach his twin, and the caterer, KC, needed a color theme to ensure he could get the linens on time. That meant a check of Vivian's notebook, but it was back at his place. One more thing for his rapidly expanding to-do-later list. Same as finalizing the menus for all events. But he wasn't about to reverse course now.

So here he was inside the rackhouse, waiting on Georgia Moure and her electrician to give him an update about the needed repairs. *Let it be good news.* Noting the pair was still in deep discussion on the other side of the vast space, he leaned against an empty bourbon barrel, pulled out his cell phone, and checked his text messages.

His mood flatlined.

The first text was a picture of Aspen, Lacey, his grandfather, and uncle sipping root beer floats at the ice cream parlor and looking more than joyful.

Caleb had had to cancel on Aspen the last two days. Fortunately, his uncle and grandpa had stepped in to help Lacey work with Aspen in the arena. But Caleb wanted to be the one to teach Aspen. To be there with Lacey. Spending time with the mother-daughter duo was the only place he'd wanted to be since Lacey left him on that sidewalk.

If ever there was a warning sign he was in way too deep, it was flashing at him now. He shoved his phone into his pocket, then joined Georgia and the electrician. He shook the electrician's hand, thanked him for his time, and watched him leave. He turned to Georgia. "Tell me this can be fixed."

"Your current electrical can be updated to satisfy the permitting requirements," Georgia said.

Caleb had liked the general contractor instantly from her straight talk to her quick action. He grinned. Finally, good news.

"But it's going to cost you." Georgia tore a paper off her clipboard, folded it, and handed it to him. "Maybe have a glass of bourbon in your hand when you read the estimate."

Caleb stuck the paper in his shirt pocket and walked outside with her to her truck. "My only concern is whether you can have the work completed and inspected in time for the wedding."

"If you've got the funds—" Georgia opened her truck door and turned back to him "—then your brother will have his reception in the rackhouse, not the tent."

"That's all I needed to know." Caleb shook her hand quickly and headed for his truck.

His phone buzzed again. More pictures filled the screen. This time it was Lacey on his Arabian Denny, riding bareback, her smile pure joy.

Caleb's mood dipped again. He knew full well that Lacey didn't need looking after, not even on a horse. But that didn't stop him from wanting to be with her all the same, watching out for his deputy. As if she was his to look out for. But that wasn't what Lacey wanted.

As for what he wanted… Those warning signals flared again. *Take the contractor out. Move on like you always do. It's what Lacey said to do.* He called out to Georgia. Her truck door was still open, and her boots rested on the truck frame.

Georgia glanced up from her phone and smiled.

She was pretty, he noticed. A true cowgirl from her scuffed cowboy boots to her well-worn hat. *Ask her out.* He rolled the words around in his mouth. Tested them out. "Anything else I should be worried about?" *Aside from my heart. Which I might be losing to my deputy.*

Georgia laughed. "Other than some minor repairs on the structure, I think we're going to be good."

Caleb nodded. If only he could claim the same for his heart. He hopped into his truck and called out, "See you tonight at Dog Days."

Georgia waved him off with a "see you there."

EMCEEING THE LAST DOG DAY event proved the distraction Caleb needed to keep his thoughts off his deputy. If only it had been more than a temporary reprieve. As it was, he'd gotten a brief hug from Aspen and a slobbery greeting from Butterscotch during a break between the agility competition and the contest for the dog face that only a mother could love. He'd caught glimpses of his deputy, still in her uniform, talking and mingling with the locals. It wasn't nearly enough.

Finally, dusk gave way to night, the last award was given out, and his emcee duties concluded. The dogs were let off leash to enjoy the temporarily fenced-in park, and the crowd lingered. Now was his chance to get to his deputy.

Caleb had Lacey in his sights but found himself waylaid by the fire chief and his family. Then by Kellie Pratt and her son, who wanted Caleb to sign his cast. Followed by friends he knew from working the rodeo.

With every delay, he watched Lacey slip farther away. And finally, Georgia stopped him. Her crew was ready to begin work at the rackhouse on Friday, which allowed for one week to finish the space. All Georgia needed was for Caleb to meet her and her crew there to let them inside Friday morning.

It was then that he saw a familiar dog bolt for the open gate on the far side of the park, followed quickly by a familiar red-haired woman in uniform. Caleb told Georgia to text him a time for Friday and took off after his deputy.

He found Lacey on her hands and knees in front of a section of tall bushes and trees.

"Need some help, Deputy?"

Lacey glanced over her shoulder. Relief passed across her face before she turned back to peer between the branches. "Butterscotch got spooked. I think it was all the chaos with the other dogs." Lacey set the dog leash beside her and sweetly called out Butterscotch's name.

The bushes didn't move.

Lacey frowned. "She's not budging. What should we do?"

"We sit with her." Caleb sat down and patted the grass beside him. "And we wait until Butterscotch is ready to come to us."

Lacey wiped her hands on her pants. "You don't have to wait with me."

"I must admit Butterscotch found a good spot." Caleb stretched his legs out. "The Last Dog Day is a bit more energetic than I recalled. I don't mind taking a moment." *With you.*

"You looked like you were in your element judging and emceeing, then leading the dog parade." She bumped her shoulder against his but didn't lean against him like he would've preferred. "You worked the crowd well and encouraged even more adoptions."

"I enjoyed it." He tipped his hat lower on his head. "In fact, I'm starting to appreciate these sorts of moments a lot." *But only the ones spent with you.* He cleared his throat. "Where is Aspen?"

"Wells took her to the diner. They wanted grilled cheese sandwiches." Lacey glanced at the bushes. "You could still catch up with them if you want to."

Oh no. His deputy wasn't chasing him off that easily. He was finally alone with her. He propped his arms behind him and leaned back. "I hear some rustling in the branches behind us. I can't leave now and risk startling Butterscotch again."

Lacey nodded silently, and her shoulders lowered. Whether she was relieved he was staying or that the dog might be coming out was up for debate.

He decided to press and find out. After all, if he opted to dive deep into the quicksand of his so-called *feels*, he sure as certain wasn't going to go it alone. Not that he had fully committed to that kind of dive quite yet. Still, it was time to find out if he'd possibly sidetracked her too. "You were right about Georgia."

Lacey yanked a weed from the grass. "That's good to hear."

Is it? She sounded far from pleased with his admission. "Georgia is quite possibly the perfect cowgirl."

There went another weed and a handful of grass. "That's why I introduced you." Her words were clipped as if stuck between her clenched teeth. "That's who I promised to find you, and I did."

But was it still only about the wager for her? Sure, the wager had given him an excuse to spend more time with Lacey. But now it wasn't the wager that kept him beside her. "Did you know Georgia just came back from a camping trip where the whole group took their horses? They rode into a remote area, camped, and went white water rafting." Caleb kept his words easy and light. "I've always wanted to do something like that."

She smashed the weed in her fingers. "I'm sure you two will have a lot of fun times together."

Except the fun I want to have is with you. The rustling started up again behind them. Caleb set his hand on Lacey's leg.

Her gaze jumped to his, but the night sky cast too many shadows across her face to read her usually expressive eyes. Still, he heard her soft inhale. Felt her relax beneath his steady touch. He whispered, "Don't move. Butterscotch is coming closer."

His words were no sooner out than a wet nose pressed against his skin, and a blond furry head burrowed underneath his arm.

Lacey grinned. Her shoulders shook. "Looks like someone else wants your attention."

Caleb straightened and showered Butterscotch with pats while Lacey clipped her leash back on. One problem solved. But what to do about his deputy?

"Butterscotch!" That cheerful shout came from Aspen.

Lacey let the dog run to Aspen. The young girl dropped to her knees to greet the dog with a whole-body hug. Lacey and Caleb walked to join Wells.

"Lacey, we need to get back on duty." Wells looked grim. "Two cars collided with an electric pole in Llyne. Knocked out the power to most of the town. Multiple accidents have been reported."

In a blink, Lacey went from relaxed and easygoing to alert and ready. Until her gaze landed on her daughter, who was rolling in the grass with Butterscotch.

Caleb touched Lacey's arm. "I can take Aspen home and wait with her."

"You don't have to." But Lacey shook her head as if realizing she had no other options. Her father was headed to Llyne too. Her ex-husband and his wife were out of town.

"I want to," Caleb urged. *Please rely on me. Let me show you I can be who you need.* That put him precariously close to the edge of those so-called *feels*. He met her gaze and said softly, "You have to get to work, Deputy. There are people who need you."

She opened her arms as if she wanted to hug him, then dropped them just as quickly. "Text me if anything comes up."

"Aspen and I are good," he assured her. "We've got a speech to write and shows to binge-watch."

"The binge-watching will be easy." Worry crossed her face, and she added, "But I'm not so sure about that speech part. She's been resistant whenever I bring it up."

"I'll see what I can do." Caleb walked with Lacey over to Aspen and Butterscotch.

"Thanks for this," Lacey said. "You're a really good…"

Do not say friend. Caleb held her gaze, willing her to find another word. Any other word.

She rolled her lips together, sighed, and said, "Just…thanks for this." Then she spun around, hugged Aspen, and explained the situation.

Caleb smiled. He would take that. And hope the night ended on an even more positive note than a handshake. Because then he just might start to believe he wasn't about to take that deep dive all alone.

CHAPTER NINETEEN

CALEB WAS AT the front door, propping it open before Lacey's boots touched the porch. He was holding a steaming mug and looked rested. Lacey held on to the image, memorized it for the days when she might need it.

But her cowboy wasn't supposed to be a part of her daily life. Not like this. Not as the person she always leaned on. The one she always looked to. She slowed her steps.

"Evening, Deputy." He pressed the mug into her hands, guided her inside, and whispered, "Aspen is asleep on the couch. Can I make you something to eat?"

Lacey shook her head. It was too much. Too homey. Her daughter curled up under a blanket on the sofa. Her cowboy beside her to help her decompress. It was everything she could want. Everything she could pretend was hers. It was like coming home to her own family—the one she always envisioned.

But she'd messed all that up before. How could she trust she'd get it right now? Lacey wrapped her hands around the hot mug and took a deep sip of the honey-sweetened tea.

Aspen sat up and rubbed her eyes. "Mom? Caleb?"

"I'm here." Lacey set her mug on the coffee table and sat on the edge of the couch. "I'm home. How about we get you to bed?"

Aspen yawned, wrapped the blanket around her shoulders, and stood up. She shuffled over to Caleb and hugged him tight.

Her whispered words were too hushed for Lacey to hear. She watched Caleb's grin, heard his "you got it," then watched the pair share a pinky promise.

Once more she felt that pull inside her. The one that wanted to step into his arms and share a group hug with the pair.

Suddenly Aspen pulled away, handed Caleb the blanket, and hurried back to the family room. She slipped on a pair of purple-tinted clear-framed eyeglasses that Lacey hadn't seen before and snatched up a different pair from the coffee table. Her words were sleepy. "Don't forget these, Caleb. Your eyes need them."

"Thanks." Caleb slipped the black frames into his front shirt pocket and wound the blanket back around Aspen.

It wasn't the eyeglasses on her daughter's face that set Lacey back.

Her daughter had fallen for Caleb. She was certain of it now.

Lacey had been so concerned about protecting her own heart, she hadn't been paying attention to Aspen's. She had to pull back for both their sakes.

"Come on, Mom," Aspen said through her yawn. "You gotta tuck me in."

Lacey blinked and followed her daughter to her bedroom. With her eyeglasses tucked into a case in the nightstand drawer, Aspen burrowed underneath the blankets and cuddled Dash, her favorite horse stuffed animal. Lacey gave her daughter one more kiss on the forehead, then slipped out.

She found Caleb in the kitchen, leaning against the counter. "All good?"

"She was asleep before I got out of her room." Lacey retrieved her tea and carried it into the kitchen. "How did you know? About Aspen's eyeglasses. I didn't."

"I had a hunch after she wouldn't look over the contest rules with me." He shrugged one shoulder. "I never liked wearing my glasses when I got them in high school. I did all my reading in my room where no one saw me wearing them."

"I should've known." About her daughter's glasses. About her daughter getting attached. Lacey rubbed her hand over the small scar on her forehead. Suddenly exhausted.

"Jeffrey probably thought Aspen told you," Caleb said. "And Aspen probably figured you knew."

"I should've guessed about the glasses." Seen the bond her daughter was forming with him. Lacey sighed. "Or noticed her case. Something." Anything that would've warned her to step in before it was too late.

"You know now." Caleb lifted the kettle from the stove and refilled her mug. "And it's not a big deal. You would've found out eventually."

He was right, and yet Lacey struggled to let it go. But that was the problem, wasn't it? She was struggling to let her cowboy go. But this was Caleb Sloan. Her all-play, no-commitment cowboy. Losing her heart to him would be a misstep she might not recover from.

Panic sent her pulse into a fast beat. Her words rushed out, bumping into each other. "You should go. I've kept you long enough. Asked too much of you already."

He set the kettle on the stove and turned to look at her. "You haven't asked anything of me yet. I offered to help."

"Still, it's late." *And you look like someone I could lean on right now. For just a minute until I get my feet back under me.* He would hold her too. She knew that deep inside her. Also knew it might be impossible to remember that it was only temporary. But she was responsible for two hearts now.

He closed the distance between them, reached up, and tucked her hair back behind her ear. His fingers barely skimmed the small bandage on her forehead. His words were gentle, his tender gaze almost her undoing. "You're right. You need to get some sleep. I can let myself out."

Or you could let me hold you. We could hold each other. But what would happen when he let her go and took her heart with him? And he would. Caleb Sloan had always claimed he was too restless to stay put long, while Lacey meant to put down roots and stick around for good. She crossed her arms over her chest. "What about you? Don't cowboys sleep?"

"Not this one." He pulled out his truck keys and grinned. "I've still got some run left in me before I call it a night."

But her cowboy had slowed down with her. Never seemed to mind either. Lacey shut down that thought. That was only her heart fooling her into believing she could change a cowboy. She picked up her tea rather than reach for him. "Night, Caleb."

He touched the brim of his hat. "Tell me you're still coming to the dandelion wine tasting event on Saturday. Grandpa Sam and Uncle Roy will be upset if you cancel."

"I'll be there," she said. "Early too. I promised Sam and Roy I'd keep an eye on you."

That drew his full smile. "Is that so?"

"Apparently they are concerned about your decorating aesthetic," she replied dryly. "It's an exclusive event, you know. They want it to feel special."

"I won't let them down," he promised and headed for the door. "Hey, Deputy, don't forget to lock up behind me." With that, he was gone.

Lacey turned the dead bolt on the door, switched off the lights, and headed to her bedroom. A quick check on Aspen, then she showered, climbed into bed, and finally secured her heart.

After all, if she gave her heart away again, she meant to do it for longer than a whim. Something more like a lifetime. And that just might be a moment too long for her cowboy.

CHAPTER TWENTY

IT WAS TIME to set his deputy straight.

It had been three days since the Last Dog Day event and their late-night rendezvous in her kitchen. Lacey hadn't ended that night with a handshake. For that, Caleb was grateful. But he had been dismissed all the same. When all he had really wanted was to be there for her. For whatever she needed.

Worse, that was the last time Caleb had been alone with his deputy. They had crossed paths at Aspen's practices. But if Lacey wasn't leaving for work, Caleb was late for a meeting. Their schedules never quite overlapped for more than a few quick conversations in passing.

He would've settled for a passing-by kiss. If it had meant they would've made time for each other soon. But that implied they were something more than friends. Something more like partners. There were those heart-tugging feelings winding through him again. Making him reconsider the appeal of having something more than a friendship with Lacey.

But Lacey had called in Caleb's mother, not him, for an assist picking up Aspen from day camp when her shift ran long.

Caleb didn't begrudge the friendship between Lacey and his mother. In truth, he appreciated that Lilian Sloan was finally showing up for her family and friends. Still, Caleb wanted

Lacey to call him. Lean on him. Let him show up for her like a partner would.

Even more, Caleb was bone-tired of his deputy asking him if he had been out with Georgia. Tired of her filling him in on another one of Georgia's thrilling trips. As if Caleb couldn't get enough of Georgia.

The truth was Caleb wasn't interested in talking about his contractor. He wanted to talk about his deputy and his feelings—the ones he was holding Lacey solely responsible for. The ones that had him twisted up tighter than the braids on a steer rope.

Oh yes, it was past time to set his deputy straight. Tonight, in fact.

Caleb just needed to find the perfect moment. When it was just him, her, and no interference.

However, that was not right now. Now, Caleb was guiding KC's catering van into the parking space behind the commercial greenhouses at Elsie and Ryan's farm. The dandelion wine tasting extravaganza was scheduled to begin in less than two hours.

Tonight was a dry run of sorts for Caleb to prove he was responsible and capable of managing projects. The rehearsal dinner and wedding reception next weekend would be the show-stopper. And proof that Caleb could add value beyond tour guide while also bringing in an additional revenue stream to Misty Grove Distillery.

After ensuring KC was situated in the greenhouse reserved for food service and dandelion wine sampling, Caleb passed through the connecting hallway into the greenhouse dubbed the dance hall.

His deputy was on a ladder, adjusting long vines of live ivy around a tall trellis in the corner where the DJ would set up. She smiled down at him. "I like those tall vases with the floating gold pearls and candles inside. The ones you put on the tables in the dining area. Very elegant."

"You don't have to sound so surprised." Caleb reached up to help her down. "The atmosphere can be elevated, even though it's only dandelion wine."

"You had a vision, didn't you?" She stepped off the ladder and studied him.

He had a vision about dancing with her under the glass ceiling of the greenhouse. The moon and stars shining through. "Again, you sound so amazed. I had an idea of what my grandpa and uncle would appreciate. I went with it."

"I like it." She set her hands on her hips and shifted her gaze around the space. "A lot."

I like you. It's those feelings. I don't typically deal in those much. But with you... Caleb cleared his throat. "Ready to go?"

"Where are we going?" She aimed her smile at him.

"Out to the dandelion pasture," he said. "I want to pick fresh dandelions for the sampling tables." *And dig into those feelings.*

"Did I hear you're heading out to the pasture?" Grandpa Sam strolled across the cement floor. "Count us in."

Another roadblock. Caleb wanted to count his family out, so he would have his deputy alone.

"Lacey will be wantin' a tour of the barn." Uncle Roy followed Sam. In his hand was what looked suspiciously like a steak French fry bundle. He stuck a bite in his mouth and grinned. "As the winemakers, we should be the ones to show Lacey around. It's more personal that way."

"I don't want to take you away from anything you're doing here," Lacey said.

"They've been snacking on the appetizers with Chef KC," Caleb said under his breath.

Lacey coughed to cover her laugh.

"Of course we were tasting with Chef KC." Uncle Roy wiped his hands on his plaid shirt. "That's called good quality control."

Except his grandfather and uncle had refused to let Caleb or anyone else in the family, for that matter, sample their dandelion wine. According to the stubborn cowboys, that was part of the evening's allure. No one could taint someone else's opinion if everyone was sampling the wine at the same time.

"Besides, Caleb has got all this well in hand." Something suspiciously close to surprise lifted his grandfather's eyebrows. Grandpa Sam nodded, more of that surprise in his murmur. "Very well, indeed."

Caleb frowned. Not his grandfather too. Did no one genuinely believe he could make tonight a success?

"There's a working waterwheel at the barn where we make our wine and a stream that divides Sloan land from Elsie's." Uncle Roy took Lacey's arm in his and walked her toward the door. "Ryan built a bridge to connect the Sloan property with this one. You can see it from the barn window."

"It's like our very own piece of paradise for our winemaking." Grandpa Sam came up to Lacey's other side. "Private and soon to be profitable."

Caleb wasn't letting his grandfather and uncle out of his sight. He hurried after the departing trio and called out, "There are no wine sales tonight. Only tastings."

"But once they've had their first sip of our elixir, they're certain to be back for more." Grandpa Sam chuckled and held the door open for them.

"Tonight starts the buzz," Uncle Roy declared. "It will only build from there like a frenzy. Everyone wants a frenzy."

No one wanted that. Caleb chuckled and immediately lost his irritation. The gang climbed into the four-seater UTV, Caleb in the driver's seat. He handed Lacey a basket he had set in the UTV bed earlier. "For the dandelions."

"We'll be sure to fill that right up," Grandpa Sam offered. "After the tour, of course."

Caleb took the fastest route out to the old barn that sat on the far corner of Sloan land. After visiting the barn and checking out the inner workings of the waterwheel, his grandfather and uncle showed Lacey around the rest of the property and took her to the bridge. The one where Ryan had proposed to Elsie after he built the bridge to join Sloan land with Elsie's family farm. Lacey was seemingly touched by the story and wanted to walk across the bridge herself.

The view of the stream and bridge was quite striking. But what captivated him most was his deputy.

As she stood in the center of the bridge, the afternoon sun highlighted her radiant smile and the stunning shades of red in her hair. His grandfather handed her a dandelion stem, its head a white puffball. They exchanged a few words. Her smile grew, and her laughter floated through the breeze. Then she closed her eyes and blew, scattering the dandelion fluff every which way.

He guessed she'd made a wish. Would've liked to have known what it was…to see if he could grant it. Maybe then his deputy would discover he had more to offer than wagers and good times.

Or he could simply tell her. Set her straight, as it were.

Caleb grabbed the basket and headed to the dandelion fields. The sooner the task was finished, the quicker he could get his deputy alone for that straight talk.

Later, back at the greenhouses, Lacey and Caleb arranged the last of Caleb's dandelions at each of the tasting tables and stepped back. Caleb turned a slow circle and nodded. "I think we're done decorating."

Lacey checked the time on her watch. "And sooner than we thought. I have plenty of time to shower, change, and check in with Wells and Aspen."

This is it. Caleb rubbed his hands together. "Since we are early, do you want to take a walk with me? Elsie and Ryan worked all summer to finish the garden maze. There's a fountain in the middle I think you'd like."

"You had me at garden maze. I've always wanted to walk through one." She grinned and motioned toward the door. "Let's go. I can't wait."

Their pace was unrushed through the maze. Partly because Lacey stopped to smell the roses and every other flowering plant along the way, declaring each one her favorite scent until she reached the next. Caleb spent the time willing his heartbeat to slow and the right words to come.

But the deeper they walked into the maze, the more tangled his tongue felt. He finally gave in and started joining Lacey, smelling one flower after the next right alongside her.

With a cornucopia of scents swirling in his head and the right words no clearer than when they'd entered, Caleb led Lacey into the center of the maze. There, water spilled over multiple tiers of a tall vintage fountain and real pink and red rose petals floated in the wide circular basin.

Lacey gasped. "This is more stunning than I imagined." She hurried over to the fountain. "It's like our own secret garden."

Caleb followed her. Felt the sweat bead on the back of his neck. "Lace, there's something I wanted to tell you."

Lacey set her finger on a pink rose petal and glided the flower over the water. The smile she aimed at him was open and gentle.

Were his palms sweaty now too? Caleb smoothed his hands over his jeans. *Get it together.* This was Lacey. An old friend. A good friend at that. Nothing to be nervous about. He cleared his throat. "I wanted to tell you…"

"I know. You need to be hosting tonight's event and won't be able to leave. I won't ask to come back out here later." Lacey swirled her fingertips through the water. "Even though this place must be even more magical at night."

"I've never been good with these sorts of things," he muttered. Heck, he had never given his heart a voice before. He had always preferred action to explanations. And fearing he was blundering this beyond repair, Caleb leaned into what he always did. Jump in first and explain later. With more conviction, he said, "But this should sum things up."

He took Lacey's hand, twirled her away from the fountain, and straight into his embrace.

Her hands landed on his shoulders. Her breath rushed out, along with a startled, "Caleb."

He wanted her breathless. Wanted her to understand what he couldn't seem to put into words. He framed her face, tipped her head up. "There are things I need to say."

Her wide gaze searched his face. "You have my attention."

Her brown eyes were enchanting. His words scattered like that dandelion fluff she'd blown into the wind earlier. But the time for wishing had passed. Finally, he managed to say, "I can't take another handshake, Lacey."

She blinked. One achingly slow sweep of her eyelashes against her cheeks.

And he was transfixed all over again. He could get lost in her. Willingly. Gladly. Every day if she let him. "And I can't take one more night thinking about what it would be like to kiss you."

"Kiss me…" One more sweep of those eyelashes. A catch of

her breath. A quiver of her mouth. Her words were more a puff of air than substance. "You want to kiss me."

Her pulse raced under his fingertips. His kept pace. "More than you could possibly know."

"But…"

"There's only one but that matters." Suddenly, he was second-guessing not making that wish. *Please, tell me I'm not wrong. That you feel this too.* "If you haven't thought about kissing me, then tell me now." *Or don't say anything. Just turn around. Walk away.*

Her eyes flared. Her breath hitched.

"Tell me, Lace," he said without pulling her closer like he wanted to. "Tell me, and we walk away now."

Her teeth nipped into her bottom lip. "What if it's a bad idea?"

"I'm quite sure it is." He smoothed his thumbs over her cheeks. "But I'm tired of running from this."

"One kiss." Her arms curved up and around his neck. Her gaze held his, bold. Direct. Fearless. "Right here. Right now."

He didn't move. Didn't speak. Knowing she was setting the parameters as if this was one of their dares. But it was so much more than a game.

"If it doesn't sit right for one of us, no hard feelings." She closed the distance between them. "We leave as friends."

There was that word again. But she was in his arms. Her fingers tangled in his hair. He leaned in, then paused when their breath collided. "Fine. Friends."

His mouth brushed hers. Just the briefest catch of their lips. More of a tease. A skim. Nothing lasting. Everything they could walk away from. Dismiss, even. Yet there was nothing friendly about the sensation spreading through him. It was more of a jolt. A permanent imprint.

His eyes snapped open. Met hers, which were large pools of wonder fixed on him. He heard her inhale. She felt it too. That rush of awareness. Still, he held back. Gave her time to retreat. To push him away. Claim she felt nothing.

She shifted, her hand suddenly cradled his cheek. Her thumb smoothed over his bottom lip. Her gaze followed as if entranced.

Oh, there would be another kiss. It was building between them. Pushing their pulses past rapid.

There would be no dismissing this kiss. No walking away and forgetting about it. It would be perfect and haunting. Friendship shattering. He should release her. Step back. His curiosity was satisfied. That was what had started this. But there was still so much left unsaid.

He gathered her close.

And she pressed more fully against him. Tightened her embrace as if anchoring them inside that garden maze in that moment with its rose-petal-strewn fountain. "Caleb Sloan, we made a deal." Her thumb paused mid-caress on his bottom lip. Her gaze lifted to his. "For a kiss."

One side of his mouth lifted. "I've never been one to back away."

"Neither have I." Her smile flashed bright.

They moved at the same time. Their lips only just connected, and shouts shattered the silence.

The first one was for Lacey. That halted them in place.

The second one was for Caleb. That forced them apart.

Another round of shouts. They spun away from each other. The thump of footsteps approached. And the moment was gone before it ever really started. Suddenly, what had been building was now nothing more than a could-have-been.

"There you guys are." Ryan jogged toward the fountain, waving a cell phone. "Lacey. There's an emergency."

"That's my phone." Lacey lunged toward Ryan. His brother tossed her phone to her, and Lacey snatched it midair.

"It's Aspen," Ryan finished and came to a stop. Worry splashed across his face. "Wells is taking Aspen to the ER right now."

Lacey swayed.

Caleb wrapped his arm around her waist, held her steady. "What happened?"

"Lacey's phone was ringing," Ryan said, his words rushed. "You left it in the greenhouse. It wouldn't stop. Elsie answered it finally. Aspen was stung by several bees on her walk with Butterscotch."

They were suddenly on the move, weaving swiftly through the maze. Ryan was on one side of Lacey, Caleb on the other. Confusion covered her words. "I don't understand. She's never been stung before?"

"She's had a reaction this time," Ryan said.

Lacey gasped.

Caleb picked up the pace and dug in his pocket for his truck key. "Ryan."

"Go. I got this," Ryan replied.

That was all that needed to be said. What had always been said between the Sloan brothers whenever one of them needed backup. His brothers would rally and take care of the evening. So Caleb could take care of Lacey and Aspen.

They were out of the maze and across the driveway in minutes. He helped a stunned Lacey into the passenger seat of his truck and shut the door. Giving a quick nod to his brother when Ryan told him to check in, Caleb climbed into the driver's seat and headed for Belleridge Regional Hospital.

He reached over and covered Lacey's clasped hands, already too cold to the touch.

She adjusted her hold, as if seeking his warmth, and looked at him. Her expression was bleak. Her face pale. Her eyes filled with alarm. "Caleb. Please hurry."

CHAPTER TWENTY-ONE

SEVERAL HOURS AFTER her frantic arrival at Belleridge Regional Hospital's emergency room, Lacey was curled around her daughter in a bed on the third-floor children's unit. She watched the slow drip of the IV attached to Aspen's arm and listened to her daughter's steady breaths.

There was nothing slow about the if-only's surging through Lacey. If only she'd called home sooner. If only she'd been at the ranch. If only she hadn't been indulging in a moment—a selfish one at that. If only she'd stayed focused on her daughter and not gotten sidetracked by wagers, crooked grins, and a no-good-for-her-heart cowboy.

The door opened, and Lacey's stepdad eased inside. He clutched a paper to-go coffee cup and looked as worn-out as Lacey felt. He settled into the chair beside the bed and took hold of Aspen's good hand. "How's our patient?"

Aspen's cheek was swollen from a beesting, as were her left palm and forearm from the other stings. Aspen whispered, her voice hoarse with worry. "What about Butterscotch, Grandpa?"

"Dr. Paige says Butterscotch will be perfectly fine soon. Same as you." Wells cleared his throat and tucked the blankets around Aspen. "Seems her face is swollen like yours, and she's getting medicine too."

"Dr. Paige will take good care of Butterscotch." Lacey

smoothed the hair from Aspen's forehead even though her fingers still trembled with concern for her daughter. "Same as the doctors are doing for you here." *Same as I promise to do from here on out. You have my word.*

"I want to see her." Aspen frowned. "What if she's scared?"

"Dr. Paige took her home to her house," Lacey said, grateful for the kind veterinarian's quick response and continuous text updates. "Riley already made a bed for Butterscotch in her bedroom."

Aspen nodded, seemingly satisfied that her new friend would know how to comfort the dog.

"Lacey, you've got a cowboy pacing the shine off the tile floor out there in the waiting room," her stepdad said, his gaze compassionate. "Might be time to put his worries to rest."

"Caleb." Aspen shifted and looked at Lacey. "He's here?"

Lacey nodded.

"Can I see him?" Aspen whispered.

"Are you sure?" Lacey asked. *Because I'm not.* "You aren't too tired, are you?" *Maybe we could rest here awhile longer. You. Me. And none of those hard, uncomfortable truths.*

Aspen shook her head. "I gotta tell Caleb about the bees' nest. And how Butterscotch found it. And how I protected her." Aspen's brow wrinkled. "Well, how I tried to."

"You were very brave," Lacey assured her and rubbed the frown from her daughter's brow. "Those bees just got startled and a little scared." *I'm scared now. Scared I don't know how to get this right.*

"'Cause the bees weren't trying to be mean," Aspen finished and wiped her hand under her nose. "They didn't know we wouldn't hurt them. I gotta tell Caleb."

There were things Lacey had to tell Caleb. The time for stalling was over. Lacey pressed a kiss against Aspen's forehead and unfolded herself from the bed. "I'll go get him."

Lacey stepped into the hall and headed for the waiting area. She found her cowboy standing at the tall windows overlooking downtown Belleridge. His back was to her. He clutched a caramel-colored stuffed pony in one hand and ran his other hand over his face, then around to massage the back of his neck. Then he stilled.

She saw her reflection in the darkened window. Knew he saw it too. He turned slowly, his gaze took her in with one long sweep from her head to her toes and back, as if assuring himself she was there and that she was fine.

Lacey ran her hands over her T-shirt. Smoothing out the wrinkles was ridiculous. She was in the same clothes she'd worn to help set up the dandelion wine tasting event. The same clothes she'd worn when he held her near the fountain. That felt like a lifetime ago. Or perhaps it was another lifetime. She pressed her palm against her stomach. "Aspen wants to see you."

He nodded and lifted the stuffed animal, gripping it with both hands while he seemed to search for his words. All the while his gaze searched hers. Finally, he said, "If she needs to rest, I can come back in the morning."

But the morning would be too late. Lacey was letting him go. Tonight. "She knows you're here. She'll be upset if you don't see her before you leave." *I'll be upset too. Even though it's for the best. But that's for later.* She motioned to the hall. "Her room is this way."

Inside the room, Caleb shook hands with Wells as Lacey's stepdad vacated his chair and gestured for Caleb to sit. Wells stepped to Lacey's side and whispered, "I'm going to get a refill. I'll be back shortly."

Lacey nodded yet never took her gaze off her cowboy and her daughter.

Aspen's face lit up at Caleb's arrival. "Caleb."

"There's my favorite cowgirl." Caleb's words were quiet, sincere, and tinged with fondness.

For her daughter. For Lacey too. But in his arms earlier, there had been more than simple affection. Lacey had wanted to be swept up in those feelings. In him. But her feet were back on the ground. Her focus back on her daughter. Where it belonged. That first knot cinched inside her chest.

"Caleb, I swatted at all the bees," Aspen said, her words urgent. "To save Butterscotch. And then we ran real fast."

Caleb scooted the chair closer to the bed. "Courageous, just like your mom."

"You think I'm like my mom?" Wonder filled Aspen's words.

"I do," Caleb said softly.

Courageous. No, she wasn't that. That knot tightened, cutting into Lacey's breath.

Delight danced in Aspen's gaze, making her eyes sparkle in the dim room.

No. Couldn't her cowboy see? Her daughter's heart was on her sleeve. Too exposed. Too open. Too easy to break. Lacey had to protect Aspen. Caleb couldn't have her daughter's heart. Not when Lacey couldn't trust her cowboy with her own. She wanted to step between the pair. Chase her cowboy out of the room. Surely that wasn't wrong. Surely that was the responsible thing to do. After all, hearts were at stake. She widened her stance as if preparing to defend her position.

Aspen was hugging her new stuffed pony, ecstatic that Dash, her favorite horse stuffie at home, now had a partner. "Now they can always be together. And make each other super happy."

Partners...but for how long? And when it all fell just a little bit short, that was when partners drifted. And the loneliness sneaked in. And the hurt. Then not even fondness and affection could hold it together. And it all crumbled. Lacey had picked up the pieces once. Vowed not to have to do that ever again.

"That's what a good partner does." Confidence tinged Caleb's words. "Makes sure his partner is always happy."

"If they aren't happy, then you gotta squeeze them real hard." Aspen hugged her pony tight against her chest with her good arm and kissed its head. "And you hang on until love makes them smile so much they glow."

Or you let them go. Certain you will smile again. And so will they, one day. Bargaining with pieces of her heart, or worse, her cowboy's was not going to make either one of them happy. And Lacey had to have her whole heart for her daughter. How else would she prove she loved her?

Caleb and Aspen discussed names for her new pony. He drew out her muted giggles more than once. Wells returned and gave Lacey a hot cup of tea.

At Aspen's first yawn, Caleb took her hand and said, "You need to sleep now."

"But I'm not tired." Aspen ruined that declaration with another yawn. "And we didn't decide on a name yet."

"I bet you'll find the perfect name in your dreams." Caleb rose and squeezed her fingers. "Night, Aspen. Dream all things happy."

"Night, Caleb," Aspen said around another yawn. "You dream happy too."

Caleb returned the chair to Wells. He set his hand on her stepdad's shoulder. The two men spoke quietly before they shared another handshake. Then Lacey set her tea on the counter and stepped out into the hall with her cowboy.

"Do you need anything?" he asked, his words hushed.

I need you to tell me how to say goodbye to you. Then remind me that this is the smart thing to do. Because when she looked at him, she wanted only to step into his embrace and find her strength again. Discover those misplaced dreams. She shook her head. "You've done enough."

"Hardly," he said. "Anyone can buy a stuffed animal."

But not just anyone gets to my heart. At least they were not supposed to. And she could not risk losing it again, only to realize too late that she was not the one he truly wanted. That all this was just another whim. She couldn't be a whim. She thrust her arm between them. "Thanks for everything, Caleb."

His chin dropped to his chest. His eyes slammed closed. Not before she saw a flash of hurt there.

Lacey held herself still. A chill seeped into her.

He lifted his gaze to her. Hurt flared and was just as swiftly banked behind a stiff composure. "Lacey Nash, we are way past handshakes."

Lacey kept her arm in place.

"Listen well, Deputy." He stepped closer until her fingertips barely touched his plaid shirt. His gaze remained fixed on her, distant and guarded. "If I take your hand now, I'm going to pull you into my arms." His words lowered below a hush. "And I'm going to kiss you to remind you who we are to each other."

Her breath hitched. Her throat went dry. Her heart raced. If she kissed him, she would be his, possibly forever. If that were possible. She curled her fingers into her cold palm and dropped her arm to her side.

"What is this, Lacey?" he asked.

"Goodbye," she blurted.

He crossed his arms over his chest. "Why?"

I'm not the one you belong with. You'll realize it soon enough. I'll ruin your fun. I have to be responsible. Always. She stressed, "So you can live the life you want, with someone like Georgia."

That distance between them fractured into a divide. "And what life is that exactly?"

"The carefree, no-commitment one you prefer. The one you've always claimed to prefer." The accusation was unfair perhaps, but she couldn't stop herself. "The very one you've been living since high school." The one that made them no good for each other. He'd resent her for reining him in. They'd become strangers. And no good could come from that.

Caleb ran his fingers over his closed mouth and started to shake his head.

"Don't deny it," she charged on. Her words were sharp inside her low tone. "In fact, tell me this. Tell me that you seriously intend to accept that full-time position at the distillery."

His lips parted. But only a thick silence settled between them.

She grimaced. "You can't tell me that. Because you can't accept that job."

"Why not?" His words were clipped.

"Because you can't commit to anything long-term," she said. "Tell me I'm wrong." *Please. I'm calling your bluff. Call mine.*

His lips pressed together.

Her short laugh was more anguished than triumphant. No use for it now. He always preferred straight talk, and he was getting it. "I can't have temporary, Caleb. Or a fling. Or take whatever this is while I wait for you to move on."

His eyes flared. He set his hands on his hips. "Is that what you think this is?"

"When has it ever been more than that with you?" she countered.

"Maybe it's more right now." His words and expression softened. "Maybe this is everything. Maybe I have no intention of moving on."

But she couldn't bet her heart—or Aspen's—on maybes. Not again. Lacey willed her tears to stand down. Still, she felt those cracks inside her heart.

"It doesn't really matter, does it?" His expression went back to stubborn and sour. "You've already decided for us both."

"I'm looking out for myself and my daughter," she said, her words sounding more like a pain-filled hiss. "That's my job as a mother."

"Right," he said. "You mean the job you think you're failing at."

She sucked in a breath.

"That's what you've convinced yourself anyway." He waved his arm between them. "That all the wrongs and mistakes in the past and the ones now are entirely your fault. Your doing." He shook his head slowly. "I'm surprised you can stand straight with all the blame you're shouldering."

"That's not fair," she charged.

"But I'm not wrong." He lifted one eyebrow. "If you're not perfect, then your love is somehow less than, isn't it?"

"Don't talk to me about love."

"Right." Impatience gave an edge to what would be his normally light tone. "Because what would a frivolous, reckless cowboy like me know about something as consequential and enduring as love?"

She was only saying what needed to be said. What they both already knew. Couldn't he see that? She whispered, "I can't be who you need."

"Funny." The corners of his mouth lifted. There was nothing easy or indifferent about his half grin. "I only ever wanted you to be you."

"This is me." She speared her arm at the closed hospital door. "I'm a mother. A deputy. I live to serve and protect. That's who I am."

"You really don't see yourself, do you?" he asked.

She thrust her fingers through her hair. "You want a happy-go-lucky cowgirl, Caleb. And that's not me anymore."

"I want the woman whose heart is bigger than this state." He stepped into her space. "I want the woman who embraces life with joy and passion and showers those she loves with the same. The one who is fearless."

I want a cowboy who will stick. She lifted her chin. "You've got the wrong person."

"Do I?" he countered.

"I have to get back to my daughter." Beside her daughter, she would surely be steady again. Not quite so numb. Surely in time this would all feel right and not so very wrong. "I'll make arrangements for Aspen to practice for the contest someplace else."

He nodded. "If that's what you think is best."

"That's exactly what I'm doing." She flattened her palm against her chest. "Making the best decision for myself and my daughter." *For our hearts.*

"Then it looks like you win, Deputy." He took a step back. "Congratulations."

The cowboy she knew faded away before her eyes. *Don't go. Tell me you can stay. Tell me I'm wrong.* Lacey curled her fingers into her palms. *Don't quit on me. On us.* The words clogged her throat. *Fight, cowboy. Don't flee.*

One more step back, and he added, "You're getting exactly what you want."

But she didn't feel like celebrating. She felt like crying. Hard and long. And soul deep. She reached blindly for the door behind her.

"Hey, Deputy," he called out, so much emptiness in his expression. "I lied earlier at the fountain."

Lacey willed the cold metal door handle to freeze out his next words. She clutched the metal harder and waited. Knew her cowboy's final words would buckle her knees. But her cowboy would not see her break. Not a crack. Not a single tear.

"It's not fine. Not even close," he said, "and if it's all the same to you, you can keep the friendship too."

Just like that, it was over.

She'd lost her cowboy, but she'd won. She'd been right all

along. The fun stopped, and he had given her up. Certainly, the rush of satisfaction would fill her soon. Any minute now, really.

Instead, tears surged all at once. Unstoppable.

Lacey sagged against the door and slid to the ground. Easier to pick up those pieces of her heart there, when she finally got around to celebrating.

CHAPTER TWENTY-TWO

LILIAN SLOAN WAS a coward.

True, she was a skilled heart surgeon known for her compassion, patience, and good judgment. She took detail-oriented to extremes. And she possessed exceptional hand-eye coordination. It was the heart-mind connection—her own—where she faltered.

After all, if she was brave, she would not have spent the last few hours lingering inside the first-floor waiting area of Belleridge Regional Hospital.

If she was brave, she would not have lied.

But she was lingering. She had lied. And she sure as certain was a coward.

The elevator doors opened in the lobby, and her youngest son stepped off. Or rather, a version of her son. This one was a far cry from the fun-loving, never-takes-himself-or-life-too-seriously son she knew Caleb to be.

Now, he looked defeated and defiant. Never a good combination, that. Lilian had felt the very same after her divorce. And then she had gone on to blaze a path that burned bridges she was now trying diligently to repair. Lilian wound her way through the empty waiting room chairs and called out, "Caleb."

"Mom." He blinked as if she had flashed a penlight directly into his eyes. Then he rubbed his forehead and seemed to finally focus on her. His frown deepened. "Where were you, dressed like that?"

Lilian passed her hand over her crisp, cream-colored blazer, sweeping down to the waist of her matching tailored, pleated trousers. The formfitting power suit was a remnant of her city life. Her armor of sorts. "I was out with a colleague from the university. An adjunct professor at the medical college there."

Caleb eyed her and remained silent.

Tell the truth, Lilian. It was a date. Lilian touched her pearl earrings. The ones she hadn't worn since she moved back to Texas and discovered the appeal of more casual jewelry. She tipped her chin up and added, "I had my phone turned off at dinner." That was true. Guilt was a powerful motivator. She finished with, "I got here as soon as I could."

Caleb finally nodded, but the motion seemed automatic as if he'd stopped listening to her.

Lilian added *distracted* to her description of her son. "But enough about me. What happened?"

"Aspen was in the backyard at their ranch with Butterscotch and decided to pick flowers." Caleb tugged off his cowboy hat and scrubbed his hand through his hair. His gaze shifted to the elevators and caught. "Butterscotch was sniffing around and stuck her nose into a beehive in the ground. Aspen was stung swatting the bees away from the dog. And now we know she's highly allergic to beestings."

Lilian let Caleb fill her in despite already having those particular details thanks to the voicemail updates that Wells had left on her phone. The one Lilian had turned off during her dinner date.

Caleb exhaled, the sound long and weary. "Aspen is fine, she's recovering now. You can go up." He cast one more dark glance at the elevators. That defiance hardened across his face before he smashed his hat back on his head. "I'm sure Wells and Lacey would like to see you."

She was quite sure that was not true. Wells had told Lilian about his feelings for her. And Lilian had gone on a date with another man. Not exactly the most appropriate response to a good guy who wanted to love her and confessed he was willing to wait for her heart to catch up.

Lilian wrapped her arm around Caleb's and said, "Maybe this is for the best." That was her inner coward speaking up again. Lilian turned them toward the exit and gave in to it. "You look like you need someone to listen. And as it happens, I have two very capable ears." *Just don't ask me about love. I tend to get that wrong and hurt the ones I love the most.*

"I don't really have anything to say." Caleb walked beside her, his movements and words stiff.

"How about we keep each other company?" Outside, Lilian inhaled the night air and forced herself not to look back. Her son needed her. And the truth was, she needed him. "I'm not quite ready to call it a night and be alone."

He paused and considered her. "Mom. Are you okay?"

I'm a coward. But that was neither here nor there. Just a recently discovered character quirk. She squeezed his arm. "Like you, I'm fine."

A frown formed between his eyebrows. "As it turns out, I have two very capable ears that can listen too."

"But like you, I don't feel much like talking," she said, trying to reassure herself as much as Caleb. She certainly didn't want her son worrying about her. "I appreciate the offer though. And when I'm ready to talk, I know where to find you."

He nodded and tucked her closer to his side as if it was suddenly them against the world. Or perhaps simply them standing united against love. Whatever it was, she welcomed the support.

"You know..." She held on to the last syllable, her high heels clicking on the pavement. "I think I'm in the mood for a nightcap, if you're up for it?"

"I have just the place." Caleb unlocked his truck and helped her inside.

Ten minutes later, Lilian and her youngest son were tucked into a back booth at the All-Day Diner sharing an order of sweet potato fries and sipping on chocolate cookie milkshakes spiked with Irish cream and vanilla vodka. They talked about the last books they'd read and the latest movies they'd enjoyed—and by silent agreement avoided the uncomfortable stuff.

It was their first real mother-son time together. If only it hadn't taken her being a coward to finally experience it, she might have been truly grateful.

CHAPTER TWENTY-THREE

THE FOLLOWING AFTERNOON, Lacey was still searching for that feeling of satisfaction. That triumph that came from doing the right thing. All she kept running into was a gaping emptiness. And a rather unpleasant discontent.

Not that she would let that interfere with her determination to stay on her path. After all, no one ever claimed that doing the right thing was easy.

Take right now, for instance. Lacey parked in her ex-husband's driveway and glanced into the back seat. Willing her smile to look light and easy. "We're here, sweetie."

Aspen plucked at her hospital band around her wrist. "Why can't I stay with you?"

Because it wasn't the right thing. Lacey wanted to remove the beehives on the property to make it as safe as possible for her daughter first. She held on to her smile. "Your dad and Sarah-Beth came home early from their trip. They're worried about you. They want to see you."

"But what about Butterscotch?" Aspen insisted. "She wants to see me. She likes to sleep with me. She'll be lonely."

Lacey was already lonely. She liked having Aspen at the ranch, sleeping in the next room where she could check on her daughter and the dog anytime she wanted. Where she could soak in her daughter's laughter and wrap herself in her spontaneous hugs. Lacey wanted to reverse out of the driveway and take her daughter back to her house.

Congratulations, you're getting exactly what you wanted. Her cowboy's words snapped through her.

Right. This was all for the best. Lacey grabbed her key fob and opened the car door. "I'll bring Butterscotch over to visit."

"Dad won't let a dog in the house," Aspen grumbled and climbed out of the back seat. "But Caleb lets Butterscotch sit on the couch with us to watch movies. And eat popcorn."

Caleb. That pang in Lacey's chest pulled against her smile, weighing it down. Lacey plucked the stuffed pony from the back seat. "Don't forget this."

Aspen shook her head and pushed the pony away. "Dreamer has gotta go home with you. She's gotta be with Dash. They're partners now."

"Right." Dreamer and Dash, the stuffed animal duo that would keep each other infinitely happy. Lacey clutched the stuffed pony against her stomach. "I will tuck them in tonight."

Aspen pressed a kiss on the stuffed pony's head. "I'll be home soon, Dreamer."

Home. One brief kiss with her cowboy, and Lacey had almost believed she'd found that. But it was more of a dream. Lacey set the pony on her passenger seat and took Aspen's hand. "Let's get you inside so you can rest and enjoy lots of pampering from Mama-Beth and your dad."

The door opened before Lacey and Aspen reached the porch. Sarah-Beth wrapped them both in a gentle embrace. "I've been so worried."

Jeffrey stepped out onto the porch and kissed Aspen's forehead. "There's my girl."

Lacey released Aspen and tucked her suddenly empty hands at her sides. "I'm sorry you had to cut your vacation short."

"Vacations can be rescheduled. Family is more important." Jeffrey lifted his gaze from Aspen to Lacey, then straightened. Something like concern washed over his face. "Lacey, we need to talk."

"I know. Not now," Lacey said. "I didn't sleep well in the hospital chair." Those sharp pieces of her broken heart had kept her awake. And that emptiness kept trying to consume her. She shifted in her running shoes as if suddenly unsteady. But she'd done the right thing. This too would pass. "I've got to pick up Butterscotch now. And I'm working tomorrow."

"Don't forget to send pictures of Butterscotch." Aspen wrapped her good arm around Lacey's waist and squeezed her. "Remember to give her lots of treats and extra hugs."

Lacey held on to her daughter, stealing one more hug for herself. "I won't forget."

"And you'll bring her over to see me," Aspen ordered.

"Yes, I will," Lacey promised.

"What about my practice?" Aspen spun to face Lacey. "Caleb promised to work with me on trotting. I almost got it."

But Caleb never promised that he'd stick. *And we can't keep falling for him. It hurts now, but it will fade.*

Lacey squatted, putting her at eye level with Aspen and closer to firm ground. "The doctor wants you to rest today. We have to follow the doctor's orders, so we don't end up back at the hospital." Lacey brushed Aspen's hair off her face. "We'll talk about practice tomorrow."

Aspen's lips pulled together. "You won't forget?"

"No." Lacey held out her little finger. "I pinky swear."

Aspen grinned. "That's what Caleb and me do."

Used to do. Lacey blanched and bit back her words. She would have that talk with her daughter soon. When she could think about her cowboy without wanting to cry. "Why don't you grab a blanket and get comfy on the couch? I heard Mama-Beth has special treats and a new movie for you to watch."

Aspen hugged Lacey one more time and headed inside.

"Are you sure you don't want to come in, Lacey?" Sarah-Beth set a comforting hand on Lacey's shoulder. Concern and compassion crossed her face. "I've got hot water for tea."

Jeffrey set an arm around his wife's waist and considered Lacey. "And if you need something stronger, Lace, we've got that too."

"I really should go." Lacey tugged on the ends of her shorts. "The dog is waiting." And her empty house. And her broken heart. She really needed to put those pieces back together.

Sarah-Beth wrapped her in another warm, tight hug. "Well, I'm grateful you were with Aspen. I would've panicked like no one's business."

Lacey had panicked. She still was panicking.

"I've never been good in hospitals," Sarah-Beth confessed.

"I've promised to hold her hand," Jeffrey said, his smile affection filled. "And not leave her side."

Sarah-Beth touched her pregnant belly. "But I could really use some of your courage, Lacey."

Everyone really needed to stop referencing Lacey's courage. They were getting her all wrong. She was simply doing what she had to do.

"Now, you go and get some rest too." Sarah-Beth released her. "Everything will look better in the morning."

"Is that a promise?" Lacey asked. How she really needed that to be true.

UNFORTUNATELY, THINGS LOOKED BLURRY, not better, the following morning. Lacey had returned home to find more care packages and baskets from friends and neighbors. The overwhelming support brought her to tears. The same thing happened when she fell onto the couch, curled up in the blanket, and inhaled her cowboy's lingering cologne. She had cried through her shower and finally cried herself to sleep.

Now her eyes were bloodshot and puffy, and everything that had once seemed so clear was out of focus. Lacey kept her sunglasses in place and headed into the sheriff's department to begin her shift. Work had helped her heal in the past. She would bury herself in it now.

Gertie slowly rose from behind the reception desk, her shrewd gaze fixed on Lacey. She lowered her microphone over her mouth and said, "Attention all units. This is a ten-zero."

Lacey slowed as she passed the end of the reception desk. *Use caution.*

"Repeat. A ten-zero," Gertie stated. "For a ten-four-four-four."

Lacey frowned. "That last one's not even a valid code." Lacey knew that much. She had memorized Gertie's entire code handbook. That one did not exist.

Lacey's stepdad opened his office door and stepped into the lobby.

Gertie tipped her platinum head, that now had lavender streaks running through it, toward Lacey. "We got ourselves a ten-four-four-four, Sheriff."

Lacey exhaled and set her hands on her hips, frustrated. "That's not a legit code."

"It's part of the *special* code list." Gertie opened and closed cabinets underneath her desk as if searching for something. Most likely another codebook.

Lacey ran her hand over her face. She could not take another code list. Not this morning, when she was grumpy, sleep-deprived, and desperate to get her mind off her cowboy. She sighed. "I can take whatever the special call is." A distraction would be more than welcome.

Gertie shook her head. "Sorry, Deputy Nash, this one is above your pay grade."

"I can handle it," Lacey insisted. She was there to serve. To do her job.

"Deputy, code ten-four-four-four is the code for heartbreak," her stepdad said gently, too much compassion swirling in his warm gaze.

Lacey gaped at him.

Gertie closed the last cabinet and set a box of tissues on the counter in front of Lacey. "If you were handling it, you wouldn't be heartbroken."

Lacey slammed her lips together and lifted her gaze to the ceiling, then brought it back to the too-perceptive dispatcher. "Gertie, please tell me you didn't just announce to the entire department that I'm heartbroken."

"No, dear." Gertie's grin was sympathetic.

Lacey exhaled. That was a relief. She certainly didn't need everyone aware of her condition. And besides, she hadn't cried since she'd woken up. She was better now. Dare she say fine, even.

Gertie nudged the box closer to Lacey. "I just announced to

the entire department that you were in the building, and they should use caution…considering your heartbreak."

Lacey wasn't sure if she should laugh, but she feared she might sound more hysterical than amused. And that might just dislodge those tears again. Instead, she tapped the tissue box back toward the dispatcher. "I don't need those." One more tap. "And you can cancel that ten-zero. And the ten-four-four-four. I'm fine."

Gertie shared a look with the sheriff.

"Perfectly fine." Lacey stretched her arms out. "I'm going to go in there and do my job. And do you know why?"

Gertie's eyebrows arched. Her stepdad held his silence.

"Because I'm fine." Lacey yanked open the door to the rest of the offices. "Now, when you have a real call, I'll take it. Because I'm fine."

Lacey let the door shut behind her. And if she wanted to tell herself she was fine until the words became an ongoing chant, well, that was her business.

After all, it was up to her to make sure her heart fell in line, and she was determined that would be sooner rather than later. Because she was *fine*.

CHAPTER TWENTY-FOUR

EVERYTHING IN CALEB'S life was back on track, exactly the way he liked it.

His deputy had been kind enough to show him that what he believed about his *so-called feelings* was true all along. *His feelings* were nothing more than a momentary distraction. And best ignored. For the past four days, Caleb had been doing just that. Quite remarkably too, if he did say so himself.

He welcomed back the old squeeze-the-fun-out-of-every-day Caleb with a flourish and much fanfare. He had worked side by side with Georgia and her construction crew every day to finish the renovation on the rackhouse in record time. He had provided breakfasts and lunches and ensured a constant stream of upbeat music and positive energy. The work was physically hard and more rewarding than he'd expected.

With respect to his evenings, well, those he spent behind the bar at The Feisty Owl, delighting customers with new drink recipes and bartending tricks. The laughter and the camaraderie fueled him and crowded out those pesky *feelings* just as he'd intended.

The few hours he gave to sleep, exhaustion kept his dreams dull and uninspiring. And when sleep eluded him, he crocheted. Was he well rested? Hardly. But that wasn't important.

He was back where he started. Where he had always been

happy. On his own. And if he couldn't be happy, he could certainly be content. Nothing wrong with content. It was better than hurt.

At the moment, he was standing inside his brand-new office at Misty Grove Distillery, having just officially accepted the position of marketing director. His family surrounded him, their faces full of pride and joy on his behalf.

The dandelion wine tasting event had been a resounding success. Plus, Carter had gotten a private preview of the renovated rackhouse that morning. It was just one day before the wedding weekend would officially kick off with the Friday night rehearsal dinner at the Sloan farmhouse. Carter had shaken Caleb's hand and said simply, "Impressive. Really impressive, little brother."

Caleb had effectively proven his family wrong and completed his career pivot. He was by all accounts a success. It should feel sweeter. Better. He accepted another round of congratulatory hugs from his family.

Soon enough it was only Caleb and his three brothers. His twin, Josh, had left with his fiancée, Vivian, to pick up the thank-you gifts they'd ordered for the wedding party. Caleb pushed more wattage into his smile and said, "There's only one thing left to do now."

"What's that?" Ryan sat in the leather chair behind Caleb's new desk, his boots stacked on the large desk and his hands tucked behind his head.

Caleb sidestepped that dull ache in his chest. "I need to get a date for this weekend."

Grant dropped his hand on Caleb's shoulder and squeezed. Approval flashed across his face. "Finally going to call Lacey then."

"Lacey?" Caleb shook his head. He had given his deputy what she wanted. And he was nothing if not obliging. He rubbed the heel of his hand against his ribs. There was nothing to hurt over after all. "I'm going to ask Georgia."

Carter turned from the wide window overlooking the wheat fields that contributed to their successful bourbon mash recipe and frowned. "Georgia?"

"My contractor." Caleb kept his words as upbeat as his fixed-in-place grin. "The one I've been working with from sunrise until way past sunset to finish the rackhouse on time."

"We know who Georgia is." Ryan lowered his boots, propped his elbows on the desk, and steepled his hands under his bearded chin. Then he considered Caleb as if he was a disruptive nine-year-old in the principal's office. "We just don't understand why you want your contractor to be your date."

"I need to take someone." Caleb shrugged. "I refuse to sit at the singles' table all weekend."

"But—" Ryan started.

"But nothing." Caleb swiped his hand through the air. He had dared to open his heart to his deputy, to take a chance. And he had ended up right where he knew he would. Left behind and alone. He ignored those feelings threatening to rush forward and said, "Georgia and I had fun this week. She's fun to be around. She'll be a fun date." And that was all the old Caleb wanted. Fun, fun, fun. No strings attached. No worries. That was how he remained content. And content was the new goal.

"We get it. Georgia is obviously fun." Carter cast a hooded glance at Grant as if looking for an assist.

Grant jumped right in. "But Georgia is not Lacey."

No. Georgia was definitely not Lacey. No one was his deputy. And if Caleb chanced to linger too long on that thought an unfamiliar fear surfaced. The one that hinted no one would ever be Lacey and his heart would never be the same without her. He set his hands on his hips. "So what's your point?"

"That she's not Lacey," Ryan repeated the obvious, his words flat and insistent.

Caleb understood perfectly fine. He understood the brief kiss he and his deputy had shared would haunt him for the rest of his days. Things between him and Lacey had never really started. Never really finished. It was all just stuck. Right at the beginning, like a misplaced question mark. But he could not—would not—get anywhere focusing on unfinished business. Therefore, he would fold his hand and move on. "You guys misread the situation between Lacey and me." The fates knew he had too. But he was clear now. "I tried to tell you that we were only friends."

Ryan turned the wedding ring on his finger, his eyebrows pulled together. Grant opened and closed his mouth. Carter touched the front of his throat as if working the correct words free.

"Look, I appreciate the concern, even though it's unnecessary. I'm good. Really good." Caleb swept his arm around the room and grinned as wide as he could. Because full smiles were a sure sign that someone was good. "I have exactly what I want. It was always about this job. And look at my office. Who wouldn't want to come to work here every day?"

Carter's jaw clenched as if he crunched down hard on his reply.

Grant didn't hold back. "What about the wager between you and Lacey?"

"We both agreed we were caught up in nostalgia," he hedged. They hadn't actually talked about the wager. But Caleb had conceded, handing over the win to Lacey. At the rate he was going, he would have close to a dozen crocheted scarves to donate to Three Springs's Rodeo Reunion silent auction. Not that it mattered. He shook his head. "But we aren't kids anymore." And the adults they were no longer saw eye to eye.

Grant kept pressing. "But it was different with Lacey. And you know it."

No. It was not different with his deputy. Caleb would not allow it to be different. Because if it was different, then that would give the whole situation more importance. And it could not be anything significant. Because then that ache in his chest—the one that hadn't let up with every single sunrise that passed—would be something more lasting. Something like a true heartbreak. But Caleb had vowed never to allow that to happen to him.

He clapped his hands together, snapped himself back into the moment. "You all need to leave now. I have to lock up, go find my contractor, and secure my wedding date."

Ryan stood slowly and approached Caleb. His other brothers stepped in behind Ryan as if offering him backup. Ryan seemed to be studying him. "You're sure you want to do that, little brother?"

"Absolutely." Caleb motioned to the door as if eager to find his contractor and start that date immediately. "It's going to be perfect. You'll see."

After all, the venue was perfect. His new position as marketing director and his new office were perfect. He was about to secure a perfect date for the most perfect wedding. And he had it on good authority from his very own deputy herself that his contractor was perfect for him.

And that was how a cowboy saved his heart. What could be more perfect than that?

CHAPTER TWENTY-FIVE

LACEY WALKED ACROSS her backyard to the porch and smiled at the familiar figure sitting in one of the two rocking chairs. Butterscotch took off running toward the new arrival. Lacey and her stepdad had shared dinner together the past five nights, ever since Aspen had been discharged from the hospital.

She was grateful for the company, though slightly concerned about Wells. Whenever she mentioned Lilian Sloan, her stepdad would give her a private smile and tell her that he was still waiting for his doc to figure things out. And then he would deftly change the subject. Same as Lacey deflected whenever the topic of Caleb came up.

Lacey dropped into the rocking chair beside her stepdad and grinned. "The beehive has been successfully relocated."

Thanks to one of Elsie's bee management contacts, Lacey's property was much safer for Aspen. Already, she was anticipating Aspen visiting. The house was too quiet. Fortunately, Lacey had seen Aspen every day.

Elsie and Ryan had insisted that Aspen's practices continue at their stables. The generous couple had even brought Caleb's Paint, Biscuit, to their stables for Aspen to keep riding. She knew Caleb was behind the horse's relocation. She owed him a thank-you, and in time she hoped she could find her way to expressing her gratitude.

"Your mom and I couldn't keep you out of that orchard behind the stables," Wells mused and shifted a burlap bag from one hand to the other. Then he rubbed Butterscotch's head, resting on his leg. "You called that area your very own secret garden. But your mom worried about snakes and spiders and every sort of woodland creature."

"What did you do?" Lacey smiled and took a handful of roasted pecans when he held the burlap bag out to her—the one she recognized from the care package the Baker sisters had dropped off.

Her stepdad's eyes sparkled. His grin grew. "I taught you to ride horses."

Lacey stilled her rocking chair, and Butterscotch scooted over for attention. Lacey gaped at her stepdad. "Seriously?"

"It's true. Your mom thought if we were riding together, I could keep an eye on you." Wells frowned, yet the delight in his gaze gave him away. "That certainly backfired, didn't it?"

Lacey dropped a few pecans into her mouth, but her silent laughter shook her shoulders.

Butterscotch stretched out between their chairs.

"You quickly became very good," Wells added. Pride flashed across his face before he tossed several pecans into his mouth. "And dare I say I taught you to be a better rider than me. I always took pride in that."

Lacey swallowed her pecans and wiped her hands together. "But Mom worried."

"Even more. She traded one worry for another." He tipped the pecan bag at Lacey and eyed her. "But your mom loved you more than her worries. She knew what made you the happiest."

"Horses." And Caleb. Lacey fixed her gaze on the dusk-filled sky. That was when she had been her happiest. On a horse, her cowboy riding shotgun. It had not mattered what they were doing. As long as Caleb had been with her, her day was better. Back then…and even more so recently. She set her chair rocking again.

"Your mom cried something fierce when we sold your horses. Longer and harder than you. Broke her heart." Her stepdad's rocking chair creaked. "She never forgave herself."

"But it was the right thing to do," Lacey said.

"Didn't make it hurt any less." He chewed on more pecans. His words were casual. "That was why she made me promise not to sell this place."

Lacey slowed again.

"Your mom worked double time before the cancer came back to pay down the mortgage," Wells explained. "She was determined it wouldn't be a burden for either of us."

The depth of her mom's love and sacrifice touched and strengthened her. Lacey wanted Aspen to know that same kind of love from her. "Why would Mom do that?"

"Because your mom always wanted you to have a place to come home to. A place to find yourself again when you needed it." Wells shook his finger at Lacey and lifted his voice an octave higher to mimic her mom's voice. "Mark my words, Wells. My girl will want horses again, and I'm going to be sure she has a place to raise them."

"That sounds like something she would say." Lacey's grin was bittersweet and wistful. "I miss her."

"Me too. Every day," he admitted and pointed to the backyard. "But she's here. You can feel her in this house. On this land. She left her mark."

Lacey inhaled and nodded. She could feel her mom in the memories inside the house and around the property. "I want to make her proud. Honor her memory." And all that her mom had done for her only daughter.

"This place wasn't the same for me without your mom." Wells reached over and took Lacey's hand in his. His gaze was compassionate, his words sincere. "It has always been better suited for a family."

A family. That was one of those dreams from a different time. But then Lacey's marriage had fallen apart, and all Lacey saw was a broken family. One that she had failed to mend. Her deployment had almost been a reprieve from all the things she couldn't fix in her marriage.

Now she was home again. This time, with her cowboy, that dream had returned and felt almost within her reach. Until she lost it again. Lacey blinked at the tears pooling in her eyes.

"You want to honor your mom, Lacey?" Wells squeezed her fingers, drawing her attention back to him. He sounded so earnest. "Fill this house with your family. Fill the stable too. Build your life and live it. Be the happiest you can be."

Her happiest always seemed to circle back to her cowboy. The one she had pushed away.

"Don't settle for anything less than your happiest," her stepdad said, holding her attention and her hand steady in his. "Your mom and I did that. We had no regrets."

Lacey already felt her own regrets building.

"If your mom was here, she would tell you to push past your fear," he continued. "You can't be scared of living and failing, Lacey."

"Mom would say that's only half a life lived," Lacey mused. Her mom had always credited Wells and Lacey for giving her a life that was overflowing. "Mom always told me: *full is the only way to live, Lacey.*"

"Your mom lived her own advice." Wells squeezed Lacey's fingers one last time, released her hand, and sat back with a sigh. "Your mom loved fully and with all her heart. We should all be as fearless as she was in life and love."

Fearless in love. Lacey ran her hands over her jeans. "I wish she was here now to show me how to do that."

"You jumped and trusted those horses all those years ago. Reached new heights with them too." Her stepdad nodded and watched her. "Trust yourself now, Lacey. You might be surprised how far you can go."

"And what if I fall?" That was the fear, wasn't it? Getting it all wrong again. Getting hurt all over again. But she wasn't exactly happy now. And hurting, yeah, she hurt more than she wanted to admit.

Wells scratched his cheek. "What did you do back then?"

Lacey grinned, relaxed at the thought. "Dusted myself off and smarted about it for a few days."

"And then," he pressed.

"Tried again until I got it," she said.

Most often she'd grabbed Caleb and made her cowboy practice jumping or whatever else she was attempting, for however long it took. Then she'd stopped turning to her cowboy, and she'd lost a piece of herself along the way. Until recently. Home again with her cowboy beside her, she had been finding herself. Like her mom had known she would all those years ago.

"Well?" her stepdad drawled.

Her mom had been fearless. It was time to follow her lead. She could keep wallowing inside her fear or get up. Try again. Maybe even get it right this time. Lacey's smile came from deep inside her. "Well, I think I'm done smartin' about it now."

"Now that's good to hear." Approval washed over her stepdad's words. "What do you intend to do about it then?"

"I'll let you know as soon as I figure it out." She stood, wrapped Wells in a warm hug, and pressed a kiss against his cheek. "Do you mind watching Butterscotch for a bit?" At her stepdad's nod, she added, "There's a conversation I need to have. It's long overdue."

Twenty minutes later, Lacey walked up to her ex-husband's front door and pressed the doorbell.

Jeffrey answered, confusion on his face. "Lacey. Everything okay?"

It wasn't, but it was going to be. "I have some things that need to be said." Lacey inhaled and lifted her chin. "And I'm going to say them now whether you want to hear them or not."

Jeffrey stepped outside and eased the front door closed. He stuck his hands in his pant pockets and looked at her. "I'm listening."

"I'm done apologizing, Jeffrey." Lacey widened her stance and wrapped her courage around her. "For our marriage falling apart. For who I am. For all the parts of me that fell short."

He opened his mouth.

Lacey went on before he could speak. "And I'm tired of carrying the blame for our divorce for both of us. There were two of us in that marriage. It's past time you apologized."

His eyebrow arched at her pause.

Lacey stopped. "I've more to say, but I'm ready to listen to you."

A small smile wavered across his face, but he cut the expression off. "I am sorry, Lacey. Sorry that I ever made you feel less than. That was never my intention. And I'm sorry you've been carrying all the blame. I wasn't the partner you needed or deserved. If anyone fell short, I did."

"Thanks." Lacey exhaled and welcomed the lightness that settled inside her. It was time to pack up the past and set it aside. Finally. "Look, Aspen is the best part of us." Lacey ticked things off on her fingers. "She is well-read, methodical, and intelligent like you. And she's brave, dedicated, and free-spirited like me. We never fully appreciated those qualities in each other. But perhaps we can appreciate them in our daughter."

"What are you saying?" he asked.

"We need to be the parents Aspen needs," she continued. "Her love for horses isn't a whim. It's not a phase. She's good, Jeffrey. And she can win this contest. But she needs our full support."

"I understand," he said simply.

Lacey quit pressing. Her ex-husband would take everything she told him now and think about it. It was enough. It was a start. A step forward. "Perhaps if we'd talked like this all those years ago, things would've been different."

Jeffrey shook his head. "We care about each other, right?"

Lacey nodded and leaned back against the railing. "Always have."

"And that's all it will ever be," Jeffrey said, his expression sincere. "Lacey, we never worked because we didn't love each other like we needed to." He touched his wedding ring. "We didn't love each other the way I love Sarah-Beth. Or the way our daughter tells me that you love Caleb Sloan."

I love Caleb Sloan. Lacey pulled back, thankful she was propped against the railing for the added support. "Exactly how does Aspen say I love Caleb?"

"Like a cowgirl loves a cowboy." Jeffrey's eyebrows raised. Amusement creased across his forehead. "Your daughter claims you smile so much you glow when you are with Caleb." Jeffrey wiped his hand across his mouth but failed to stall his grin. "Apparently, Caleb glows just the same. Like you both apparently swallowed the sun."

Lacey searched for Aspen's words to Caleb in the hospital.

You hang on until love makes them smile so much they glow.
Lacey glowed. Caleb glowed. Who else had seen it?

She had felt it. The quick pulse. The giddiness. The butter-flies. And that warmth that infused her from the inside out. With her cowboy. Or thinking about her cowboy. Her heart was full. So full she glowed.

But then she had gotten scared. Closed those blinders. Closed out her cowboy. And lost her light. She wanted it back, wanted her cowboy back. She wanted to love so much she glowed. Lacey pressed her hands to her cheeks. Lacey loved Caleb. *I. Love. My. Cowboy.*

Jeffrey considered her. "Aspen is not wrong, is she?"

Lacey lowered her hands, revealing her wide grin. Her cheeks heated. Warmed to what she hoped was a glow. "I think Aspen might just be smarter than both of us."

"That's a given." Jeffrey took Lacey's hand and pulled her in for a quick hug. Then he leaned back to look at her and asked, "Now what are you going to do about it?"

"Mind if I take Aspen for a little bit?" Lacey's smile sank through her like sunshine warming her skin. "I'll have her home by bedtime."

"No need. I promised you three weeks with our daughter." Jeffrey opened the front door and grinned. "By my count, there is still more than a week left."

"Thanks, Jeffrey." Lacey touched his arm before he stepped inside and decided to press her luck. That was the gift of being in love. Insatiable positive vibes. "You will be at Aspen's con-test, won't you?"

"Wouldn't miss it." Jeffrey motioned her into the house. "If Sarah-Beth and I can help, please let us know."

"Thanks. That means a lot, but I think I've got this." And she believed it. She turned and walked into the family room where Aspen was stretched out on the couch. "Aspen, I need your help. It's really important."

"Mom." Aspen sprang up and peeked over the back of the couch. "Mom, what is it?"

"I'm going to need my best cowgirl to help me catch a cow-boy," Lacey announced.

"Yes!" Aspen thrust her arms over her head, cheered, and danced around the couch. She rushed to Lacey and wrapped her arms around Lacey's waist. "I told you cowgirls belong with cowboys."

Lacey wanted that to be true. For the first time ever, she was going to bet everything on love. And offer her cowboy a proposal he could not refuse.

CHAPTER TWENTY-SIX

THE REHEARSAL DINNER party departed for the Sloan family pond in a flurry of UTVs filled with supplies. Caleb's brothers had already headed over to the pond to light the firepit and prepare for an evening of swimming and water games.

Caleb waved off the last crowded UTV. The tires kicked up dust from the dirt trail, which mixed with the boisterous laughter of the guests. And Caleb realized he was alone for the first time all week. He inhaled and welcomed the sudden silence, broken only by the soft cadence of nature's nighttime choir.

A movement near the stables caught his attention. The stable door opened. A shadowed figure entered and clicked shut the door behind them. But he was supposed to be alone. Caleb frowned and headed for the stable barn.

Just inside the door, he came to a quick halt. "Mom. What are you doing?"

His mother wrestled with a saddle outside Winston's stall. The older brown quarter horse eyed his mother with a mixture of disinterest and boredom. "I figure there is no time like the present to break in a new saddle."

"Why aren't you at the pond with the rest of the rehearsal party?" Caleb moved to his mother's side and eased the saddle out of her grip.

"Why aren't you?" she countered and propped her hands on her hips.

"Wasn't in the mood," Caleb admitted.

"Me either." Lilian tipped her head toward Winston's stall. "Can you please saddle Winston?"

Caleb never budged. "Mom, how long has it been since you rode a horse?"

"Since before you were born." She swiped her fingers across her forehead and frowned. "About the same amount of time since I was last in love."

Last in love. Caleb let that comment slide. For now.

"But I'm only interested in facing one fear today." She fluttered her hand in the air. "I'm sure it will come back to me. Now, if you won't saddle Winston for me, I'll do it myself."

Caleb walked into Winston's stall and saddled the patient gelding. When he was finished, he stepped out and said, "You're not riding for your first time in over thirty years alone. Give me a minute." Caleb grabbed the bridle outside Whiskey Moon's stall. His horse shook his head and whinnied his pleasure at an evening ride.

Caleb led his Palomino out of his stall, then opened Winston's stall to guide him out.

His mother took Winston's reins and asked, "Don't you need a saddle?"

"Whiskey Moon and I prefer bareback." He opened the wide double barn doors at the end of the stables and walked the horses outside. "He never quite adjusted to the saddle. We have a better connection without it."

"I know something about not adjusting to things." Lilian stroked the Palomino's neck. "We would certainly get along well, I think."

Caleb nodded and wondered again at his mother's peculiar mood. He helped her into her saddle, made quick adjustments to her stirrups, then handed her the reins. Mounted on Whiskey Moon, he led the horses toward the recently harvested wheat fields and the flat roads that cut through them. Slowing his horse, he reined in beside his mom, keeping the pace at an easy walk.

His mom shifted in her saddle and glanced at him. "By the way, where is your date?"

"You mean Georgia?" Caleb shrugged. "She found a better connection with Vivian's cousin tonight."

His mother considered him, her eyebrows arched. "You don't seem all that bothered."

"Not in the least." Caleb frowned and added, "Georgia actually told me I had a broken heart that I needed to fix." That was after the contractor admitted she had agreed to be Caleb's date to see the decorated rackhouse. Apparently, her cousin needed a venue for her engagement party, and Georgia was scouting locations.

His mother pressed her lips together.

Caleb swept his hand over his blue Paisley print shirt and continued to defend himself. "There's nothing about me that screams broken heart." He was dressed as he always was. Better, even, in his dress jeans, clean boots, and fully ironed button-down dress shirt. "I'm the same as I've always been."

"Your hair is in need of a trim," his mother said lightly.

Caleb drew back. There was something fragile about his mother's grin. As if it was on the verge of collapsing without her full focus. Caleb was more than content to shift the focus away from himself. "Mom, were you serious back in the stables?"

"About not having ridden since before you were born?" His mother adjusted the reins in her hands. A wrinkle formed between her eyebrows. "I thought I wasn't doing too bad. Does it show that much?"

"You look fine. Comfortable in fact," he said. But it was her bruised heart showing that worried Caleb. "I was talking about the last time you were in love. I'm assuming that would have been with my dad."

"You would be correct." There was that fragile movement of her lips again. Just a fleeting lift, then it was gone. "After my divorce, I convinced myself that being in love was more of a hindrance than an asset. So I tucked away my heart."

Caleb knew a little something about convincing himself of things like that. He'd spent the past week convincing himself he had made the right decision. That he did not miss his deputy.

That he was better off alone. And he was almost completely convinced. *Almost.* He shifted his weight on his horse's back.

"I've never told anyone this," his mother said, her words measured, her gaze fixed on the horizon. "I panicked after my divorce. I had lost my husband to someone better. Someone who said and did all the right things. I wasn't enough for him. So I couldn't imagine how I would ever be enough for my own kids. Or anyone else for that matter."

This was not the conversation he had been expecting. Caleb flexed his fingers around the reins. "Is that why you went to medical school?"

"I went to medical school to become someone my family could be proud of," she said simply.

"But you never came back to give us the chance to be proud of you," he countered.

"Your grandparents gave you more than I ever could those first few years," she confessed.

"What about later?" Caleb asked.

"I came back." She slanted her gaze toward him. "I watched you play baseball with Josh. You were quite good as the catcher."

He lifted his eyebrows in surprise. She had been there.

"I watched you and your brothers in the rodeo in high school too," she added.

He searched his memory of the ballparks and the arenas. Of the parents crowded on the bleachers. Would he have recognized her? Probably not. He'd been too focused on his brothers, his teammates, and his coaches. And then celebrating his successes with his grandparents. They'd been his world. Yet the image of her alone on those cold bleachers, so close yet so far, bothered him. "Why stick to the bleachers?"

"I sidelined myself," she admitted. "I had already hurt you, but you were thriving. So were your brothers. I didn't want to cause more havoc. And I had a life in New York to return to."

"But what about you?" he asked. "Weren't you hurting?" Just like she seemed to be hurting right now.

She straightened in her saddle. "Nothing I didn't deserve."

"So what was New York then?" he asked. "Some kind of self-imposed penance?"

"I thought the more patients I helped—the more people I saved—the more it would offset the pain I caused within my own family."

"Did it?" he pressed.

"No." Her shoulders lowered. Her words were dry. "I fully realize the irony. A renowned heart surgeon who can't heal her own heart. Tragic, really."

Or lonely. All these years on her own. Alone. But his mother was home with her family again. Still, Lacey had confessed she'd been lonely even in her marriage. But family should be enough. He was counting on it for himself. He rolled his shoulders against the emptiness inside him. The one that had opened up when his deputy had walked out.

But he'd been fine before. Before he'd known what life could be with someone like Lacey beside him. He cleared his throat. "Mom, what happened with Wells?"

"He wanted to love me," she said softly.

Caleb blinked. His deputy had pushed him away, never given him the chance to love her. "And that's a bad thing."

"For someone who hurts those she loves, yes." Her gaze was bleak. "And his words made me panic all over again. Foolish at my age, I know."

"Not so foolish," he said. "But you deserve to be loved and to maybe let yourself love, no matter your age."

"Thank you for that." She reached over and touched his knee. "You deserve the very same."

"Lacey didn't trust that I could love her." He guided the horses down the road that circled back to the stables and added, "Or that I even know how to love."

"I don't believe that." She patted his knee again and returned her grip to her reins. "I've seen you with our family. You know how to love, Caleb, deeply and with everything you have."

"Why do I feel a but in there?"

"But you choose not to love like that," she added. "The same as me."

"I never thought I would say this." Caleb paused and slanted his gaze at his mom, his words wry. "But we are a lot alike. It seems we are both bad at love. And neither of us can seem to get out of our heart's own way."

His mother chuckled. "What should we do about it?"

"Nothing," Caleb stated when she glanced at him. "I think we should stick to things we are good at, and let that be enough." If that emptiness wasn't stretching out endlessly before him, he might have convinced himself.

"I suppose we can't be any more miserable than we are now," his mother sighed.

"That's true," Caleb said and allowed the silence—and that sudden melancholy—to surround them.

They made their way back to the stables and came face-to-horse with an exasperated Grandpa Sam. His arms were crossed over his chest, and his deep frown disappeared into his beard. Worse, he stood in the stable doorway, blocking their entrance. It was clear no one was getting around Sam Sloan tonight. At least not until he had his say.

"Look at the pair of you." Grandpa Sam motioned between them, his movement brusque. "More alike than you want to admit."

Caleb held back from informing his grandfather that he and his mom had only just admitted their similarities. His grandfather was obviously in a mood. *Stirred up*, his gran Claire would've said. Then she would've added, *You'd best hear him out. Every word. After all, you caused it.*

"We went for a ride," Lilian said pleasantly. "Spent a lovely time together."

"You should be happy, Grandpa." Caleb dismounted and helped his mother off her horse. "That's progress for us."

"That's nothing." Grandpa Sam took the reins of Lilian's horse, his disappointment showing. "This was nothing more than two hearts on the run."

"It was a slow walk," Caleb said, purposely misunderstanding his grandfather. "Mom hasn't ridden in a while."

"Walk or gallop, it's all the same," Grandpa Sam insisted. "I suppose you supported each other's decisions too. Came to a mutual agreement that love wasn't worth the trouble."

Caleb avoided looking at his mother, certain his grandpa would catch their guilty stares.

It hardly mattered. His grandfather had already guessed correctly. He would've called it his keen eye for perception. Grandpa Sam rolled right on, "Don't go denying it either. Of course that's what you did. You are two hearts on the run, just like I said."

"Things didn't work out for either of us," Caleb argued, trying to sound reasonable. Same as he had when he'd been a kid and his antics stirred up his grandfather. Besides, things didn't work all the time for lots of folks. "That's just the way it is. We aren't running."

"You sure as heck aren't fighting either." Sam waggled his finger at Caleb, then aimed his frown at Caleb's mother. "And if you aren't fighting, then you're…"

"Running," his mother said simply.

"Now you're catching on, Lily-Bee." Sam's eyebrows hitched higher on his forehead. "And if you keep going, you sure are going to end where you did last time."

"Alone," his mother sighed.

Caleb was fine with alone. Or rather he wanted to be fine with it. He had been fine before his deputy swept back into his life and showed him he might be better off with her.

"When you came back, you told me this time was about doing things different," Sam said to Caleb's mother and smoothed his fingers through his beard. "And yet this looks an awful lot like more of the same from where I'm standing."

"Old habits," his mother said weakly.

Like a locked-down heart. Caleb pressed his hand into his ribs. *You choose not to love.*

"Get a new habit," Sam ordered, but then his face broke out in a grin. "You might find it suits you better."

Caleb was starting to forgive his mother as he began to understand her more. He supposed he was even opening his heart to his mother. That was certainly a point in his favor. He was doing something different. But opening his heart to love? That might be a change too far.

"You mean like running *to* something instead of *away*." His mother's smile blossomed.

His grandfather's gaze sparked. "Now you just might be catching on, Lily-Bee."

"I think I need to go," his mother said, suddenly a flurry of excited movement. "I know what I need to do."

"I'll see to your horse," Sam said and hitched his thumb at Caleb. "There's more work to be done here."

"Thanks, Dad." His mother hugged his grandpa.

Grandpa Sam said, "I put a bottle of bourbon I pinched from Carter's private collection and a dessert from Tess in your car already. Tess and I decided it was all for a good cause."

"I hope it's enough." Caleb's mother laughed, turned, and framed Caleb's face in her hands. "Thank you for giving me this time with you. It was exactly what I needed."

Caleb wrapped his mother in a tight hug. It was the first genuine embrace mother and son had shared. "Maybe we can ride together again soon. I can show you more of the trails."

"I would love that." With a quick wave, his mother fairly ran to her sports car. One honk of her horn, and her taillights disappeared down the driveway.

Grandpa Sam stroked Winston's head, then led the horse to his stall. "Let's get these horses to bed for the night so we can put our feet up."

"I can handle it." Caleb opened the stall door and walked his horse inside. "You can head up to the house."

"We'll do this together," Grandpa Sam insisted, "then we'll sit down together too. You've been running on your own far too long. It's a pace you can't sustain."

But that hardly meant Caleb wasn't going to keep trying. They worked together, brushing down the horses, cleaning the tack, and sweeping the stalls. Once they had fresh water in the buckets and hay on the floor, there was nothing more to do. Minutes later, Grandpa Sam pressed a whiskey glass into Caleb's hand and sat in the chair beside Caleb on the back porch of the farmhouse.

Caleb dragged the coffee table closer and rested his boots

on top. He wouldn't deny it felt good to sit down. But he wasn't fooled that his grandfather had nothing more to say to him.

Grandpa Sam sipped his bourbon and rested his boots on the table too. He didn't leave Caleb waiting long before he asked, "Do you know why your grandma always wanted you to sit still? Why it was so important to her?"

"She was tired of chasing me around," Caleb said dryly, adding a tease to his words to lighten the mood.

"She never did complain about that," Sam said. "Always claimed it was the best kind of exercise. She didn't know she was doing it."

Caleb chuckled.

"Your gran wanted you to sit because she worried you were too busy to stop and take stock." Grandpa Sam swirled the single ice cube in his glass. "She worried you weren't checking in to make sure your heart and your head were in alignment."

But Caleb had been too busy on purpose. That was how he outran his heart. Not stopping to take stock kept him from getting hurt. Just look at recent events. He took a deep sip of his bourbon. "My heart and mind haven't ever seen eye to eye." Same as him and his deputy.

"You haven't ever given your heart a proper chance." Grandpa Sam frowned.

That sounded awfully close to what his mother had claimed. "There's nothing wrong with my choices."

"That's your mind speaking for you." Grandpa Sam's laughter was low and knowing. "Listen closer and hear what your heart wants."

His heart wanted his deputy. Wanted a life spent with her. His heart wanted to love and be loved. He cradled his whiskey glass in his hands. "What if love isn't enough?"

"You won't really know if it is or isn't unless you give her your heart," Grandpa Sam mused. "All of it. Not just a piece. Not with conditions. No holding back."

Caleb tipped his head back and stared at the sky. Could he love like that? His heart wanted to try. Lacey deserved nothing less than everything he had to give. "That's quite the risk, isn't it?"

"I've never seen you back away from a risk." Grandpa Sam grinned at him. "Or an adventure. And falling in love just might be the last adventure you need."

He couldn't deny the appeal of taking this adventure with Lacey. He could only imagine what he could accomplish with her next to him. What they might build together.

"Only one question really needs to be answered." His grandpa eyed him over the rim of his glass. "Do you love her or not? Because that's the beginning and the end. The rest is just details."

Love her. Love his deputy. Caleb shifted and rested his elbows on his knees. Closed his eyes and finally took stock. And there, at the core, was the truth. Just waiting for Caleb to accept it. To embrace it. To honor it.

He loved her. It was that simple and that complicated. It was that freeing and that anchoring. And it was everything. Absolutely everything.

He supposed he had always loved Lacey. From the first time he met her. But what had once been affection and admiration was now something deeper. Stronger. Enduring. Oh yes, he loved his deputy.

But his deputy did not know it.

Caleb's eyes snapped open and fixed on his grandpa. "I messed up, Grandpa. Badly."

"It would not be called falling in love if the path was free of potholes." Grandpa Sam's arm draped around Caleb's shoulders. "We all stumbled on our way to love. I can assure you of that."

But Caleb hadn't stumbled. He had not even tried. He had not fought. Instead he had walked away. As if Lacey was not worth the trouble. "I let her down. I'm quite sure I hurt her and…" A different sort of panic simmered inside Caleb. A fear that he might have lost Lacey before he had even fought for her.

"That's the funny thing about love." Grandpa Sam patted Caleb's shoulder. "The ones that truly love you, well, they keep on loving you even when you shut 'em out good and tight."

Please, let my grandfather be right. "Then I can fix this," Caleb said. He could still fight for love. For his heart and Lacey's. "I can still make things right."

"Can't guarantee it will be easy." Grandpa Sam clinked his glass against Caleb's. "But I can guarantee it will be worthwhile."

"Grandpa, I don't think I can do this alone," Caleb admitted. This time the stakes were too high. Lacey mattered too much. And winning her back meant going in with everything he had.

"You haven't been alone." Grandpa Sam beamed at him. "Your family has always been in your corner. We've been waiting for you to turn around and need us."

He was about to take the biggest risk of his life and put his heart on the line. He should be nervous. Scared. Unsure.

Instead, Caleb grinned and decided to double down on his heart and Lacey's, counting on love to win them an adventure of a lifetime.

CHAPTER TWENTY-SEVEN

AND THEN THERE was one. A single Sloan brother left standing. Though if Caleb had his way, he wouldn't be single for long. But that would have to wait for now.

Tonight was about celebrating his twin and his new wife. The ceremony had gone off without a hitch, and now the reception was doing the same. Standing by the bar in the back of the renovated rackhouse, Caleb lifted his champagne glass along with the other guests in a final toast to the ecstatic couple.

Josh twirled his bride around the dance floor under the hundreds of fairy lights Caleb had personally strung from the ceiling. His twin swung his new wife into his arms for a tender kiss, then they bowed to the crowd with a flourish. Thanking their guests for sharing in their special day, the couple encouraged everyone to continue celebrating even though they were heading out. Josh swept Vivian into his arms. The cheers filled the rackhouse as the couple took their leave.

Ryan approached Caleb and quickly swapped Caleb's champagne flute with a tumbler glass. Grant appeared at Caleb's other side and poured bourbon into Caleb's glass with the efficiency of a professional server. Suddenly, Carter, Grandpa Sam, and Uncle Roy were there, holding out their glasses for their own splash of bourbon. And then the glasses clinked together.

"Now that's a proper drink for a toast." Uncle Roy waggled his eyebrows and sipped his bourbon.

"Didn't feel right to be in the rackhouse and not sipping what was made here," Grandpa Sam added, a twinkle in his gaze.

"We're missing someone." Caleb glanced around the tables, found the woman he was looking for, and smiled. He called out, "Lilian Sloan. You're needed near the bar."

Their mother excused herself from her table, where she sat with her date, Sheriff Wells Hopson, and the Baker sisters.

Caleb poured a glass for his mother and handed it to her. He cleared his throat and said, "I'd like to make a toast to family. For always having my back. And believing in me all along."

"If you'd asked us sooner, we would've told you we believed in you." Grandpa Sam clinked his glass against Caleb's. "You just weren't believing in yourself."

"I am now." Caleb raised his glass again. "Thanks to all of you."

"Fine then, I'm going to speak on behalf of your gran Claire and myself," Grandpa Sam said, his words rough, his gaze tender. He reached over and took hold of Lilian's hand. "I don't believe I could be more proud of this family and who you have become. Brothers. Leaders. Fathers. Husbands." He slanted his gaze to Lilian. "Mother. Daughter." He paused and sniffed. "Sure makes an old cowboy like me look back and say: *what a fulfilling journey I've had.* And I owe it all to my family."

Caleb dabbed at his damp eyes, noticing his brothers and mom doing the same. He grinned at his grandfather. "We wouldn't be here without you, Grandpa and Gran Claire. There are no words for the love we have for you."

There was a round of here, here's from his brothers.

"Caleb Sloan, I'm too old to cry," Grandpa Sam said but ruined his statement by tapping the back of his hand against his eye. "And I love you all more."

The Sloan family shared a group hug and another toast to Josh and Vivian, promising to fill Josh in on Grandpa Sam's heartfelt words.

"Now then, this is supposed to be a celebration. We need to be getting to it." Grandpa Sam smoothed his hand over his leather bolo tie. "If you'll excuse me, I'm going to see if Breezy still has a step in her two-step."

"I'll see you out there." Uncle Roy chuckled. "Gayle already promised me a dance."

Caleb's brothers drifted off to find their wives and join the others on the dance floor. Caleb turned to his mother and held out his arm. "Do you think Wells would mind if I borrowed you for a dance?"

His mother smiled and wrapped her arm around his. "I would mind more if we didn't dance."

With that, Caleb guided his mother to the dance floor for a two-step followed by a country swing. When the band shifted into a slow song, Caleb handed his mother off to Wells for a waltz and made his way back to the bar.

Several songs later, Caleb was still leaning against the bar, chatting with the friendly bartender that Chef KC had hired. His back was to the room, but his boot tapped to the beat of the lively music.

Wells stepped up beside Caleb, asked the bartender for a refill, then turned toward Caleb. "I have something for you."

Caleb straightened when Wells extended his arm and placed something in Caleb's hand. Caleb gaped at the white gold diamond ring resting in his open palm. He lifted his startled gaze to the sheriff, now his mother's boyfriend.

"That's the wedding ring Lacey's mom wore." Wells smiled, his expression sincere and open. "I was going to wait to give it to you. But I was talking to Lilian, and well, in case you want it sooner, now you have it."

Caleb ran his fingertip over the solitary diamond. It was heavier than he would've expected. At one time, he would have refused the gesture. Backed away swiftly and steadily. Now he leaned in, curled his fingers around the ring as if to protect it. Because it was everything he wanted now. "I was going to ask for your blessing after I earned your daughter's heart." Caleb had already worked out his approach. He only needed Josh and Vivian's wedding to conclude, and then he would start getting the affairs of his own heart sorted.

Wells grinned. "You have my and Lacey's mom's blessing."

"I'm honored." Caleb hoped Lacey would be too, when he finally put his love-for-the-win plan into play. He tucked the ring safely into his pocket, then reached out and shook the sheriff's hand. "Not that you need it, but you and my mom have my blessing too."

"That means more than you know." Wells pumped Caleb's hand one more time. He tipped his head to the stage and the band who was winding down another set. "I heard a rumor that there's a special request coming up. You won't want to miss it."

LACEY WAS EARLY. And anxious. More anxious than early, really.

Standing on the moonlit grounds of Misty Grove Distillery, she rolled up to the balls of her feet in her new indigo suede cowboy boots and back to her heels. She shook her arms at her sides. Shrugged her shoulders. Rolled her head to one side, then the other. Nothing dislodged the nerves.

She touched her cowboy hat. Smoothed her fingers over her flowy wrap dress and fiddled with the bow resting on her left hip. Still, her pulse only raced faster.

"Mom," Aspen whispered.

Lacey spun around, grateful for her daughter's familiar face. "How do I look?"

"Like the prettiest cowgirl ever." Aspen beamed at her.

Lacey inhaled, felt herself settle slightly. "Is he still inside?"

Aspen's grin grew wider. "Yup. And now it's time to catch a cowboy, Mom."

"I don't know if I can." Lacey's boots felt stuck in the gravel and dirt.

Her win-back-her-cowboy strategy had seemed like an excellent one when she first came up with it. She had garnered the support of her family and her cowboy's family, and that had only emboldened her. What wasn't to like? It would be surprising, heartfelt, and romantic. Except if Lacey couldn't go through with it, the entire thing would be nothing more than an almost-good idea that didn't win her anything.

Suddenly, a pair of thin arms wound around Lacey, and she found herself wrapped in her daughter's version of a bear hug. "Just hold on, Mom. I'll squeeze you until you glow."

Tears pooled in Lacey's eyes. She embraced Aspen and held on, grateful for the blessing of her daughter and her constant love. Mother and daughter stayed like that for another minute before Lacey kissed Aspen's head. "That was exactly what I needed."

"You feel better, right?" Aspen peered up at her.

"Immensely." The fullness in her chest steadied Lacey like nothing ever had. She reached down and took Aspen's hand. "But if it's okay with you, I could really use your support to walk out on that stage."

"I won't let go, Mom. I promise." Aspen clutched Lacey's hand tighter and studied her. "Do you want my glasses to read the words, Mom?"

"No, but thanks." Lacey laughed. "I have the lyrics memorized. I just need my voice to remember to sing the correct words."

"Grandpa Swells says it doesn't matter if you get the words right." Aspen swung their arms forward and back between them. "So long as you sing from your heart."

"I think that's the best advice I've heard." She would lead with her heart and convince her cowboy to follow.

Lacey walked with Aspen toward the side door of the renovated rackhouse. The one glowing with soft dim light and filled with the Sloan family and their guests.

Aspen pressed her ear against the door. "The music is slowing, Mom." Aspen clapped her hands and shimmied in place. "Wait till they hear you sing. They're gonna be so surprised."

The side door creaked open before Lacey's nerves could sweep through her again. Elsie popped her head out, her smile brighter than the full moon, and motioned to them. "Come on. Ryan is already onstage. It's time."

Aspen's hand was back inside Lacey's, and her daughter was tugging her through the door before Lacey's second thoughts could snag her. She was on the stage with the band, a microphone pressed into her free hand and being introduced by Ryan Sloan before her reservations could catch her. Aspen never left her side. Never loosened her grip.

And all of a sudden, the entire rackhouse quieted. Ryan

nodded to Lacey and picked up his own microphone. And Lacey turned.

All eyes were on her. But she had eyes for only one. She scanned the crowd, searching until… There. Near the back. *My cowboy.*

And just like that, everything else fell away around her. The onlookers. Her nerves. Her doubts.

Her cowboy had her in his sights. He was moving forward, his gaze locked on hers. Lacey squeezed Aspen's hand to let her know she was alright. Aspen squeezed back, then slipped her hand free and headed off the stage.

Lacey lifted the microphone in both hands and, with her cowboy her only view, said, "Caleb Sloan. This one is for you."

That half grin—the one reserved only for her—dipped into his cheek. He kept coming toward her as if he had no intention of stopping until he got her.

The band started playing behind her. Ryan filled in the harmony. The music swirled around her, through her, and when Lacey opened her mouth, she sang from her heart. A country love song about being better than she was, stronger than ever, and who she wanted to be because of his love.

Her cowboy never lost track of her. She never lost him. When he finally reached her, her hand found his. And still Lacey sang, her love for her cowboy spilling into every lyric.

He raised her arm, pressed the gentlest, most perfect kiss against her fingers. Then he flattened her palm over his heart and covered her hand with his. His gaze had a certain sheen. She was sure hers did too. And if someone wanted to know what love looked like, Lacey would've said her cowboy. Right there. In that moment. The one she imprinted on her heart.

Lacey finished the song. Applause swelled toward the ceiling. Someone took the microphone from Lacey's hand. But her attention was on her cowboy, her only focus getting closer to him. He was of the same mind as his arm came around her waist and he gathered her to him.

Her gaze traveled over his face. Finally, she managed a breathless, "Caleb."

"Speechless," he finally whispered. His tone was raw and

honest. "You leave me speechless." There was an intensity to his gaze. "Beautiful. Your voice. You. You're so beautiful. Inside. Out."

A tear slipped free and slid down her cheek. "You've always seen me. Always accepted me just as I am."

"My cowgirl." He caught her tear with his thumb. His expression was achingly tender. "I don't deserve you."

Lacey curved her arms around him and held on. "You should know, cowboy, that I have no intention of letting go this time."

"There will be a fight if you do," he promised. "I'm holding on too. I'm going to be the cowboy you deserve."

His words lightened her. Encouraged her. She tangled her fingers in his hair and playfully asked, "Out of curiosity, how do you plan to do that?"

"By loving you like you've never been loved before," he said, his words serious.

But his touch was gentle and steady on her cheek. And the affection in his gaze was more than she had anticipated. Her pulse jumped.

"I love you, Lacey Nash," he said, simply and effortlessly. "You're my reason. The start and the ending. It's you. It's always been you."

Lacey's heart soared. She would have joined it if Caleb's arms weren't anchoring her to him. Right where she wanted to be. And suddenly, speaking from her heart came naturally. Easily. "You should know I love you too, Caleb Sloan. And I have plans to love you like you've never been loved before."

"I do believe that's the first time I've ever been swept off my boots. I think I like it." Caleb dropped his head back and shouted his love for her to the entire venue, then pinned his gaze on her again. "I had a strategy to win you back. I organized it all."

"But I got to you first." Lacey smiled, feeling herself glow.

Caleb released her and patted the pockets of his dress pants. "I was going to do this... Well, it doesn't matter when because I don't want to wait any longer. I can't wait."

"Caleb." Lacey searched his face, wanted back into his arms where the world felt right.

He dropped to one knee. Right there in the middle of the

dance floor, with his family and friends watching, with her daughter and stepdad looking on. Then he reached into his pocket and held out a ring to her.

Lacey gasped. She knew that ring. Her tears fell in earnest then.

"Lacey, I'm tired of sitting back and hearing about everyone being in love," he started, his gaze searching hers. "I'm ready to experience love. With you."

Lacey was already nodding. She was ready too. With him.

Caleb's grin spread, and his face glowed. "Lacey Nash, will you marry me?"

This time it was Lacey shouting a resounding yes to the crowd and launching herself into her cowboy's arms. Amid the claps and congratulations from their friends and family, their lips collided for a kiss that opened hearts and promised a love that spanned a lifetime.

Lacey pulled away long enough for Caleb to slide the ring onto her finger. She framed his face and spoke through her tears. "I love you, Caleb."

Caleb kissed her again and linked their hands together. "Ready for an adventure like you've never seen, cowgirl?"

Lacey pulled him closer and said, "Always, but only if it's with my favorite cowboy."

EPILOGUE

Two weeks later...

LILIAN SLOAN RUBBED her palms on her jeans and shifted on the metal bench in the Three Springs Rodeo arena. "I don't believe I've ever been this nervous before."

"Doc, you're a heart surgeon. Steady hands are required. You couldn't afford nerves on the job." Wells leaned closer and took her hand in his.

"But now I'm retired," Lilian said and linked their hands until they were palm to palm. "And it seems all those nerves I ignored for so many years are coming out now."

"How about we keep each other steady?" Wells chuckled and covered their joined hands with his other. Just the way Lilian liked. Wells added, "I'm a bit nervous too."

Lilian gaped at him.

"What? It's my granddaughter, riding a horse on her own in an arena with a crowd watching," Wells confessed. "This is her first ever Junior Royal Rodeo court parade."

Pride was clear on her sheriff's face. And Lilian admitted to feeling a bit of it too. After all, she had been assisting Aspen with her preparations for her two-minute speech in the competition. Lilian wanted to believe her support and guidance had helped Aspen secure her spot on the Royal Rodeo Court as a first-time entrant.

"Okay. Okay." Lacey slid onto the bench beside Lilian and rubbed her hands together. "It's almost time for the parade to start. I'm so nervous."

Caleb joined them, wrapped his arm around Lacey's waist, and pulled her close. "Aspen is going to be great. She's riding Biscuit. They both have matching ribbons in their braids. And they make a stunning pair."

"You can say that because you got to be back there with Aspen while she prepared for the parade." Lacey kissed Caleb, then frowned at him. "I'm still not pleased about that."

"The rules of the royal court explicitly state one adult chaperone is allowed backstage." Caleb kissed Lacey back, then chuckled. "I can't help it that Aspen chose me as her one person."

"She chose you as her chaperone," Lacey corrected. "And she already told me I could be there with her next time."

"Actually, dear, she promised me." Lilian fought to keep her grin in place. "I have a text right here from Aspen."

Lacey read the text on Lilian's phone screen and shook her head. "She did. Aspen invited Nan Lily to be her chaperone for tomorrow's parade."

Lilian had helped Aspen prepare for the competition, and in turn, Aspen had helped Lilian finally choose her name. From here on out, the grandkids would call her Nan Lily. Lilian thought it had a nice ring to it, especially when Aspen used it right before she greeted Lilian with one of her all-encompassing hugs.

"I'm sure you will get a turn." Lilian tucked her phone away and nudged Wells. "Right, Wells? Lacey will get a turn to be chaperone, won't she?"

"Not likely," Wells admitted but then laughed at Lacey's stunned expression. "Aspen told me that her mom makes her too nervous, so she can't be around her beforehand."

Caleb chuckled. "Aspen told me that too."

"What do I do?" Lacey crossed her arms over her chest.

"Apparently you worry too much, dear." Lilian placed a gentle hand on Lacey's leg. "And you fuss with Aspen and the horse and every little thing."

"Now I know exactly how my mom felt all those years ago." Lacey buried her face in her hands and her shoulders suddenly shook. "How did she handle this?"

Wells leaned around Lilian and said, "She shared it."

Lacey lifted her head and grinned. She linked one hand with Caleb's and her other with Lilian's and said with a new confidence, "Then that's exactly what I'm going to do. Share my worries with my family because we are stronger together."

Family. The word filled Lilian and warmed her. She was home. With family. And stronger for it. Finally, she was right where she belonged.

* * * * *